SECONDHAND HEROES

THE LAST BATTLE

JUSTIN LAROCCA HANSEN

DIAL BOOKS FOR YOUNG READERS

FOR MY WIFE, RAYDENE, WHO WAS THERE FOR EVERY PANEL, PAGE, AND PAINTING

DIAL BOOKS FOR YOUNG READERS
PENGUIN YOUNG READERS GROUP
AN IMPRINT OF PENGUIN RANDOM HOUSE LLC
375 HUDSON STREET, NEW YORK, NY 10014

MANUFACTURED IN CHINA
ISBN 9780803740969 PAPERBACK

1 3 5 7 9 10 8 6 4 2

TEXT SET IN CCWILDWORDS

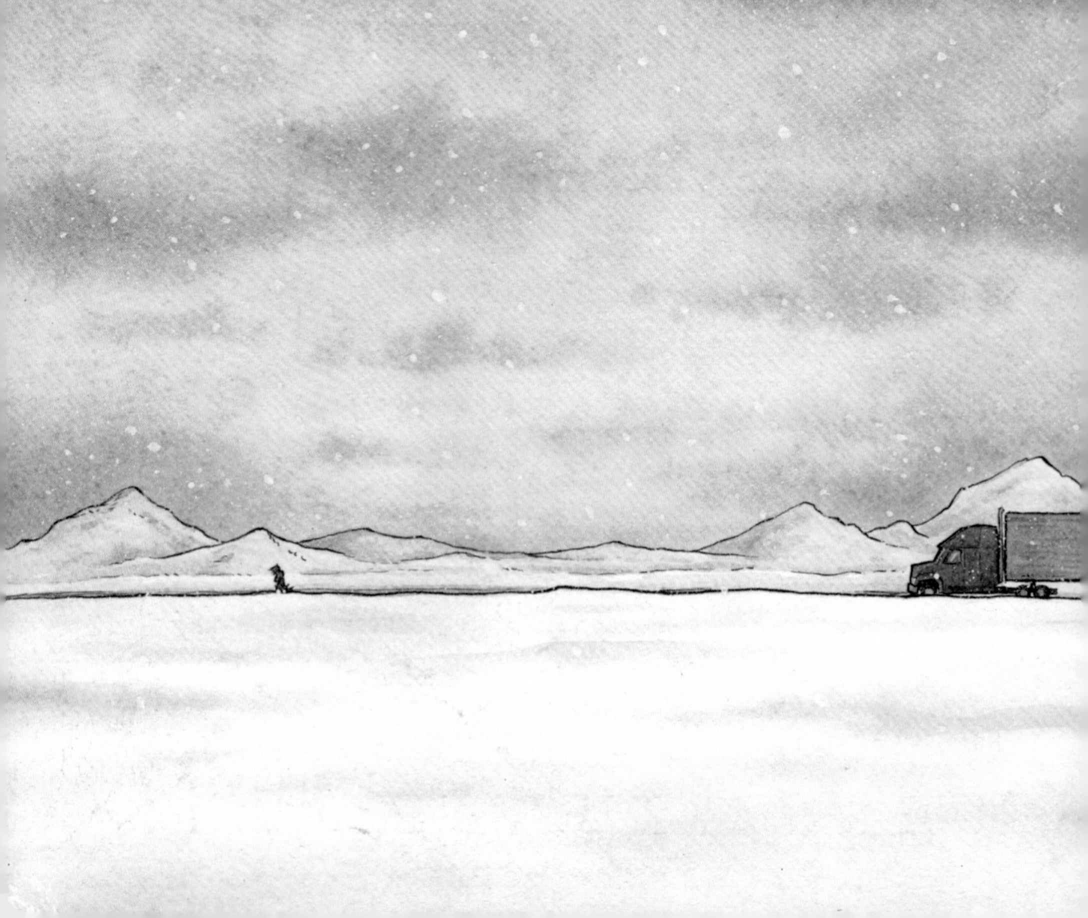

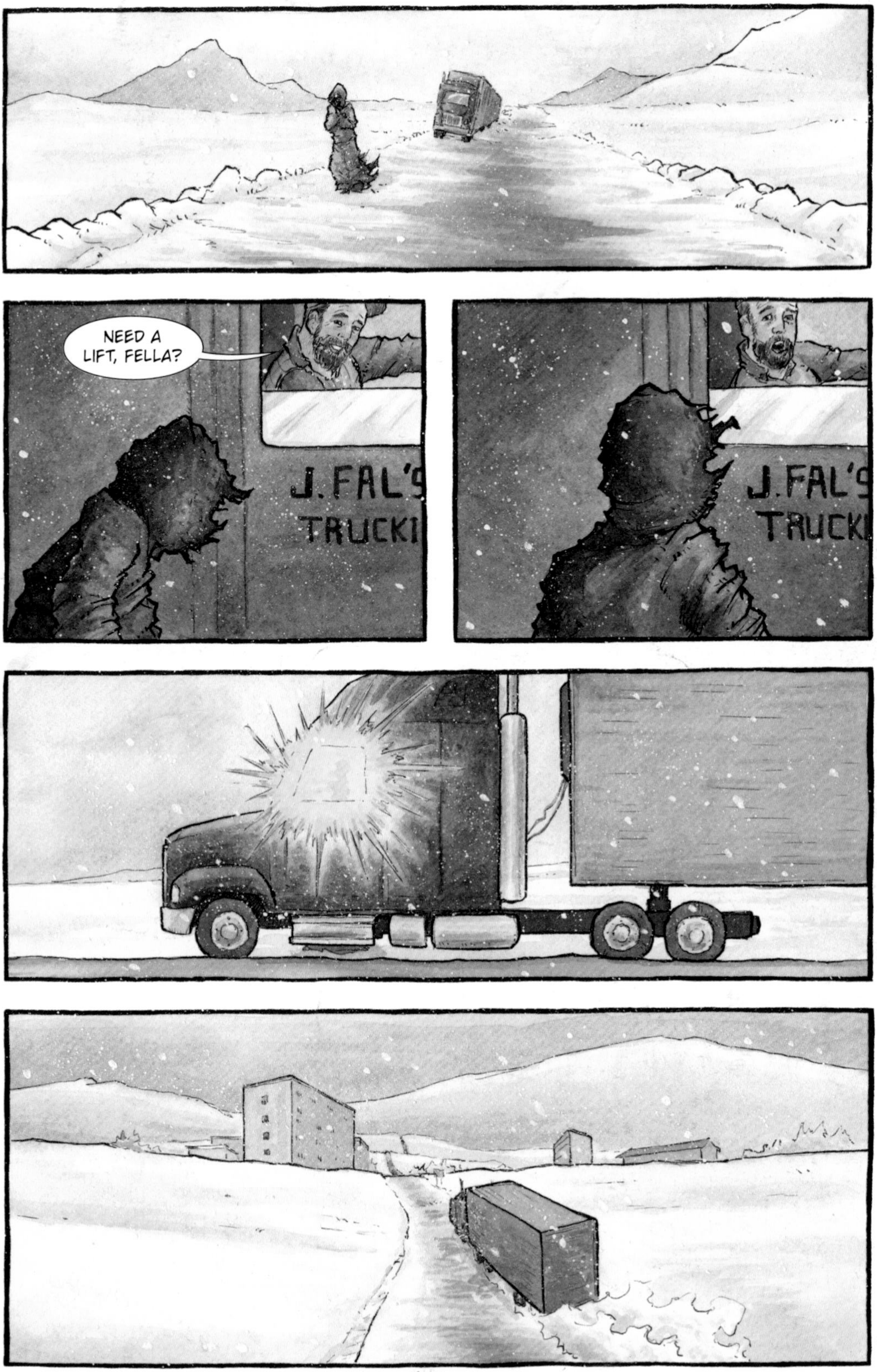
NEED A LIFT, FELLA?
J. FAL'S
TRUCKI
J. FAL'S
TRUCKI

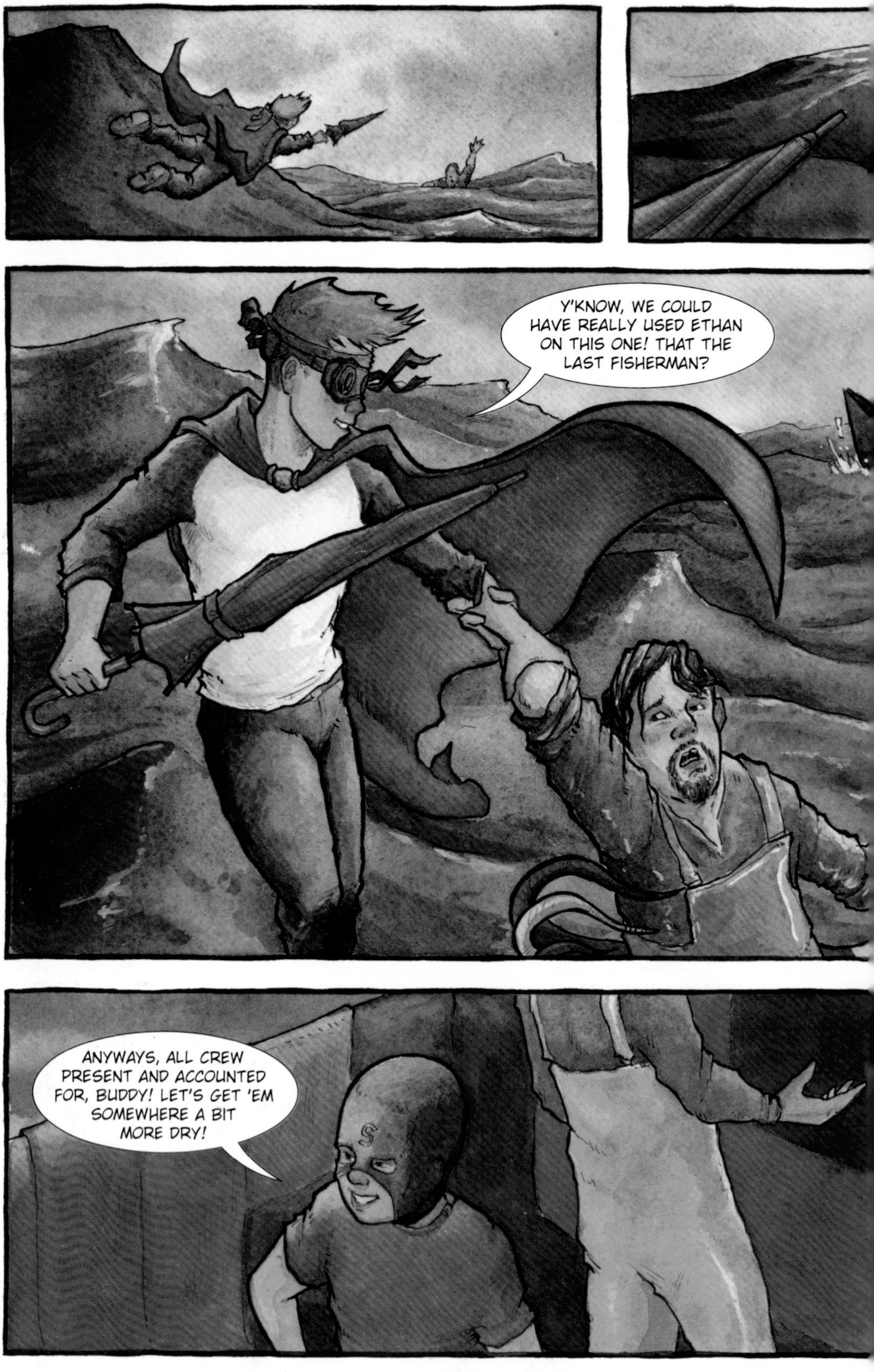
Y'KNOW, WE COULD HAVE REALLY USED ETHAN ON THIS ONE! THAT THE LAST FISHERMAN?
ANYWAYS, ALL CREW PRESENT AND ACCOUNTED FOR, BUDDY! LET'S GET 'EM SOMEWHERE A BIT MORE DRY!

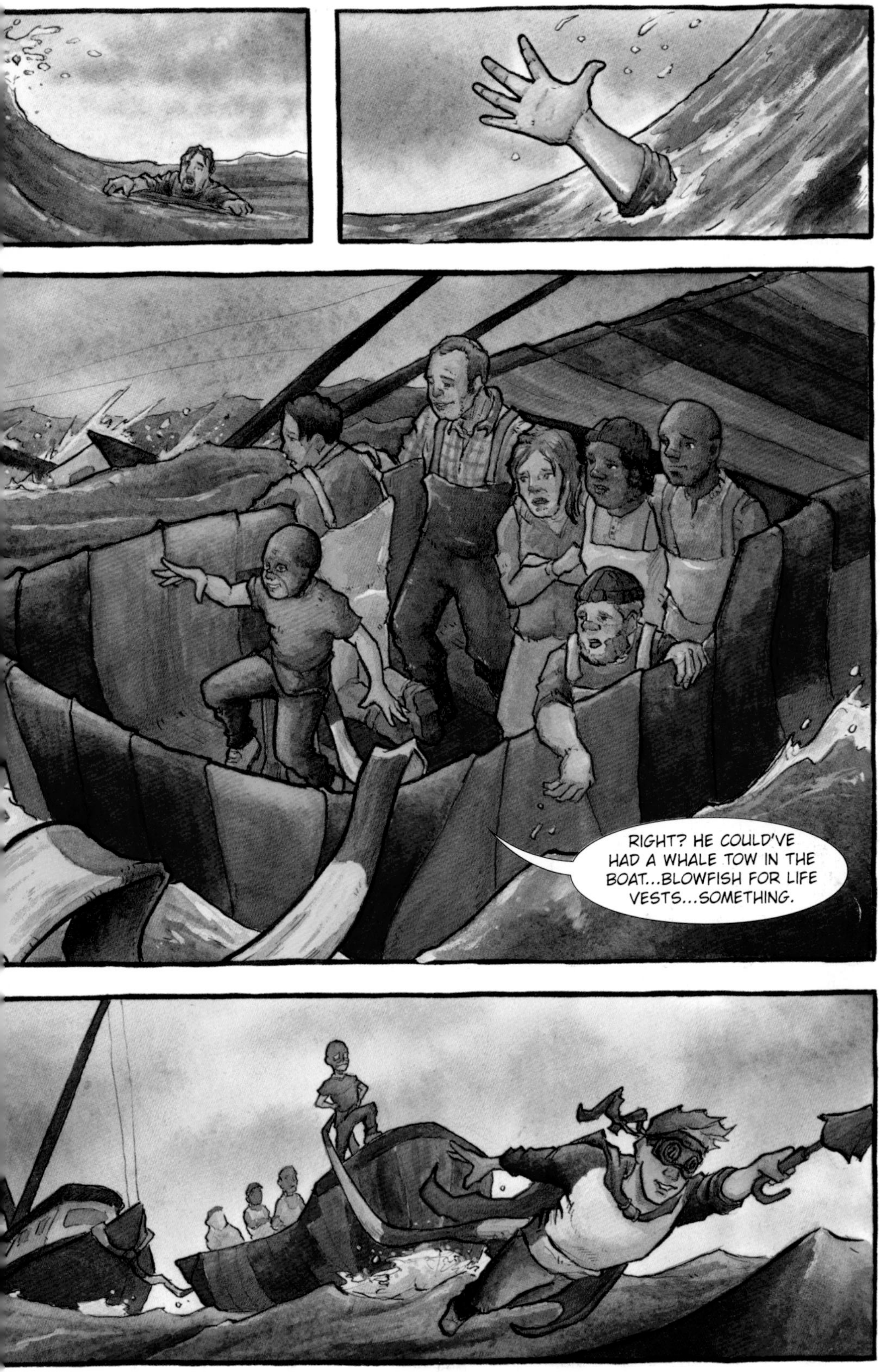
RIGHT? HE COULD'VE HAD A WHALE TOW IN THE BOAT...BLOWFISH FOR LIFE VESTS...SOMETHING.

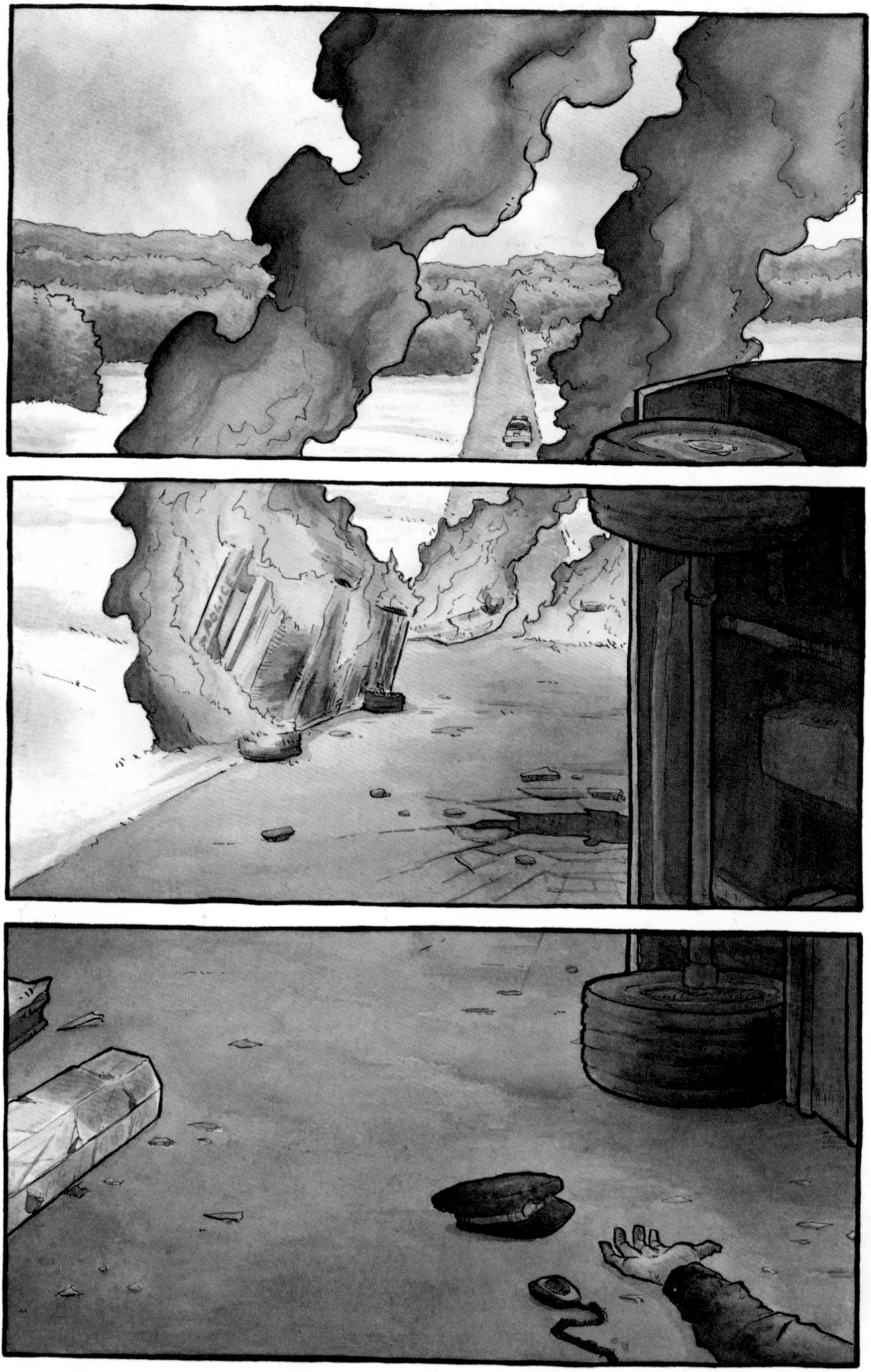
POLICE

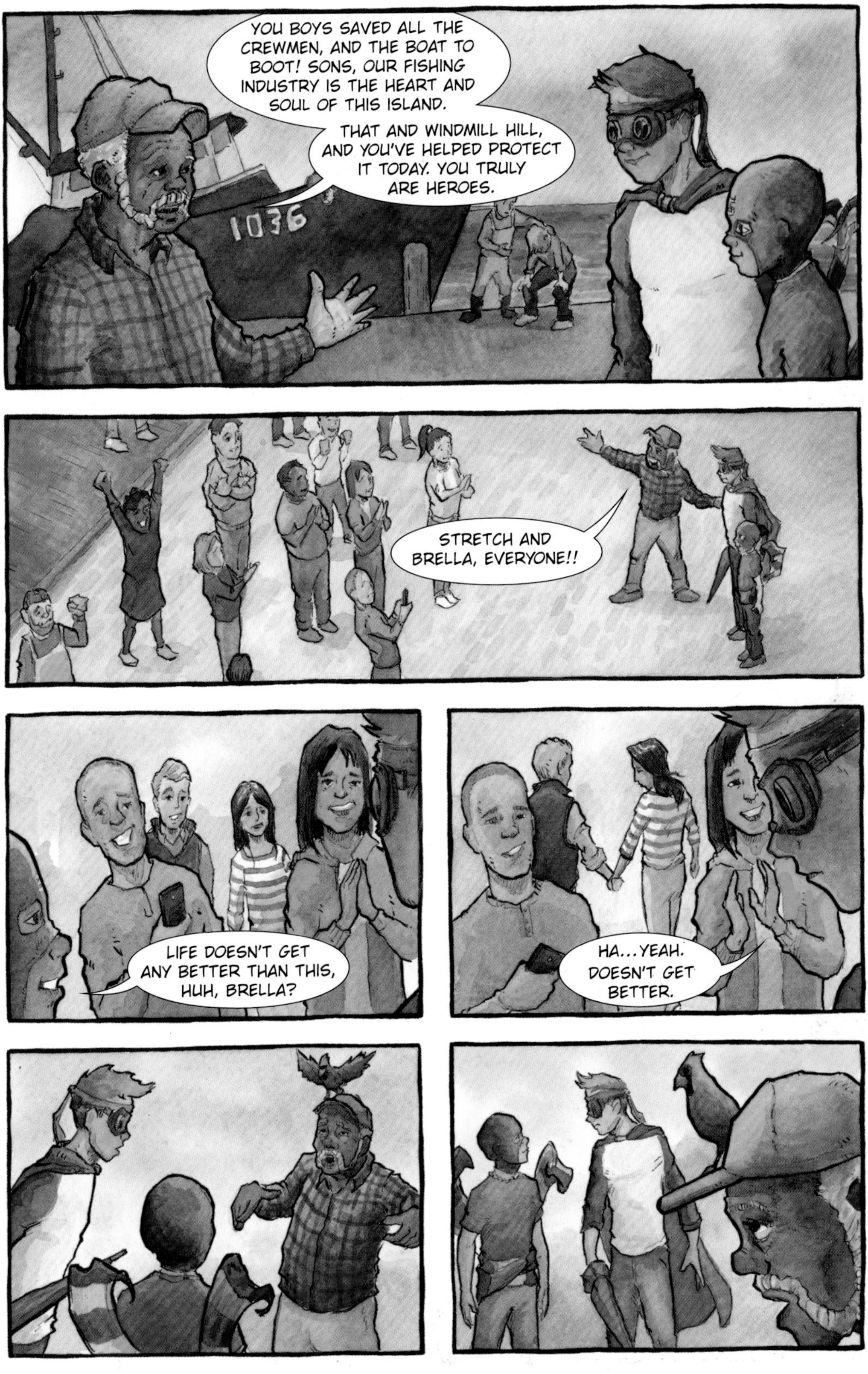
YOU BOYS SAVED ALL THE CREWMEN, AND THE BOAT TO BOOT! SONS, OUR FISHING INDUSTRY IS THE HEART AND SOUL OF THIS ISLAND.
THAT AND WINDMILL HILL, AND YOU'VE HELPED PROTECT IT TODAY. YOU TRULY ARE HEROES.
1036
STRETCH AND BRELLA, EVERYONE!!
LIFE DOESN'T GET ANY BETTER THAN THIS, HUH, BRELLA?
HA...YEAH. DOESN'T GET BETTER.

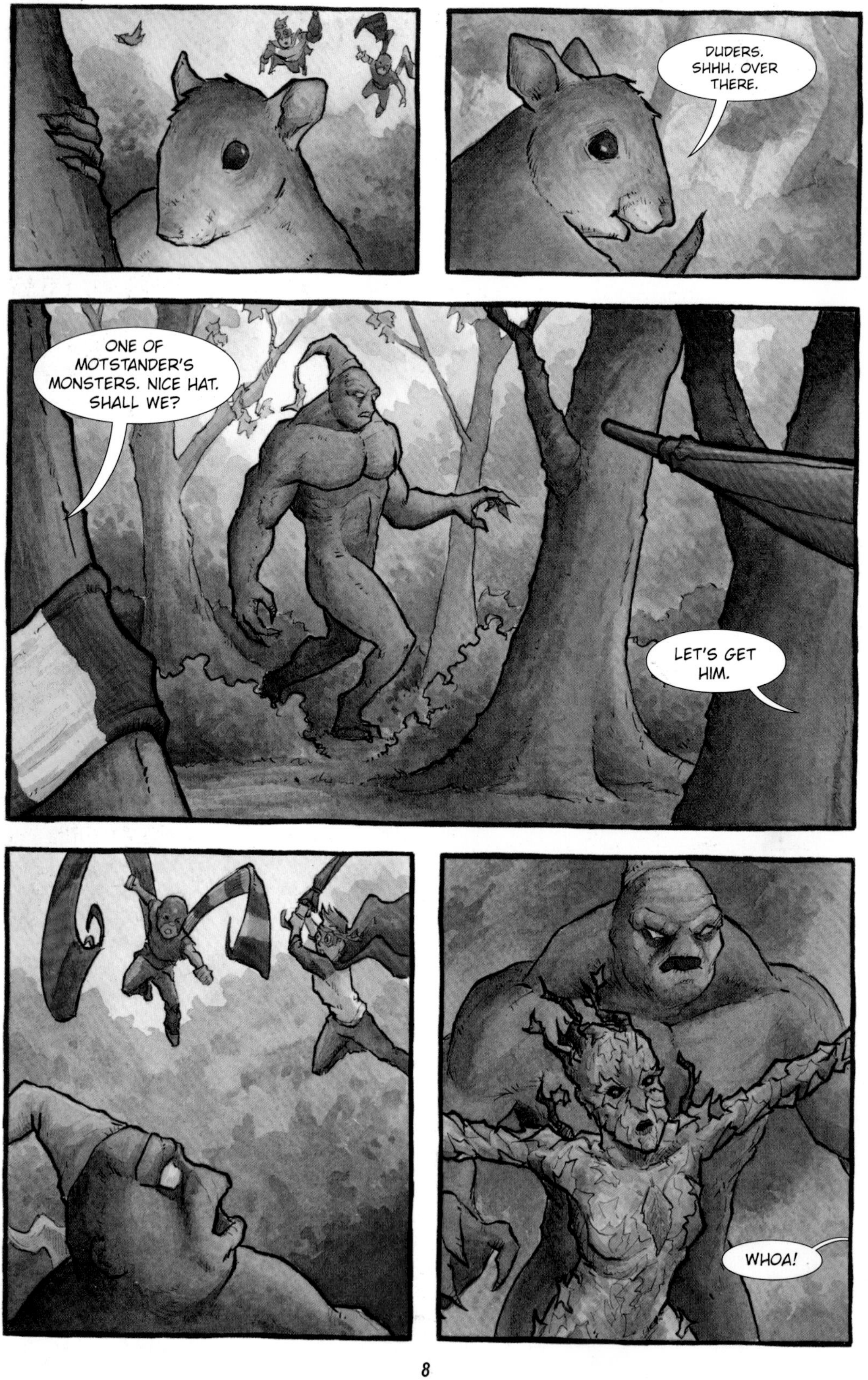
DUDERS. SHHH. OVER THERE.
ONE OF MOTSTANDER'S MONSTERS. NICE HAT. SHALL WE?
LET'S GET HIM.
WHOA!

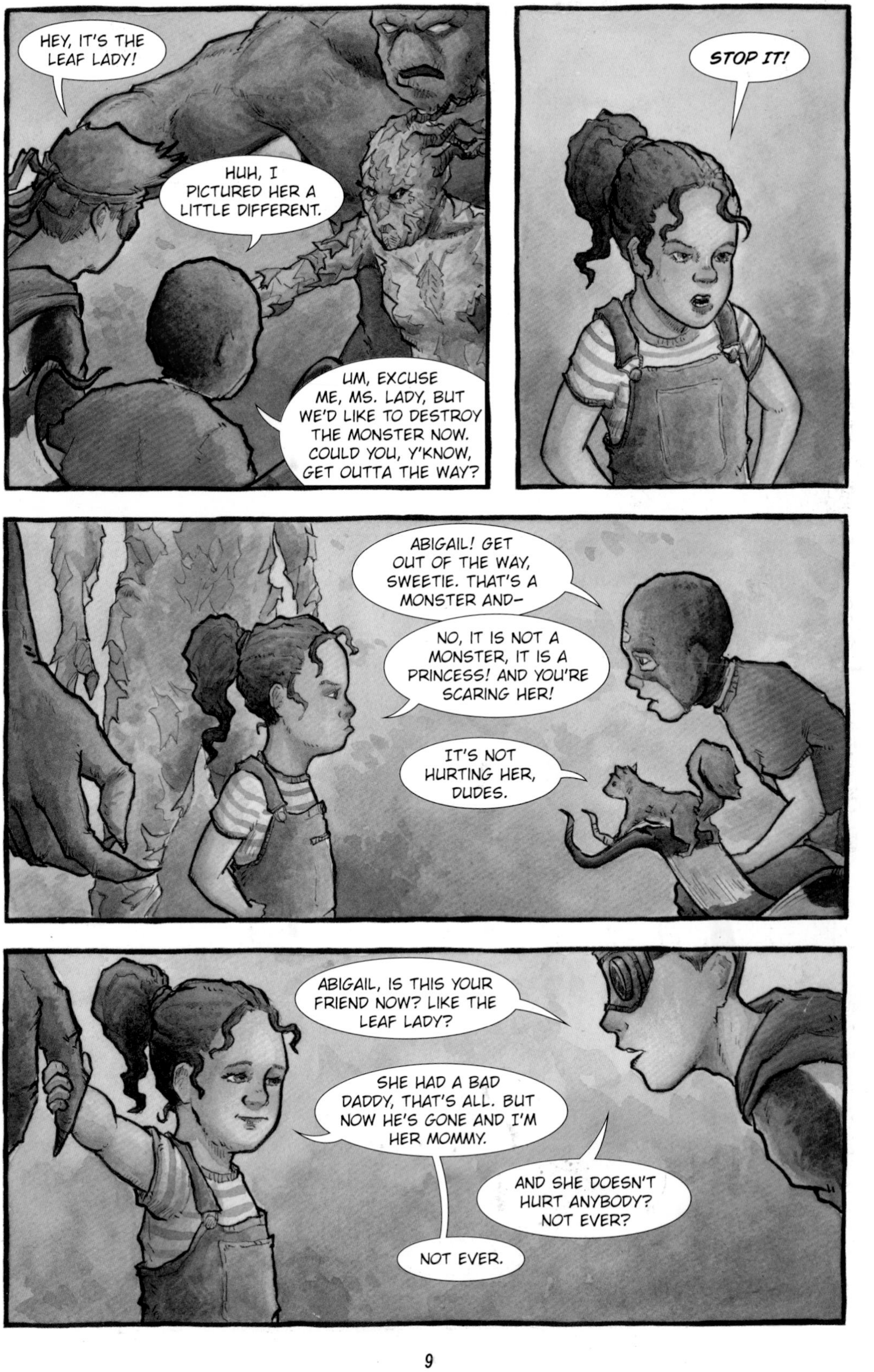
HEY, IT'S THE LEAF LADY!
HUH, I PICTURED HER A LITTLE DIFFERENT.
UM, EXCUSE ME, MS. LADY, BUT WE'D LIKE TO DESTROY THE MONSTER NOW. COULD YOU, Y'KNOW, GET OUTTA THE WAY?
STOP IT!
ABIGAIL! GET OUT OF THE WAY, SWEETIE. THAT'S A MONSTER AND–
NO, IT IS NOT A MONSTER, IT IS A PRINCESS! AND YOU'RE SCARING HER!
IT'S NOT HURTING HER, DUDES.
ABIGAIL, IS THIS YOUR FRIEND NOW? LIKE THE LEAF LADY?
SHE HAD A BAD DADDY, THAT'S ALL. BUT NOW HE'S GONE AND I'M HER MOMMY.
AND SHE DOESN'T HURT ANYBODY? NOT EVER?
NOT EVER.

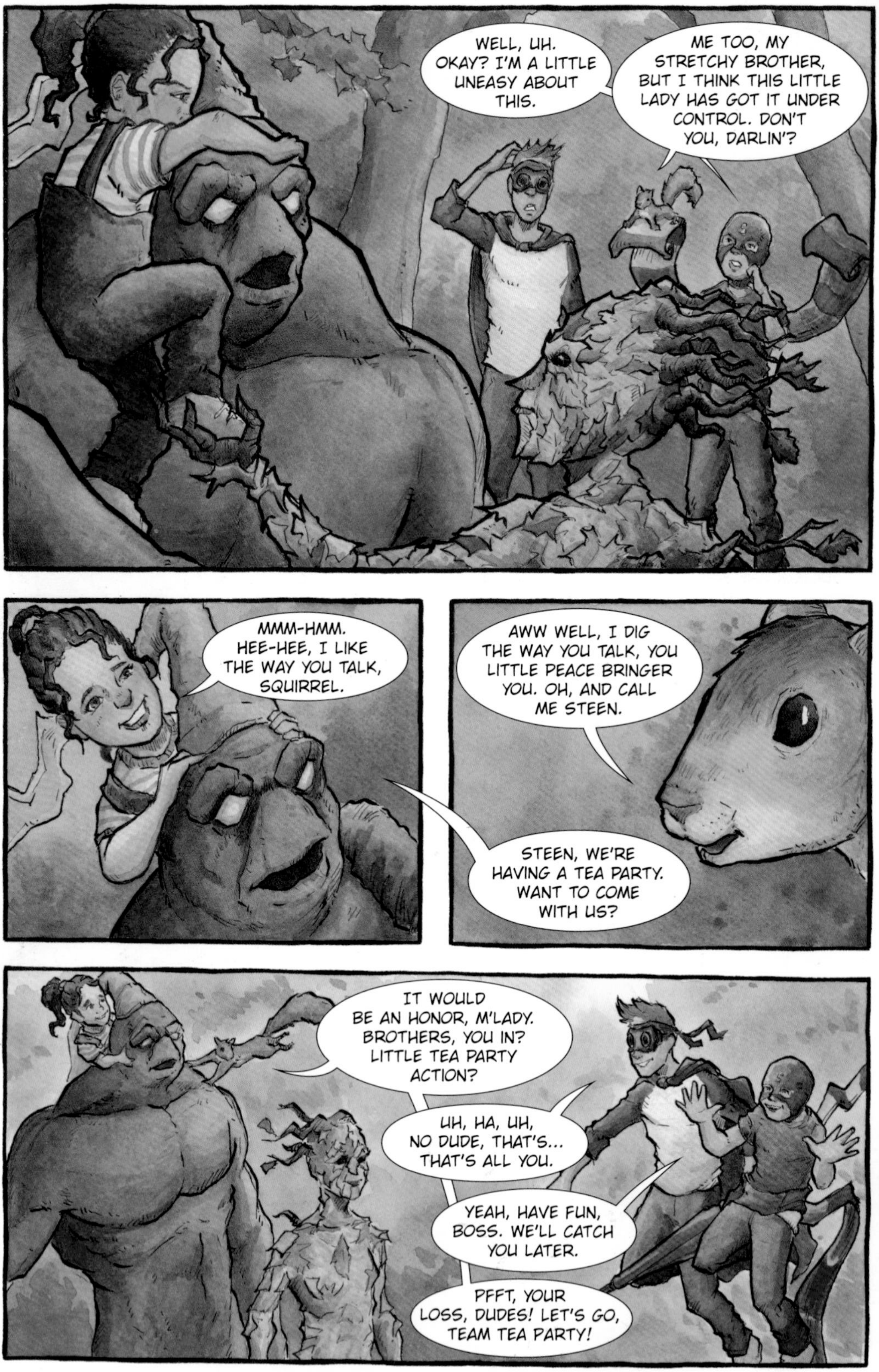
WELL, UH. OKAY? I'M A LITTLE UNEASY ABOUT THIS.
ME TOO, MY STRETCHY BROTHER, BUT I THINK THIS LITTLE LADY HAS GOT IT UNDER CONTROL. DON'T YOU, DARLIN'?
MMM-HMM. HEE-HEE, I LIKE THE WAY YOU TALK, SQUIRREL.
AWW WELL, I DIG THE WAY YOU TALK, YOU LITTLE PEACE BRINGER YOU. OH, AND CALL ME STEEN.
STEEN, WE'RE HAVING A TEA PARTY. WANT TO COME WITH US?
IT WOULD BE AN HONOR, M'LADY. BROTHERS, YOU IN? LITTLE TEA PARTY ACTION?
UH, HA, UH, NO DUDE, THAT'S... THAT'S ALL YOU.
YEAH, HAVE FUN, BOSS. WE'LL CATCH YOU LATER.
PFFT, YOUR LOSS, DUDES! LET'S GO, TEAM TEA PARTY!

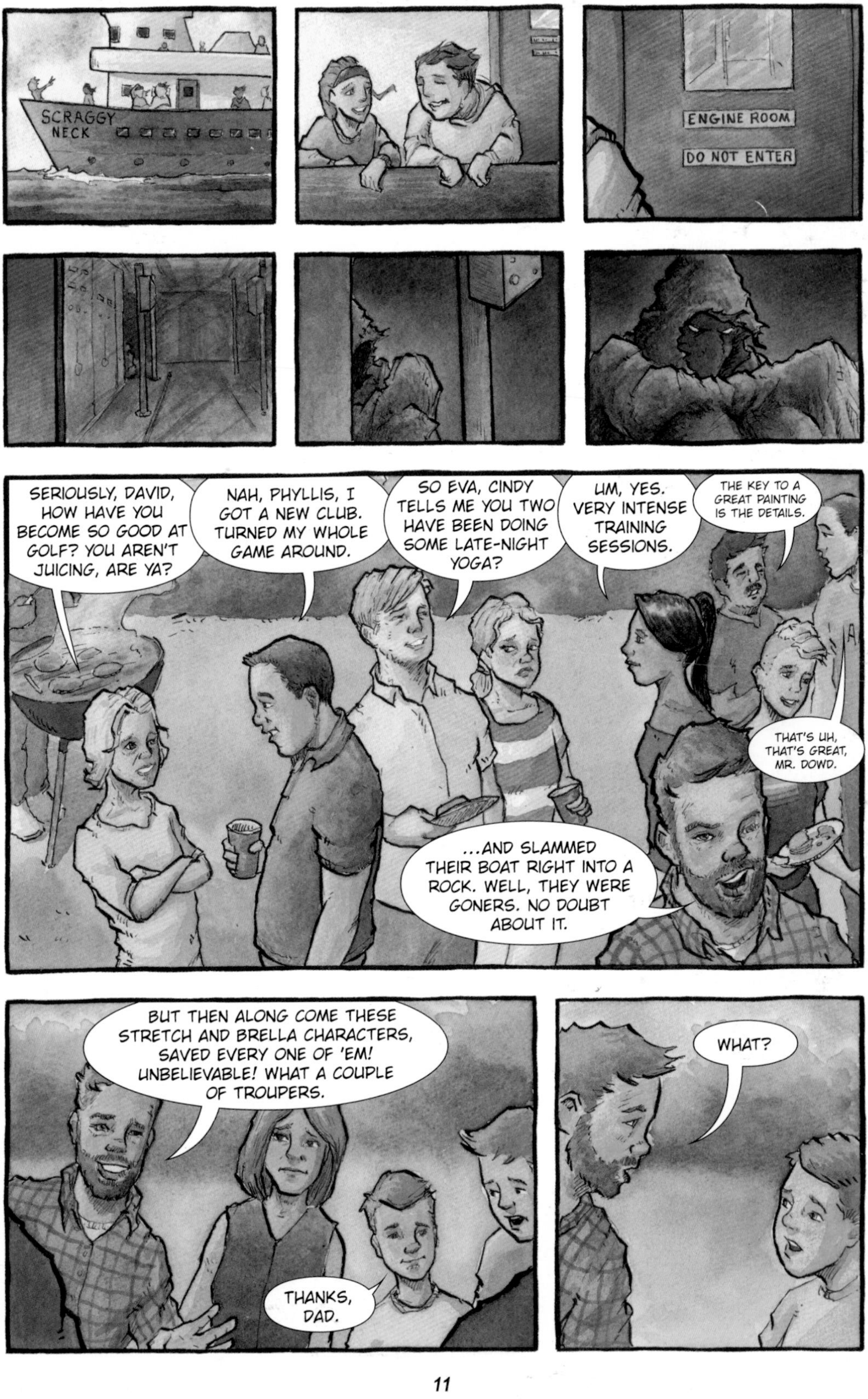
SCRAGGY NECK
ENGINE ROOM
DO NOT ENTER
SERIOUSLY, DAVID, HOW HAVE YOU BECOME SO GOOD AT GOLF? YOU AREN'T JUICING, ARE YA?
NAH, PHYLLIS, I GOT A NEW CLUB. TURNED MY WHOLE GAME AROUND.
SO EVA, CINDY TELLS ME YOU TWO HAVE BEEN DOING SOME LATE-NIGHT YOGA?
UM, YES. VERY INTENSE TRAINING SESSIONS.
THE KEY TO A GREAT PAINTING IS THE DETAILS.
THAT'S UH, THAT'S GREAT, MR. DOWD.
...AND SLAMMED THEIR BOAT RIGHT INTO A ROCK. WELL, THEY WERE GONERS. NO DOUBT ABOUT IT.
BUT THEN ALONG COME THESE STRETCH AND BRELLA CHARACTERS, SAVED EVERY ONE OF 'EM! UNBELIEVABLE! WHAT A COUPLE OF TROUPERS.
THANKS, DAD.
WHAT?

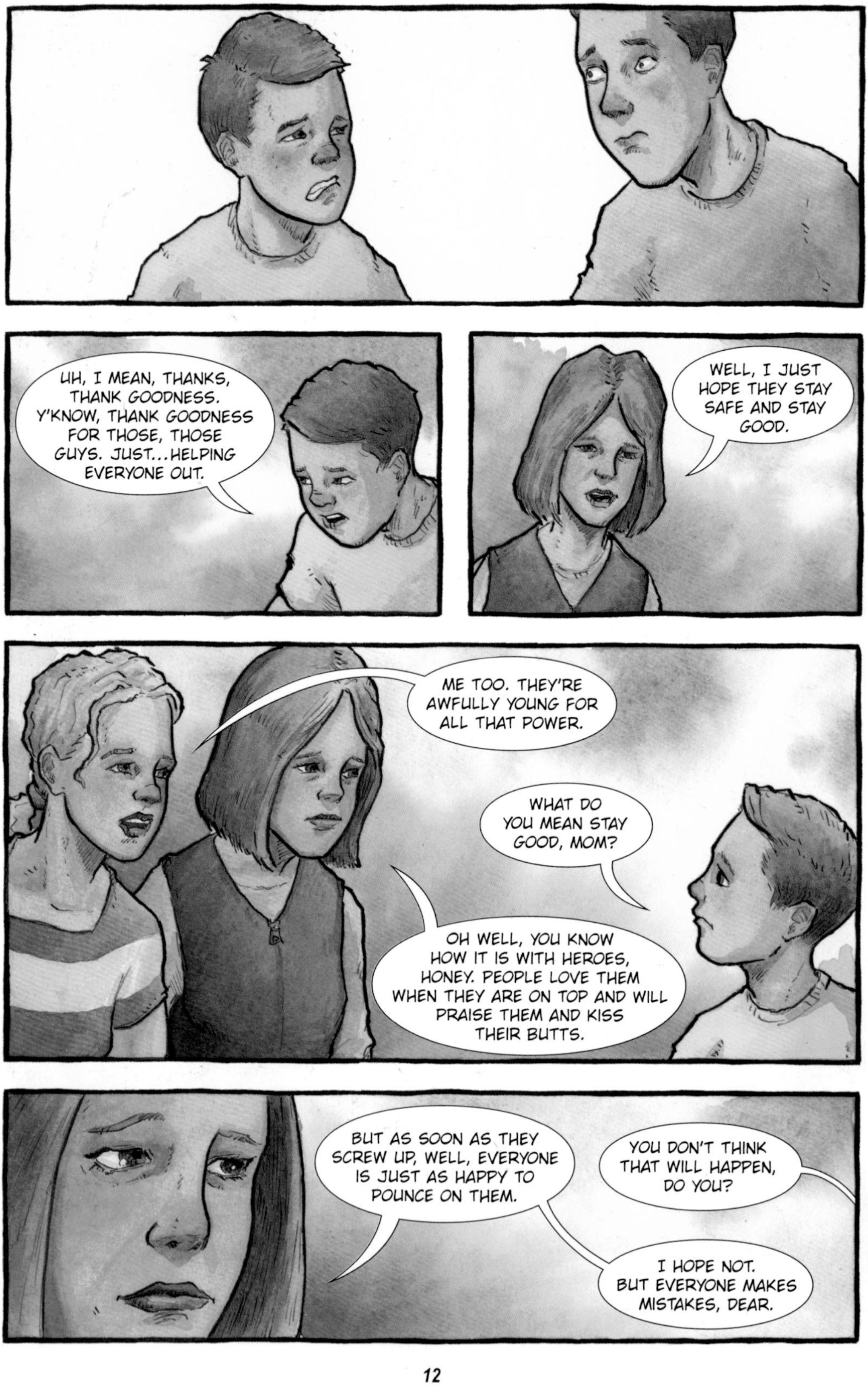
UH, I MEAN, THANKS, THANK GOODNESS. Y'KNOW, THANK GOODNESS FOR THOSE, THOSE GUYS. JUST...HELPING EVERYONE OUT.
WELL, I JUST HOPE THEY STAY SAFE AND STAY GOOD.
ME TOO. THEY'RE AWFULLY YOUNG FOR ALL THAT POWER.
WHAT DO YOU MEAN STAY GOOD, MOM?
OH WELL, YOU KNOW HOW IT IS WITH HEROES, HONEY. PEOPLE LOVE THEM WHEN THEY ARE ON TOP AND WILL PRAISE THEM AND KISS THEIR BUTTS.
BUT AS SOON AS THEY SCREW UP, WELL, EVERYONE IS JUST AS HAPPY TO POUNCE ON THEM.
YOU DON'T THINK THAT WILL HAPPEN, DO YOU?
I HOPE NOT. BUT EVERYONE MAKES MISTAKES, DEAR.

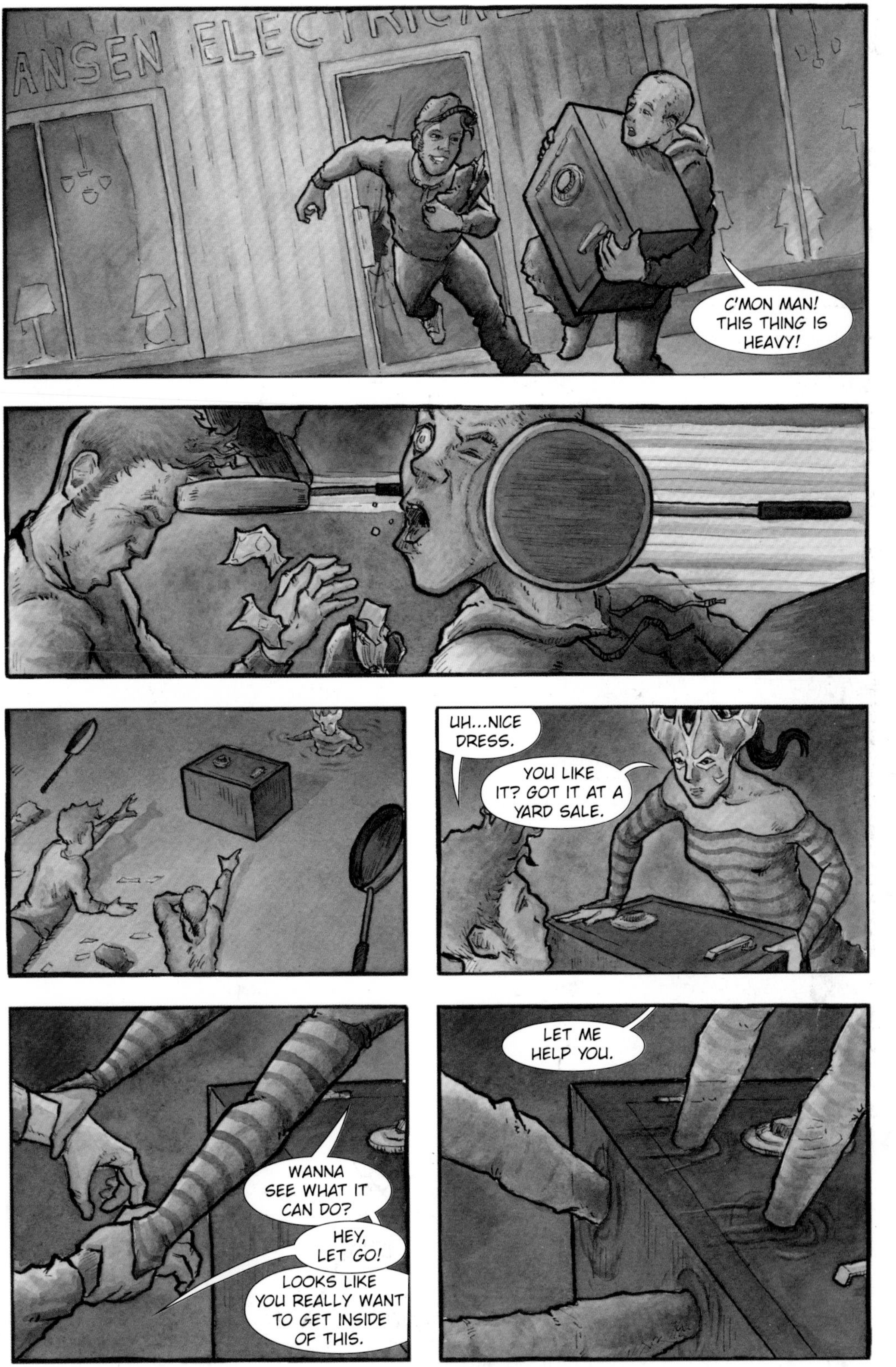
ANSEN ELECTRICAL
C'MON MAN! THIS THING IS HEAVY!
UH...NICE DRESS.
YOU LIKE IT? GOT IT AT A YARD SALE.
WANNA SEE WHAT IT CAN DO?
HEY, LET GO!
LOOKS LIKE YOU REALLY WANT TO GET INSIDE OF THIS.
LET ME HELP YOU.

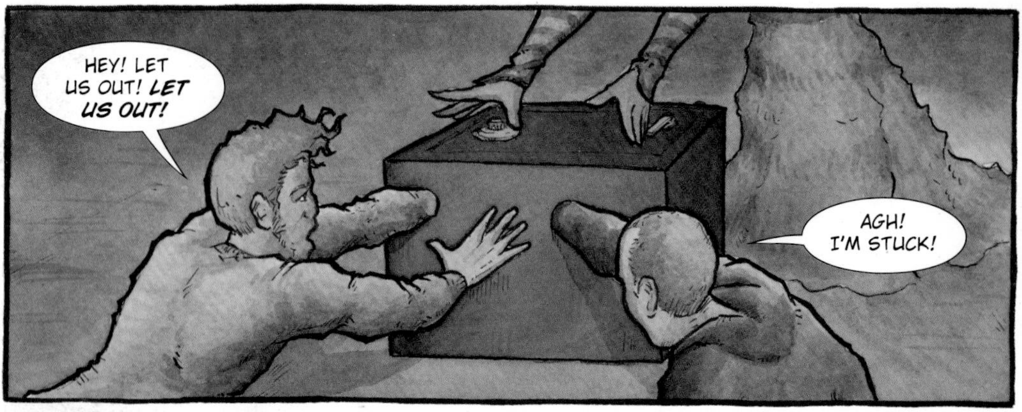
HEY! LET US OUT! LET US OUT!
AGH! I'M STUCK!

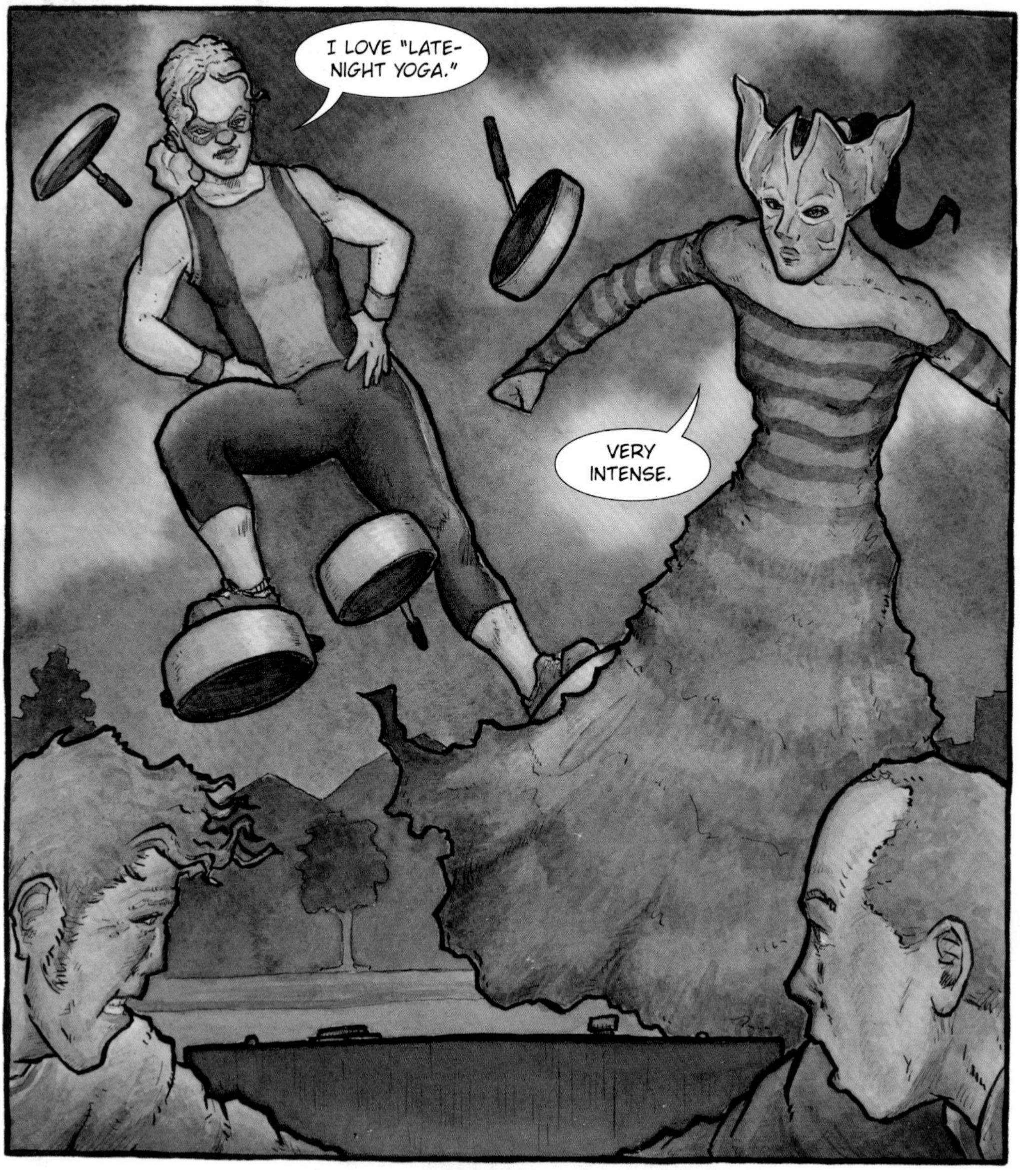
I LOVE "LATE-NIGHT YOGA."
VERY INTENSE.

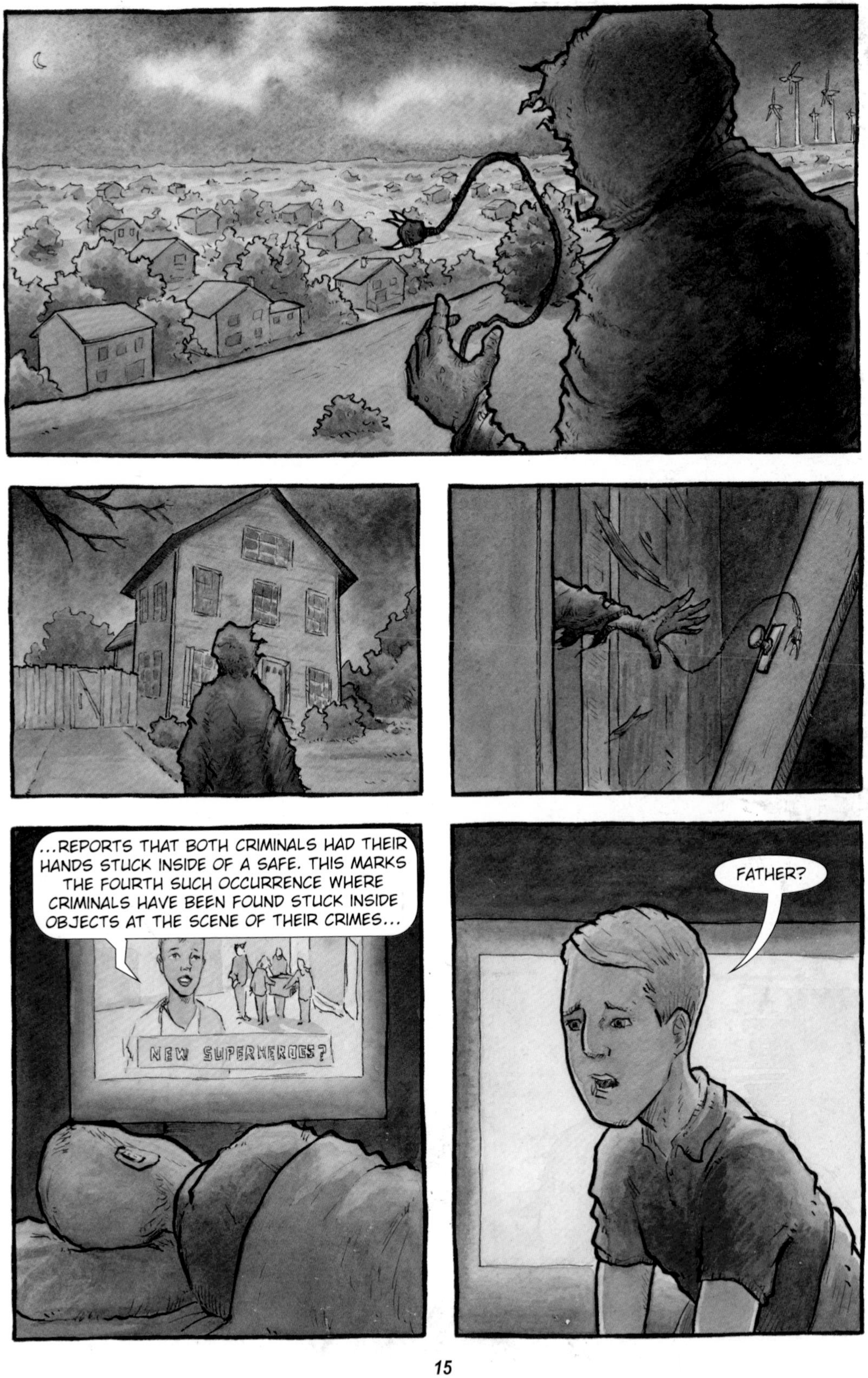
...REPORTS THAT BOTH CRIMINALS HAD THEIR HANDS STUCK INSIDE OF A SAFE. THIS MARKS THE FOURTH SUCH OCCURRENCE WHERE CRIMINALS HAVE BEEN FOUND STUCK INSIDE OBJECTS AT THE SCENE OF THEIR CRIMES...
NEW SUPERHEROES?
FATHER?

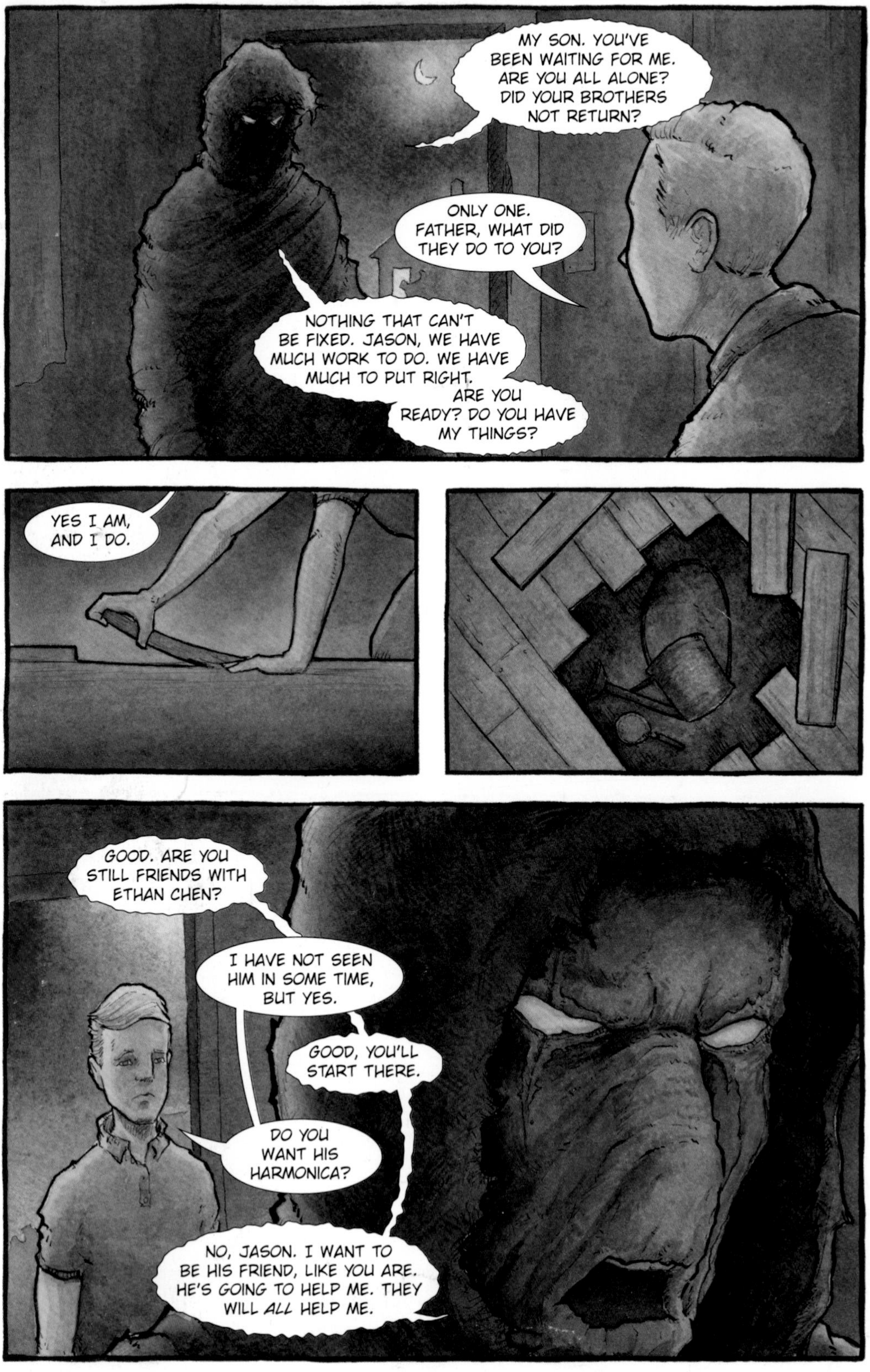
MY SON. YOU'VE BEEN WAITING FOR ME. ARE YOU ALL ALONE? DID YOUR BROTHERS NOT RETURN?
ONLY ONE. FATHER, WHAT DID THEY DO TO YOU?
NOTHING THAT CAN'T BE FIXED. JASON, WE HAVE MUCH WORK TO DO. WE HAVE MUCH TO PUT RIGHT.
ARE YOU READY? DO YOU HAVE MY THINGS?
YES I AM, AND I DO.
GOOD. ARE YOU STILL FRIENDS WITH ETHAN CHEN?
I HAVE NOT SEEN HIM IN SOME TIME, BUT YES.
GOOD, YOU'LL START THERE.
DO YOU WANT HIS HARMONICA?
NO, JASON. I WANT TO BE HIS FRIEND, LIKE YOU ARE. HE'S GOING TO HELP ME. THEY WILL *ALL* HELP ME.

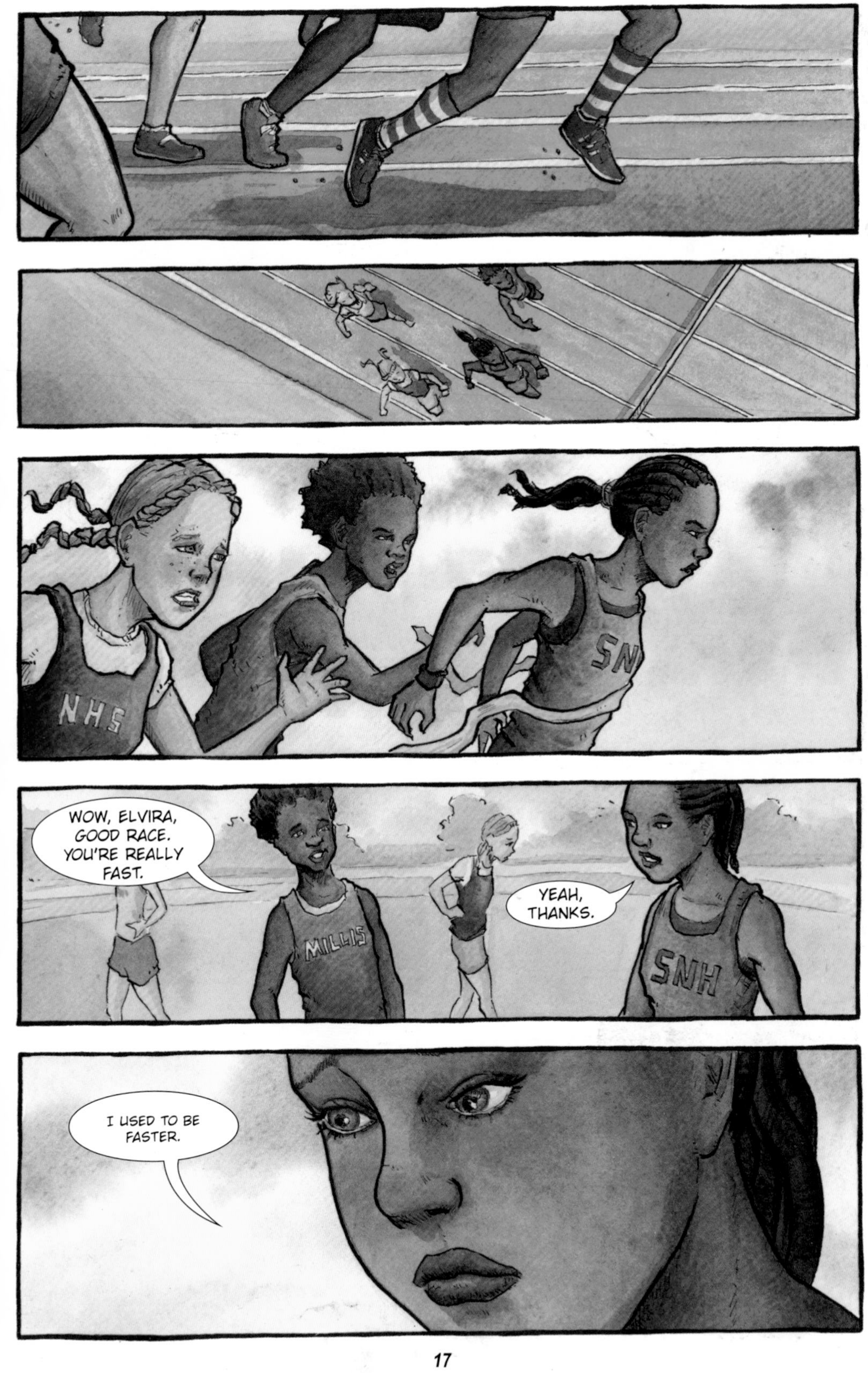
NHS
SNH
WOW, ELVIRA, GOOD RACE. YOU'RE REALLY FAST.
YEAH, THANKS.
MILLIS
SNH
I USED TO BE FASTER.

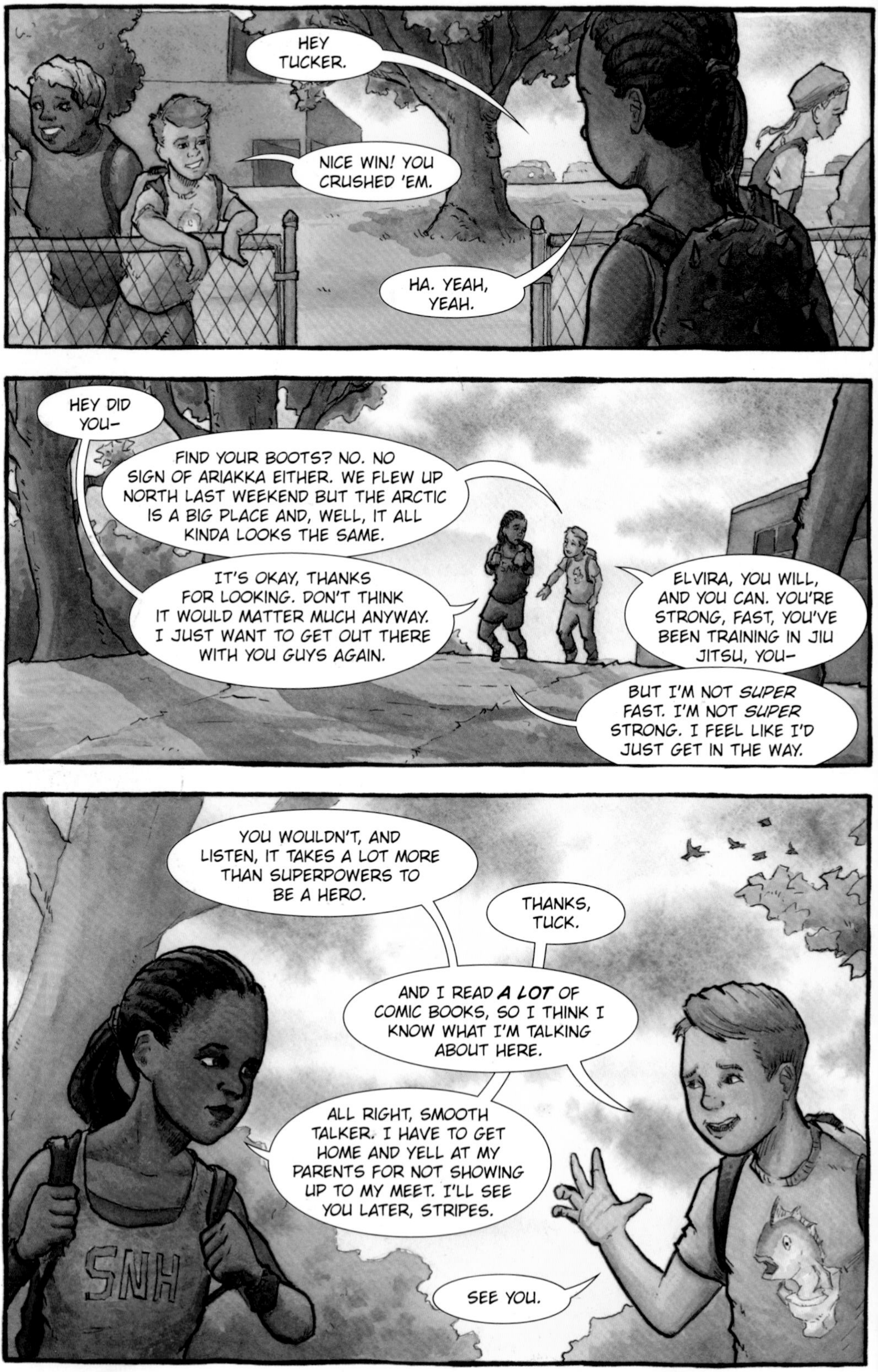
HEY TUCKER.
NICE WIN! YOU CRUSHED 'EM.
HA. YEAH, YEAH.
HEY DID YOU–
FIND YOUR BOOTS? NO. NO SIGN OF ARIAKKA EITHER. WE FLEW UP NORTH LAST WEEKEND BUT THE ARCTIC IS A BIG PLACE AND, WELL, IT ALL KINDA LOOKS THE SAME.
IT'S OKAY, THANKS FOR LOOKING. DON'T THINK IT WOULD MATTER MUCH ANYWAY. I JUST WANT TO GET OUT THERE WITH YOU GUYS AGAIN.
ELVIRA, YOU WILL, AND YOU CAN. YOU'RE STRONG, FAST, YOU'VE BEEN TRAINING IN JIU JITSU, YOU–
BUT I'M NOT *SUPER* FAST. I'M NOT *SUPER* STRONG. I FEEL LIKE I'D JUST GET IN THE WAY.
YOU WOULDN'T, AND LISTEN, IT TAKES A LOT MORE THAN SUPERPOWERS TO BE A HERO.
THANKS, TUCK.
AND I READ ***A LOT*** OF COMIC BOOKS, SO I THINK I KNOW WHAT I'M TALKING ABOUT HERE.
ALL RIGHT, SMOOTH TALKER. I HAVE TO GET HOME AND YELL AT MY PARENTS FOR NOT SHOWING UP TO MY MEET. I'LL SEE YOU LATER, STRIPES.
SEE YOU.

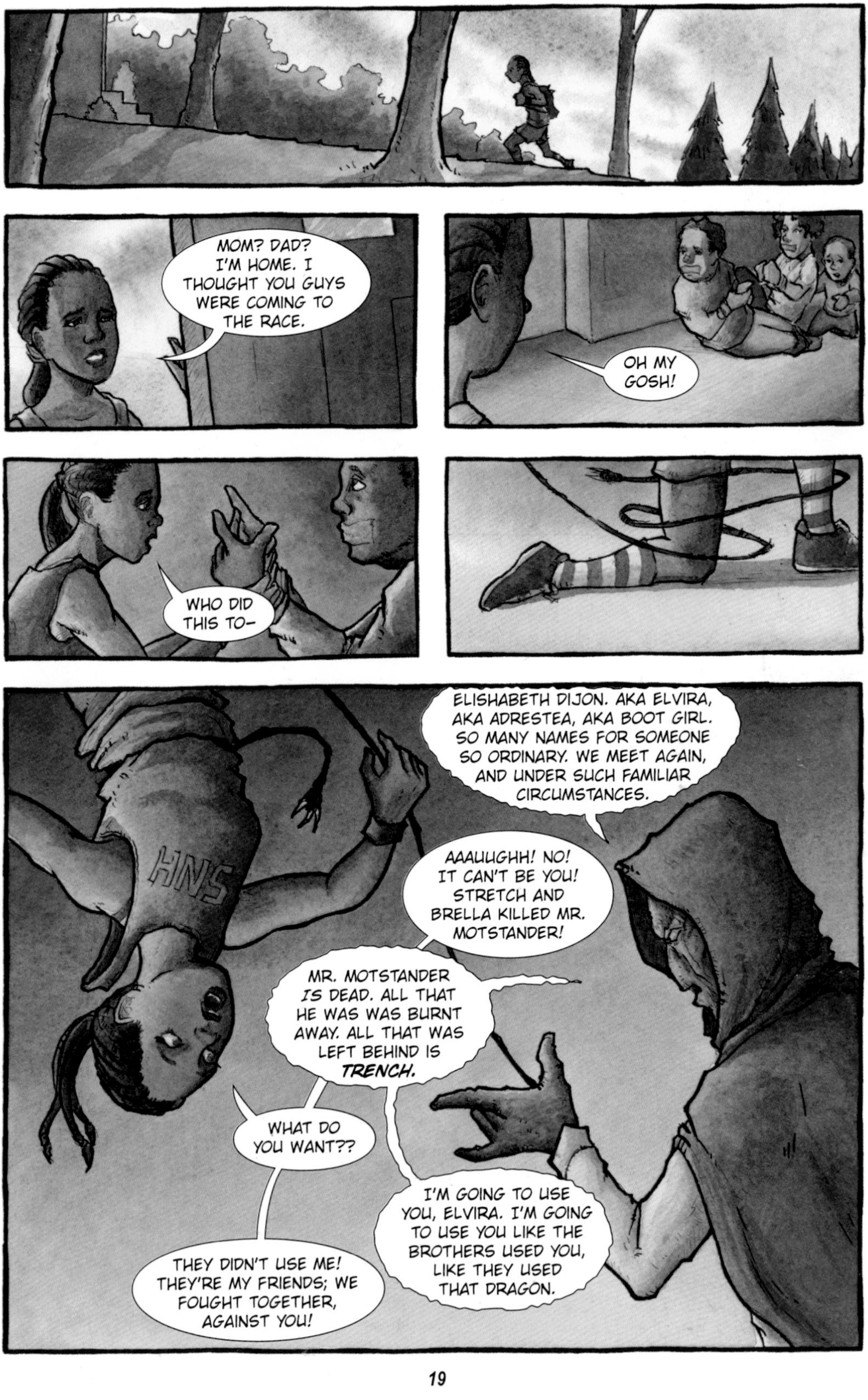
MOM? DAD? I'M HOME. I THOUGHT YOU GUYS WERE COMING TO THE RACE.
OH MY GOSH!
WHO DID THIS TO—
ELISHABETH DIJON. AKA ELVIRA, AKA ADRESTEA, AKA BOOT GIRL. SO MANY NAMES FOR SOMEONE SO ORDINARY. WE MEET AGAIN, AND UNDER SUCH FAMILIAR CIRCUMSTANCES.
AAAUUGHH! NO! IT CAN'T BE YOU! STRETCH AND BRELLA KILLED MR. MOTSTANDER!
MR. MOTSTANDER *IS* DEAD. ALL THAT HE WAS WAS BURNT AWAY. ALL THAT WAS LEFT BEHIND IS ***TRENCH.***
WHAT DO YOU WANT??
I'M GOING TO USE YOU, ELVIRA. I'M GOING TO USE YOU LIKE THE BROTHERS USED YOU, LIKE THEY USED THAT DRAGON.
THEY DIDN'T USE ME! THEY'RE MY FRIENDS; WE FOUGHT TOGETHER, AGAINST YOU!

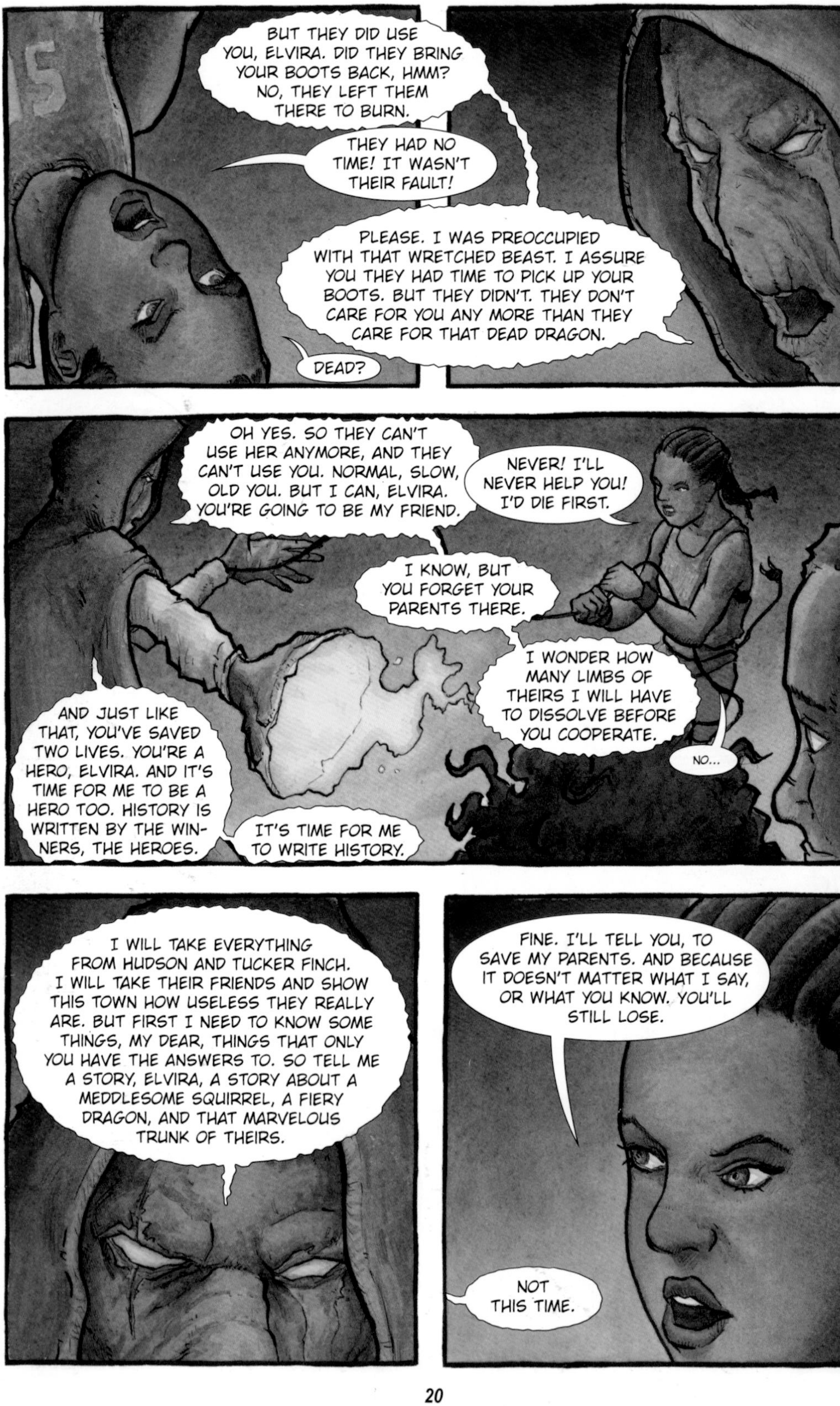

BUT THEY DID USE YOU, ELVIRA. DID THEY BRING YOUR BOOTS BACK, HMM? NO, THEY LEFT THEM THERE TO BURN.
THEY HAD NO TIME! IT WASN'T THEIR FAULT!
PLEASE. I WAS PREOCCUPIED WITH THAT WRETCHED BEAST. I ASSURE YOU THEY HAD TIME TO PICK UP YOUR BOOTS. BUT THEY DIDN'T. THEY DON'T CARE FOR YOU ANY MORE THAN THEY CARE FOR THAT DEAD DRAGON.
DEAD?
OH YES. SO THEY CAN'T USE HER ANYMORE, AND THEY CAN'T USE YOU. NORMAL, SLOW, OLD YOU. BUT I CAN, ELVIRA. YOU'RE GOING TO BE MY FRIEND.
NEVER! I'LL NEVER HELP YOU! I'D DIE FIRST.
I KNOW, BUT YOU FORGET YOUR PARENTS THERE.
I WONDER HOW MANY LIMBS OF THEIRS I WILL HAVE TO DISSOLVE BEFORE YOU COOPERATE.
NO...
AND JUST LIKE THAT, YOU'VE SAVED TWO LIVES. YOU'RE A HERO, ELVIRA. AND IT'S TIME FOR ME TO BE A HERO TOO. HISTORY IS WRITTEN BY THE WIN-NERS, THE HEROES.
IT'S TIME FOR ME TO WRITE HISTORY.
I WILL TAKE EVERYTHING FROM HUDSON AND TUCKER FINCH. I WILL TAKE THEIR FRIENDS AND SHOW THIS TOWN HOW USELESS THEY REALLY ARE. BUT FIRST I NEED TO KNOW SOME THINGS, MY DEAR, THINGS THAT ONLY YOU HAVE THE ANSWERS TO. SO TELL ME A STORY, ELVIRA, A STORY ABOUT A MEDDLESOME SQUIRREL, A FIERY DRAGON, AND THAT MARVELOUS TRUNK OF THEIRS.
FINE. I'LL TELL YOU, TO SAVE MY PARENTS. AND BECAUSE IT DOESN'T MATTER WHAT I SAY, OR WHAT YOU KNOW. YOU'LL STILL LOSE.
NOT THIS TIME.

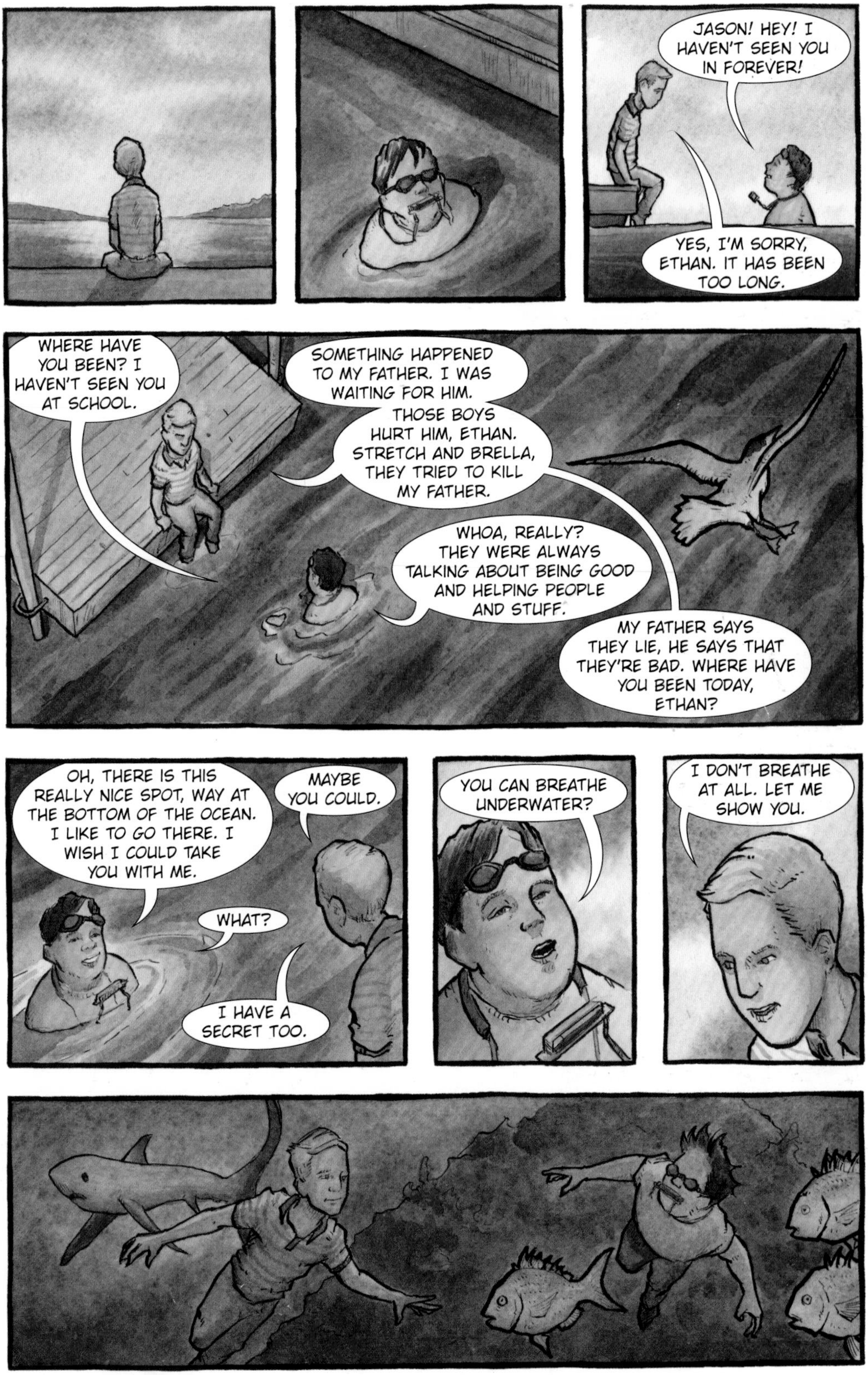
JASON! HEY! I HAVEN'T SEEN YOU IN FOREVER!
YES, I'M SORRY, ETHAN. IT HAS BEEN TOO LONG.
WHERE HAVE YOU BEEN? I HAVEN'T SEEN YOU AT SCHOOL.
SOMETHING HAPPENED TO MY FATHER. I WAS WAITING FOR HIM.
THOSE BOYS HURT HIM, ETHAN. STRETCH AND BRELLA, THEY TRIED TO KILL MY FATHER.
WHOA, REALLY? THEY WERE ALWAYS TALKING ABOUT BEING GOOD AND HELPING PEOPLE AND STUFF.
MY FATHER SAYS THEY LIE, HE SAYS THAT THEY'RE BAD. WHERE HAVE YOU BEEN TODAY, ETHAN?
OH, THERE IS THIS REALLY NICE SPOT, WAY AT THE BOTTOM OF THE OCEAN. I LIKE TO GO THERE. I WISH I COULD TAKE YOU WITH ME.
MAYBE YOU COULD.
WHAT?
I HAVE A SECRET TOO.
YOU CAN BREATHE UNDERWATER?
I DON'T BREATHE AT ALL. LET ME SHOW YOU.

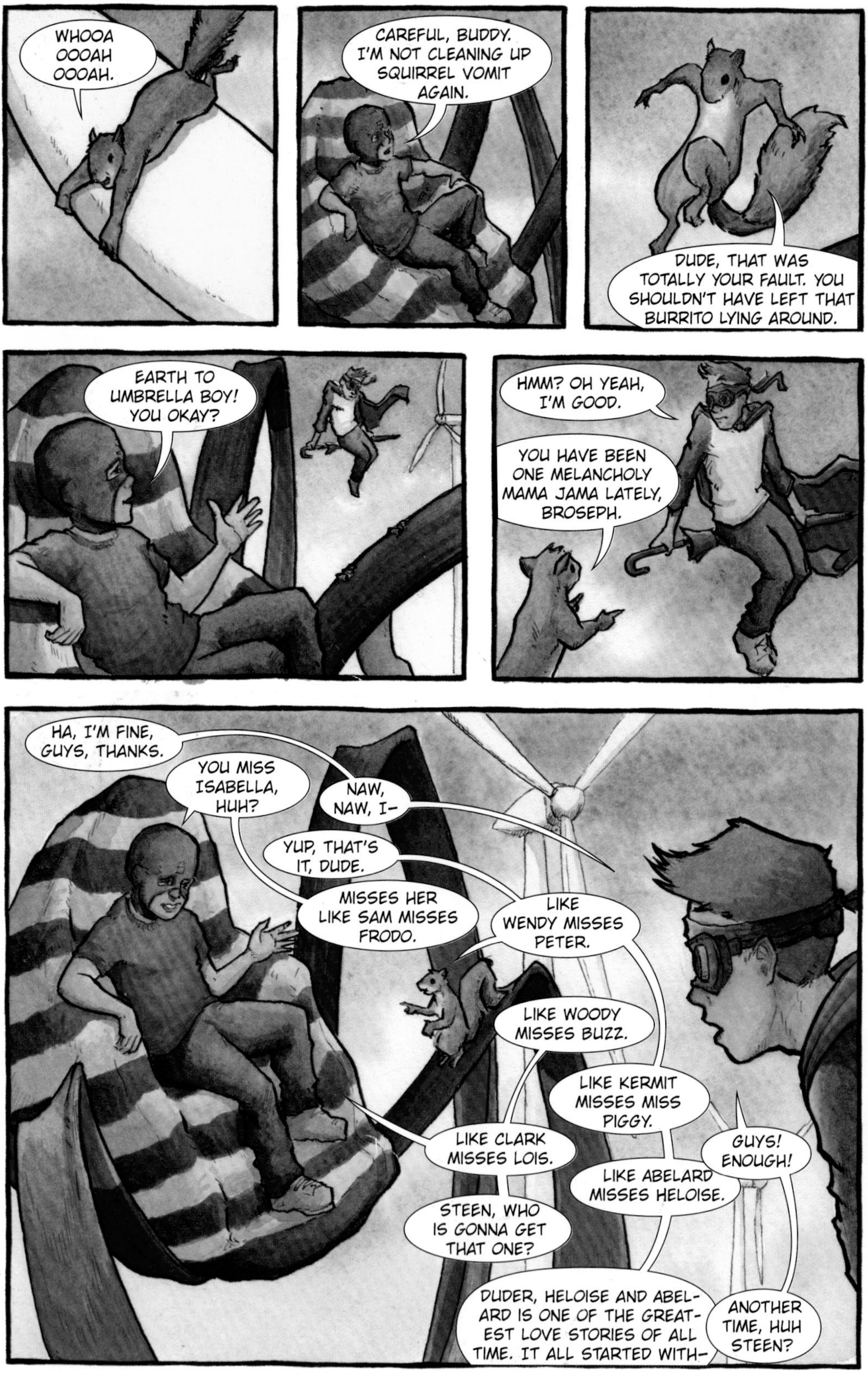
WHOOA OOOAH OOOAH.
CAREFUL, BUDDY. I'M NOT CLEANING UP SQUIRREL VOMIT AGAIN.
DUDE, THAT WAS TOTALLY YOUR FAULT. YOU SHOULDN'T HAVE LEFT THAT BURRITO LYING AROUND.
EARTH TO UMBRELLA BOY! YOU OKAY?
HMM? OH YEAH, I'M GOOD.
YOU HAVE BEEN ONE MELANCHOLY MAMA JAMA LATELY, BROSEPH.
HA, I'M FINE, GUYS, THANKS.
YOU MISS ISABELLA, HUH?
NAW, NAW, I-
YUP, THAT'S IT, DUDE.
MISSES HER LIKE SAM MISSES FRODO.
LIKE WENDY MISSES PETER.
LIKE WOODY MISSES BUZZ.
LIKE KERMIT MISSES MISS PIGGY.
LIKE CLARK MISSES LOIS.
LIKE ABELARD MISSES HELOISE.
STEEN, WHO IS GONNA GET THAT ONE?
GUYS! ENOUGH!
DUDER, HELOISE AND ABEL-ARD IS ONE OF THE GREAT-EST LOVE STORIES OF ALL TIME. IT ALL STARTED WITH-
ANOTHER TIME, HUH STEEN?

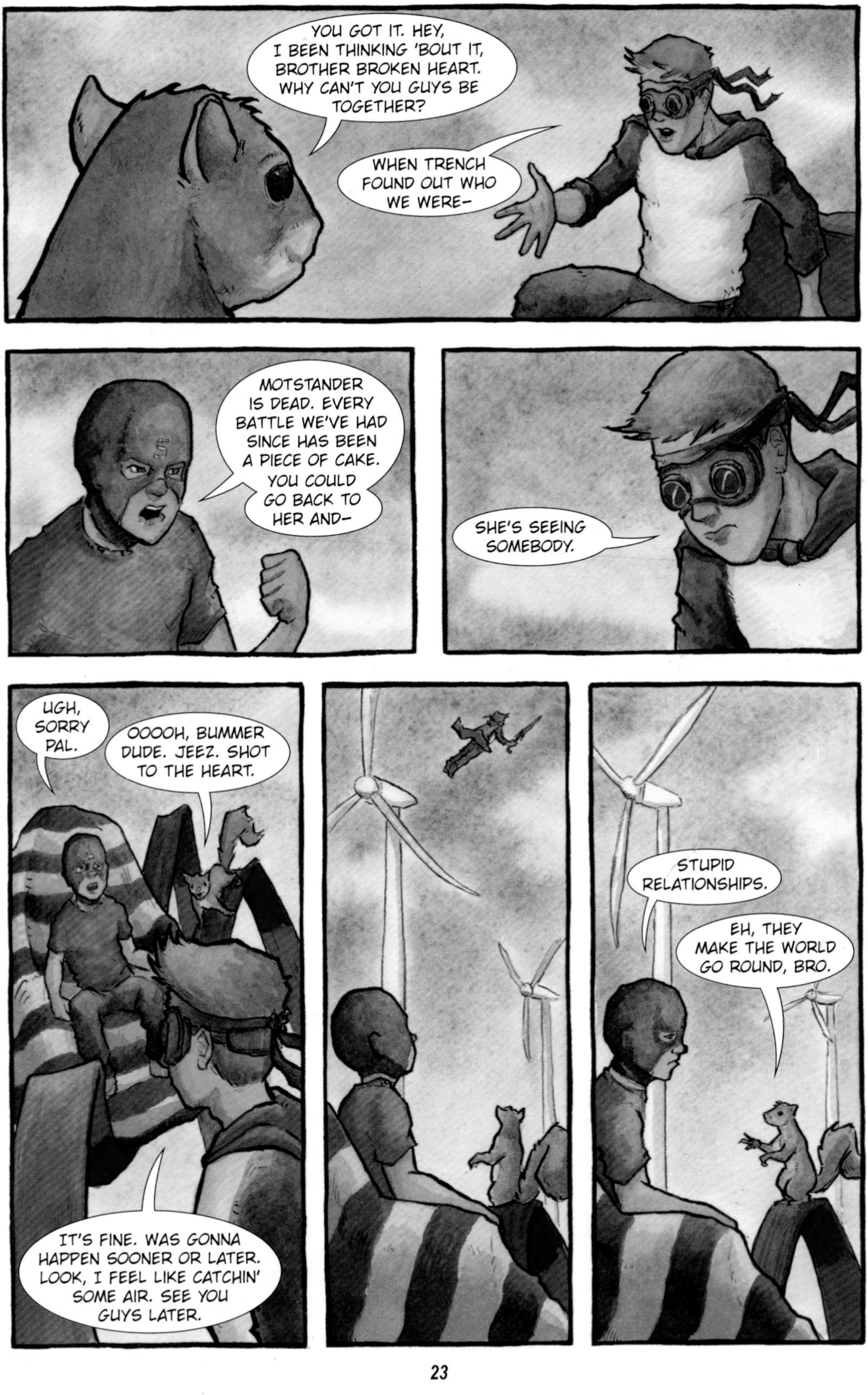
YOU GOT IT. HEY, I BEEN THINKING 'BOUT IT, BROTHER BROKEN HEART. WHY CAN'T YOU GUYS BE TOGETHER?
WHEN TRENCH FOUND OUT WHO WE WERE–
MOTSTANDER IS DEAD. EVERY BATTLE WE'VE HAD SINCE HAS BEEN A PIECE OF CAKE. YOU COULD GO BACK TO HER AND–
SHE'S SEEING SOMEBODY.
UGH, SORRY PAL.
OOOOH, BUMMER DUDE. JEEZ. SHOT TO THE HEART.
IT'S FINE. WAS GONNA HAPPEN SOONER OR LATER. LOOK, I FEEL LIKE CATCHIN' SOME AIR. SEE YOU GUYS LATER.
STUPID RELATIONSHIPS.
EH, THEY MAKE THE WORLD GO ROUND, BRO.

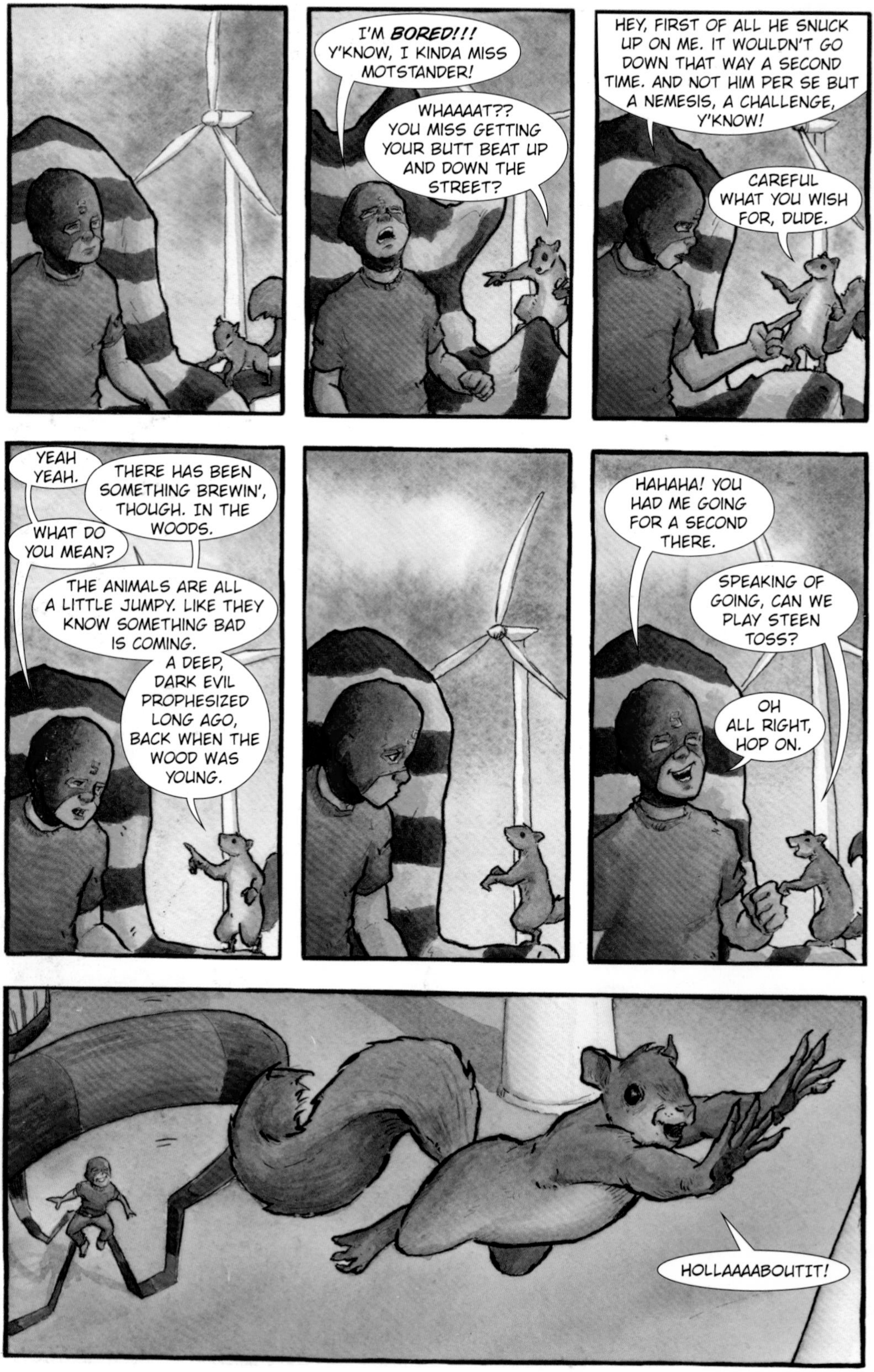
I'M *BORED!!!* Y'KNOW, I KINDA MISS MOTSTANDER!
WHAAAAT?? YOU MISS GETTING YOUR BUTT BEAT UP AND DOWN THE STREET?
HEY, FIRST OF ALL HE SNUCK UP ON ME. IT WOULDN'T GO DOWN THAT WAY A SECOND TIME. AND NOT HIM PER SE BUT A NEMESIS, A CHALLENGE, Y'KNOW!
CAREFUL WHAT YOU WISH FOR, DUDE.
YEAH YEAH.
THERE HAS BEEN SOMETHING BREWIN', THOUGH. IN THE WOODS.
WHAT DO YOU MEAN?
THE ANIMALS ARE ALL A LITTLE JUMPY. LIKE THEY KNOW SOMETHING BAD IS COMING.
A DEEP, DARK EVIL PROPHESIZED LONG AGO, BACK WHEN THE WOOD WAS YOUNG.
HAHAHA! YOU HAD ME GOING FOR A SECOND THERE.
SPEAKING OF GOING, CAN WE PLAY STEEN TOSS?
OH ALL RIGHT, HOP ON.
HOLLAAAABOUTIT!

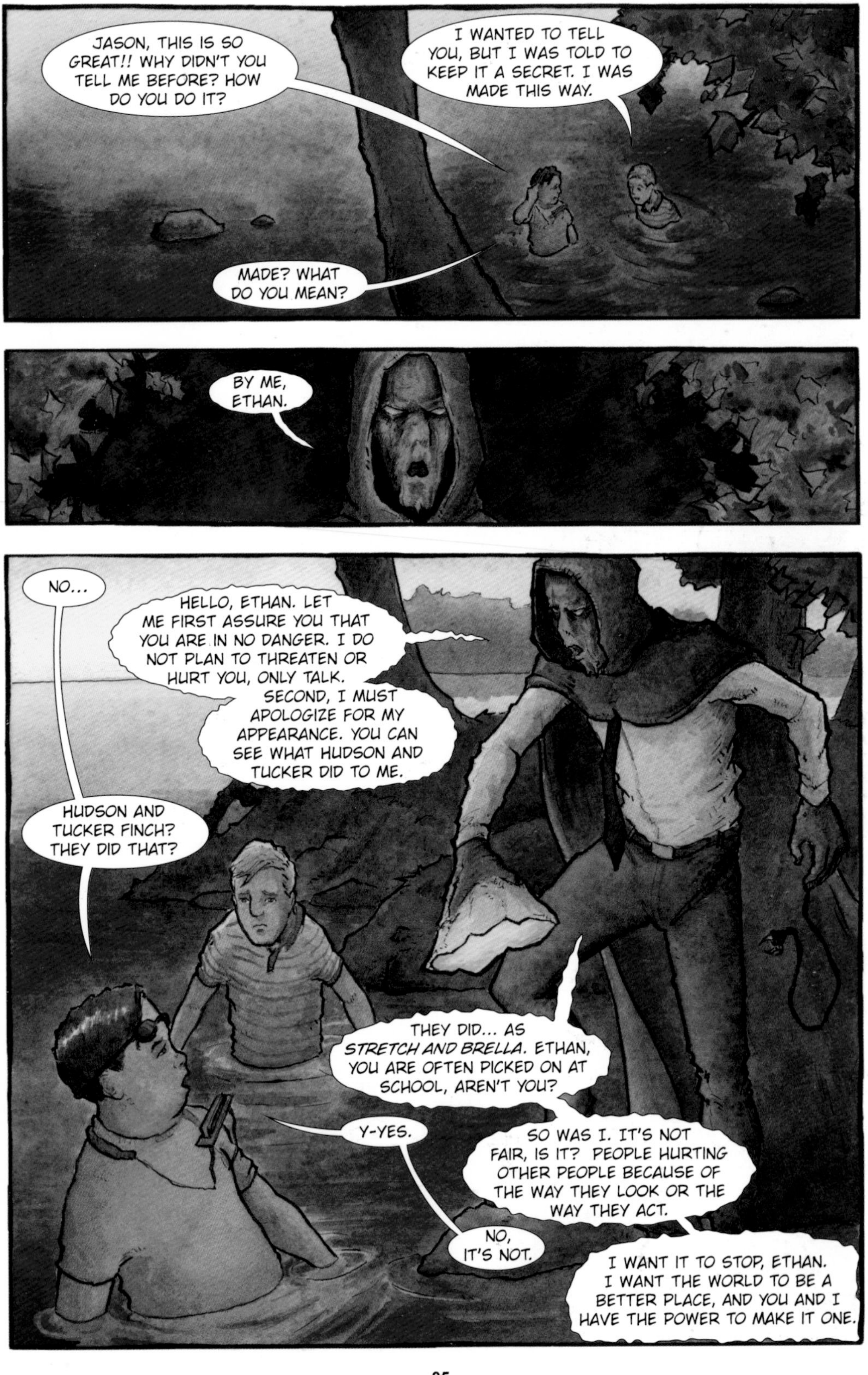
JASON, THIS IS SO GREAT!! WHY DIDN'T YOU TELL ME BEFORE? HOW DO YOU DO IT?
I WANTED TO TELL YOU, BUT I WAS TOLD TO KEEP IT A SECRET. I WAS MADE THIS WAY.
MADE? WHAT DO YOU MEAN?
BY ME, ETHAN.
NO...
HELLO, ETHAN. LET ME FIRST ASSURE YOU THAT YOU ARE IN NO DANGER. I DO NOT PLAN TO THREATEN OR HURT YOU, ONLY TALK.
SECOND, I MUST APOLOGIZE FOR MY APPEARANCE. YOU CAN SEE WHAT HUDSON AND TUCKER DID TO ME.
HUDSON AND TUCKER FINCH? THEY DID THAT?
THEY DID... AS *STRETCH AND BRELLA*. ETHAN, YOU ARE OFTEN PICKED ON AT SCHOOL, AREN'T YOU?
Y-YES.
SO WAS I. IT'S NOT FAIR, IS IT? PEOPLE HURTING OTHER PEOPLE BECAUSE OF THE WAY THEY LOOK OR THE WAY THEY ACT.
NO, IT'S NOT.
I WANT IT TO STOP, ETHAN. I WANT THE WORLD TO BE A BETTER PLACE, AND YOU AND I HAVE THE POWER TO MAKE IT ONE.

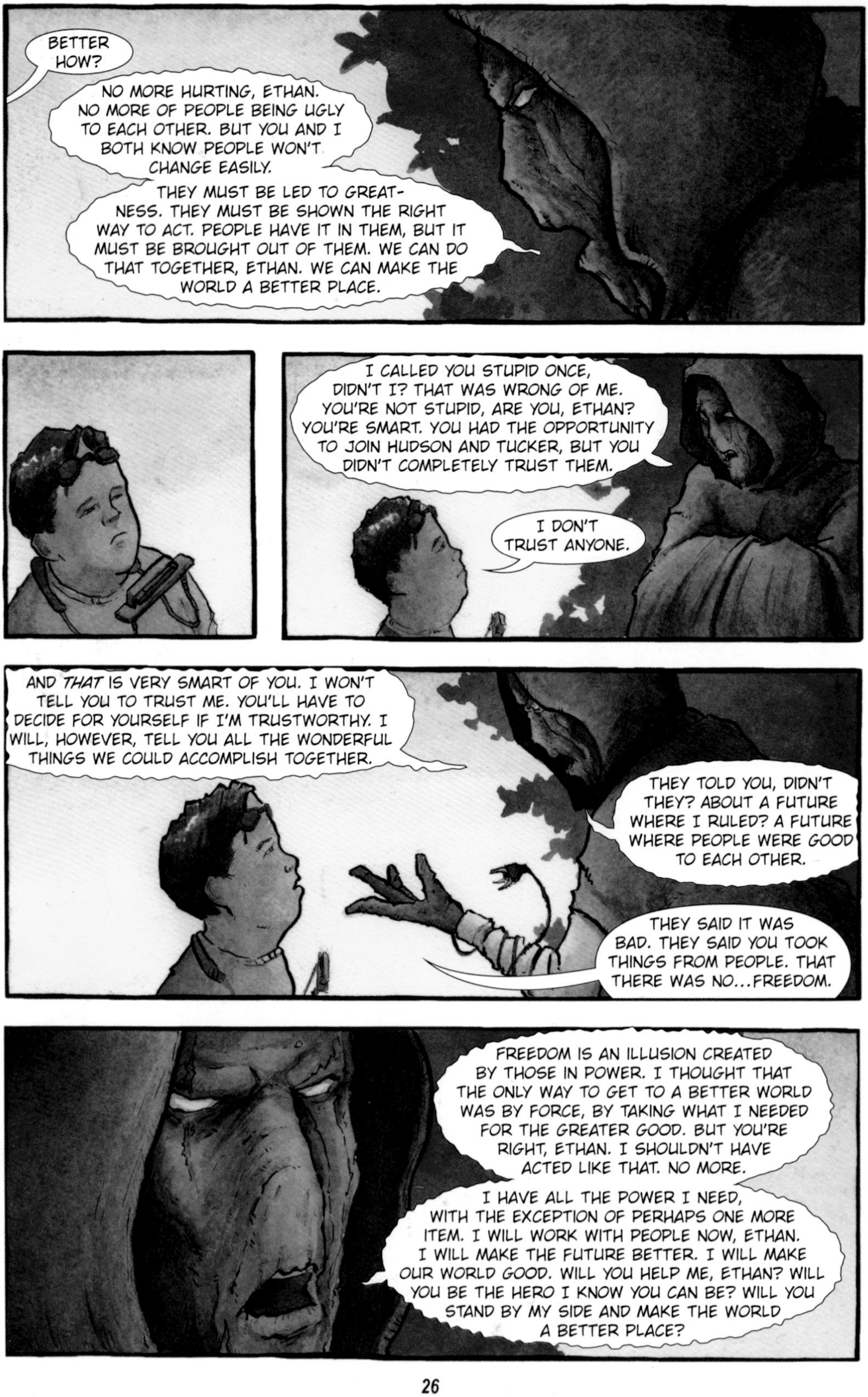
BETTER HOW?
NO MORE HURTING, ETHAN. NO MORE OF PEOPLE BEING UGLY TO EACH OTHER. BUT YOU AND I BOTH KNOW PEOPLE WON'T CHANGE EASILY.
THEY MUST BE LED TO GREAT-NESS. THEY MUST BE SHOWN THE RIGHT WAY TO ACT. PEOPLE HAVE IT IN THEM, BUT IT MUST BE BROUGHT OUT OF THEM. WE CAN DO THAT TOGETHER, ETHAN. WE CAN MAKE THE WORLD A BETTER PLACE.
I CALLED YOU STUPID ONCE, DIDN'T I? THAT WAS WRONG OF ME. YOU'RE NOT STUPID, ARE YOU, ETHAN? YOU'RE SMART. YOU HAD THE OPPORTUNITY TO JOIN HUDSON AND TUCKER, BUT YOU DIDN'T COMPLETELY TRUST THEM.
I DON'T TRUST ANYONE.
AND *THAT* IS VERY SMART OF YOU. I WON'T TELL YOU TO TRUST ME. YOU'LL HAVE TO DECIDE FOR YOURSELF IF I'M TRUSTWORTHY. I WILL, HOWEVER, TELL YOU ALL THE WONDERFUL THINGS WE COULD ACCOMPLISH TOGETHER.
THEY TOLD YOU, DIDN'T THEY? ABOUT A FUTURE WHERE I RULED? A FUTURE WHERE PEOPLE WERE GOOD TO EACH OTHER.
THEY SAID IT WAS BAD. THEY SAID YOU TOOK THINGS FROM PEOPLE. THAT THERE WAS NO...FREEDOM.
FREEDOM IS AN ILLUSION CREATED BY THOSE IN POWER. I THOUGHT THAT THE ONLY WAY TO GET TO A BETTER WORLD WAS BY FORCE, BY TAKING WHAT I NEEDED FOR THE GREATER GOOD. BUT YOU'RE RIGHT, ETHAN. I SHOULDN'T HAVE ACTED LIKE THAT. NO MORE.
I HAVE ALL THE POWER I NEED, WITH THE EXCEPTION OF PERHAPS ONE MORE ITEM. I WILL WORK WITH PEOPLE NOW, ETHAN. I WILL MAKE THE FUTURE BETTER. I WILL MAKE OUR WORLD GOOD. WILL YOU HELP ME, ETHAN? WILL YOU BE THE HERO I KNOW YOU CAN BE? WILL YOU STAND BY MY SIDE AND MAKE THE WORLD A BETTER PLACE?

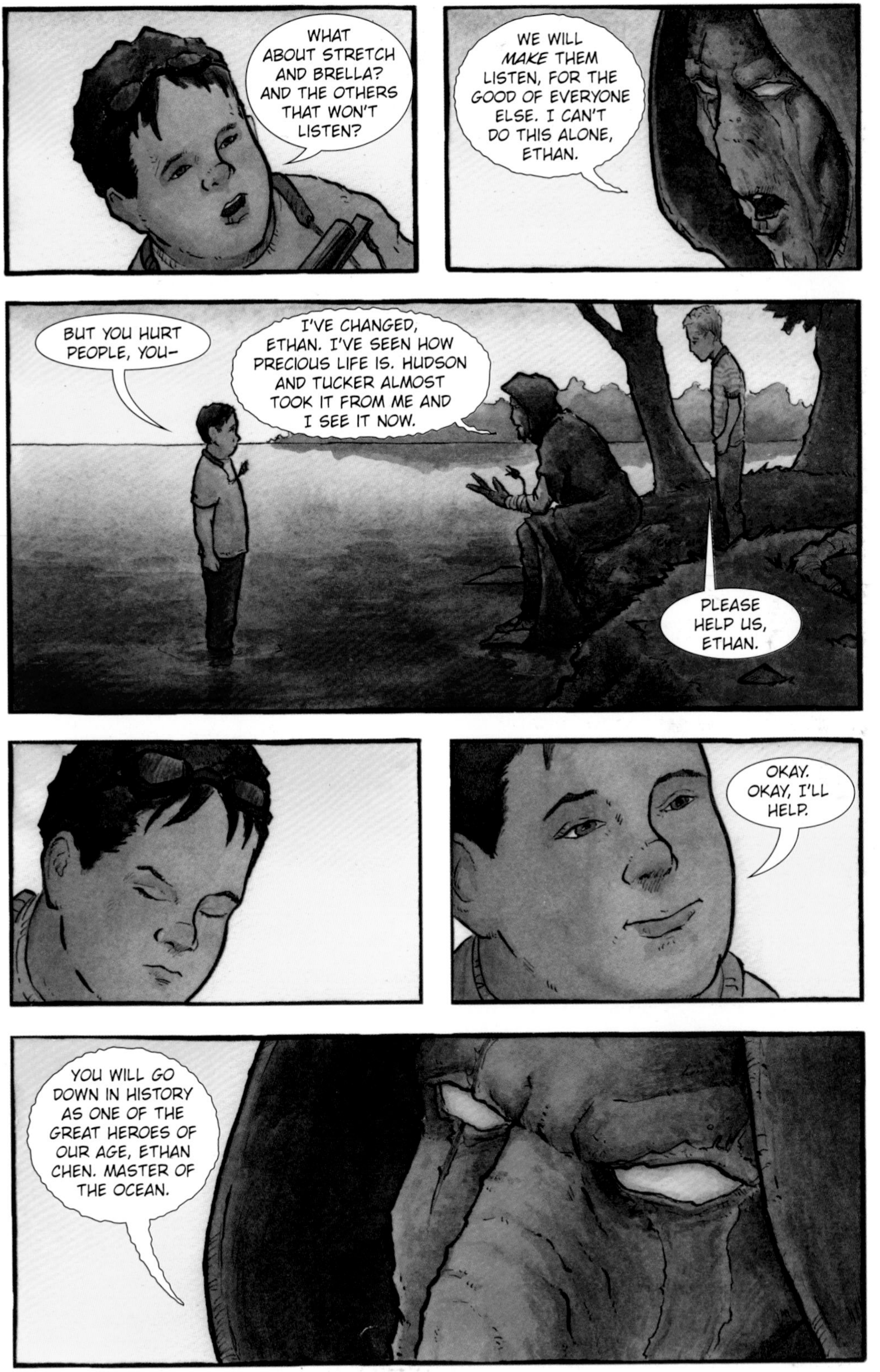
WHAT ABOUT STRETCH AND BRELLA? AND THE OTHERS THAT WON'T LISTEN?
WE WILL *MAKE* THEM LISTEN, FOR THE GOOD OF EVERYONE ELSE. I CAN'T DO THIS ALONE, ETHAN.
BUT YOU HURT PEOPLE, YOU–
I'VE CHANGED, ETHAN. I'VE SEEN HOW PRECIOUS LIFE IS. HUDSON AND TUCKER ALMOST TOOK IT FROM ME AND I SEE IT NOW.
PLEASE HELP US, ETHAN.
OKAY. OKAY, I'LL HELP.
YOU WILL GO DOWN IN HISTORY AS ONE OF THE GREAT HEROES OF OUR AGE, ETHAN CHEN. MASTER OF THE OCEAN.

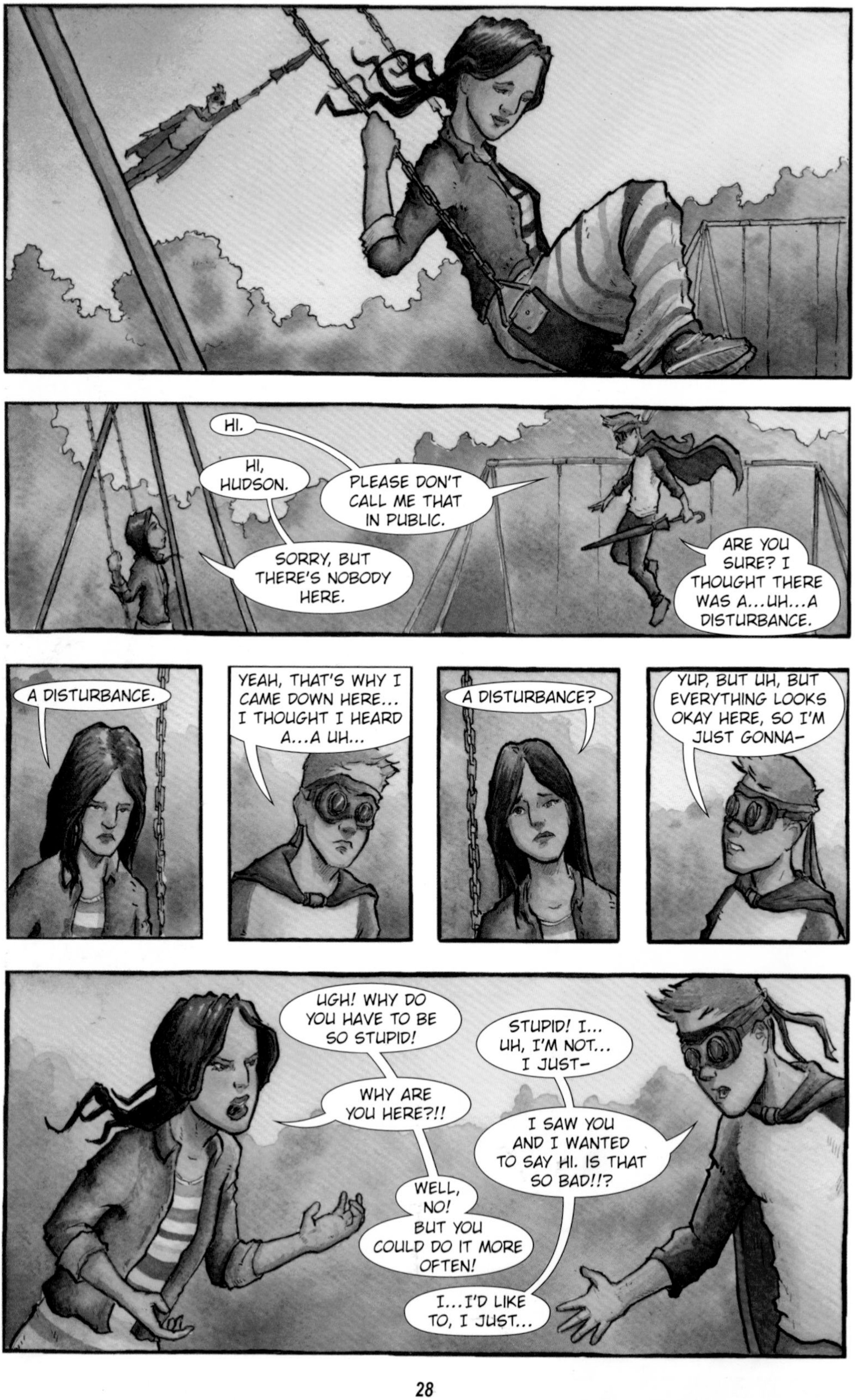
HI.
HI, HUDSON.
PLEASE DON'T CALL ME THAT IN PUBLIC.
SORRY, BUT THERE'S NOBODY HERE.
ARE YOU SURE? I THOUGHT THERE WAS A...UH...A DISTURBANCE.
A DISTURBANCE.
YEAH, THAT'S WHY I CAME DOWN HERE... I THOUGHT I HEARD A...A UH...
A DISTURBANCE?
YUP, BUT UH, BUT EVERYTHING LOOKS OKAY HERE, SO I'M JUST GONNA-
UGH! WHY DO YOU HAVE TO BE SO STUPID!
STUPID! I... UH, I'M NOT... I JUST-
WHY ARE YOU HERE?!!
I SAW YOU AND I WANTED TO SAY HI. IS THAT SO BAD!!?
WELL, NO! BUT YOU COULD DO IT MORE OFTEN!
I...I'D LIKE TO, I JUST...

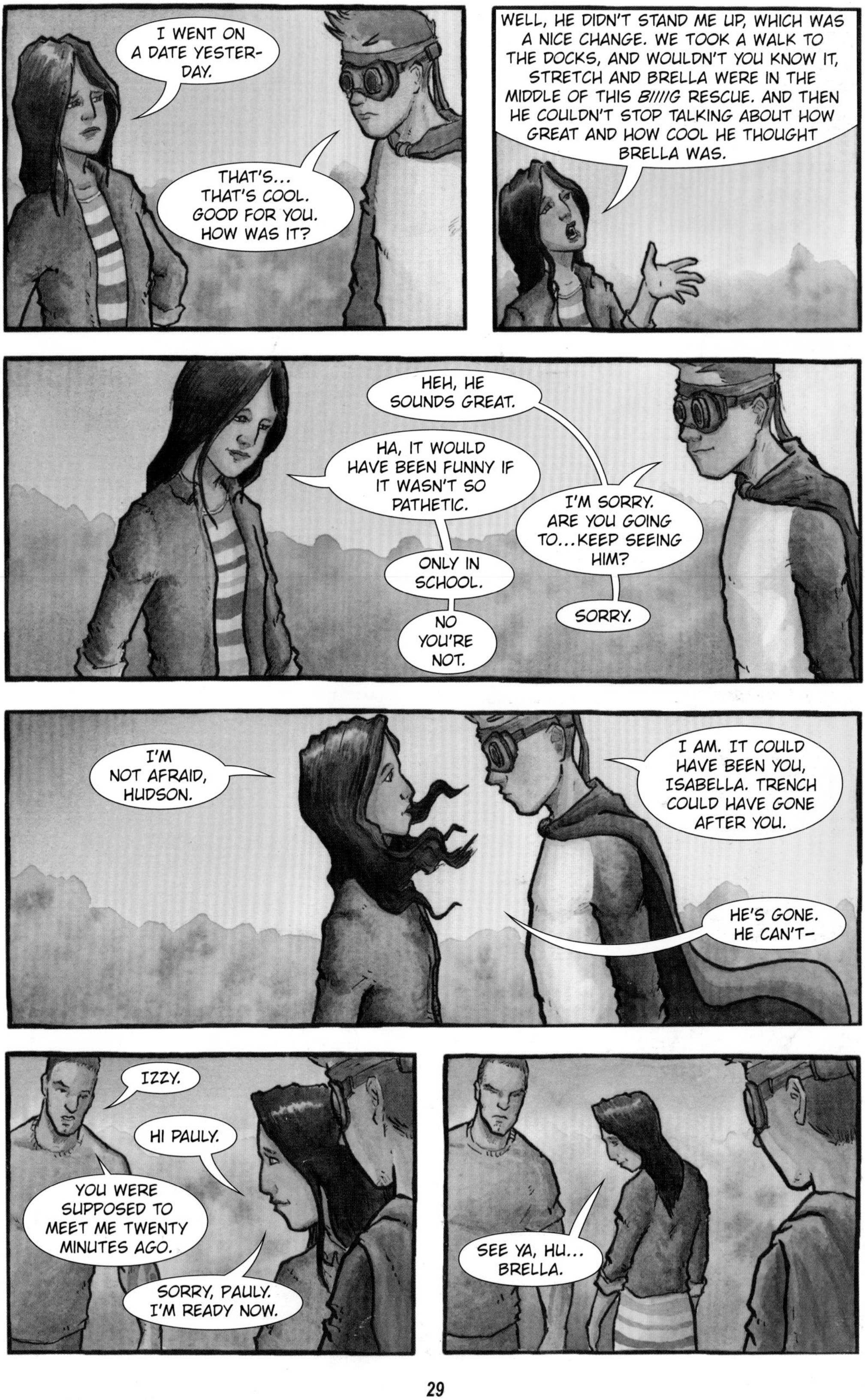

I WENT ON A DATE YESTERDAY.
THAT'S... THAT'S COOL. GOOD FOR YOU. HOW WAS IT?
WELL, HE DIDN'T STAND ME UP, WHICH WAS A NICE CHANGE. WE TOOK A WALK TO THE DOCKS, AND WOULDN'T YOU KNOW IT, STRETCH AND BRELLA WERE IN THE MIDDLE OF THIS *BIIIIG* RESCUE. AND THEN HE COULDN'T STOP TALKING ABOUT HOW GREAT AND HOW COOL HE THOUGHT BRELLA WAS.
HEH, HE SOUNDS GREAT.
HA, IT WOULD HAVE BEEN FUNNY IF IT WASN'T SO PATHETIC.
I'M SORRY. ARE YOU GOING TO...KEEP SEEING HIM?
ONLY IN SCHOOL.
SORRY.
NO YOU'RE NOT.
I'M NOT AFRAID, HUDSON.
I AM. IT COULD HAVE BEEN YOU, ISABELLA. TRENCH COULD HAVE GONE AFTER YOU.
HE'S GONE. HE CAN'T-
IZZY.
HI PAULY.
YOU WERE SUPPOSED TO MEET ME TWENTY MINUTES AGO.
SORRY, PAULY. I'M READY NOW.
SEE YA, HU... BRELLA.

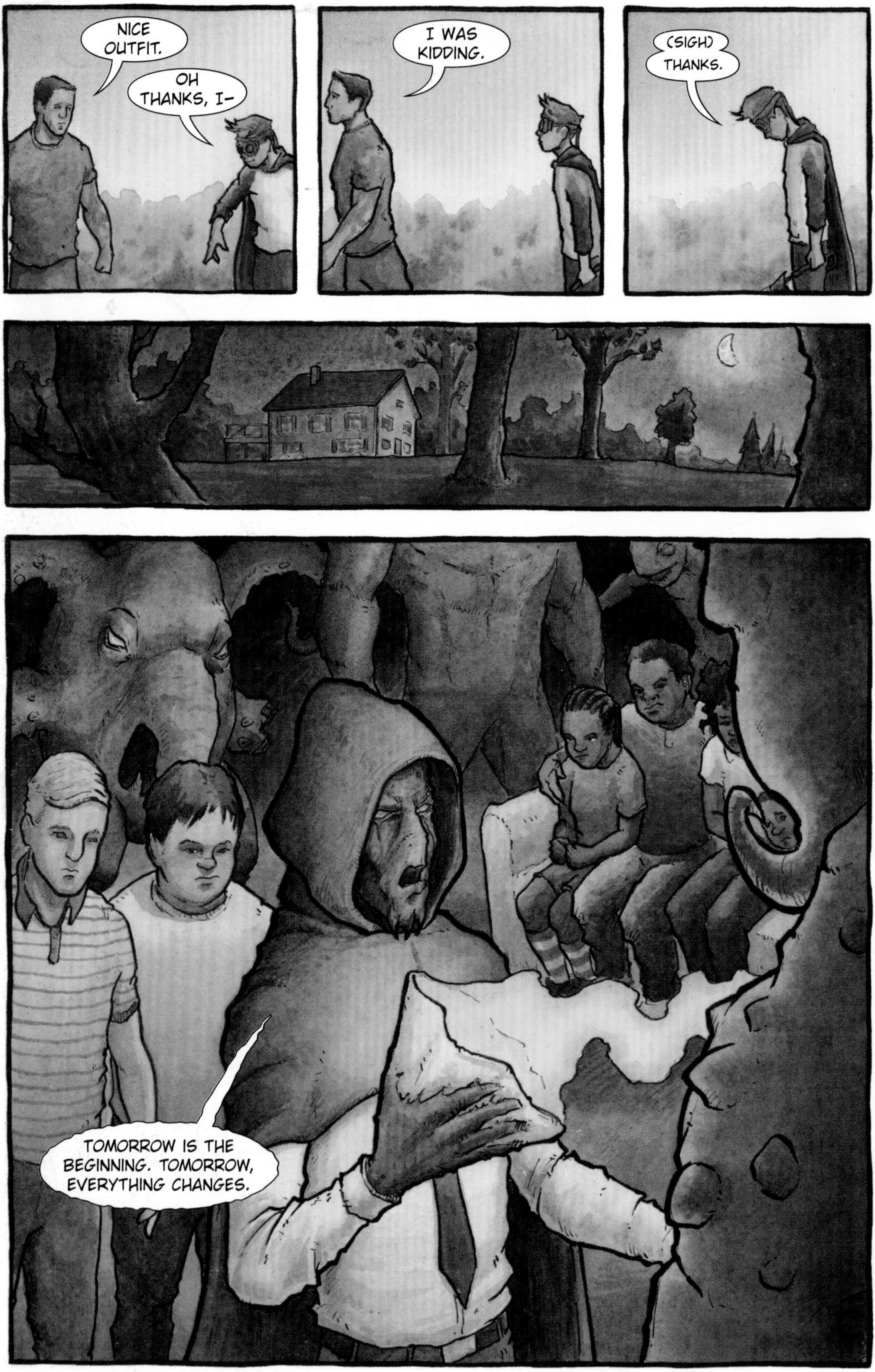
NICE OUTFIT.
OH THANKS, I-
I WAS KIDDING.
(SIGH) THANKS.
TOMORROW IS THE BEGINNING. TOMORROW, EVERYTHING CHANGES.

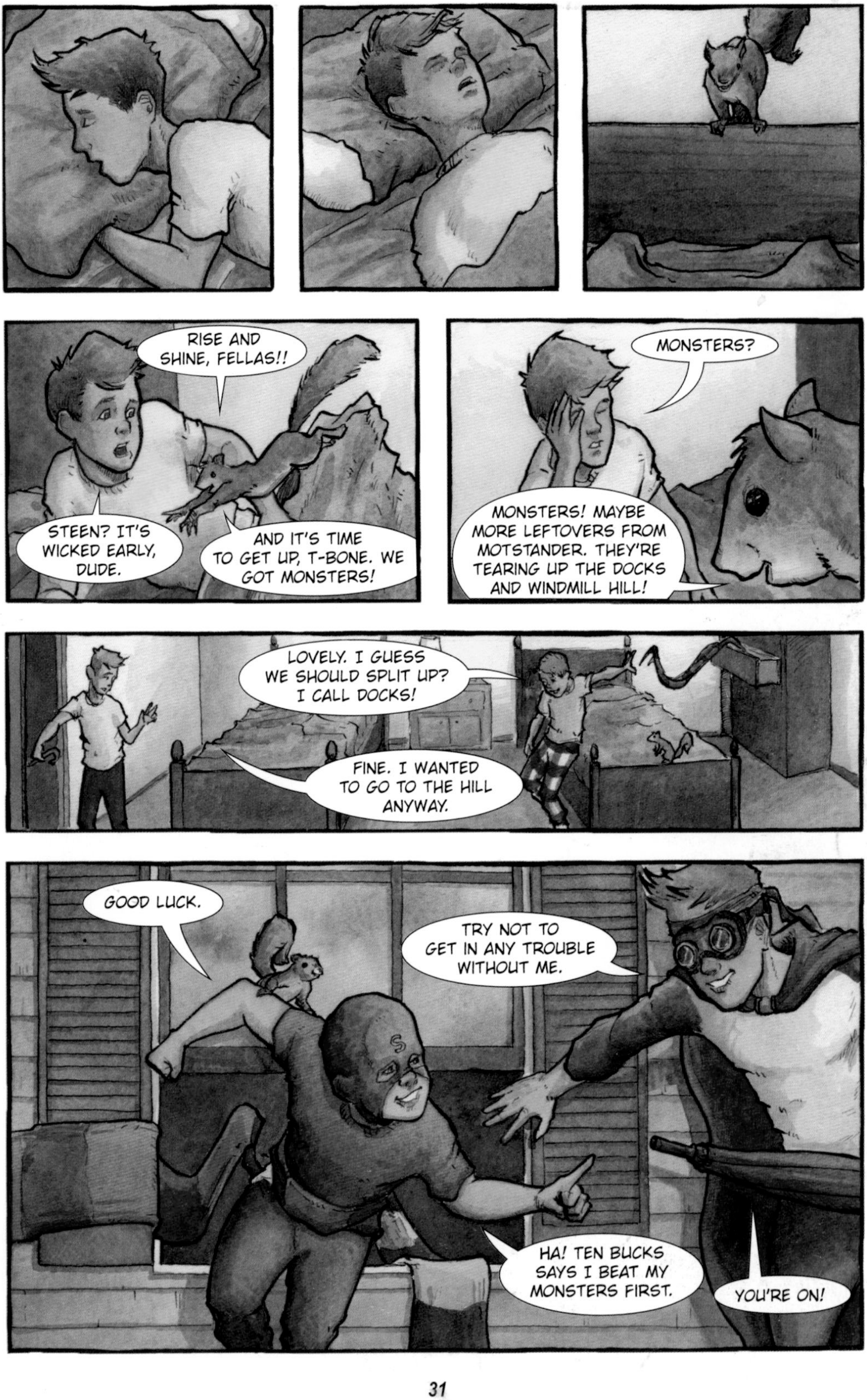
RISE AND SHINE, FELLAS!!
STEEN? IT'S WICKED EARLY, DUDE.
AND IT'S TIME TO GET UP, T-BONE. WE GOT MONSTERS!
MONSTERS?
MONSTERS! MAYBE MORE LEFTOVERS FROM MOTSTANDER. THEY'RE TEARING UP THE DOCKS AND WINDMILL HILL!
LOVELY. I GUESS WE SHOULD SPLIT UP? I CALL DOCKS!
FINE. I WANTED TO GO TO THE HILL ANYWAY.
GOOD LUCK.
TRY NOT TO GET IN ANY TROUBLE WITHOUT ME.
HA! TEN BUCKS SAYS I BEAT MY MONSTERS FIRST.
YOU'RE ON!

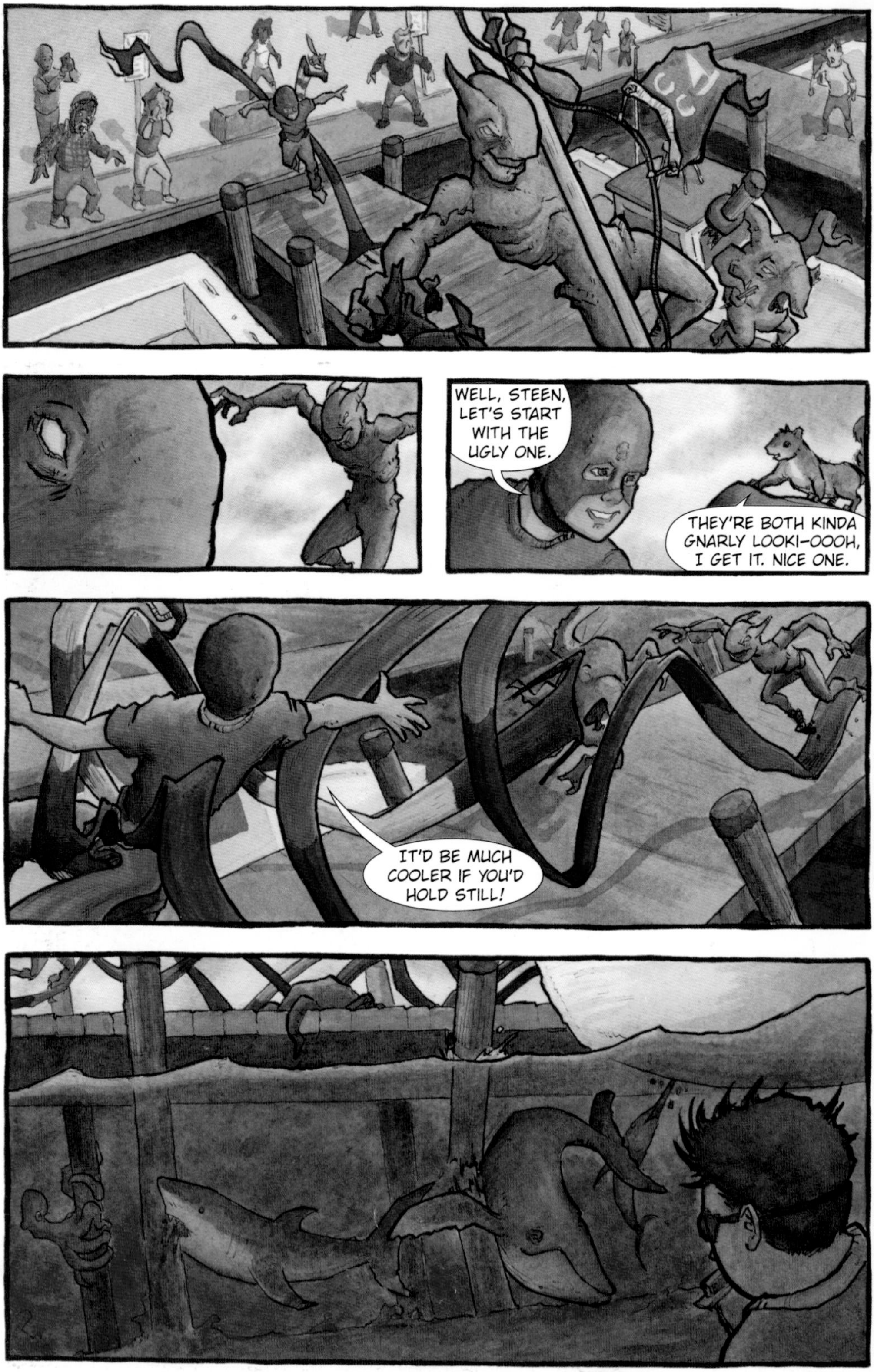
WELL, STEEN, LET'S START WITH THE UGLY ONE.
THEY'RE BOTH KINDA GNARLY LOOKI–OOOH, I GET IT. NICE ONE.
IT'D BE MUCH COOLER IF YOU'D HOLD STILL!

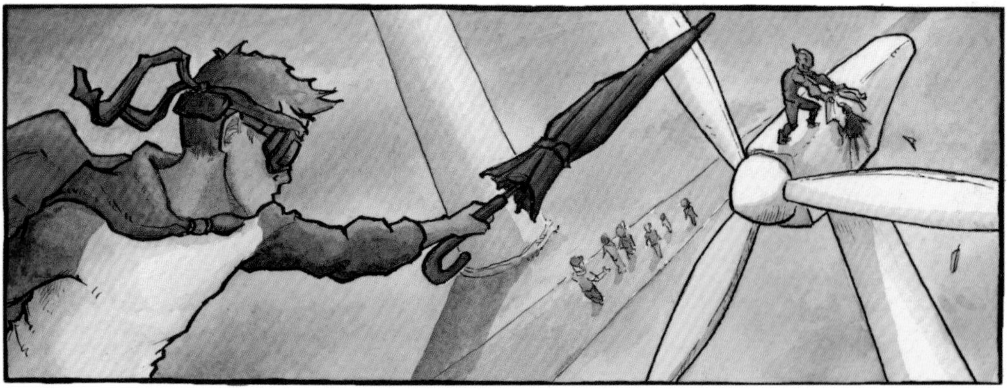

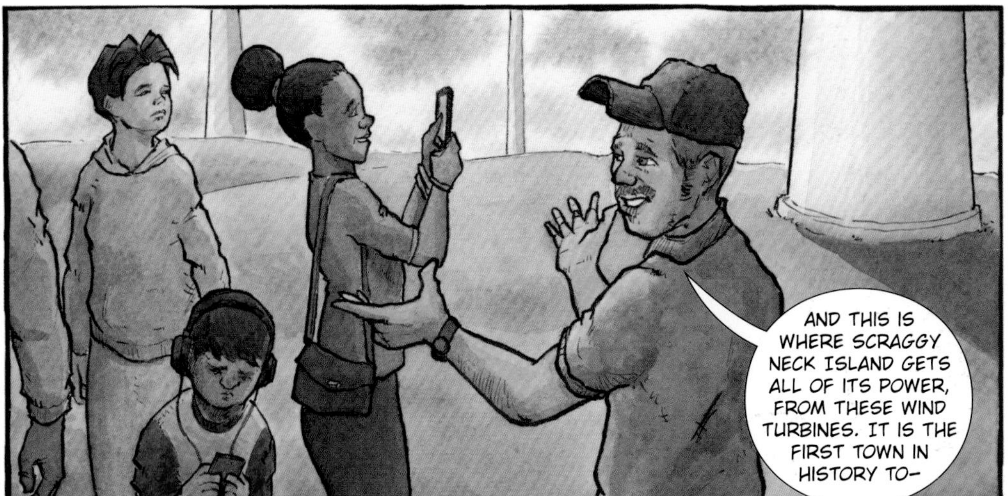
AND THIS IS WHERE SCRAGGY NECK ISLAND GETS ALL OF ITS POWER, FROM THESE WIND TURBINES. IT IS THE FIRST TOWN IN HISTORY TO–

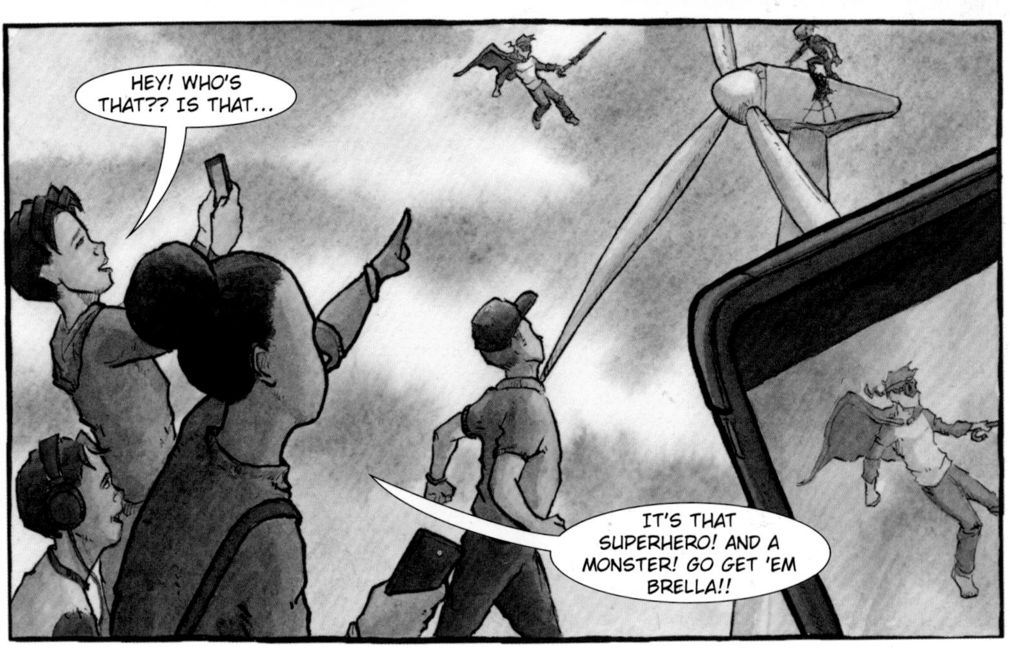
HEY! WHO'S THAT?? IS THAT...
IT'S THAT SUPERHERO! AND A MONSTER! GO GET 'EM BRELLA!!

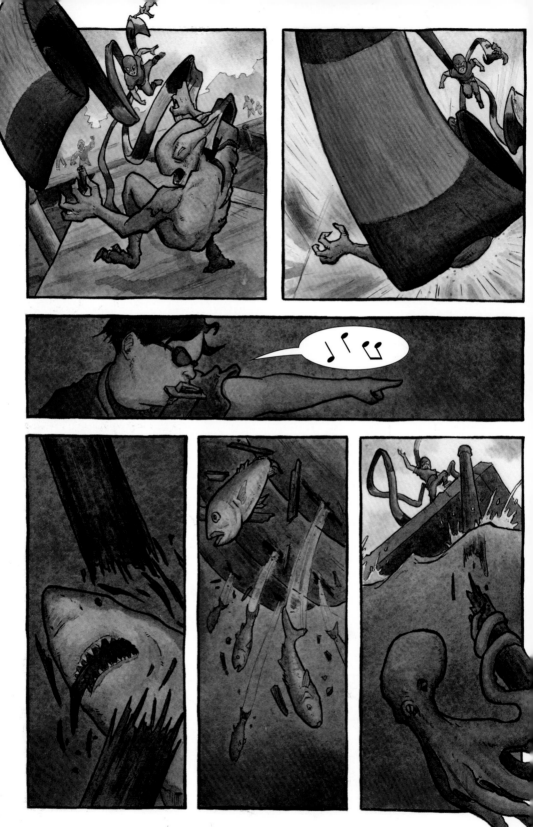

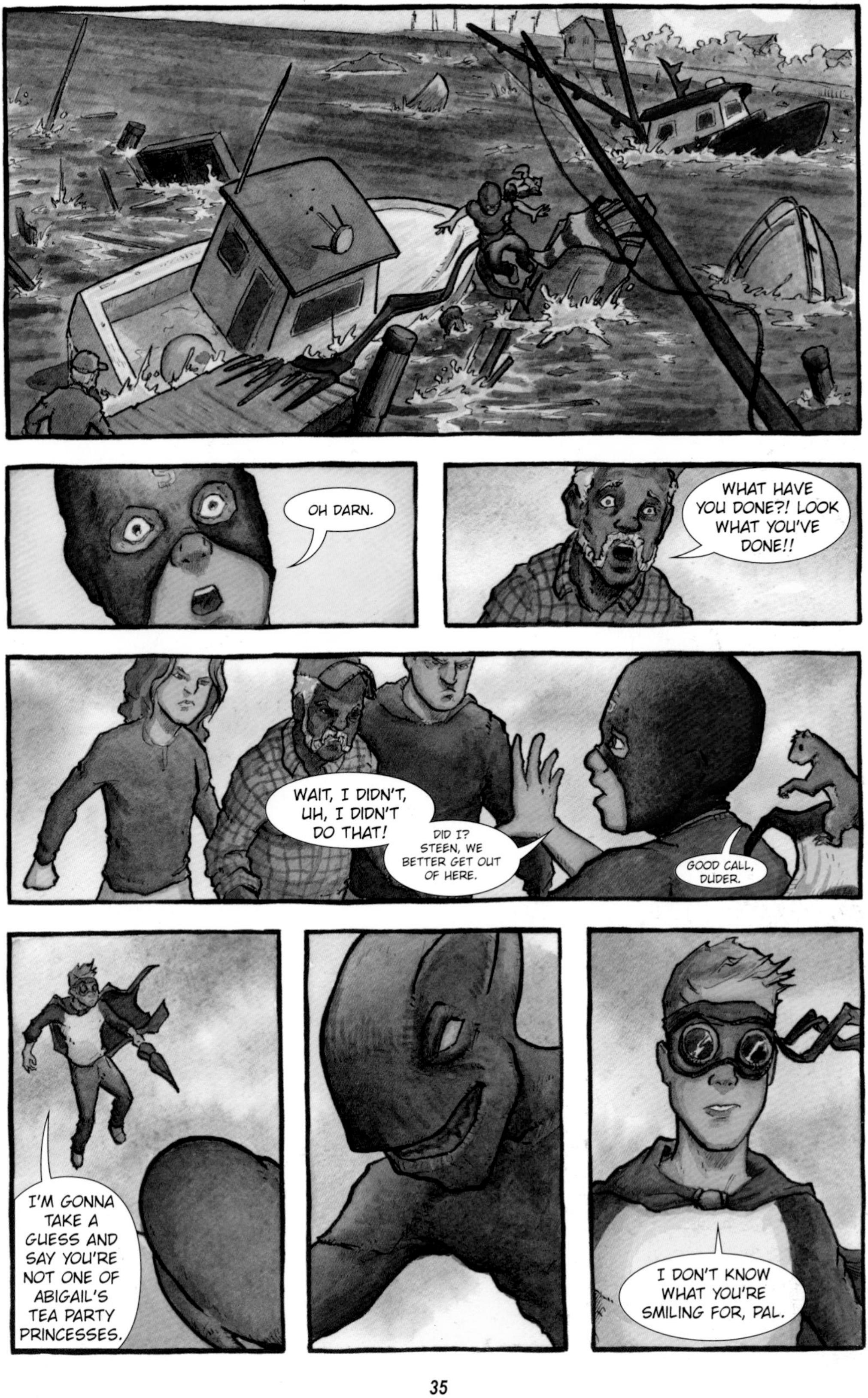
OH DARN.
WHAT HAVE YOU DONE?! LOOK WHAT YOU'VE DONE!!
WAIT, I DIDN'T, UH, I DIDN'T DO THAT!
DID I? STEEN, WE BETTER GET OUT OF HERE.
GOOD CALL, DUDER.
I'M GONNA TAKE A GUESS AND SAY YOU'RE NOT ONE OF ABIGAIL'S TEA PARTY PRINCESSES.
I DON'T KNOW WHAT YOU'RE SMILING FOR, PAL.

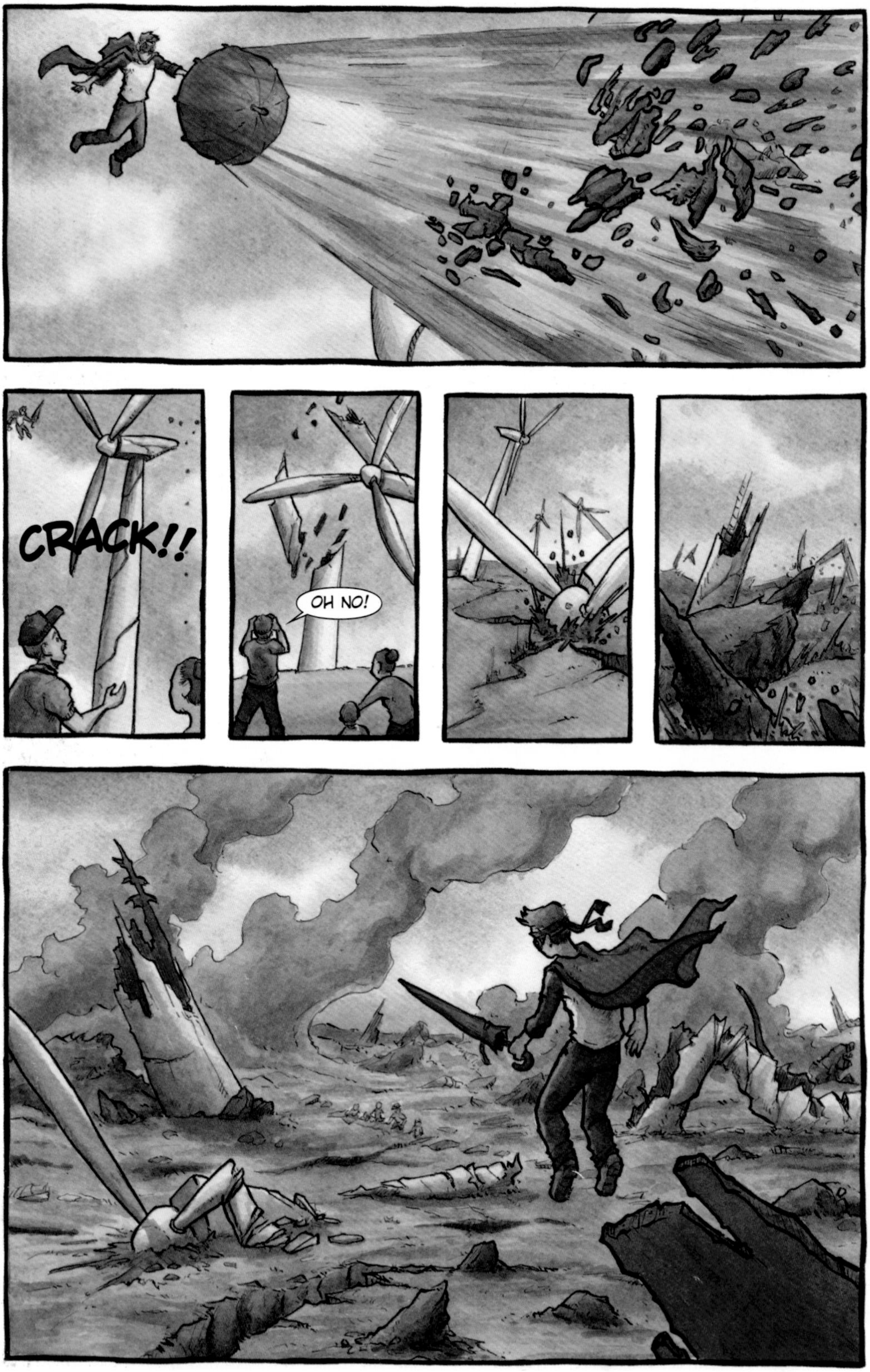
CRACK!!
OH NO!

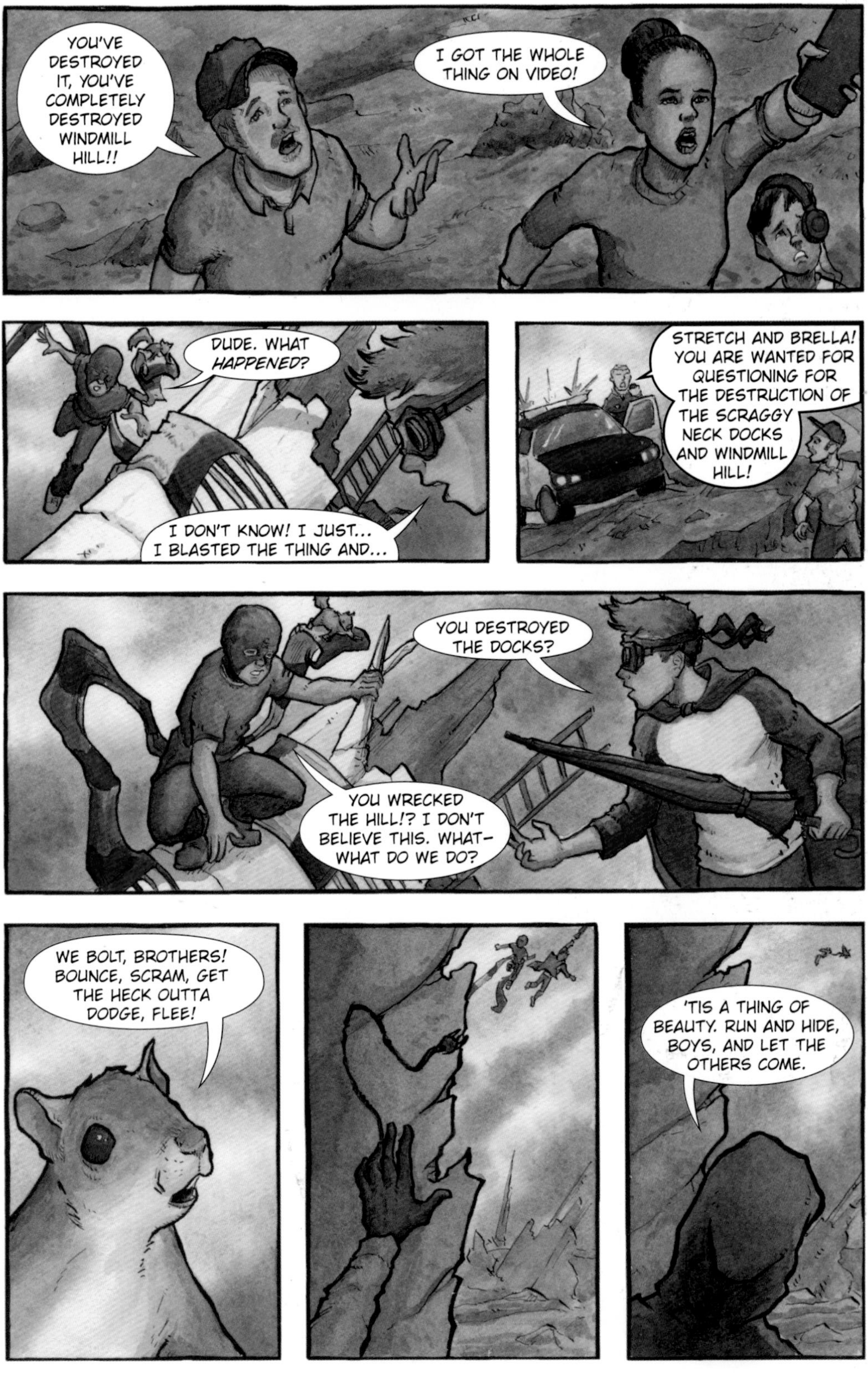
YOU'VE DESTROYED IT, YOU'VE COMPLETELY DESTROYED WINDMILL HILL!!
I GOT THE WHOLE THING ON VIDEO!
DUDE. WHAT *HAPPENED?*
I DON'T KNOW! I JUST... I BLASTED THE THING AND...
STRETCH AND BRELLA! YOU ARE WANTED FOR QUESTIONING FOR THE DESTRUCTION OF THE SCRAGGY NECK DOCKS AND WINDMILL HILL!
YOU DESTROYED THE DOCKS?
YOU WRECKED THE HILL!? I DON'T BELIEVE THIS. WHAT-WHAT DO WE DO?
WE BOLT, BROTHERS! BOUNCE, SCRAM, GET THE HECK OUTTA DODGE, FLEE!
'TIS A THING OF BEAUTY. RUN AND HIDE, BOYS, AND LET THE OTHERS COME.

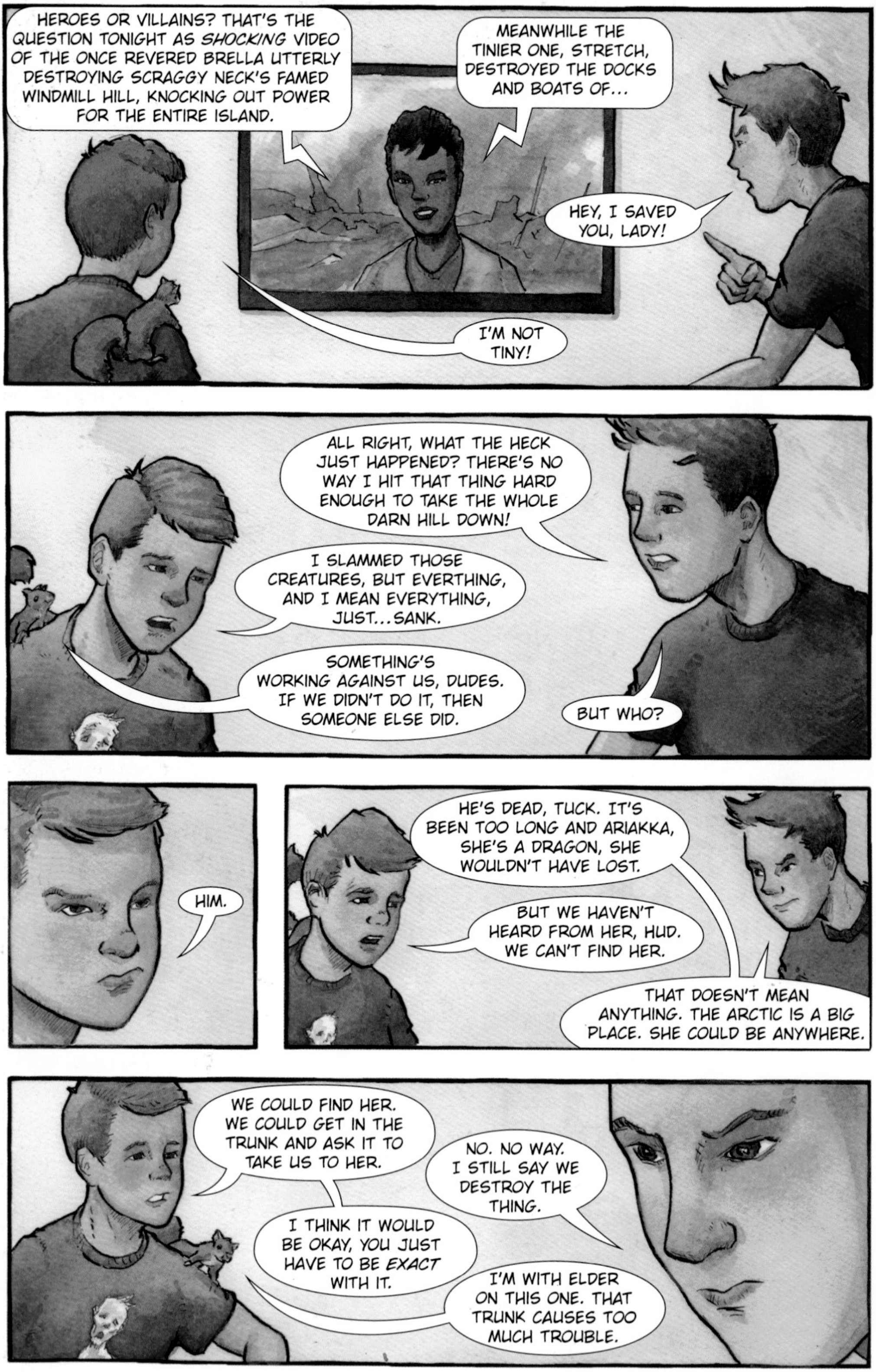
HEROES OR VILLAINS? THAT'S THE QUESTION TONIGHT AS *SHOCKING* VIDEO OF THE ONCE REVERED BRELLA UTTERLY DESTROYING SCRAGGY NECK'S FAMED WINDMILL HILL, KNOCKING OUT POWER FOR THE ENTIRE ISLAND.
MEANWHILE THE TINIER ONE, STRETCH, DESTROYED THE DOCKS AND BOATS OF...
HEY, I SAVED YOU, LADY!
I'M NOT TINY!
ALL RIGHT, WHAT THE HECK JUST HAPPENED? THERE'S NO WAY I HIT THAT THING HARD ENOUGH TO TAKE THE WHOLE DARN HILL DOWN!
I SLAMMED THOSE CREATURES, BUT EVERTHING, AND I MEAN EVERYTHING, JUST...SANK.
SOMETHING'S WORKING AGAINST US, DUDES. IF WE DIDN'T DO IT, THEN SOMEONE ELSE DID.
BUT WHO?
HIM.
HE'S DEAD, TUCK. IT'S BEEN TOO LONG AND ARIAKKA, SHE'S A DRAGON, SHE WOULDN'T HAVE LOST.
BUT WE HAVEN'T HEARD FROM HER, HUD. WE CAN'T FIND HER.
THAT DOESN'T MEAN ANYTHING. THE ARCTIC IS A BIG PLACE. SHE COULD BE ANYWHERE.
WE COULD FIND HER. WE COULD GET IN THE TRUNK AND ASK IT TO TAKE US TO HER.
NO. NO WAY. I STILL SAY WE DESTROY THE THING.
I THINK IT WOULD BE OKAY, YOU JUST HAVE TO BE *EXACT* WITH IT.
I'M WITH ELDER ON THIS ONE. THAT TRUNK CAUSES TOO MUCH TROUBLE.

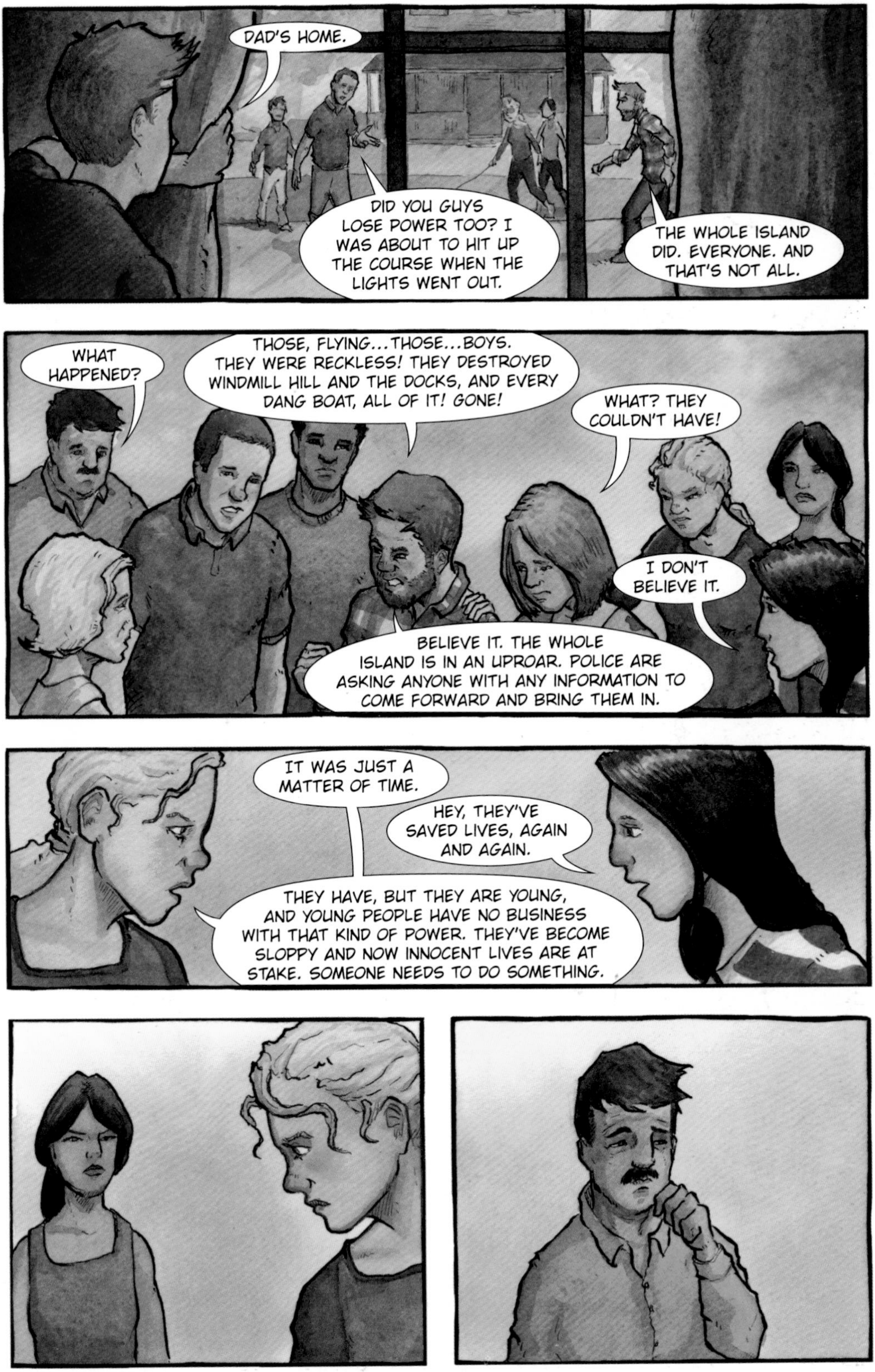
DAD'S HOME.
DID YOU GUYS LOSE POWER TOO? I WAS ABOUT TO HIT UP THE COURSE WHEN THE LIGHTS WENT OUT.
THE WHOLE ISLAND DID. EVERYONE. AND THAT'S NOT ALL.
WHAT HAPPENED?
THOSE, FLYING... THOSE... BOYS. THEY WERE RECKLESS! THEY DESTROYED WINDMILL HILL AND THE DOCKS, AND EVERY DANG BOAT, ALL OF IT! GONE!
WHAT? THEY COULDN'T HAVE!
I DON'T BELIEVE IT.
BELIEVE IT. THE WHOLE ISLAND IS IN AN UPROAR. POLICE ARE ASKING ANYONE WITH ANY INFORMATION TO COME FORWARD AND BRING THEM IN.
IT WAS JUST A MATTER OF TIME.
HEY, THEY'VE SAVED LIVES, AGAIN AND AGAIN.
THEY HAVE, BUT THEY ARE YOUNG, AND YOUNG PEOPLE HAVE NO BUSINESS WITH THAT KIND OF POWER. THEY'VE BECOME SLOPPY AND NOW INNOCENT LIVES ARE AT STAKE. SOMEONE NEEDS TO DO SOMETHING.

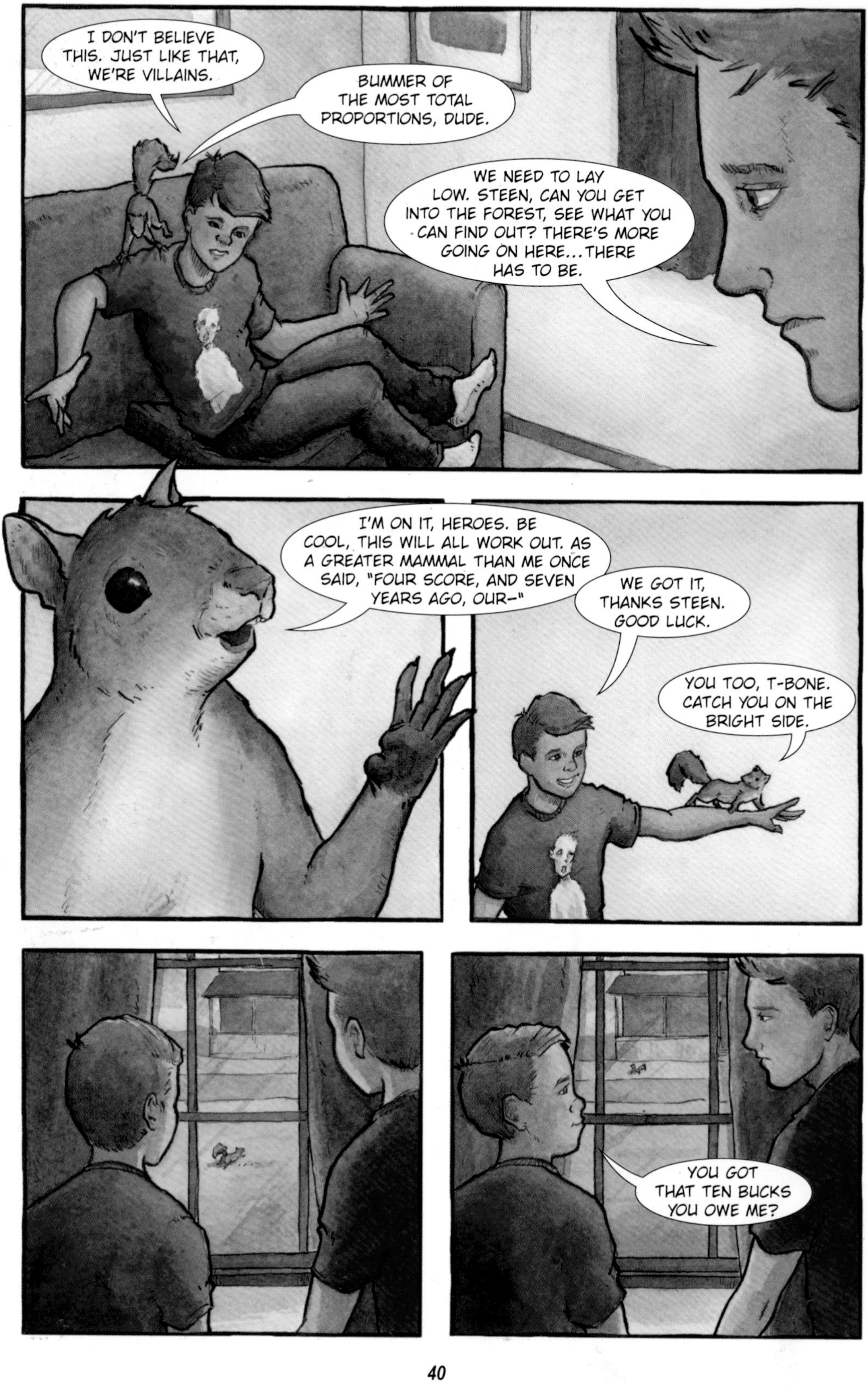
I DON'T BELIEVE THIS. JUST LIKE THAT, WE'RE VILLAINS.
BUMMER OF THE MOST TOTAL PROPORTIONS, DUDE.
WE NEED TO LAY LOW. STEEN, CAN YOU GET INTO THE FOREST, SEE WHAT YOU CAN FIND OUT? THERE'S MORE GOING ON HERE... THERE HAS TO BE.
I'M ON IT, HEROES. BE COOL, THIS WILL ALL WORK OUT. AS A GREATER MAMMAL THAN ME ONCE SAID, "FOUR SCORE, AND SEVEN YEARS AGO, OUR–"
WE GOT IT, THANKS STEEN. GOOD LUCK.
YOU TOO, T-BONE. CATCH YOU ON THE BRIGHT SIDE.
YOU GOT THAT TEN BUCKS YOU OWE ME?

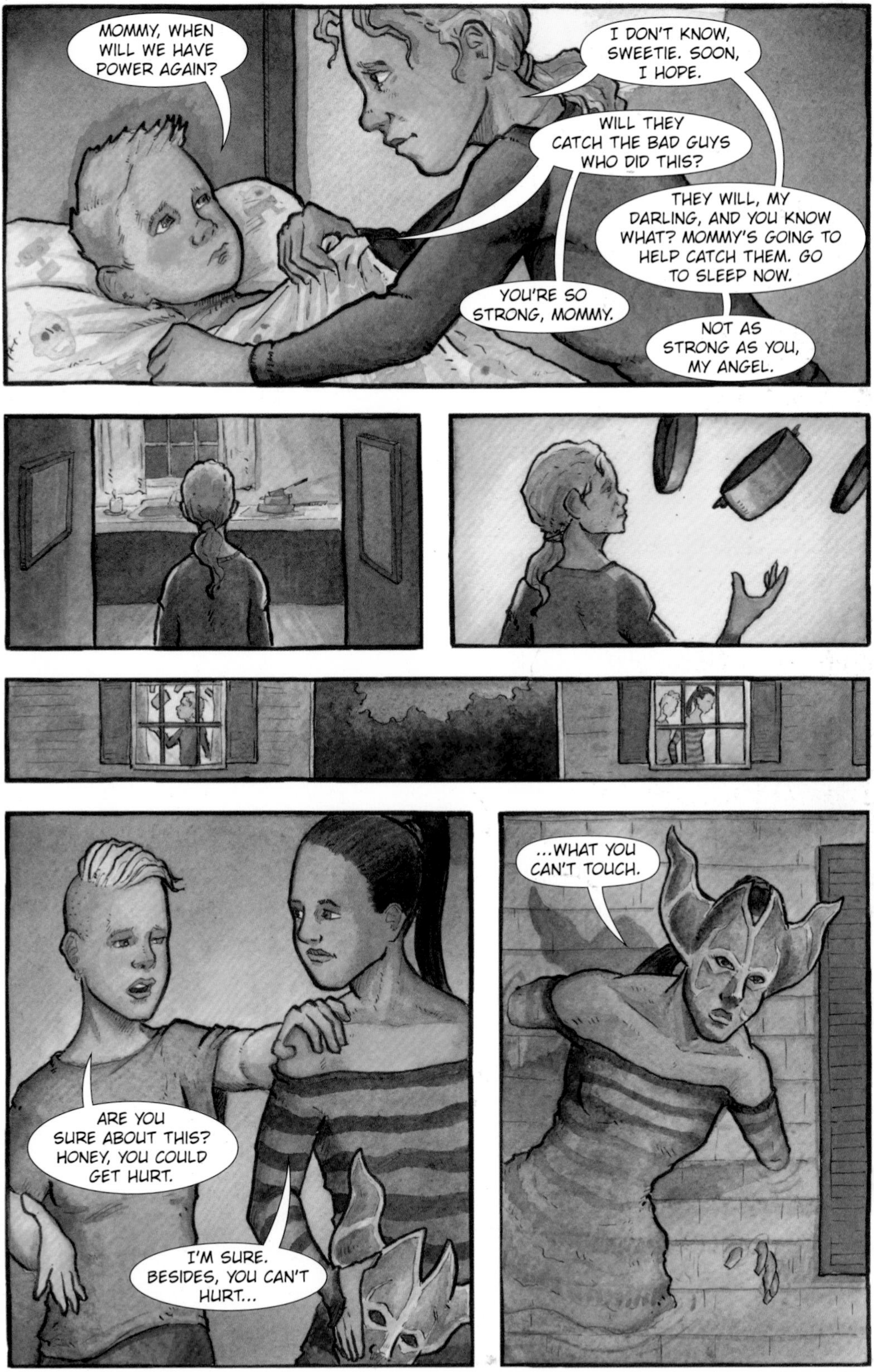
MOMMY, WHEN WILL WE HAVE POWER AGAIN?
I DON'T KNOW, SWEETIE. SOON, I HOPE.
WILL THEY CATCH THE BAD GUYS WHO DID THIS?
THEY WILL, MY DARLING, AND YOU KNOW WHAT? MOMMY'S GOING TO HELP CATCH THEM. GO TO SLEEP NOW.
YOU'RE SO STRONG, MOMMY.
NOT AS STRONG AS YOU, MY ANGEL.
ARE YOU SURE ABOUT THIS? HONEY, YOU COULD GET HURT.
I'M SURE. BESIDES, YOU CAN'T HURT...
...WHAT YOU CAN'T TOUCH.

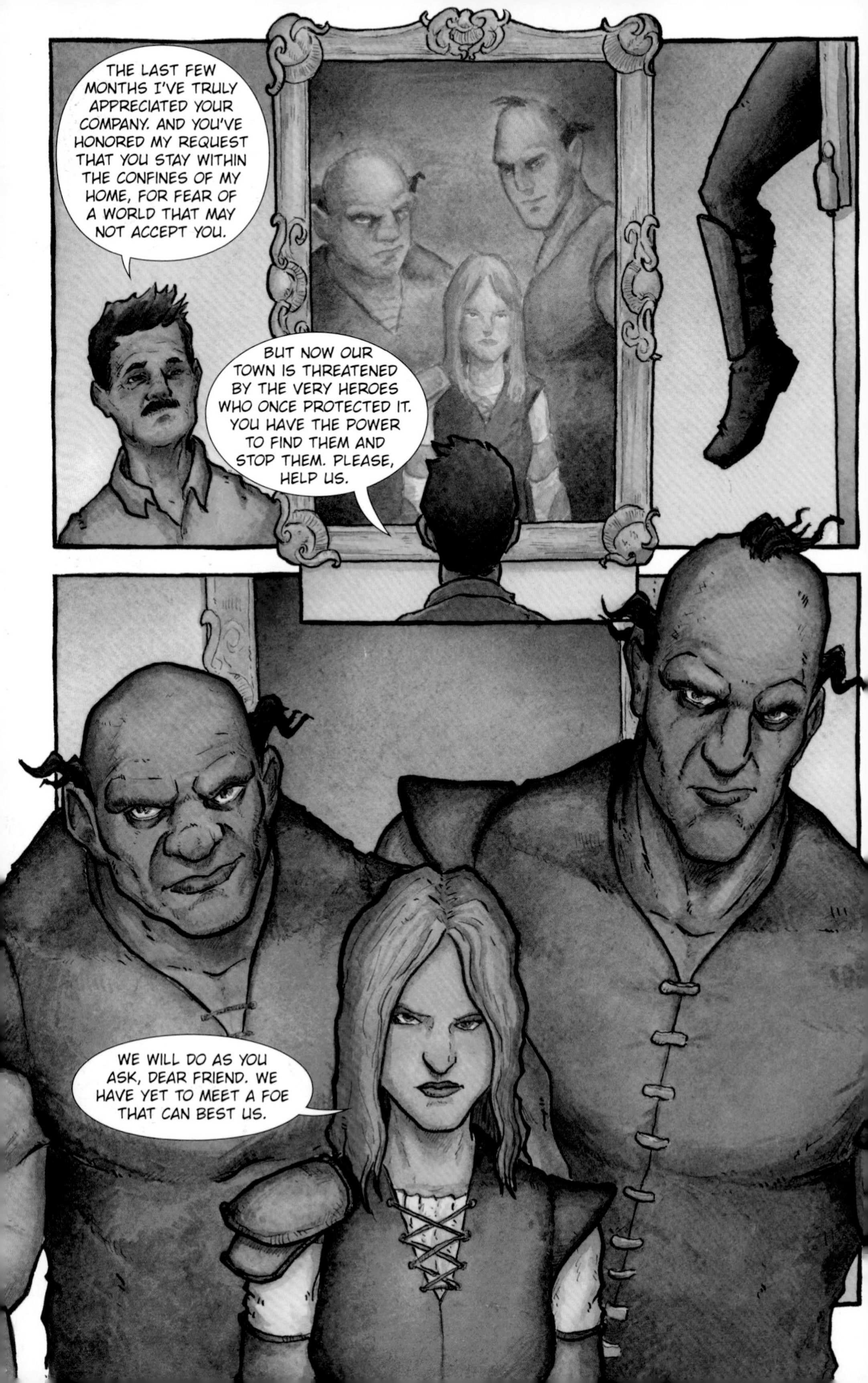
THE LAST FEW MONTHS I'VE TRULY APPRECIATED YOUR COMPANY. AND YOU'VE HONORED MY REQUEST THAT YOU STAY WITHIN THE CONFINES OF MY HOME, FOR FEAR OF A WORLD THAT MAY NOT ACCEPT YOU.
BUT NOW OUR TOWN IS THREATENED BY THE VERY HEROES WHO ONCE PROTECTED IT. YOU HAVE THE POWER TO FIND THEM AND STOP THEM. PLEASE, HELP US.
WE WILL DO AS YOU ASK, DEAR FRIEND. WE HAVE YET TO MEET A FOE THAT CAN BEST US.

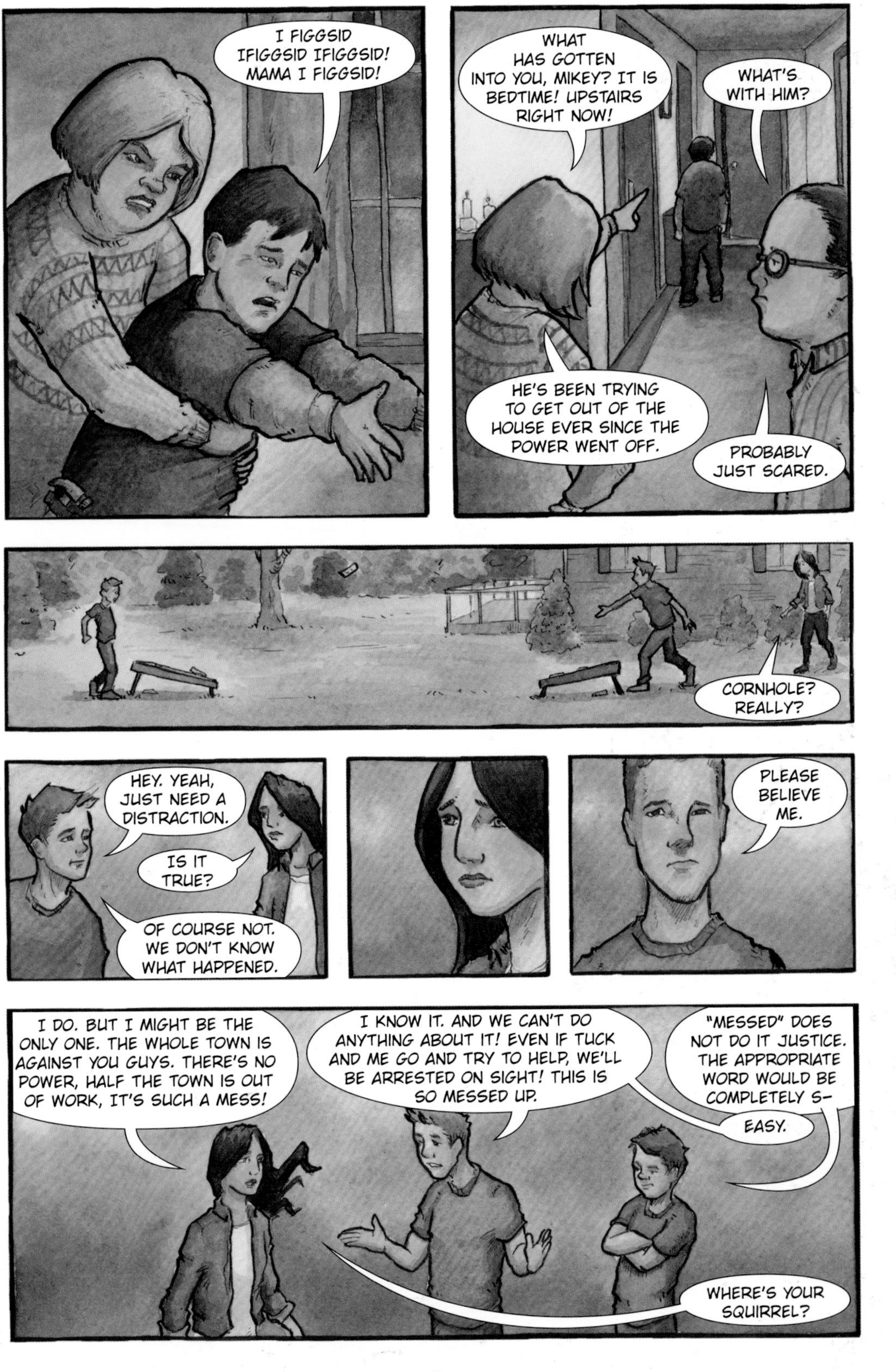
I FIGGSID IFIGGSID IFIGGSID! MAMA I FIGGSID!
WHAT HAS GOTTEN INTO YOU, MIKEY? IT IS BEDTIME! UPSTAIRS RIGHT NOW!
WHAT'S WITH HIM?
HE'S BEEN TRYING TO GET OUT OF THE HOUSE EVER SINCE THE POWER WENT OFF.
PROBABLY JUST SCARED.
CORNHOLE? REALLY?
HEY. YEAH, JUST NEED A DISTRACTION.
IS IT TRUE?
OF COURSE NOT. WE DON'T KNOW WHAT HAPPENED.
PLEASE BELIEVE ME.
I DO. BUT I MIGHT BE THE ONLY ONE. THE WHOLE TOWN IS AGAINST YOU GUYS. THERE'S NO POWER, HALF THE TOWN IS OUT OF WORK, IT'S SUCH A MESS!
I KNOW IT. AND WE CAN'T DO ANYTHING ABOUT IT! EVEN IF TUCK AND ME GO AND TRY TO HELP, WE'LL BE ARRESTED ON SIGHT! THIS IS SO MESSED UP.
"MESSED" DOES NOT DO IT JUSTICE. THE APPROPRIATE WORD WOULD BE COMPLETELY S–
EASY.
WHERE'S YOUR SQUIRREL?

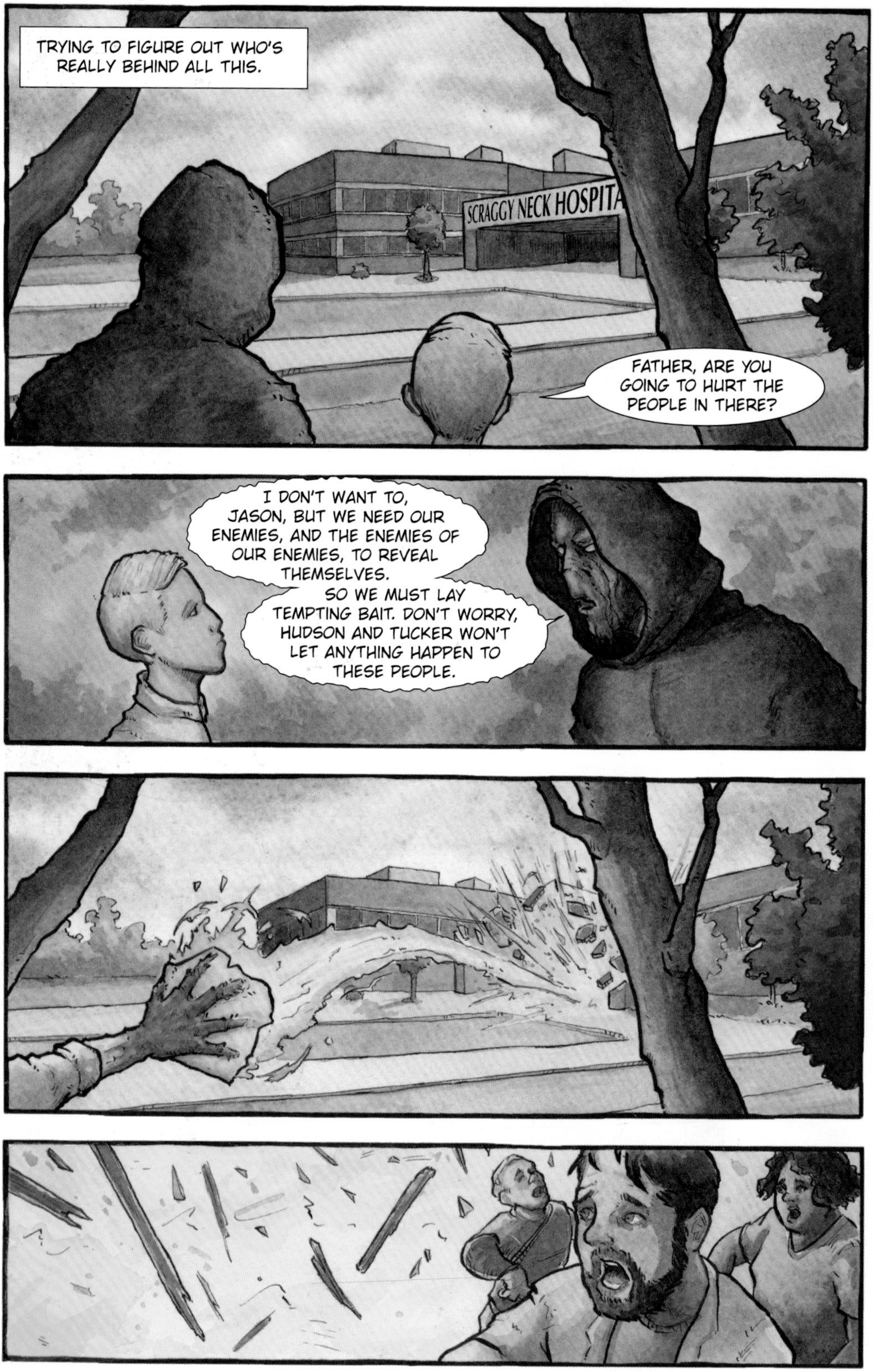
TRYING TO FIGURE OUT WHO'S REALLY BEHIND ALL THIS.
SCRAGGY NECK HOSPITA
FATHER, ARE YOU GOING TO HURT THE PEOPLE IN THERE?
I DON'T WANT TO, JASON, BUT WE NEED OUR ENEMIES, AND THE ENEMIES OF OUR ENEMIES, TO REVEAL THEMSELVES.
SO WE MUST LAY TEMPTING BAIT. DON'T WORRY, HUDSON AND TUCKER WON'T LET ANYTHING HAPPEN TO THESE PEOPLE.

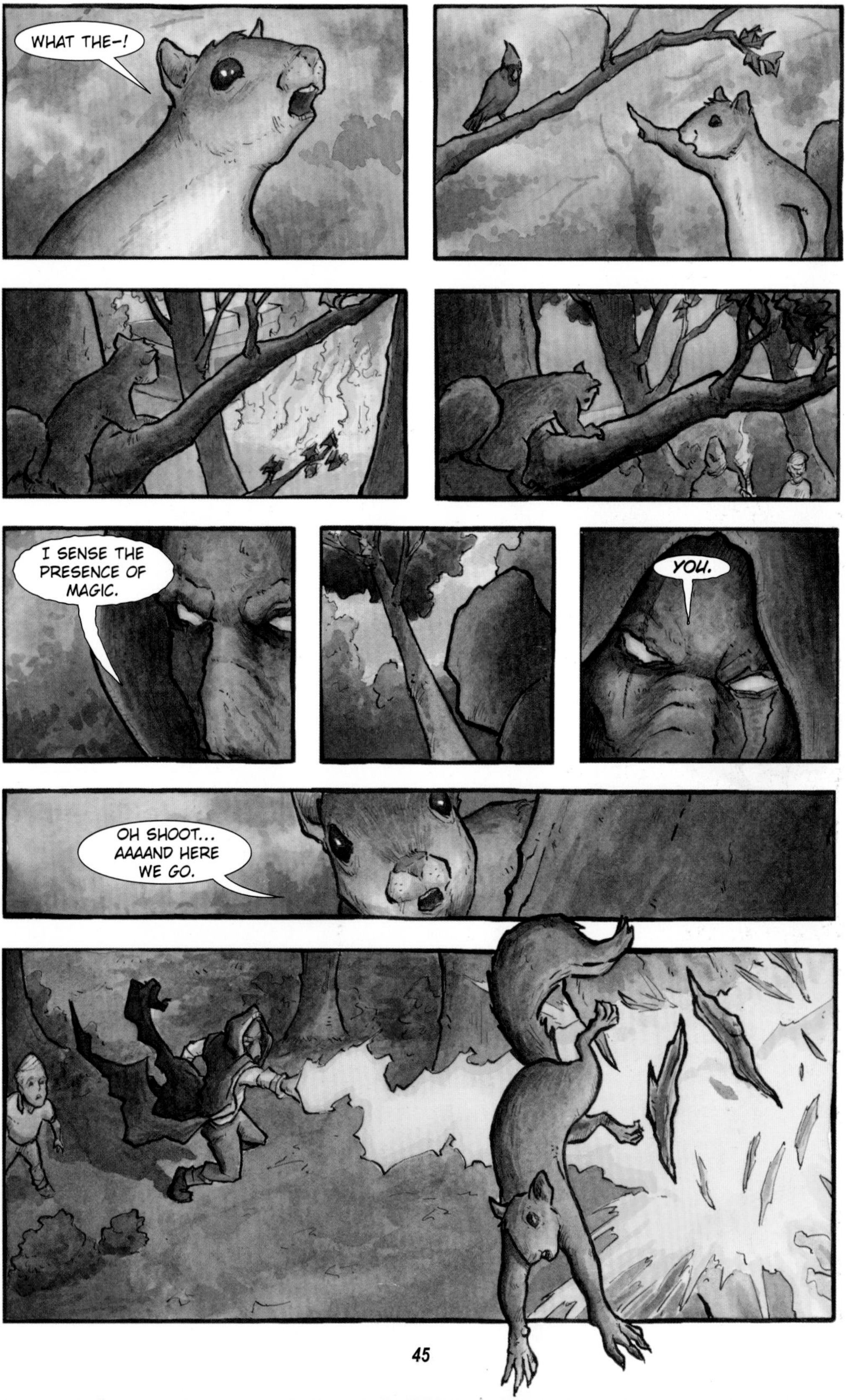
WHAT THE-!
I SENSE THE PRESENCE OF MAGIC.
YOU.
OH SHOOT... AAAAND HERE WE GO.

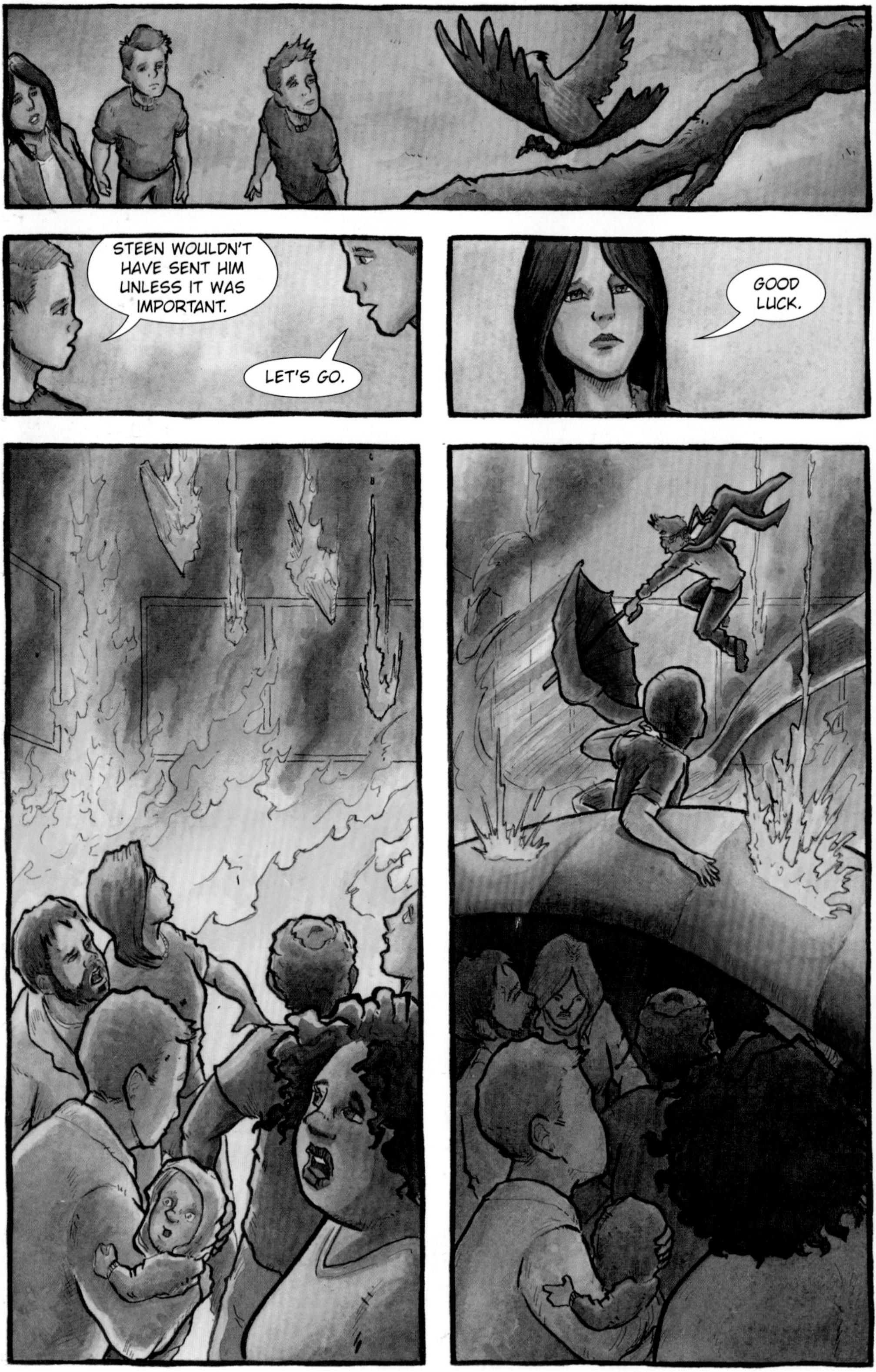
STEEN WOULDN'T HAVE SENT HIM UNLESS IT WAS IMPORTANT.
LET'S GO.
GOOD LUCK.

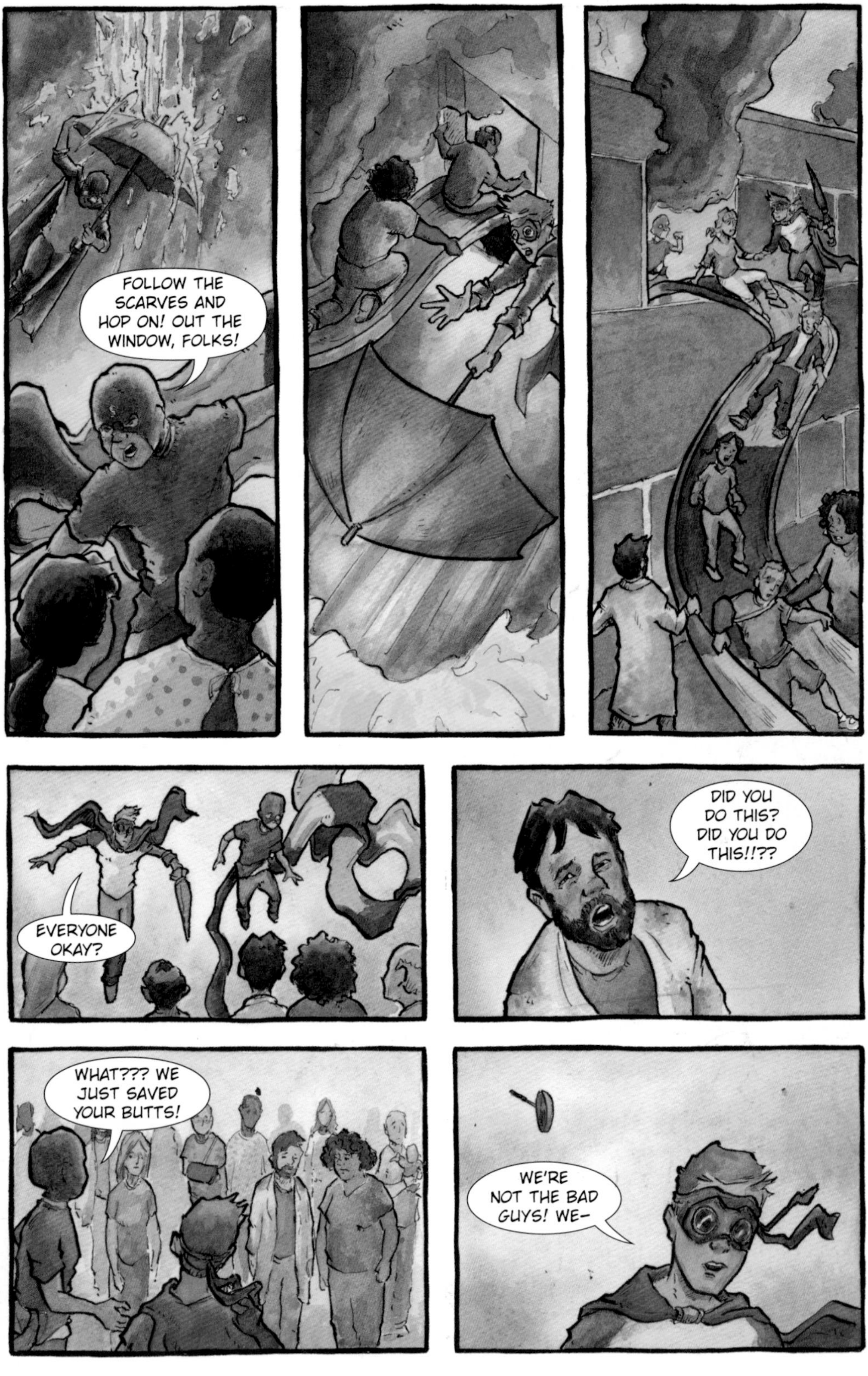
FOLLOW THE SCARVES AND HOP ON! OUT THE WINDOW, FOLKS!
EVERYONE OKAY?
DID YOU DO THIS? DID YOU DO THIS!!??
WHAT??? WE JUST SAVED YOUR BUTTS!
WE'RE NOT THE BAD GUYS! WE-

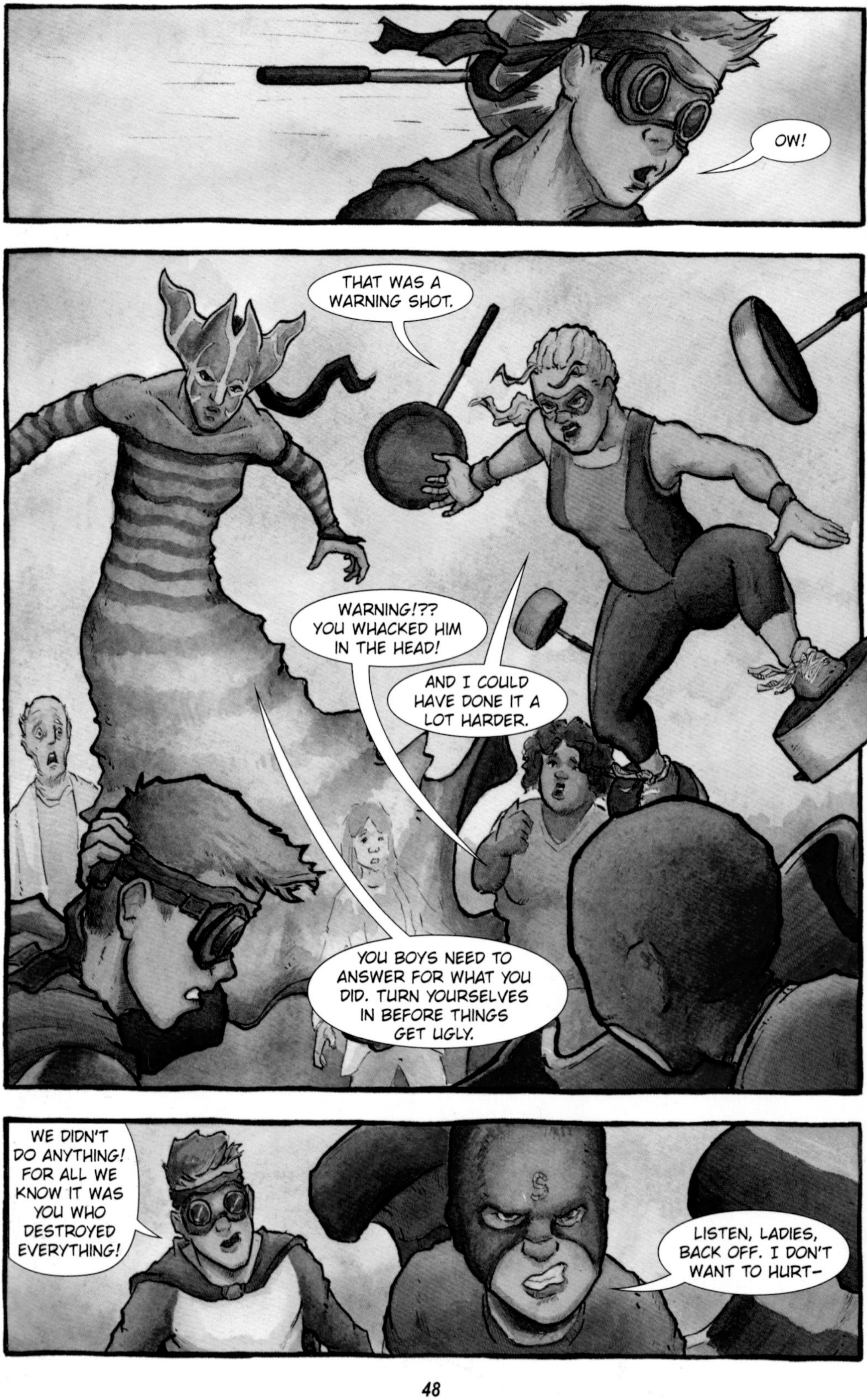
OW!
THAT WAS A WARNING SHOT.
WARNING!?? YOU WHACKED HIM IN THE HEAD!
AND I COULD HAVE DONE IT A LOT HARDER.
YOU BOYS NEED TO ANSWER FOR WHAT YOU DID. TURN YOURSELVES IN BEFORE THINGS GET UGLY.
WE DIDN'T DO ANYTHING! FOR ALL WE KNOW IT WAS YOU WHO DESTROYED EVERYTHING!
LISTEN, LADIES, BACK OFF. I DON'T WANT TO HURT–

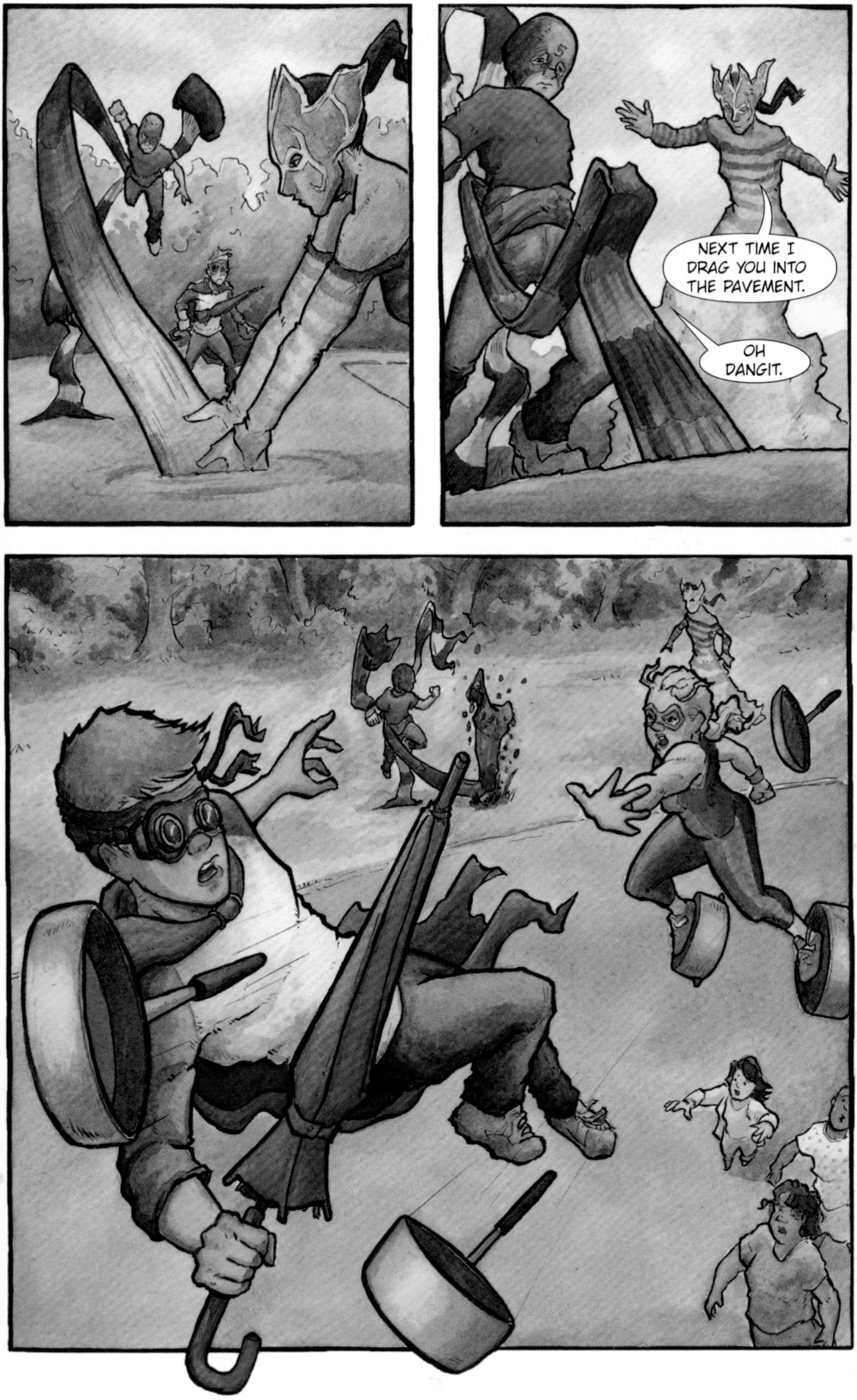
NEXT TIME I DRAG YOU INTO THE PAVEMENT.
OH DANGIT.

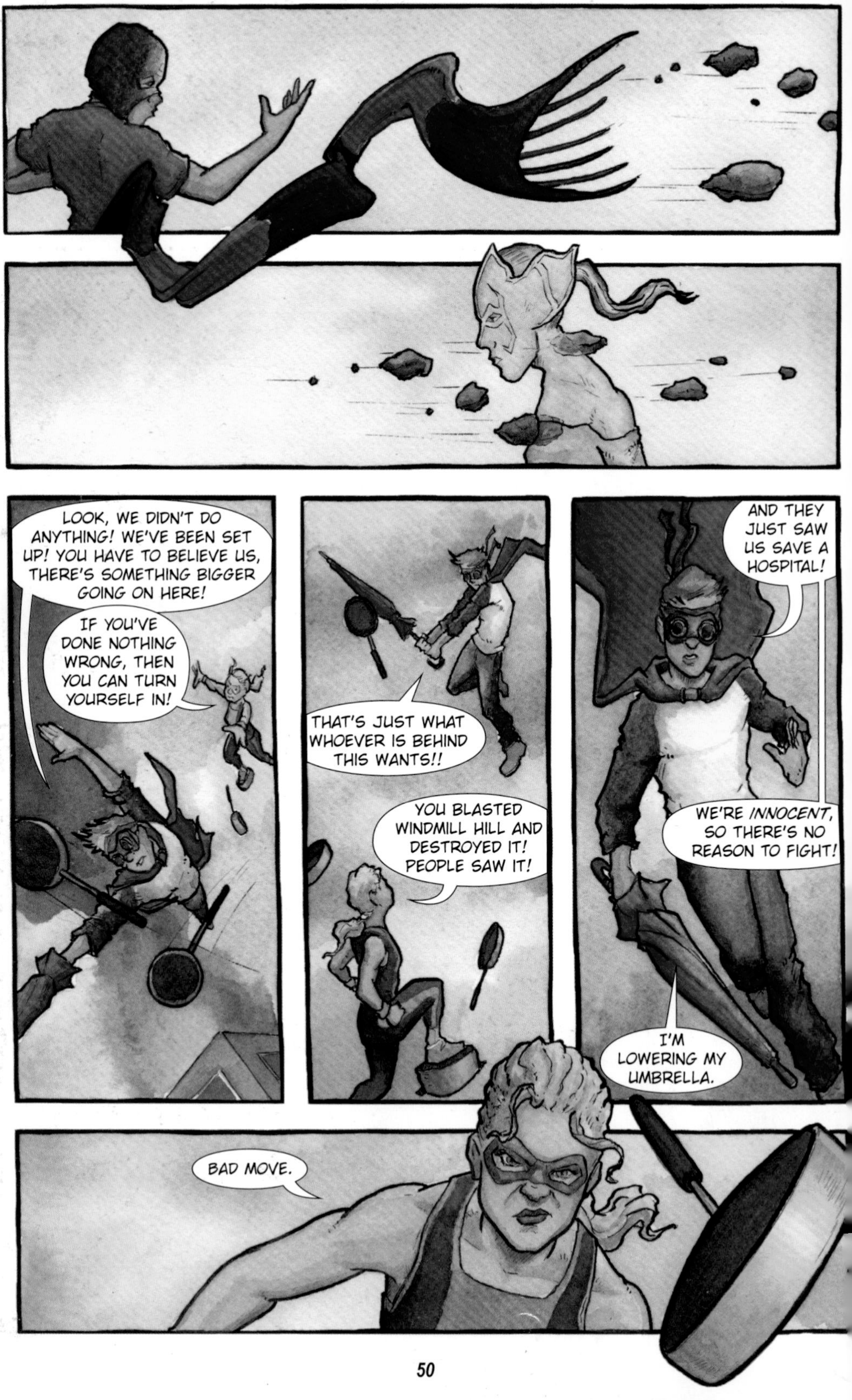
LOOK, WE DIDN'T DO ANYTHING! WE'VE BEEN SET UP! YOU HAVE TO BELIEVE US, THERE'S SOMETHING BIGGER GOING ON HERE!
IF YOU'VE DONE NOTHING WRONG, THEN YOU CAN TURN YOURSELF IN!
THAT'S JUST WHAT WHOEVER IS BEHIND THIS WANTS!!
YOU BLASTED WINDMILL HILL AND DESTROYED IT! PEOPLE SAW IT!
AND THEY JUST SAW US SAVE A HOSPITAL!
WE'RE *INNOCENT*, SO THERE'S NO REASON TO FIGHT!
I'M LOWERING MY UMBRELLA.
BAD MOVE.

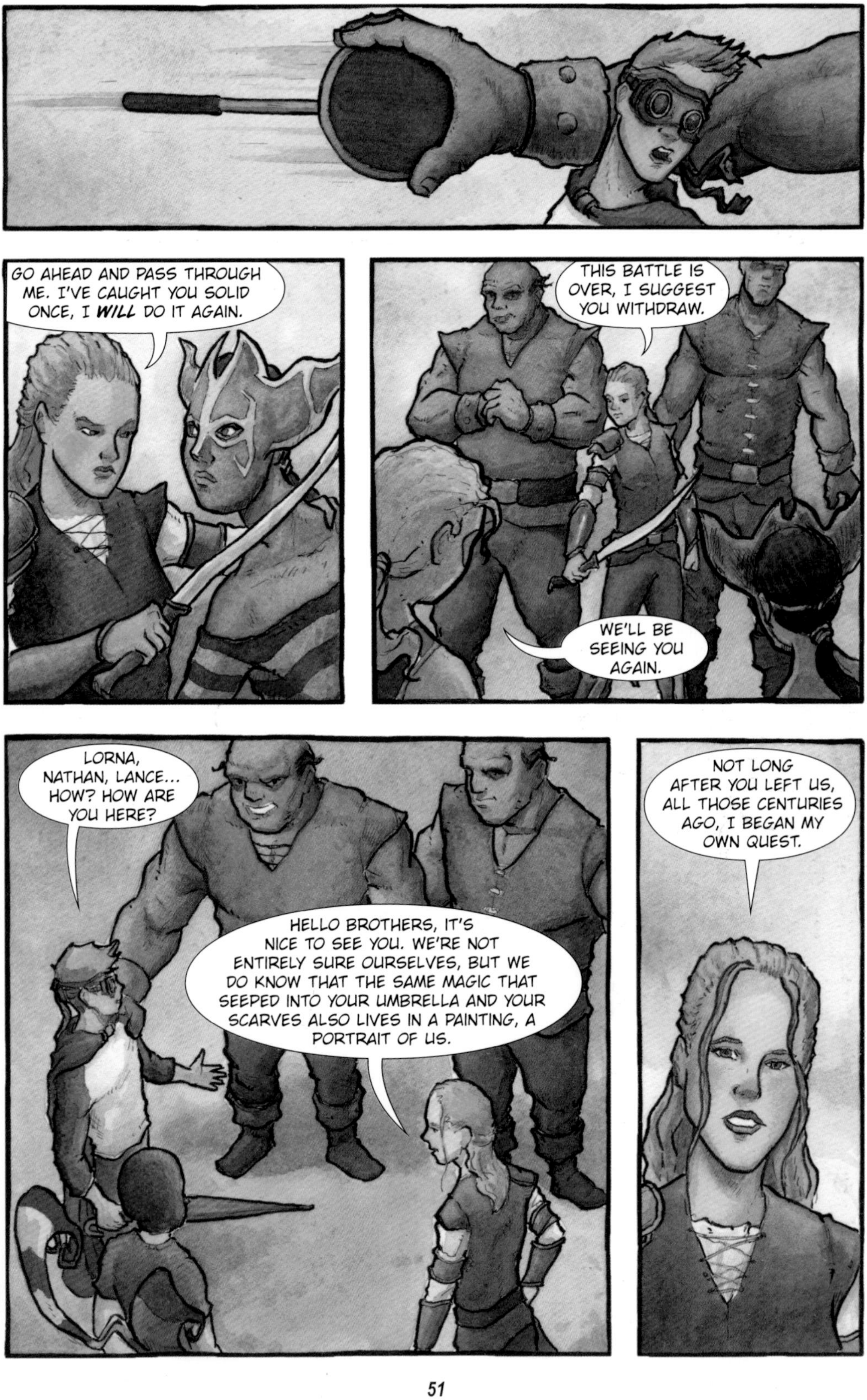
GO AHEAD AND PASS THROUGH ME. I'VE CAUGHT YOU SOLID ONCE, I ***WILL*** DO IT AGAIN.
THIS BATTLE IS OVER, I SUGGEST YOU WITHDRAW.
WE'LL BE SEEING YOU AGAIN.
LORNA, NATHAN, LANCE... HOW? HOW ARE YOU HERE?
HELLO BROTHERS, IT'S NICE TO SEE YOU. WE'RE NOT ENTIRELY SURE OURSELVES, BUT WE DO KNOW THAT THE SAME MAGIC THAT SEEPED INTO YOUR UMBRELLA AND YOUR SCARVES ALSO LIVES IN A PAINTING, A PORTRAIT OF US.
NOT LONG AFTER YOU LEFT US, ALL THOSE CENTURIES AGO, I BEGAN MY OWN QUEST.

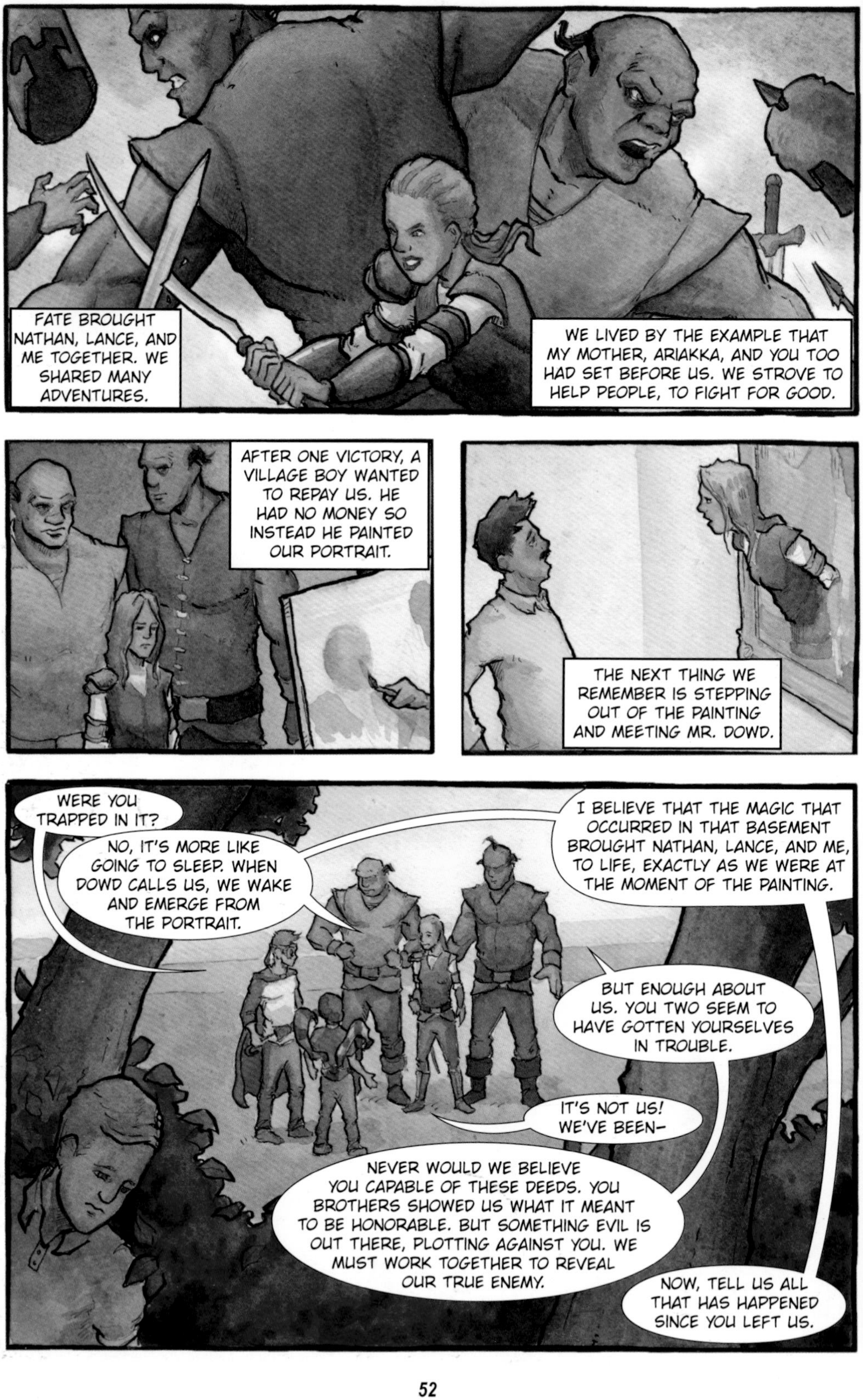
FATE BROUGHT NATHAN, LANCE, AND ME TOGETHER. WE SHARED MANY ADVENTURES.
WE LIVED BY THE EXAMPLE THAT MY MOTHER, ARIAKKA, AND YOU TOO HAD SET BEFORE US. WE STROVE TO HELP PEOPLE, TO FIGHT FOR GOOD.
AFTER ONE VICTORY, A VILLAGE BOY WANTED TO REPAY US. HE HAD NO MONEY SO INSTEAD HE PAINTED OUR PORTRAIT.
THE NEXT THING WE REMEMBER IS STEPPING OUT OF THE PAINTING AND MEETING MR. DOWD.
WERE YOU TRAPPED IN IT?
NO, IT'S MORE LIKE GOING TO SLEEP. WHEN DOWD CALLS US, WE WAKE AND EMERGE FROM THE PORTRAIT.
I BELIEVE THAT THE MAGIC THAT OCCURRED IN THAT BASEMENT BROUGHT NATHAN, LANCE, AND ME, TO LIFE, EXACTLY AS WE WERE AT THE MOMENT OF THE PAINTING.
BUT ENOUGH ABOUT US. YOU TWO SEEM TO HAVE GOTTEN YOURSELVES IN TROUBLE.
IT'S NOT US! WE'VE BEEN–
NEVER WOULD WE BELIEVE YOU CAPABLE OF THESE DEEDS. YOU BROTHERS SHOWED US WHAT IT MEANT TO BE HONORABLE. BUT SOMETHING EVIL IS OUT THERE, PLOTTING AGAINST YOU. WE MUST WORK TOGETHER TO REVEAL OUR TRUE ENEMY.
NOW, TELL US ALL THAT HAS HAPPENED SINCE YOU LEFT US.

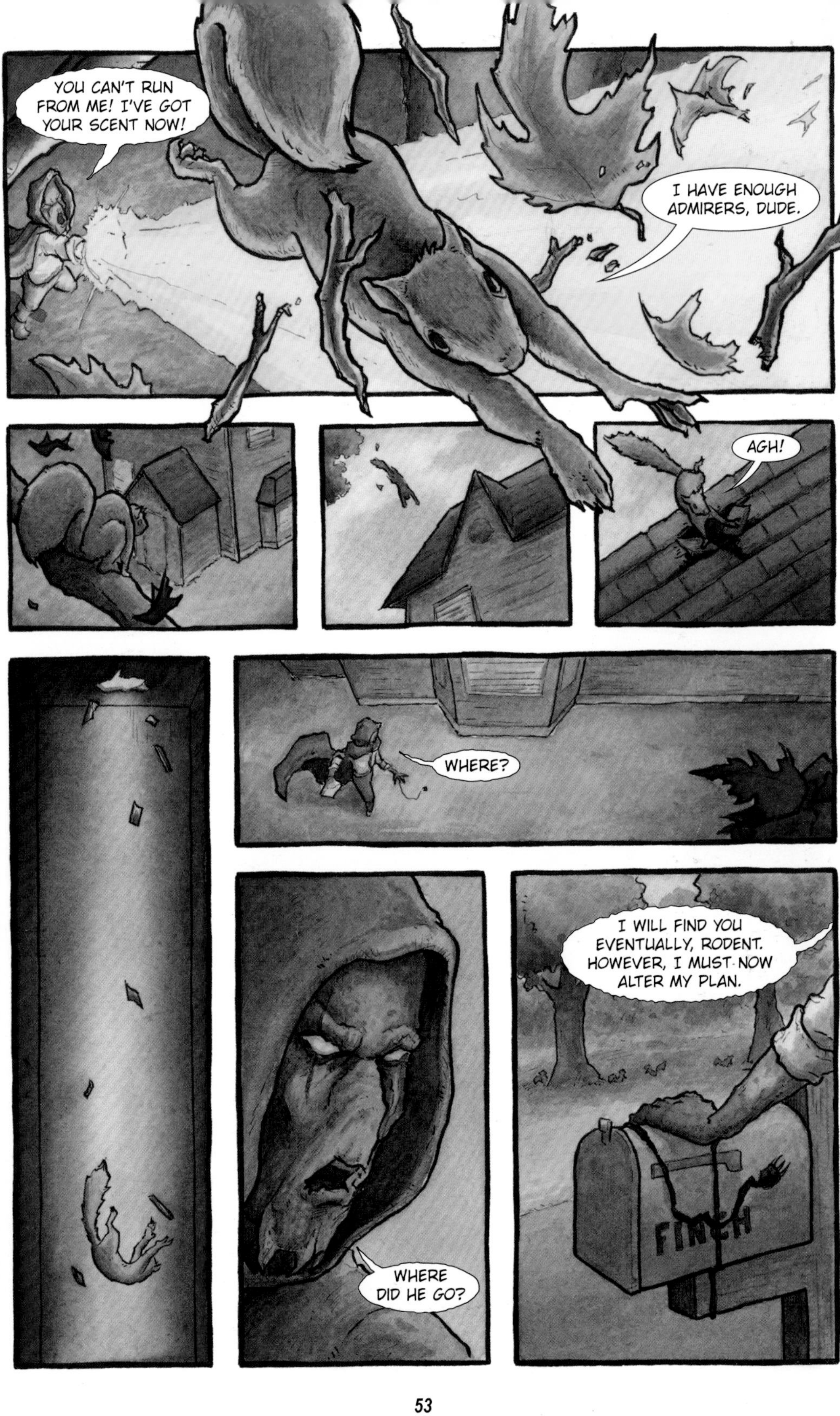
YOU CAN'T RUN FROM ME! I'VE GOT YOUR SCENT NOW!
I HAVE ENOUGH ADMIRERS, DUDE.
AGH!
WHERE?
WHERE DID HE GO?
I WILL FIND YOU EVENTUALLY, RODENT. HOWEVER, I MUST NOW ALTER MY PLAN.
FINCH

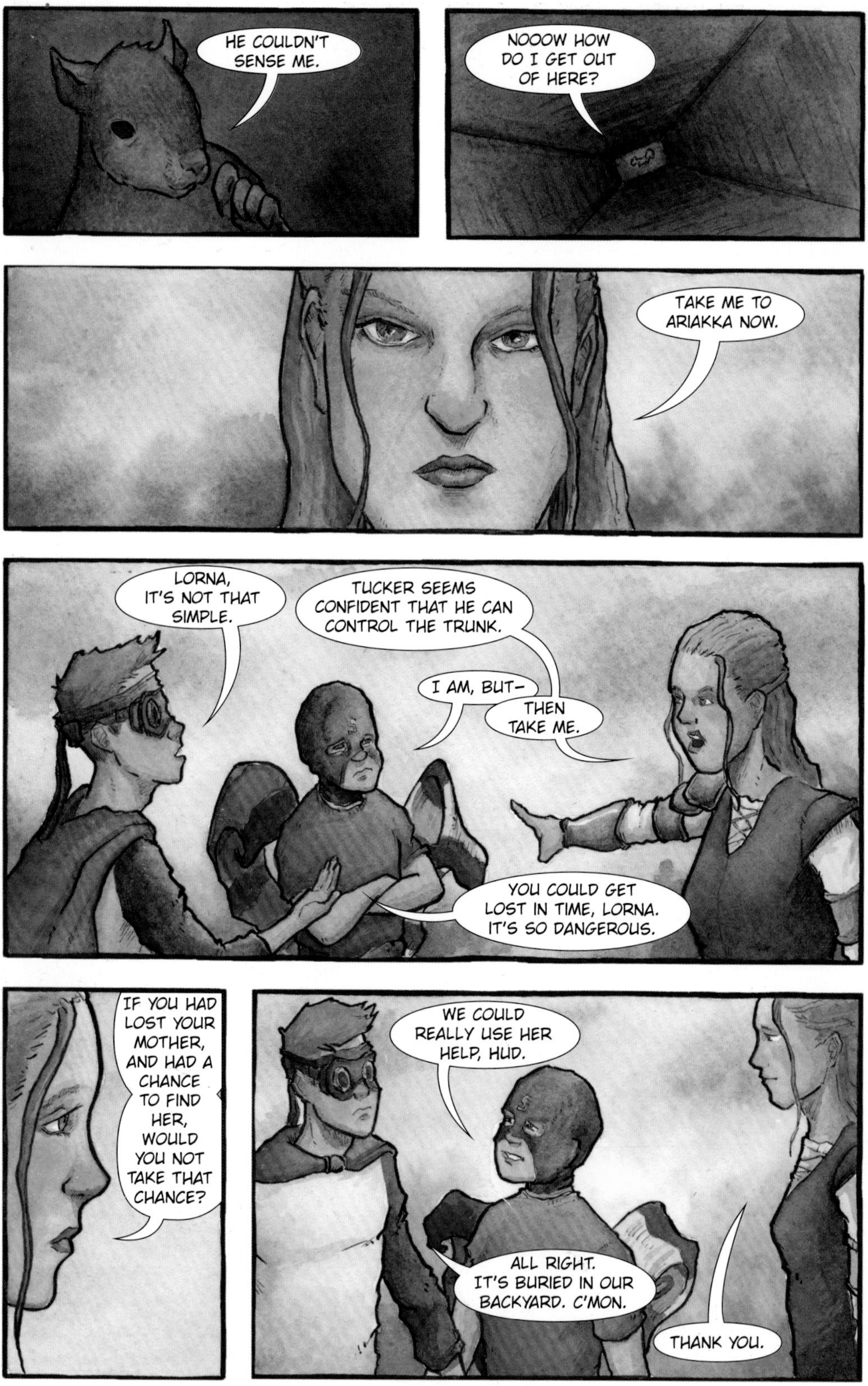
HE COULDN'T SENSE ME.
NOOOW HOW DO I GET OUT OF HERE?
TAKE ME TO ARIAKKA NOW.
LORNA, IT'S NOT THAT SIMPLE.
TUCKER SEEMS CONFIDENT THAT HE CAN CONTROL THE TRUNK.
I AM, BUT–
THEN TAKE ME.
YOU COULD GET LOST IN TIME, LORNA. IT'S SO DANGEROUS.
IF YOU HAD LOST YOUR MOTHER, AND HAD A CHANCE TO FIND HER, WOULD YOU NOT TAKE THAT CHANCE?
WE COULD REALLY USE HER HELP, HUD.
ALL RIGHT. IT'S BURIED IN OUR BACKYARD. C'MON.
THANK YOU.

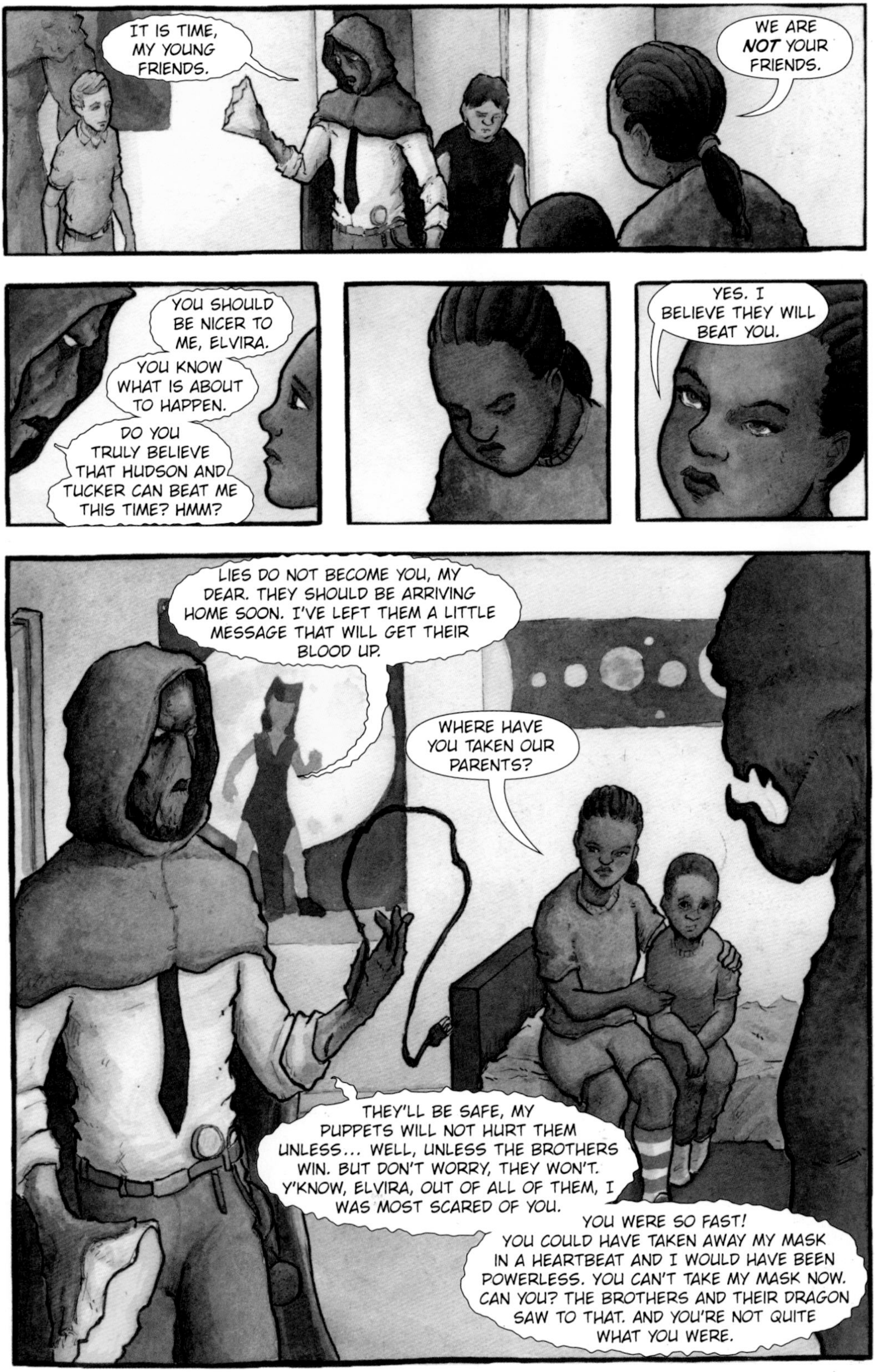
IT IS TIME, MY YOUNG FRIENDS.
WE ARE **NOT** YOUR FRIENDS.
YOU SHOULD BE NICER TO ME, ELVIRA.
YOU KNOW WHAT IS ABOUT TO HAPPEN.
DO YOU TRULY BELIEVE THAT HUDSON AND TUCKER CAN BEAT ME THIS TIME? HMM?
YES. I BELIEVE THEY WILL BEAT YOU.
LIES DO NOT BECOME YOU, MY DEAR. THEY SHOULD BE ARRIVING HOME SOON. I'VE LEFT THEM A LITTLE MESSAGE THAT WILL GET THEIR BLOOD UP.
WHERE HAVE YOU TAKEN OUR PARENTS?
THEY'LL BE SAFE, MY PUPPETS WILL NOT HURT THEM UNLESS... WELL, UNLESS THE BROTHERS WIN. BUT DON'T WORRY, THEY WON'T. Y'KNOW, ELVIRA, OUT OF ALL OF THEM, I WAS MOST SCARED OF YOU.
YOU WERE SO FAST! YOU COULD HAVE TAKEN AWAY MY MASK IN A HEARTBEAT AND I WOULD HAVE BEEN POWERLESS. YOU CAN'T TAKE MY MASK NOW. CAN YOU? THE BROTHERS AND THEIR DRAGON SAW TO THAT. AND YOU'RE NOT QUITE WHAT YOU WERE.

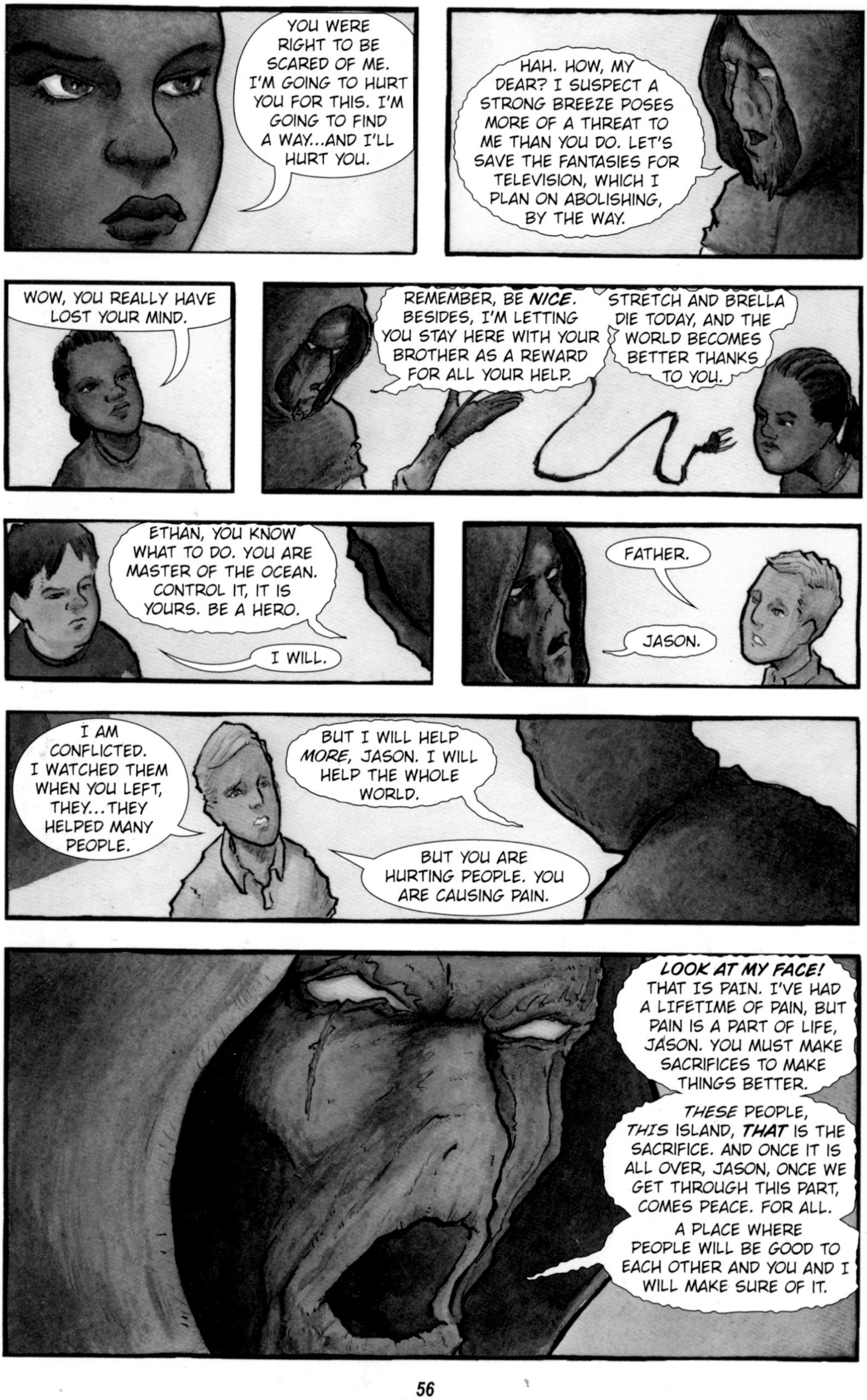

YOU WERE RIGHT TO BE SCARED OF ME. I'M GOING TO HURT YOU FOR THIS. I'M GOING TO FIND A WAY...AND I'LL HURT YOU.
HAH. HOW, MY DEAR? I SUSPECT A STRONG BREEZE POSES MORE OF A THREAT TO ME THAN YOU DO. LET'S SAVE THE FANTASIES FOR TELEVISION, WHICH I PLAN ON ABOLISHING, BY THE WAY.
WOW, YOU REALLY HAVE LOST YOUR MIND.
REMEMBER, BE NICE. BESIDES, I'M LETTING YOU STAY HERE WITH YOUR BROTHER AS A REWARD FOR ALL YOUR HELP.
STRETCH AND BRELLA DIE TODAY, AND THE WORLD BECOMES BETTER THANKS TO YOU.
ETHAN, YOU KNOW WHAT TO DO. YOU ARE MASTER OF THE OCEAN. CONTROL IT, IT IS YOURS. BE A HERO.
I WILL.
FATHER.
JASON.
I AM CONFLICTED. I WATCHED THEM WHEN YOU LEFT, THEY...THEY HELPED MANY PEOPLE.
BUT I WILL HELP MORE, JASON. I WILL HELP THE WHOLE WORLD.
BUT YOU ARE HURTING PEOPLE. YOU ARE CAUSING PAIN.
LOOK AT MY FACE! THAT IS PAIN. I'VE HAD A LIFETIME OF PAIN, BUT PAIN IS A PART OF LIFE, JASON. YOU MUST MAKE SACRIFICES TO MAKE THINGS BETTER.
THESE PEOPLE, THIS ISLAND, THAT IS THE SACRIFICE. AND ONCE IT IS ALL OVER, JASON, ONCE WE GET THROUGH THIS PART, COMES PEACE. FOR ALL.
A PLACE WHERE PEOPLE WILL BE GOOD TO EACH OTHER AND YOU AND I WILL MAKE SURE OF IT.

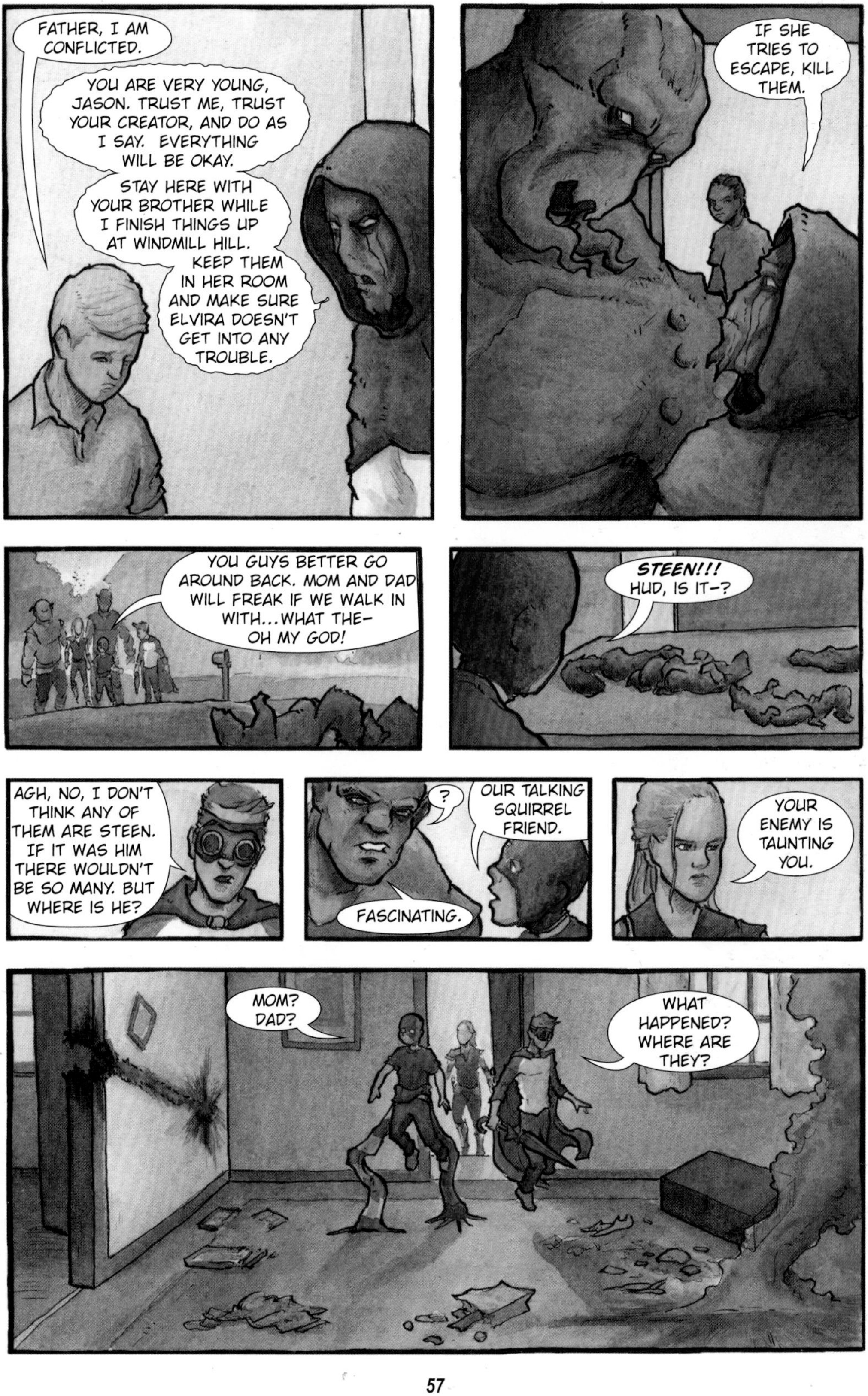
FATHER, I AM CONFLICTED.
YOU ARE VERY YOUNG, JASON. TRUST ME, TRUST YOUR CREATOR, AND DO AS I SAY. EVERYTHING WILL BE OKAY.
STAY HERE WITH YOUR BROTHER WHILE I FINISH THINGS UP AT WINDMILL HILL.
KEEP THEM IN HER ROOM AND MAKE SURE ELVIRA DOESN'T GET INTO ANY TROUBLE.
IF SHE TRIES TO ESCAPE, KILL THEM.
YOU GUYS BETTER GO AROUND BACK. MOM AND DAD WILL FREAK IF WE WALK IN WITH...WHAT THE– OH MY GOD!
STEEN!!! HUD, IS IT–?
AGH, NO, I DON'T THINK ANY OF THEM ARE STEEN. IF IT WAS HIM THERE WOULDN'T BE SO MANY. BUT WHERE IS HE?
?
OUR TALKING SQUIRREL FRIEND.
FASCINATING.
YOUR ENEMY IS TAUNTING YOU.
MOM? DAD?
WHAT HAPPENED? WHERE ARE THEY?

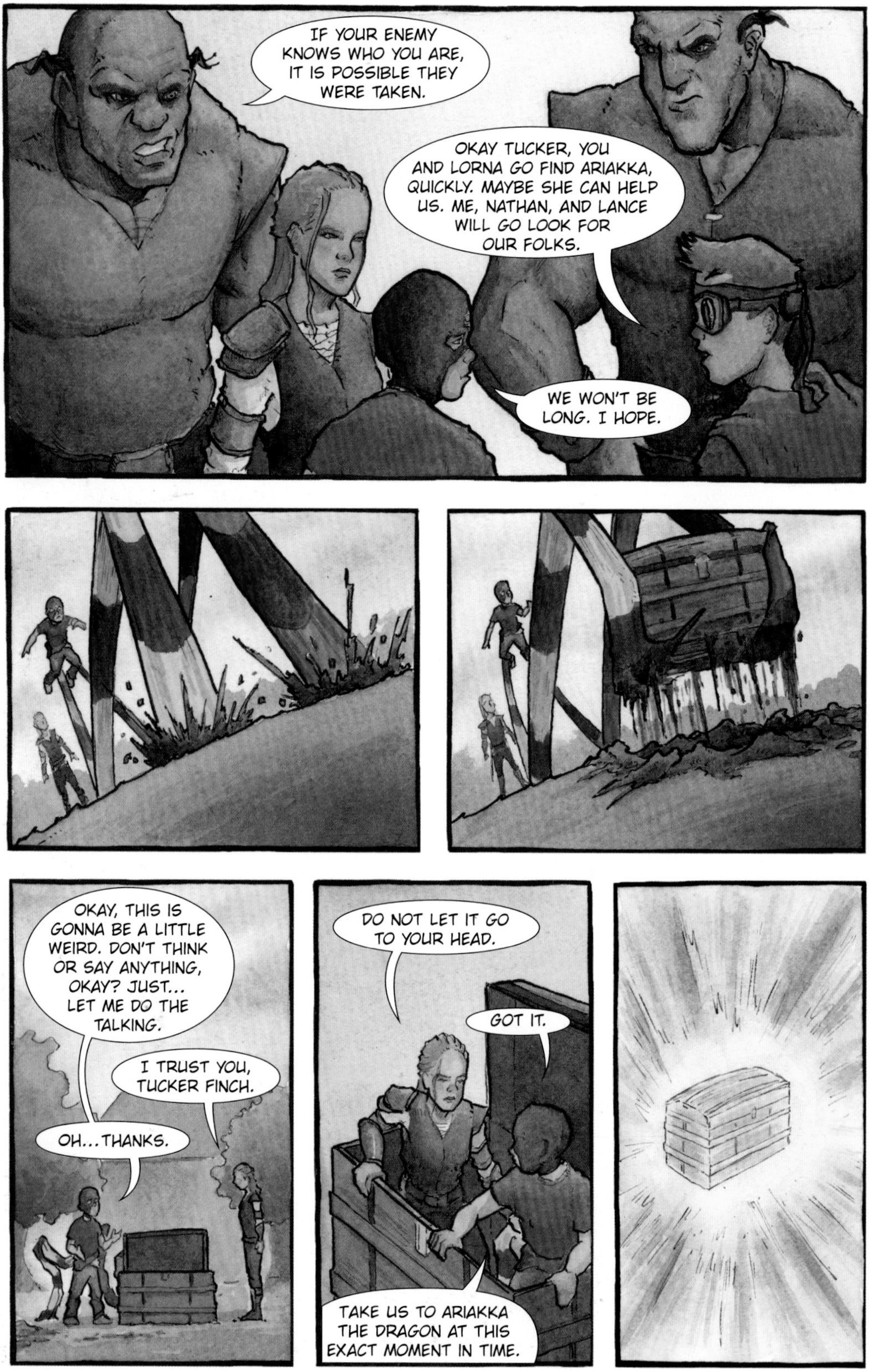
IF YOUR ENEMY KNOWS WHO YOU ARE, IT IS POSSIBLE THEY WERE TAKEN.
OKAY TUCKER, YOU AND LORNA GO FIND ARIAKKA, QUICKLY. MAYBE SHE CAN HELP US. ME, NATHAN, AND LANCE WILL GO LOOK FOR OUR FOLKS.
WE WON'T BE LONG. I HOPE.
OKAY, THIS IS GONNA BE A LITTLE WEIRD. DON'T THINK OR SAY ANYTHING, OKAY? JUST... LET ME DO THE TALKING.
I TRUST YOU, TUCKER FINCH.
OH...THANKS.
DO NOT LET IT GO TO YOUR HEAD.
GOT IT.
TAKE US TO ARIAKKA THE DRAGON AT THIS EXACT MOMENT IN TIME.

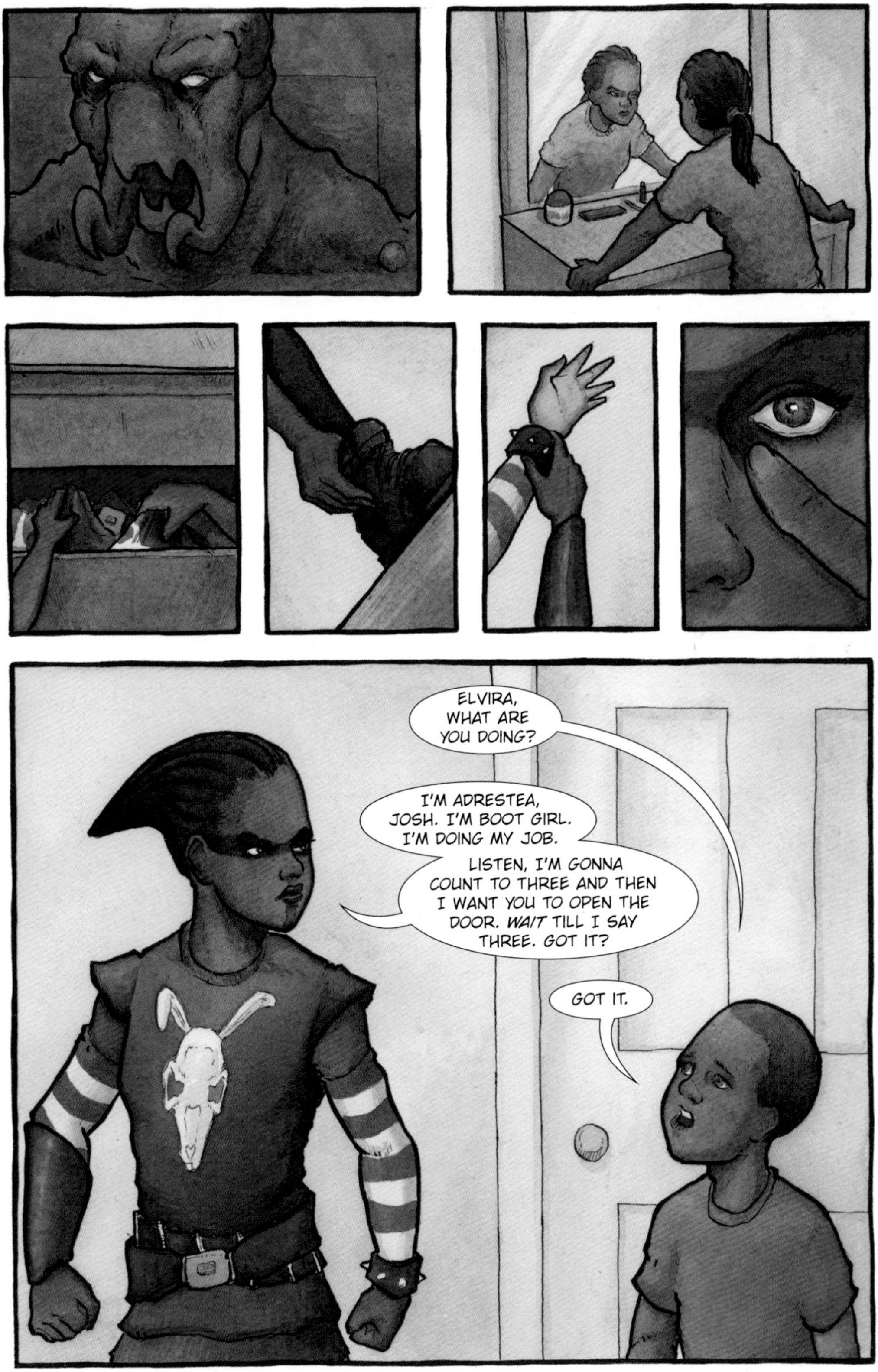
ELVIRA, WHAT ARE YOU DOING?
I'M ADRESTEA, JOSH. I'M BOOT GIRL. I'M DOING MY JOB.
LISTEN, I'M GONNA COUNT TO THREE AND THEN I WANT YOU TO OPEN THE DOOR. *WAIT* TILL I SAY THREE. GOT IT?
GOT IT.

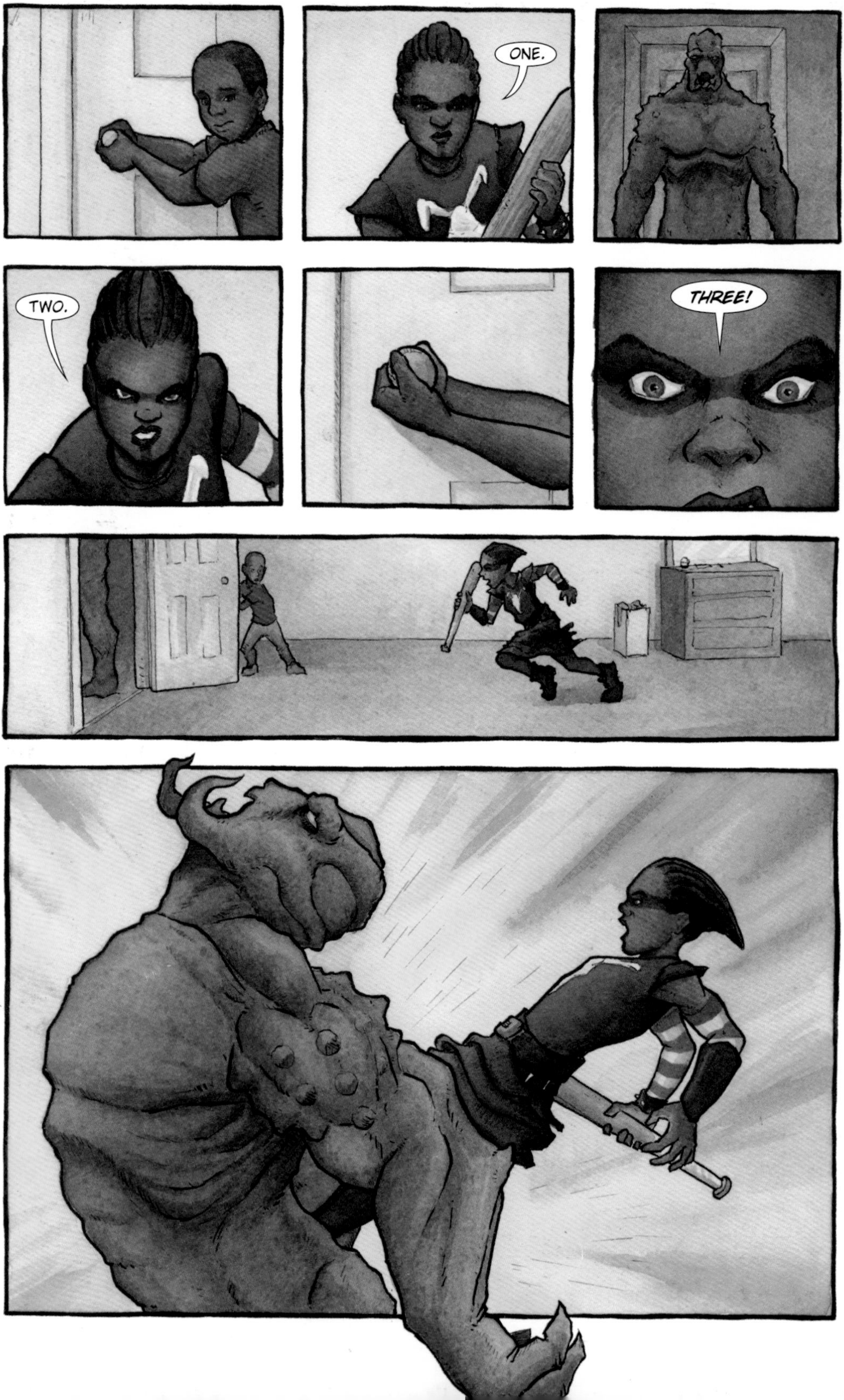
ONE.
TWO.
THREE!

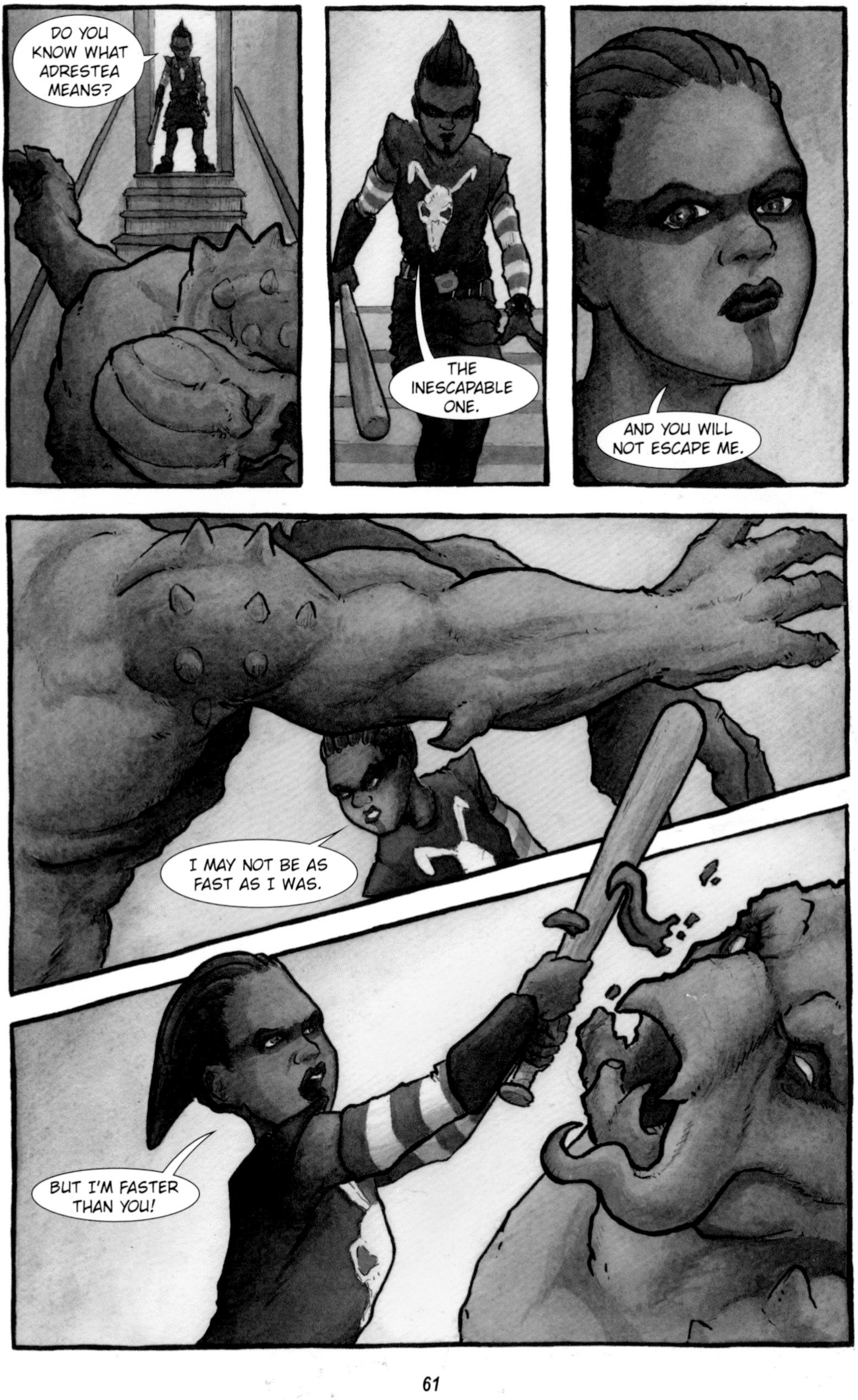
DO YOU KNOW WHAT ADRESTEA MEANS?
THE INESCAPABLE ONE.
AND YOU WILL NOT ESCAPE ME.
I MAY NOT BE AS FAST AS I WAS.
BUT I'M FASTER THAN YOU!

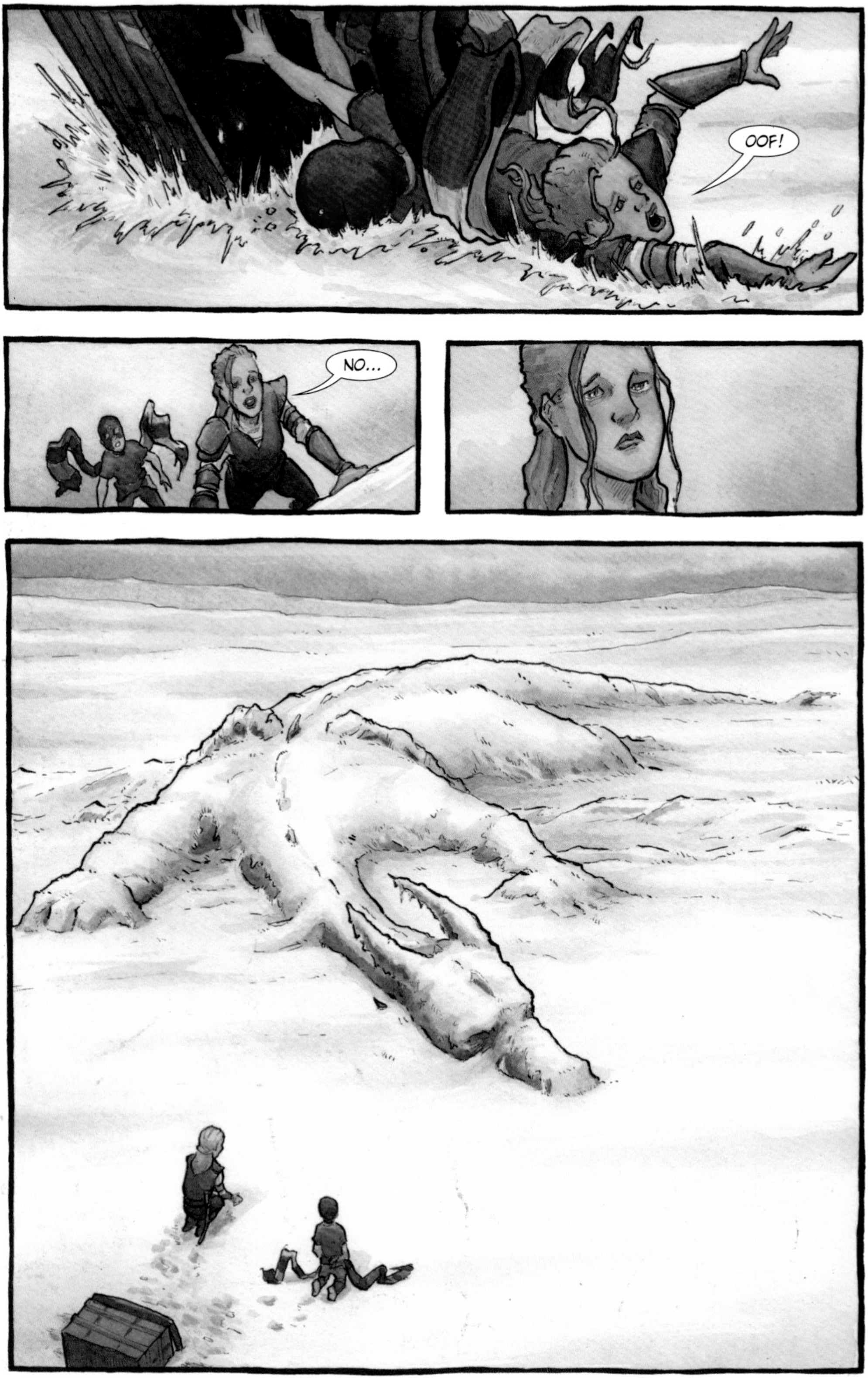
OOF!
NO...

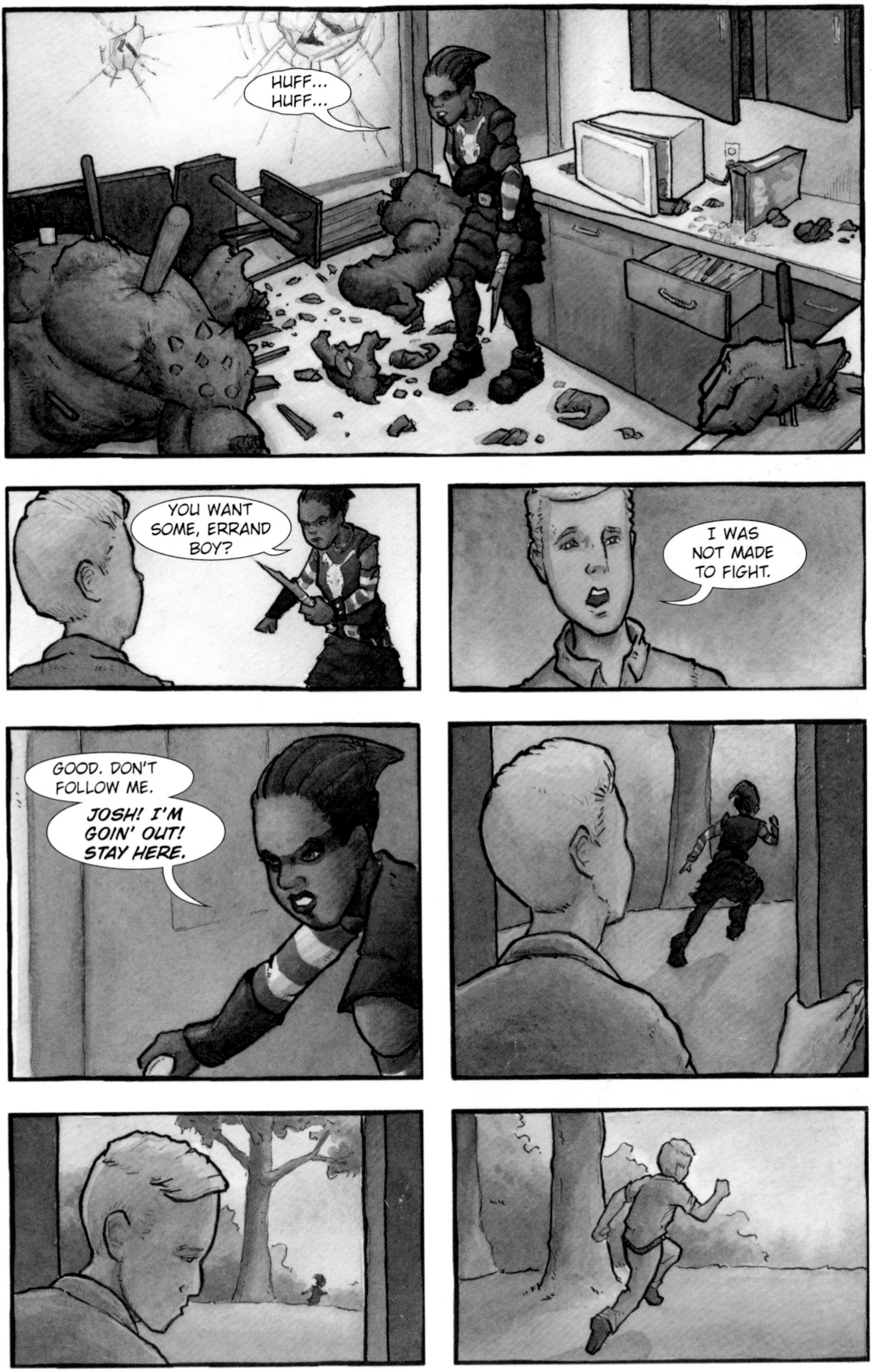
HUFF... HUFF...
YOU WANT SOME, ERRAND BOY?
I WAS NOT MADE TO FIGHT.
GOOD. DON'T FOLLOW ME.
JOSH! I'M GOIN' OUT! STAY HERE.

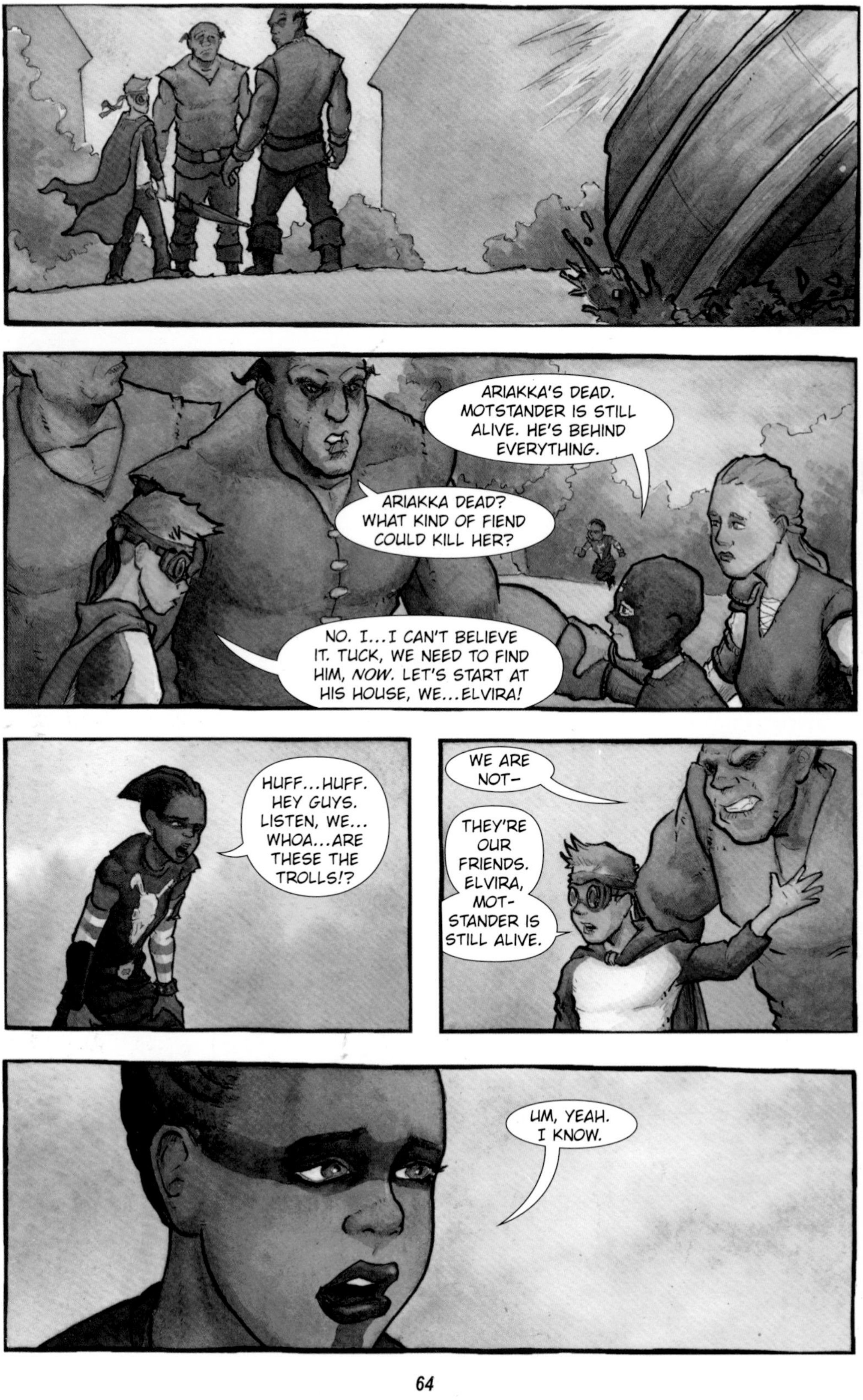
ARIAKKA'S DEAD. MOTSTANDER IS STILL ALIVE. HE'S BEHIND EVERYTHING.
ARIAKKA DEAD? WHAT KIND OF FIEND COULD KILL HER?
NO. I...I CAN'T BELIEVE IT. TUCK, WE NEED TO FIND HIM, *NOW*. LET'S START AT HIS HOUSE, WE...ELVIRA!
HUFF...HUFF. HEY GUYS. LISTEN, WE... WHOA...ARE THESE THE TROLLS!?
WE ARE NOT-
THEY'RE OUR FRIENDS. ELVIRA, MOT-STANDER IS STILL ALIVE.
UM, YEAH. I KNOW.

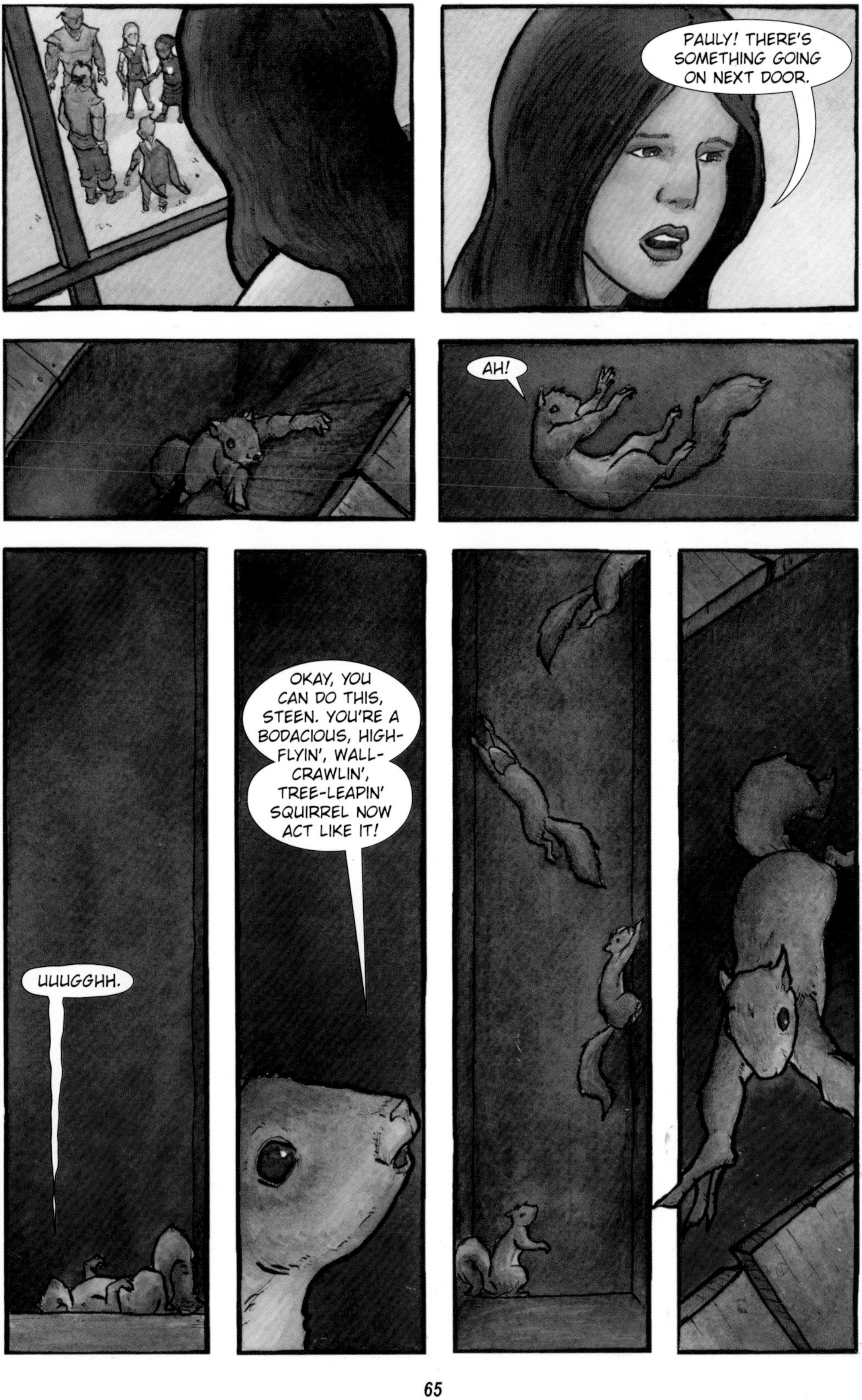
PAULY! THERE'S SOMETHING GOING ON NEXT DOOR.
AH!
UUUGGHH.
OKAY, YOU CAN DO THIS, STEEN. YOU'RE A BODACIOUS, HIGH-FLYIN', WALL-CRAWLIN',
TREE-LEAPIN' SQUIRREL NOW ACT LIKE IT!

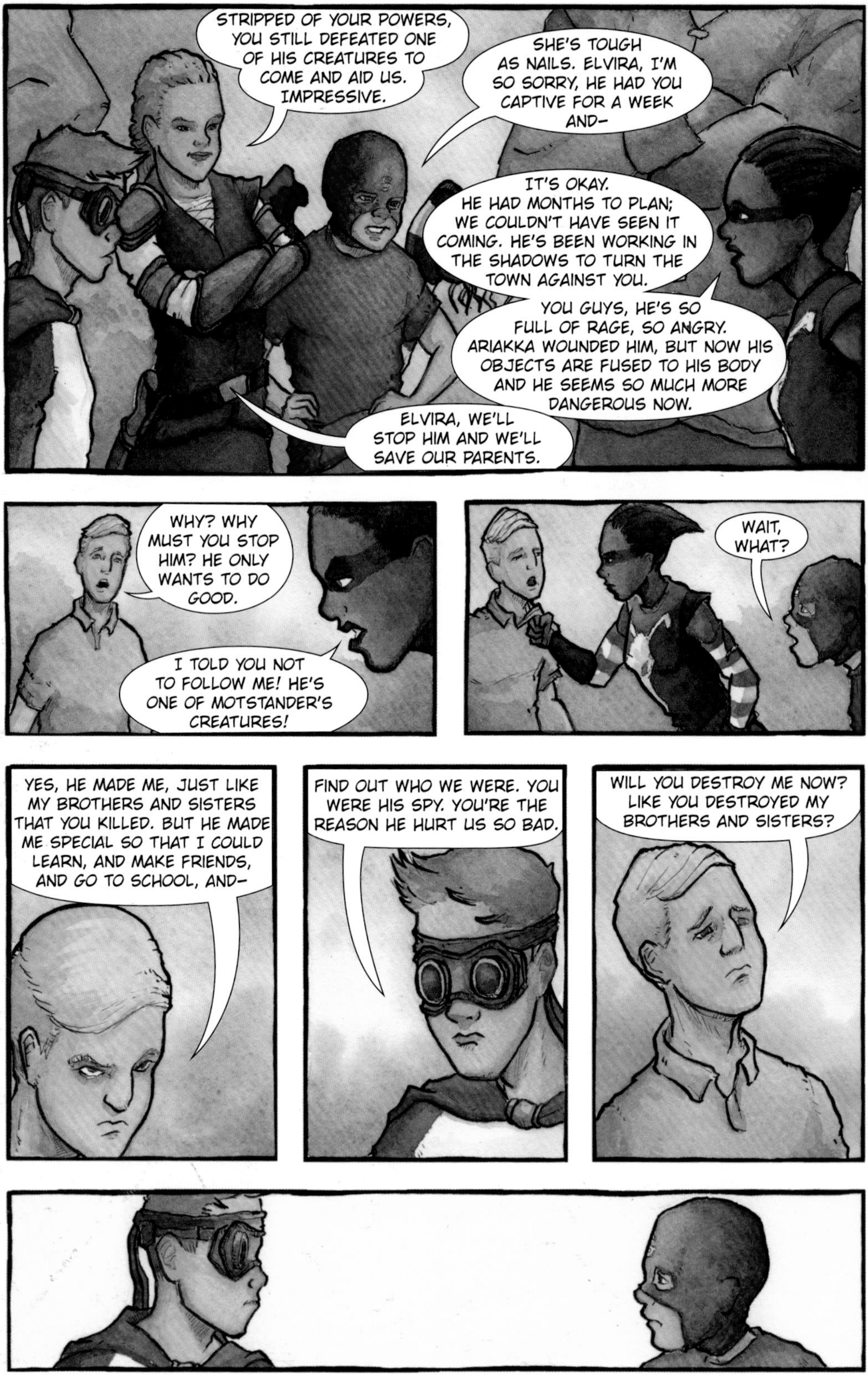
STRIPPED OF YOUR POWERS, YOU STILL DEFEATED ONE OF HIS CREATURES TO COME AND AID US. IMPRESSIVE.
SHE'S TOUGH AS NAILS. ELVIRA, I'M SO SORRY, HE HAD YOU CAPTIVE FOR A WEEK AND–
IT'S OKAY. HE HAD MONTHS TO PLAN; WE COULDN'T HAVE SEEN IT COMING. HE'S BEEN WORKING IN THE SHADOWS TO TURN THE TOWN AGAINST YOU.
YOU GUYS, HE'S SO FULL OF RAGE, SO ANGRY. ARIAKKA WOUNDED HIM, BUT NOW HIS OBJECTS ARE FUSED TO HIS BODY AND HE SEEMS SO MUCH MORE DANGEROUS NOW.
ELVIRA, WE'LL STOP HIM AND WE'LL SAVE OUR PARENTS.
WHY? WHY MUST YOU STOP HIM? HE ONLY WANTS TO DO GOOD.
I TOLD YOU NOT TO FOLLOW ME! HE'S ONE OF MOTSTANDER'S CREATURES!
WAIT, WHAT?
YES, HE MADE ME, JUST LIKE MY BROTHERS AND SISTERS THAT YOU KILLED. BUT HE MADE ME SPECIAL SO THAT I COULD LEARN, AND MAKE FRIENDS, AND GO TO SCHOOL, AND–
FIND OUT WHO WE WERE. YOU WERE HIS SPY. YOU'RE THE REASON HE HURT US SO BAD.
WILL YOU DESTROY ME NOW? LIKE YOU DESTROYED MY BROTHERS AND SISTERS?

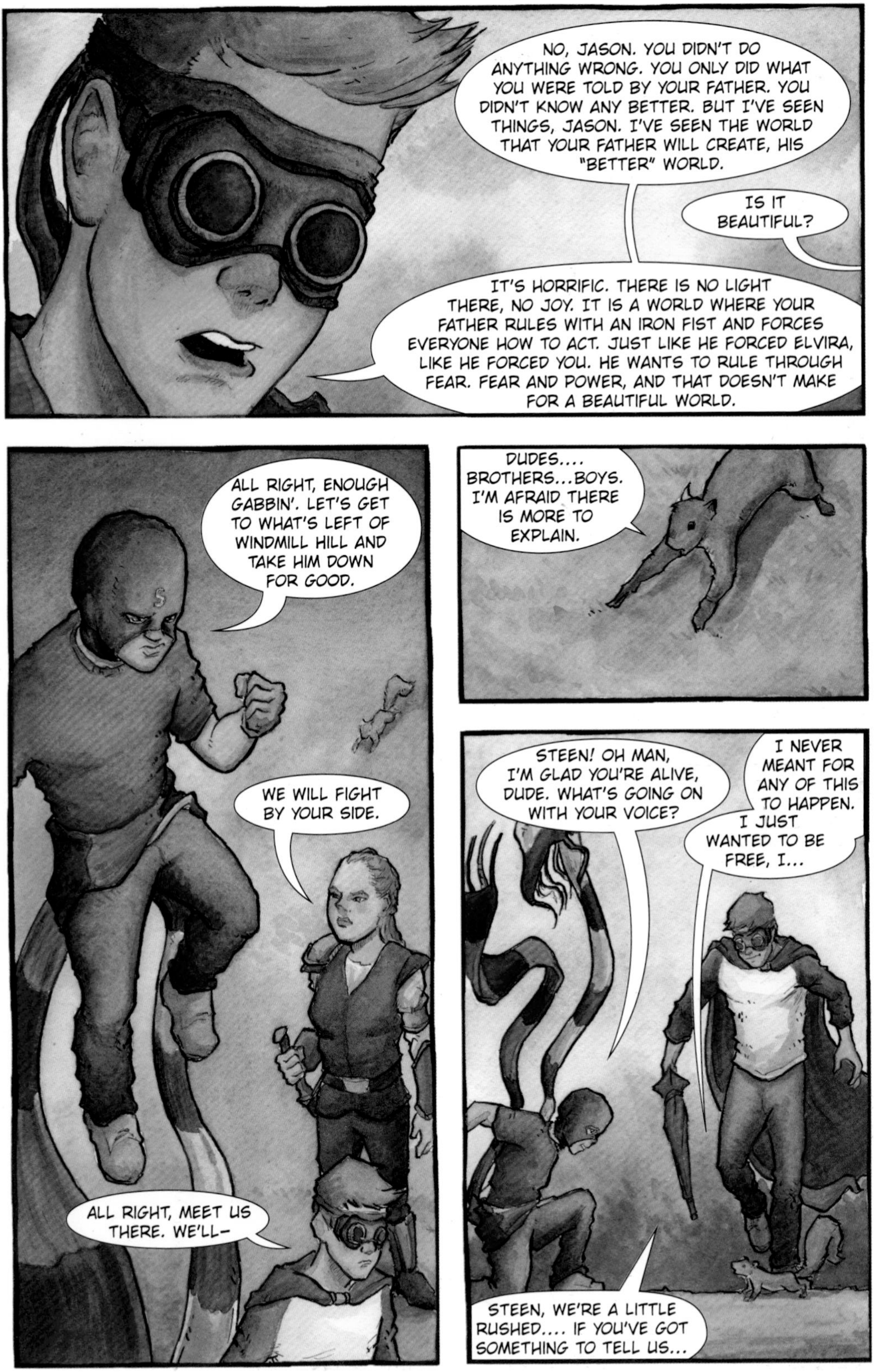
NO, JASON. YOU DIDN'T DO ANYTHING WRONG. YOU ONLY DID WHAT YOU WERE TOLD BY YOUR FATHER. YOU DIDN'T KNOW ANY BETTER. BUT I'VE SEEN THINGS, JASON. I'VE SEEN THE WORLD THAT YOUR FATHER WILL CREATE, HIS "BETTER" WORLD.
IS IT BEAUTIFUL?
IT'S HORRIFIC. THERE IS NO LIGHT THERE, NO JOY. IT IS A WORLD WHERE YOUR FATHER RULES WITH AN IRON FIST AND FORCES EVERYONE HOW TO ACT. JUST LIKE HE FORCED ELVIRA, LIKE HE FORCED YOU. HE WANTS TO RULE THROUGH FEAR. FEAR AND POWER, AND THAT DOESN'T MAKE FOR A BEAUTIFUL WORLD.
ALL RIGHT, ENOUGH GABBIN'. LET'S GET TO WHAT'S LEFT OF WINDMILL HILL AND TAKE HIM DOWN FOR GOOD.
WE WILL FIGHT BY YOUR SIDE.
ALL RIGHT, MEET US THERE. WE'LL–
DUDES.... BROTHERS...BOYS. I'M AFRAID THERE IS MORE TO EXPLAIN.
STEEN! OH MAN, I'M GLAD YOU'RE ALIVE, DUDE. WHAT'S GOING ON WITH YOUR VOICE?
I NEVER MEANT FOR ANY OF THIS TO HAPPEN.
I JUST WANTED TO BE FREE, I...
STEEN, WE'RE A LITTLE RUSHED.... IF YOU'VE GOT SOMETHING TO TELL US...

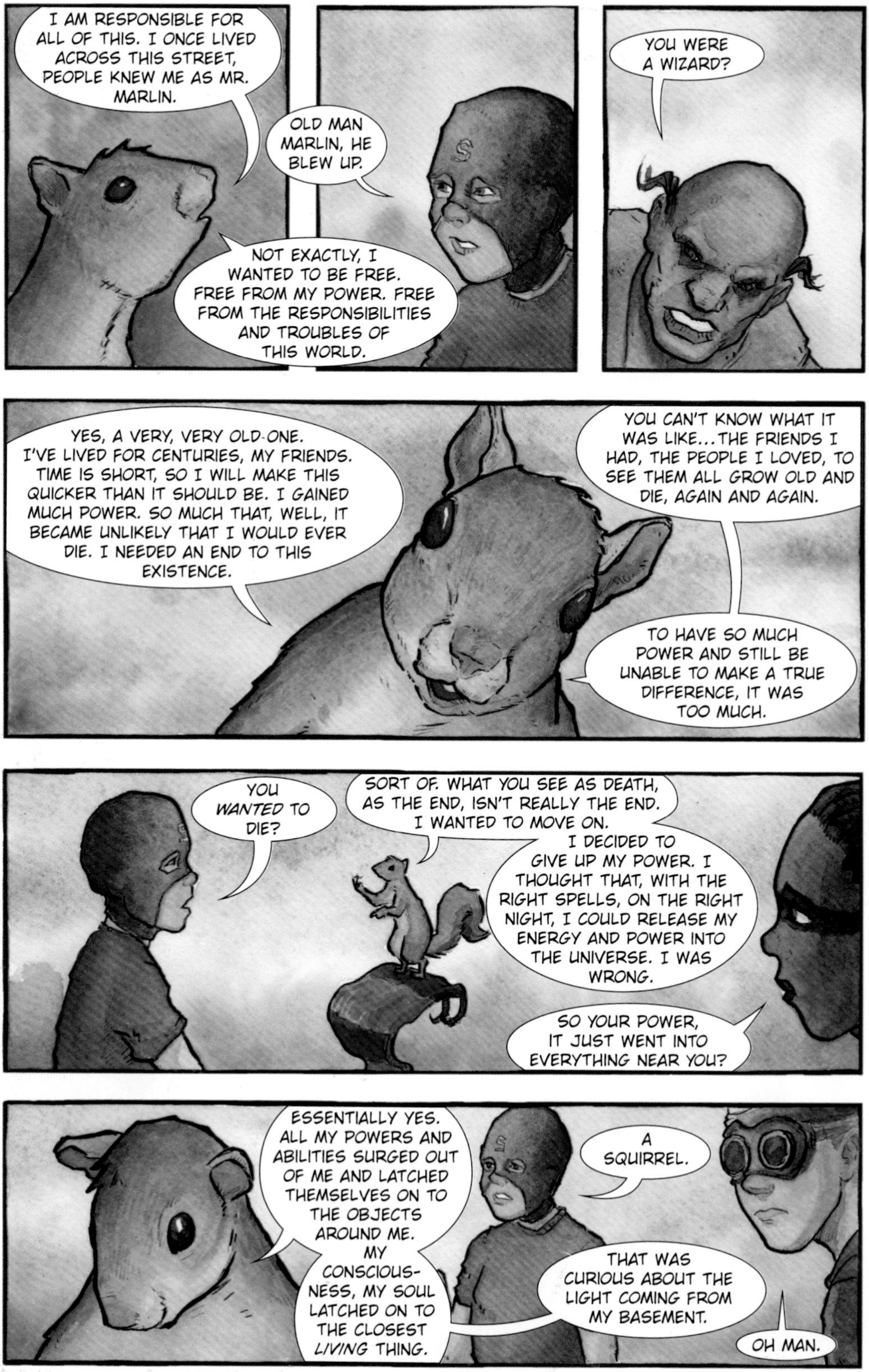
I AM RESPONSIBLE FOR ALL OF THIS. I ONCE LIVED ACROSS THIS STREET, PEOPLE KNEW ME AS MR. MARLIN.
OLD MAN MARLIN, HE BLEW UP.
NOT EXACTLY, I WANTED TO BE FREE. FREE FROM MY POWER. FREE FROM THE RESPONSIBILITIES AND TROUBLES OF THIS WORLD.
YOU WERE A WIZARD?
YES, A VERY, VERY OLD ONE. I'VE LIVED FOR CENTURIES, MY FRIENDS. TIME IS SHORT, SO I WILL MAKE THIS QUICKER THAN IT SHOULD BE. I GAINED MUCH POWER. SO MUCH THAT, WELL, IT BECAME UNLIKELY THAT I WOULD EVER DIE. I NEEDED AN END TO THIS EXISTENCE.
YOU CAN'T KNOW WHAT IT WAS LIKE...THE FRIENDS I HAD, THE PEOPLE I LOVED, TO SEE THEM ALL GROW OLD AND DIE, AGAIN AND AGAIN.
TO HAVE SO MUCH POWER AND STILL BE UNABLE TO MAKE A TRUE DIFFERENCE, IT WAS TOO MUCH.
YOU *WANTED* TO DIE?
SORT OF. WHAT YOU SEE AS DEATH, AS THE END, ISN'T REALLY THE END. I WANTED TO MOVE ON.
I DECIDED TO GIVE UP MY POWER. I THOUGHT THAT, WITH THE RIGHT SPELLS, ON THE RIGHT NIGHT, I COULD RELEASE MY ENERGY AND POWER INTO THE UNIVERSE. I WAS WRONG.
SO YOUR POWER, IT JUST WENT INTO EVERYTHING NEAR YOU?
ESSENTIALLY YES. ALL MY POWERS AND ABILITIES SURGED OUT OF ME AND LATCHED THEMSELVES ON TO THE OBJECTS AROUND ME.
MY CONSCIOUS-NESS, MY SOUL LATCHED ON TO THE CLOSEST *LIVING* THING.
A SQUIRREL.
THAT WAS CURIOUS ABOUT THE LIGHT COMING FROM MY BASEMENT.
OH MAN.

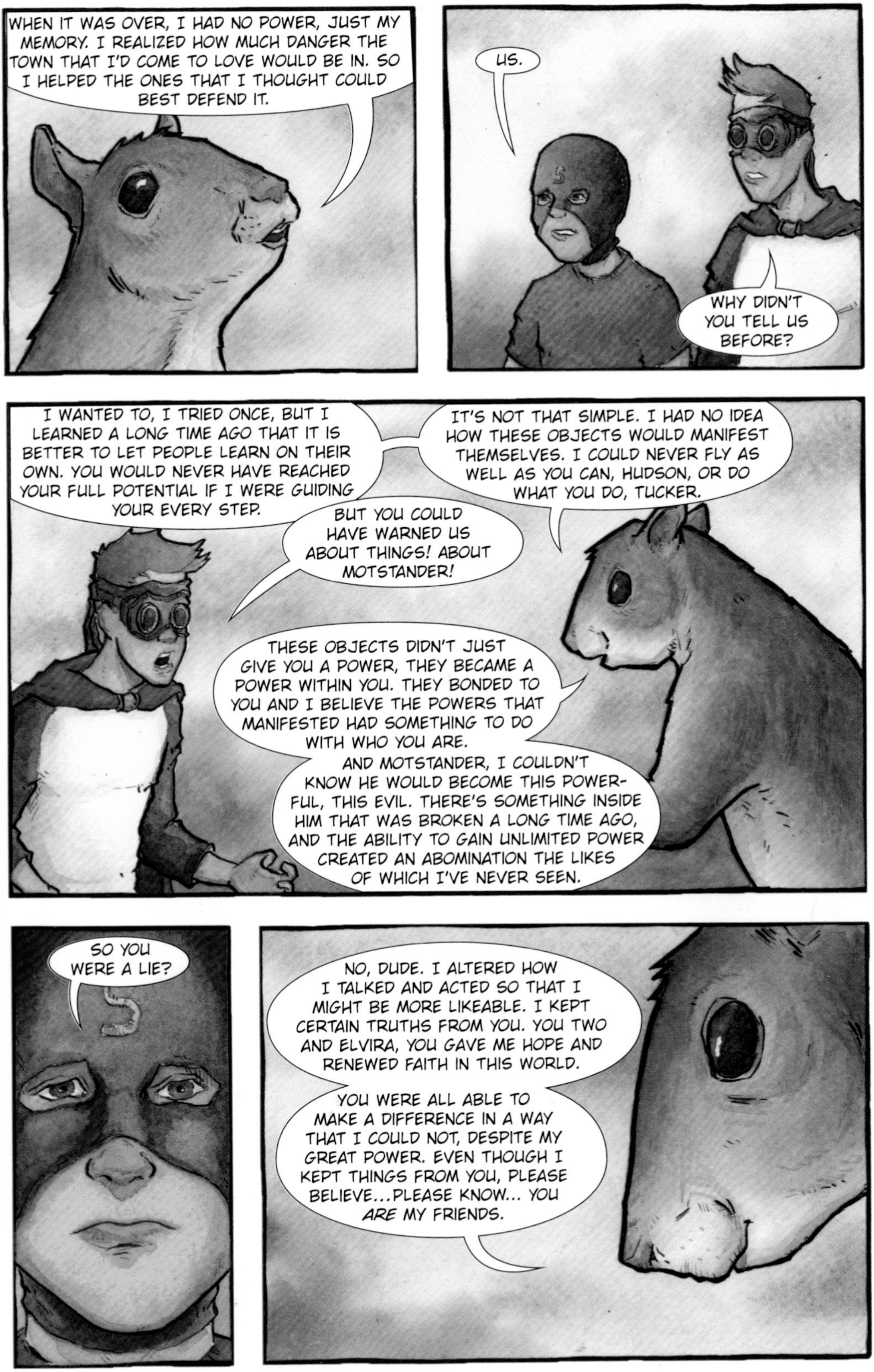
WHEN IT WAS OVER, I HAD NO POWER, JUST MY MEMORY. I REALIZED HOW MUCH DANGER THE TOWN THAT I'D COME TO LOVE WOULD BE IN. SO I HELPED THE ONES THAT I THOUGHT COULD BEST DEFEND IT.
US.
WHY DIDN'T YOU TELL US BEFORE?
I WANTED TO, I TRIED ONCE, BUT I LEARNED A LONG TIME AGO THAT IT IS BETTER TO LET PEOPLE LEARN ON THEIR OWN. YOU WOULD NEVER HAVE REACHED YOUR FULL POTENTIAL IF I WERE GUIDING YOUR EVERY STEP.
IT'S NOT THAT SIMPLE. I HAD NO IDEA HOW THESE OBJECTS WOULD MANIFEST THEMSELVES. I COULD NEVER FLY AS WELL AS YOU CAN, HUDSON, OR DO WHAT YOU DO, TUCKER.
BUT YOU COULD HAVE WARNED US ABOUT THINGS! ABOUT MOTSTANDER!
THESE OBJECTS DIDN'T JUST GIVE YOU A POWER, THEY BECAME A POWER WITHIN YOU. THEY BONDED TO YOU AND I BELIEVE THE POWERS THAT MANIFESTED HAD SOMETHING TO DO WITH WHO YOU ARE.
AND MOTSTANDER, I COULDN'T KNOW HE WOULD BECOME THIS POWER-FUL, THIS EVIL. THERE'S SOMETHING INSIDE HIM THAT WAS BROKEN A LONG TIME AGO, AND THE ABILITY TO GAIN UNLIMITED POWER CREATED AN ABOMINATION THE LIKES OF WHICH I'VE NEVER SEEN.
SO YOU WERE A LIE?
NO, DUDE. I ALTERED HOW I TALKED AND ACTED SO THAT I MIGHT BE MORE LIKEABLE. I KEPT CERTAIN TRUTHS FROM YOU. YOU TWO AND ELVIRA, YOU GAVE ME HOPE AND RENEWED FAITH IN THIS WORLD.
YOU WERE ALL ABLE TO MAKE A DIFFERENCE IN A WAY THAT I COULD NOT, DESPITE MY GREAT POWER. EVEN THOUGH I KEPT THINGS FROM YOU, PLEASE BELIEVE...PLEASE KNOW... YOU *ARE* MY FRIENDS.

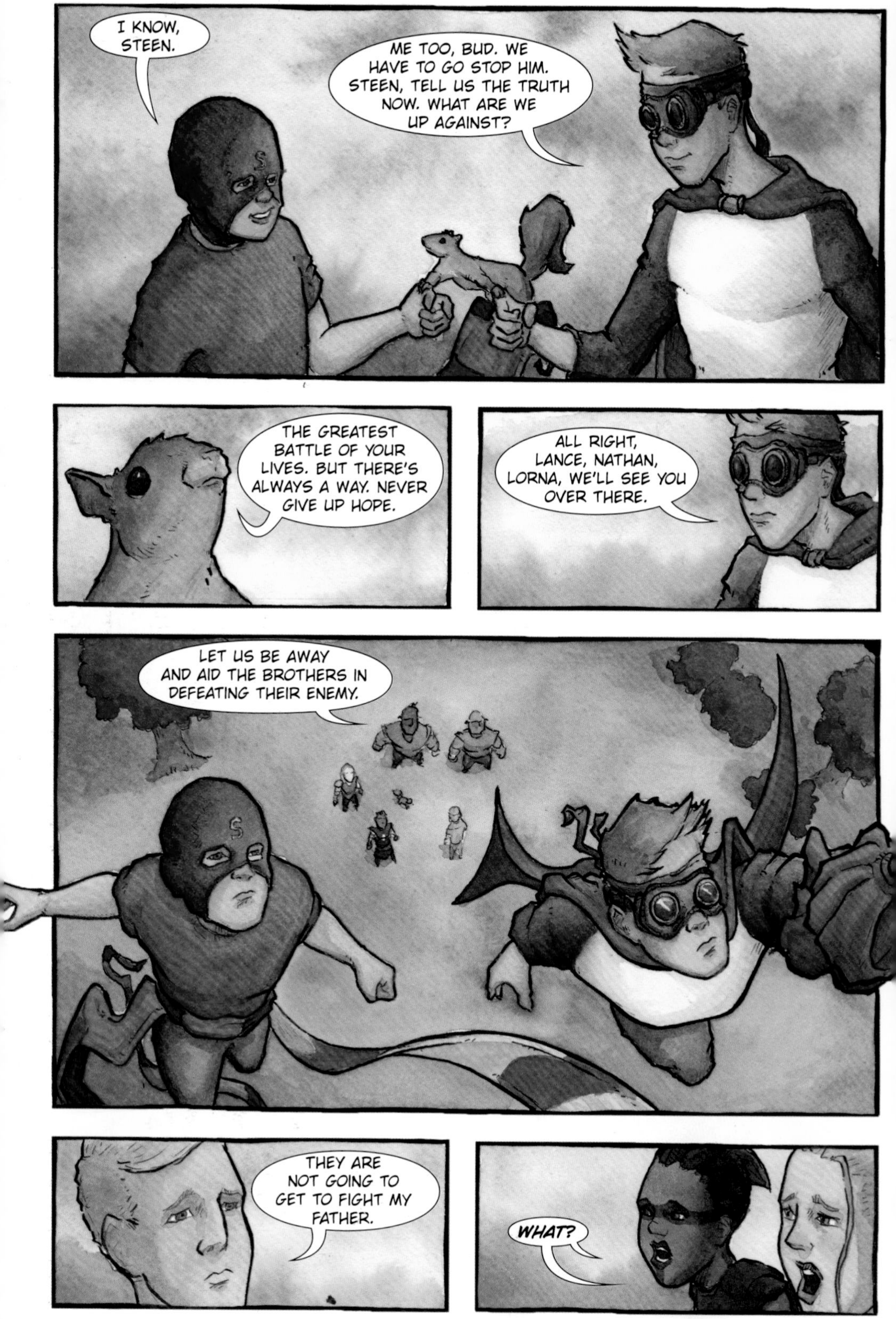

I KNOW, STEEN.
ME TOO, BUD. WE HAVE TO GO STOP HIM. STEEN, TELL US THE TRUTH NOW. WHAT ARE WE UP AGAINST?
THE GREATEST BATTLE OF YOUR LIVES. BUT THERE'S ALWAYS A WAY. NEVER GIVE UP HOPE.
ALL RIGHT, LANCE, NATHAN, LORNA, WE'LL SEE YOU OVER THERE.
LET US BE AWAY AND AID THE BROTHERS IN DEFEATING THEIR ENEMY.
THEY ARE NOT GOING TO GET TO FIGHT MY FATHER.
WHAT?

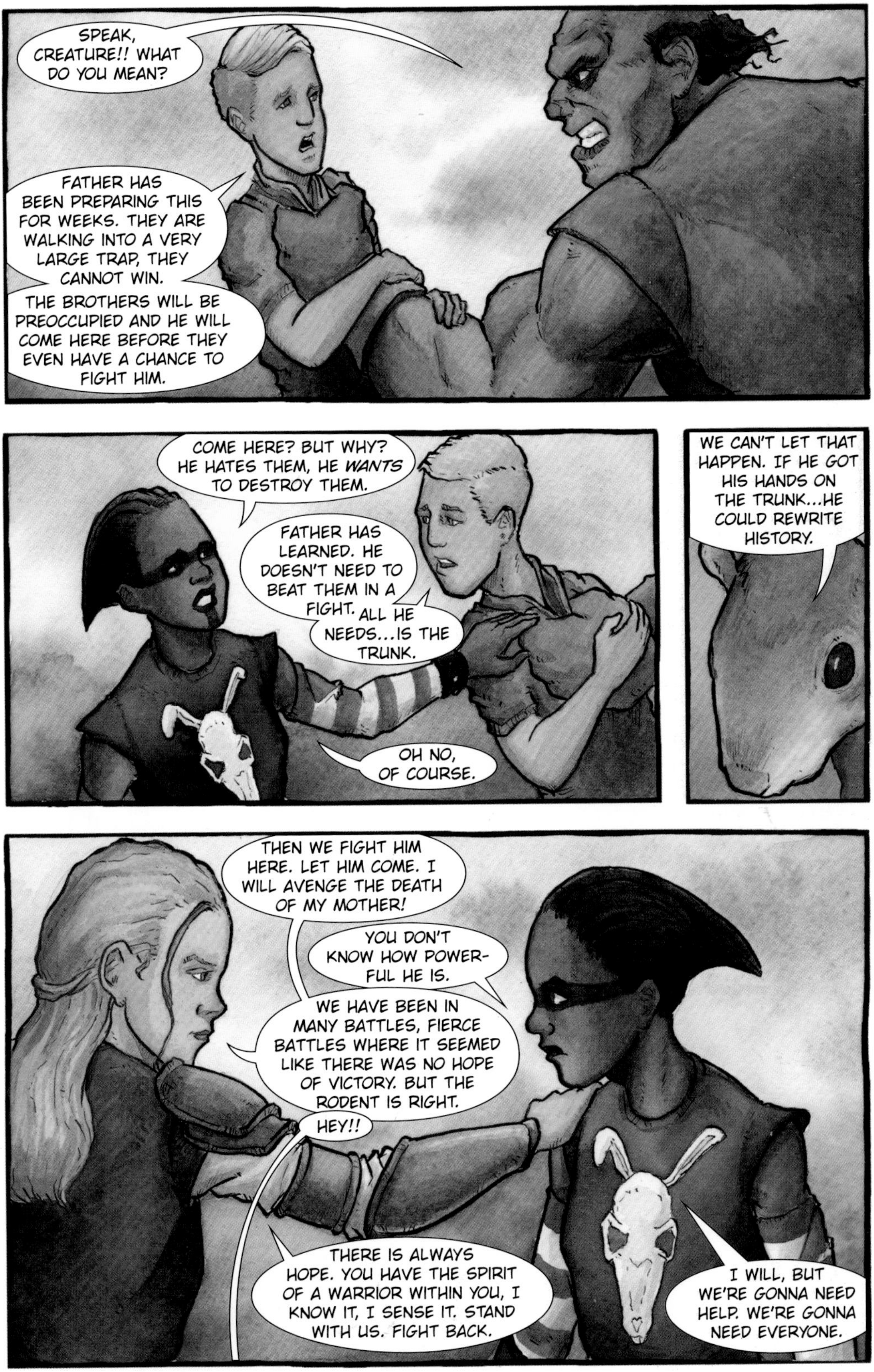
SPEAK, CREATURE!! WHAT DO YOU MEAN?
FATHER HAS BEEN PREPARING THIS FOR WEEKS. THEY ARE WALKING INTO A VERY LARGE TRAP, THEY CANNOT WIN.
THE BROTHERS WILL BE PREOCCUPIED AND HE WILL COME HERE BEFORE THEY EVEN HAVE A CHANCE TO FIGHT HIM.
COME HERE? BUT WHY? HE HATES THEM, HE *WANTS* TO DESTROY THEM.
FATHER HAS LEARNED. HE DOESN'T NEED TO BEAT THEM IN A FIGHT.
ALL HE NEEDS...IS THE TRUNK.
OH NO, OF COURSE.
WE CAN'T LET THAT HAPPEN. IF HE GOT HIS HANDS ON THE TRUNK...HE COULD REWRITE HISTORY.
THEN WE FIGHT HIM HERE. LET HIM COME. I WILL AVENGE THE DEATH OF MY MOTHER!
YOU DON'T KNOW HOW POWER-FUL HE IS.
WE HAVE BEEN IN MANY BATTLES, FIERCE BATTLES WHERE IT SEEMED LIKE THERE WAS NO HOPE OF VICTORY. BUT THE RODENT IS RIGHT.
HEY!!
THERE IS ALWAYS HOPE. YOU HAVE THE SPIRIT OF A WARRIOR WITHIN YOU, I KNOW IT, I SENSE IT. STAND WITH US. FIGHT BACK.
I WILL, BUT WE'RE GONNA NEED HELP. WE'RE GONNA NEED EVERYONE.

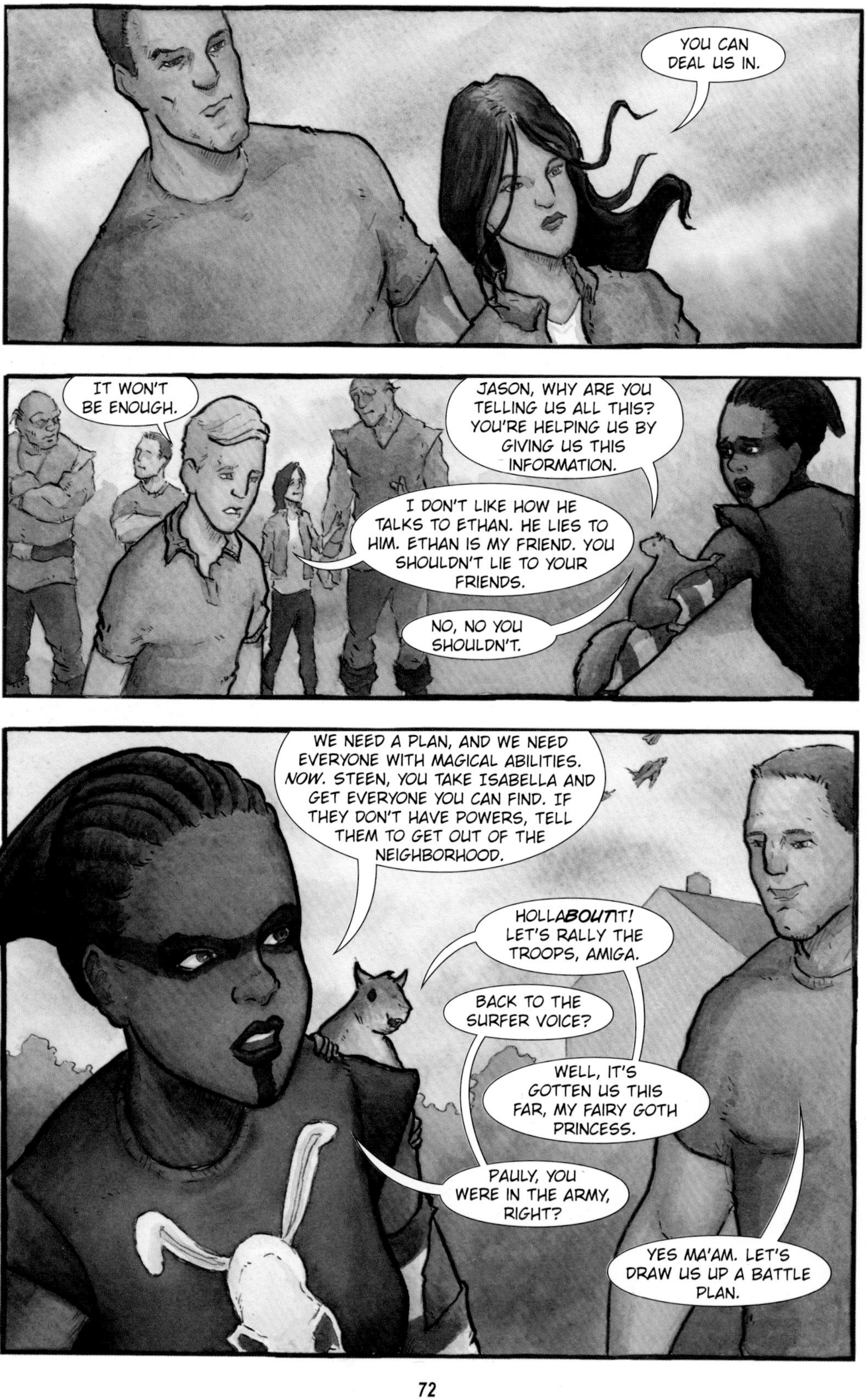
YOU CAN DEAL US IN.
IT WON'T BE ENOUGH.
JASON, WHY ARE YOU TELLING US ALL THIS? YOU'RE HELPING US BY GIVING US THIS INFORMATION.
I DON'T LIKE HOW HE TALKS TO ETHAN. HE LIES TO HIM. ETHAN IS MY FRIEND. YOU SHOULDN'T LIE TO YOUR FRIENDS.
NO, NO YOU SHOULDN'T.
WE NEED A PLAN, AND WE NEED EVERYONE WITH MAGICAL ABILITIES. *NOW*. STEEN, YOU TAKE ISABELLA AND GET EVERYONE YOU CAN FIND. IF THEY DON'T HAVE POWERS, TELL THEM TO GET OUT OF THE NEIGHBORHOOD.
HOLLA***BOUT***IT! LET'S RALLY THE TROOPS, AMIGA.
BACK TO THE SURFER VOICE?
WELL, IT'S GOTTEN US THIS FAR, MY FAIRY GOTH PRINCESS.
PAULY, YOU WERE IN THE ARMY, RIGHT?
YES MA'AM. LET'S DRAW US UP A BATTLE PLAN.

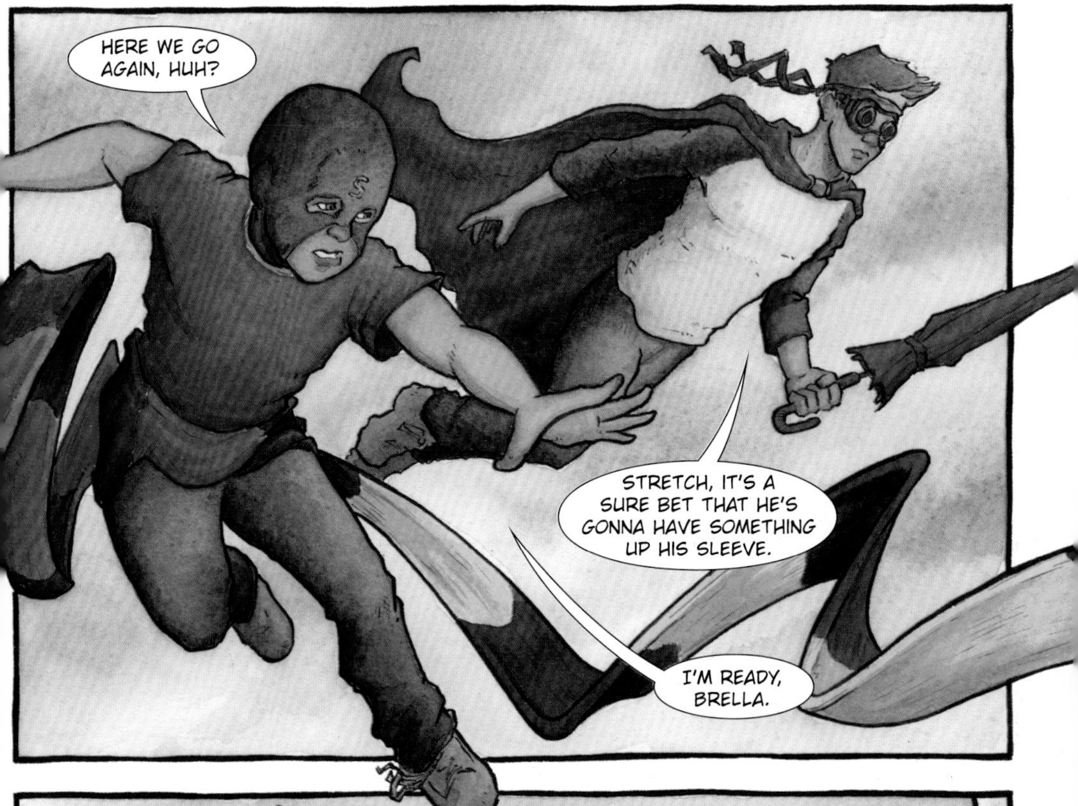
HERE WE GO AGAIN, HUH?
STRETCH, IT'S A SURE BET THAT HE'S GONNA HAVE SOMETHING UP HIS SLEEVE.
I'M READY, BRELLA.

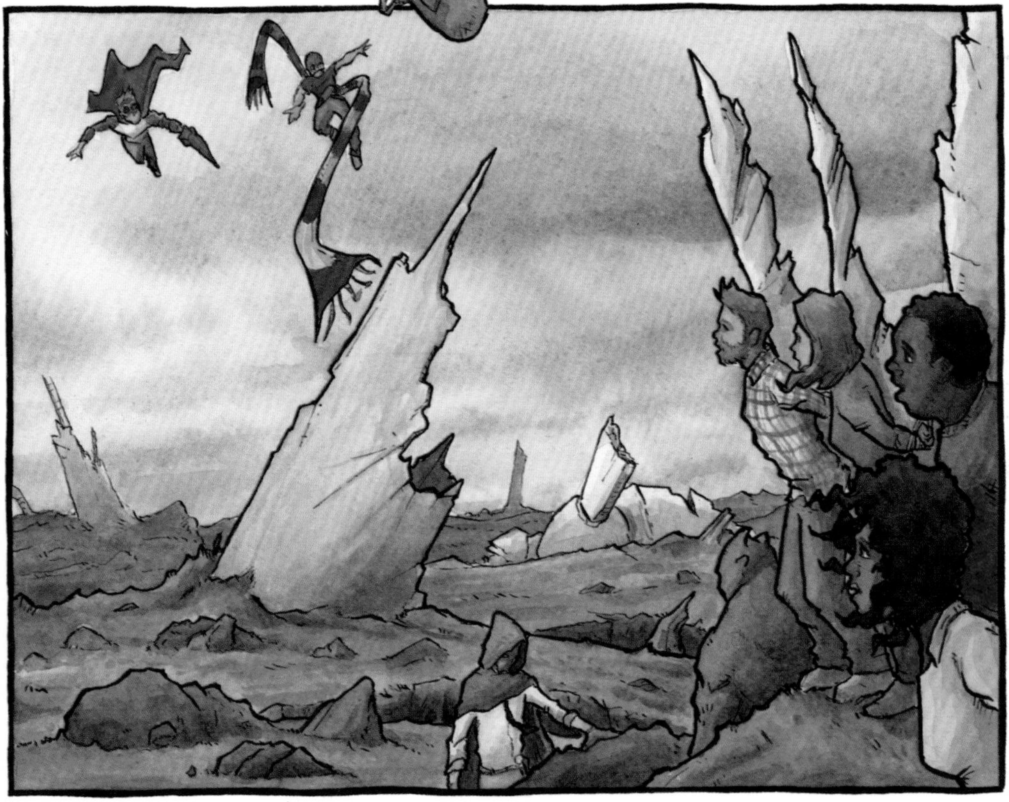

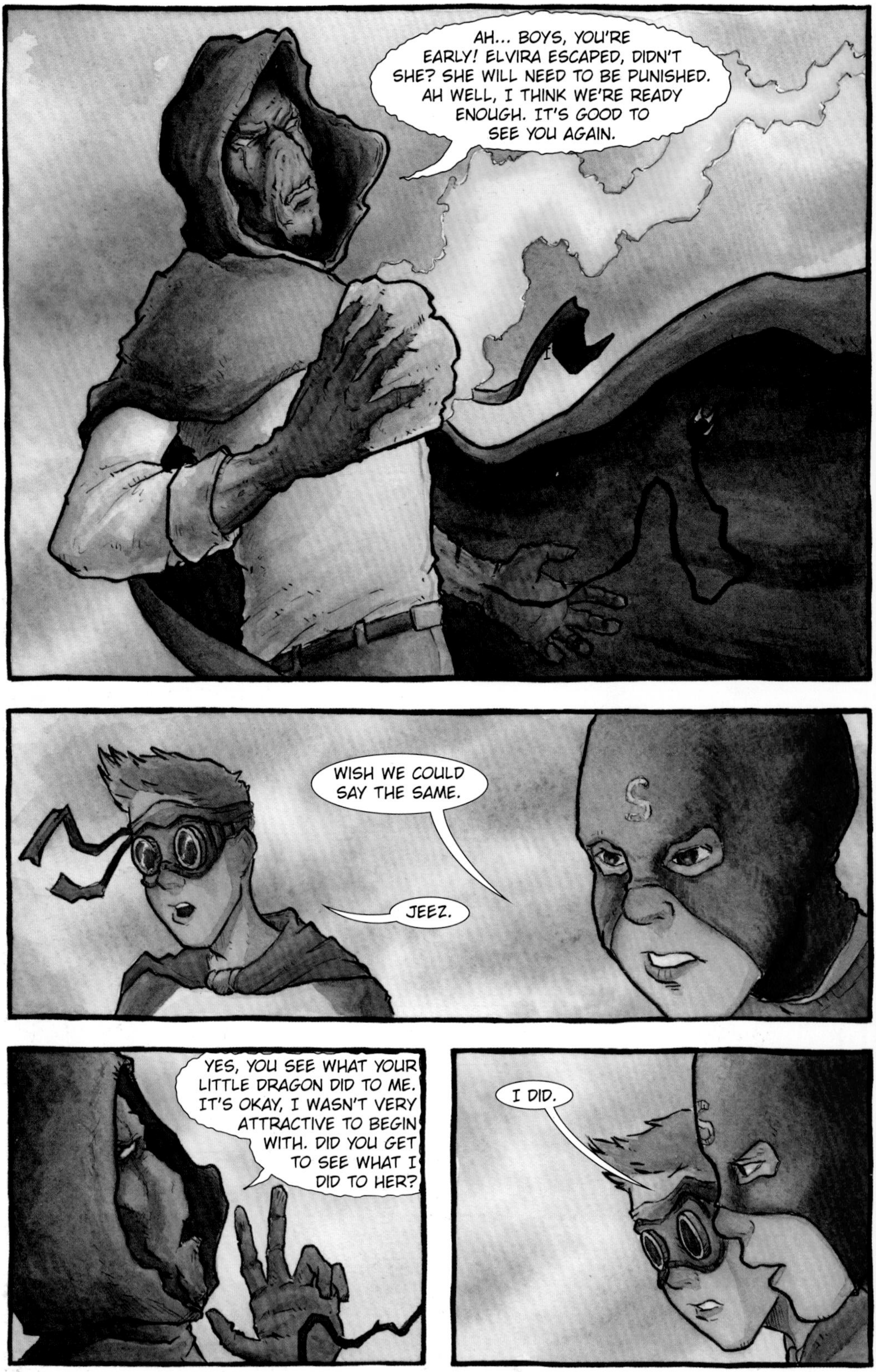
AH... BOYS, YOU'RE EARLY! ELVIRA ESCAPED, DIDN'T SHE? SHE WILL NEED TO BE PUNISHED. AH WELL, I THINK WE'RE READY ENOUGH. IT'S GOOD TO SEE YOU AGAIN.
WISH WE COULD SAY THE SAME.
JEEZ.
YES, YOU SEE WHAT YOUR LITTLE DRAGON DID TO ME. IT'S OKAY, I WASN'T VERY ATTRACTIVE TO BEGIN WITH. DID YOU GET TO SEE WHAT I DID TO HER?
I DID.

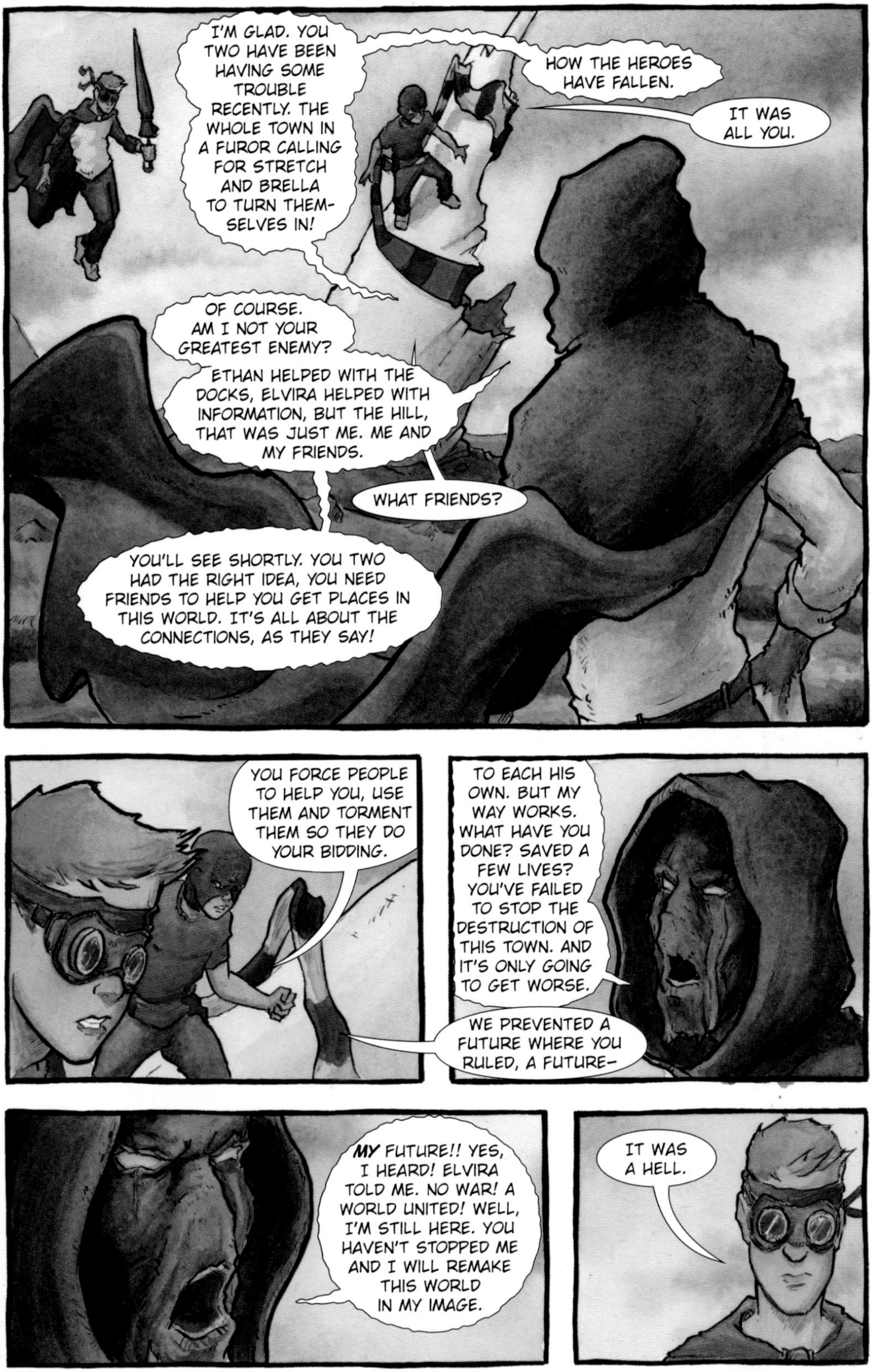
HOW THE HEROES HAVE FALLEN.
IT WAS ALL YOU.
I'M GLAD. YOU TWO HAVE BEEN HAVING SOME TROUBLE RECENTLY. THE WHOLE TOWN IN A FUROR CALLING FOR STRETCH AND BRELLA TO TURN THEM-SELVES IN!
OF COURSE. AM I NOT YOUR GREATEST ENEMY?
ETHAN HELPED WITH THE DOCKS, ELVIRA HELPED WITH INFORMATION, BUT THE HILL, THAT WAS JUST ME. ME AND MY FRIENDS.
WHAT FRIENDS?
YOU'LL SEE SHORTLY. YOU TWO HAD THE RIGHT IDEA, YOU NEED FRIENDS TO HELP YOU GET PLACES IN THIS WORLD. IT'S ALL ABOUT THE CONNECTIONS, AS THEY SAY!
YOU FORCE PEOPLE TO HELP YOU, USE THEM AND TORMENT THEM SO THEY DO YOUR BIDDING.
TO EACH HIS OWN. BUT MY WAY WORKS. WHAT HAVE YOU DONE? SAVED A FEW LIVES? YOU'VE FAILED TO STOP THE DESTRUCTION OF THIS TOWN. AND IT'S ONLY GOING TO GET WORSE.
WE PREVENTED A FUTURE WHERE YOU RULED, A FUTURE–
MY FUTURE!! YES, I HEARD! ELVIRA TOLD ME. NO WAR! A WORLD UNITED! WELL, I'M STILL HERE. YOU HAVEN'T STOPPED ME AND I WILL REMAKE THIS WORLD IN MY IMAGE.
IT WAS A HELL.

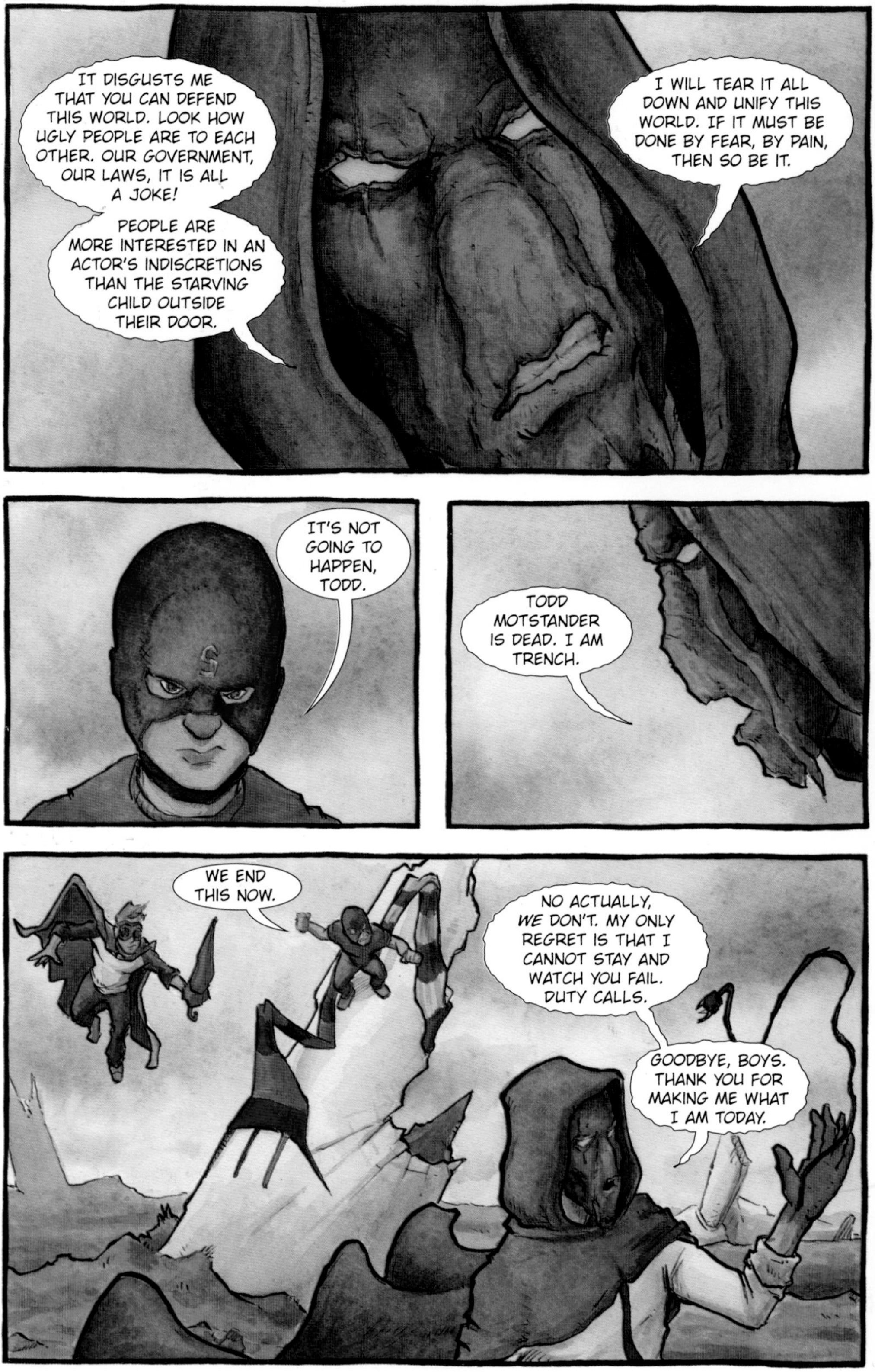
IT DISGUSTS ME THAT YOU CAN DEFEND THIS WORLD. LOOK HOW UGLY PEOPLE ARE TO EACH OTHER. OUR GOVERNMENT, OUR LAWS, IT IS ALL A JOKE!
PEOPLE ARE MORE INTERESTED IN AN ACTOR'S INDISCRETIONS THAN THE STARVING CHILD OUTSIDE THEIR DOOR.
I WILL TEAR IT ALL DOWN AND UNIFY THIS WORLD. IF IT MUST BE DONE BY FEAR, BY PAIN, THEN SO BE IT.
IT'S NOT GOING TO HAPPEN, TODD.
TODD MOTSTANDER IS DEAD. I AM TRENCH.
WE END THIS NOW.
NO ACTUALLY, *WE* DON'T. MY ONLY REGRET IS THAT I CANNOT STAY AND WATCH YOU FAIL. DUTY CALLS.
GOODBYE, BOYS. THANK YOU FOR MAKING ME WHAT I AM TODAY.

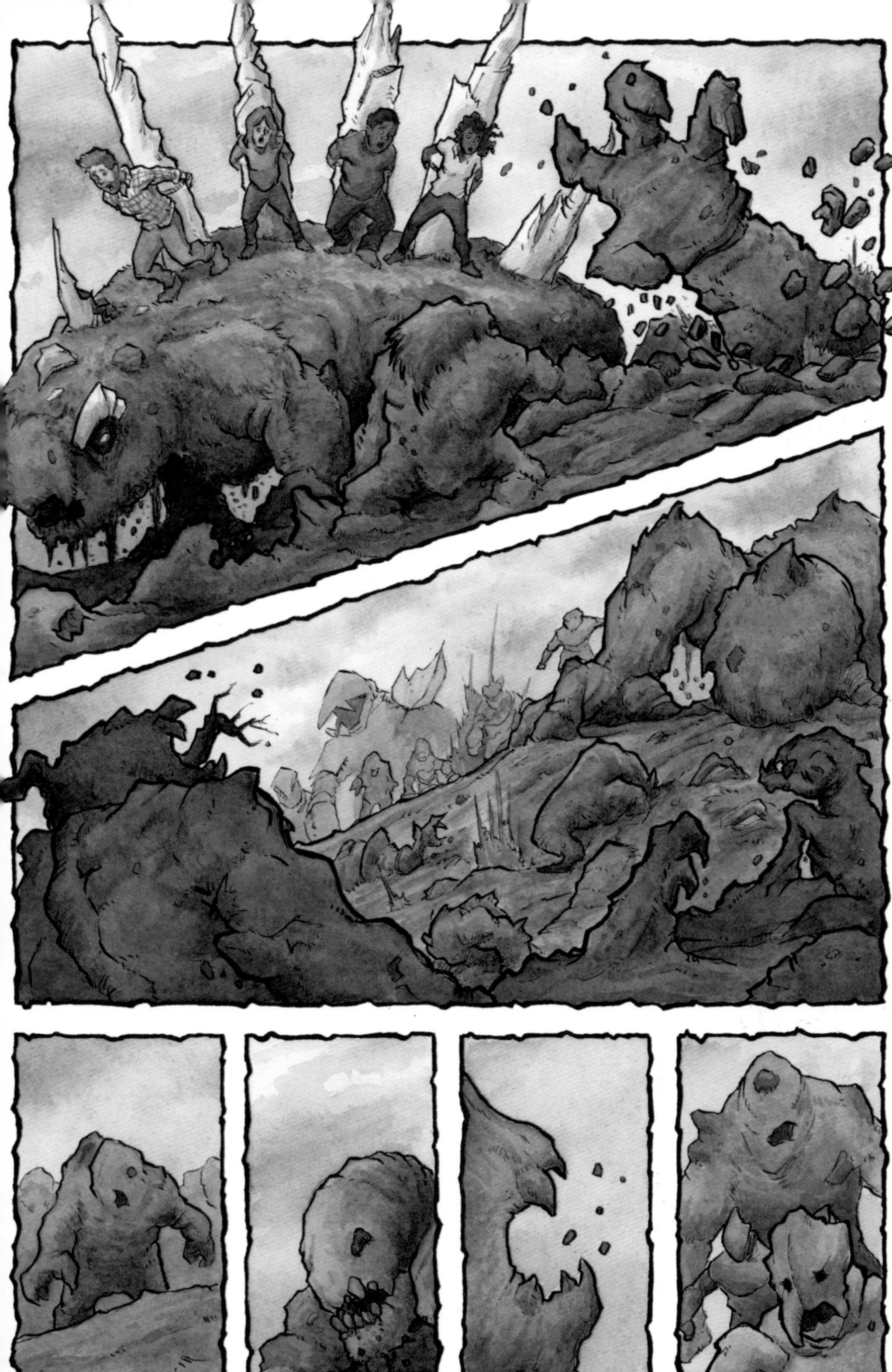

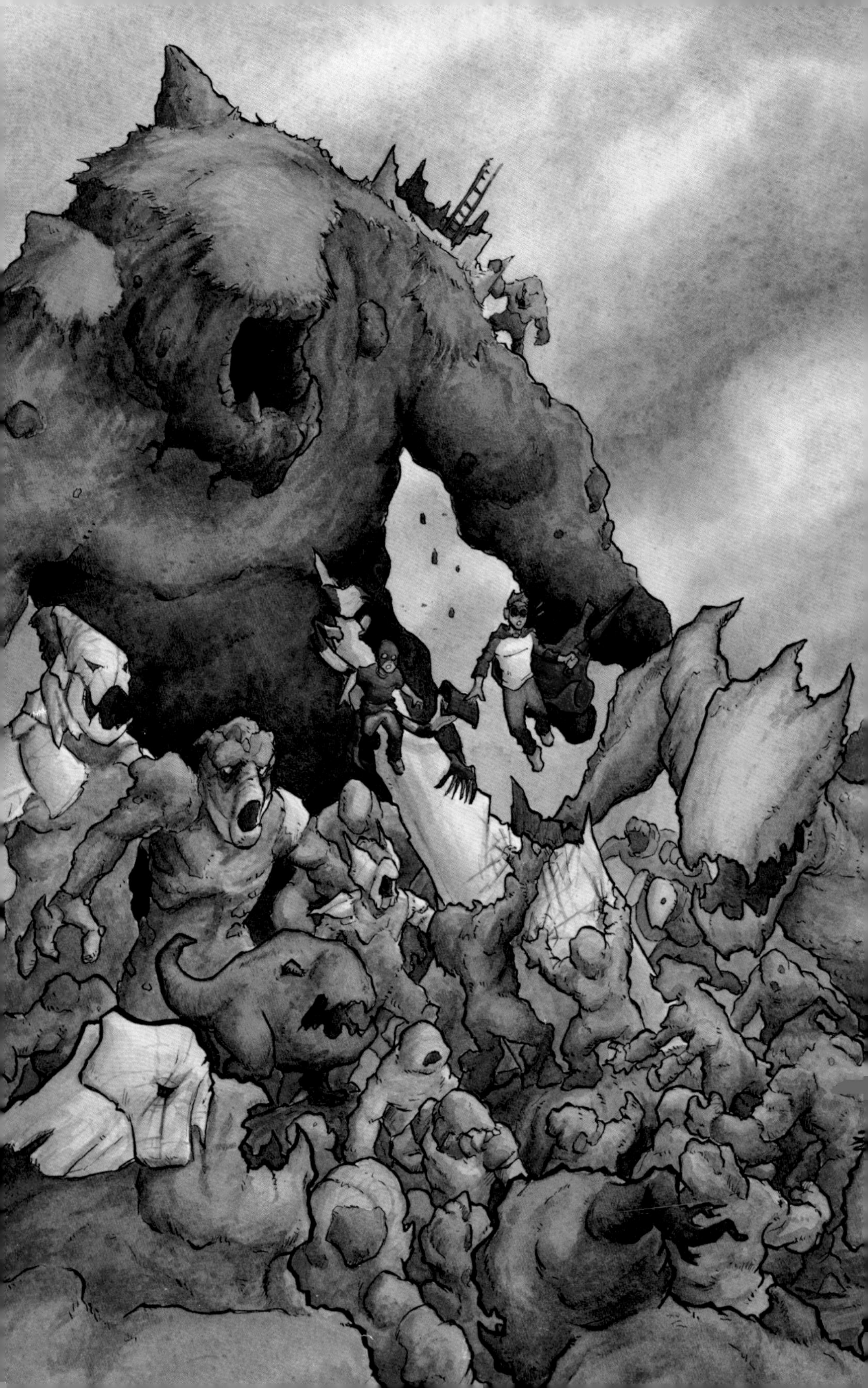

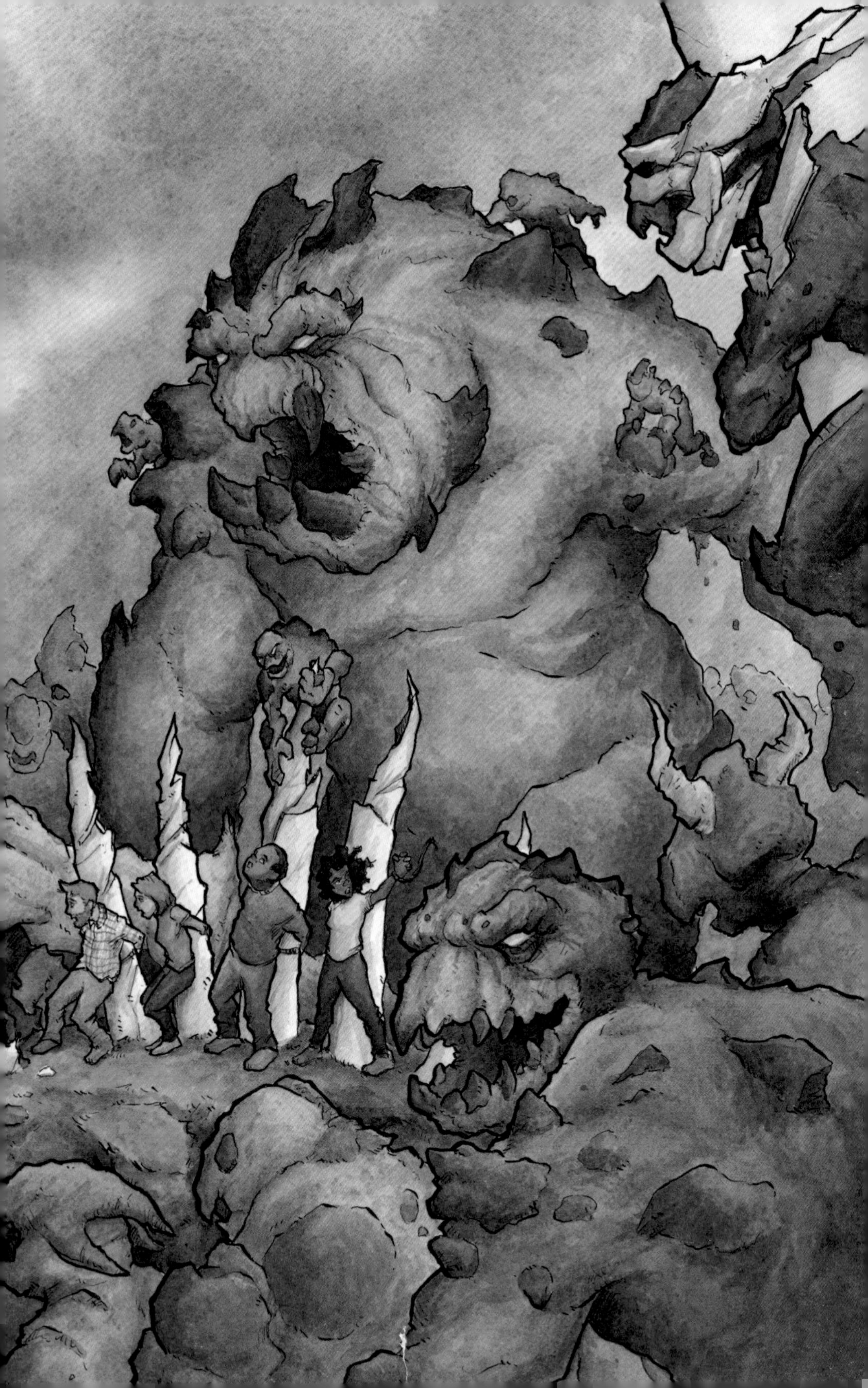

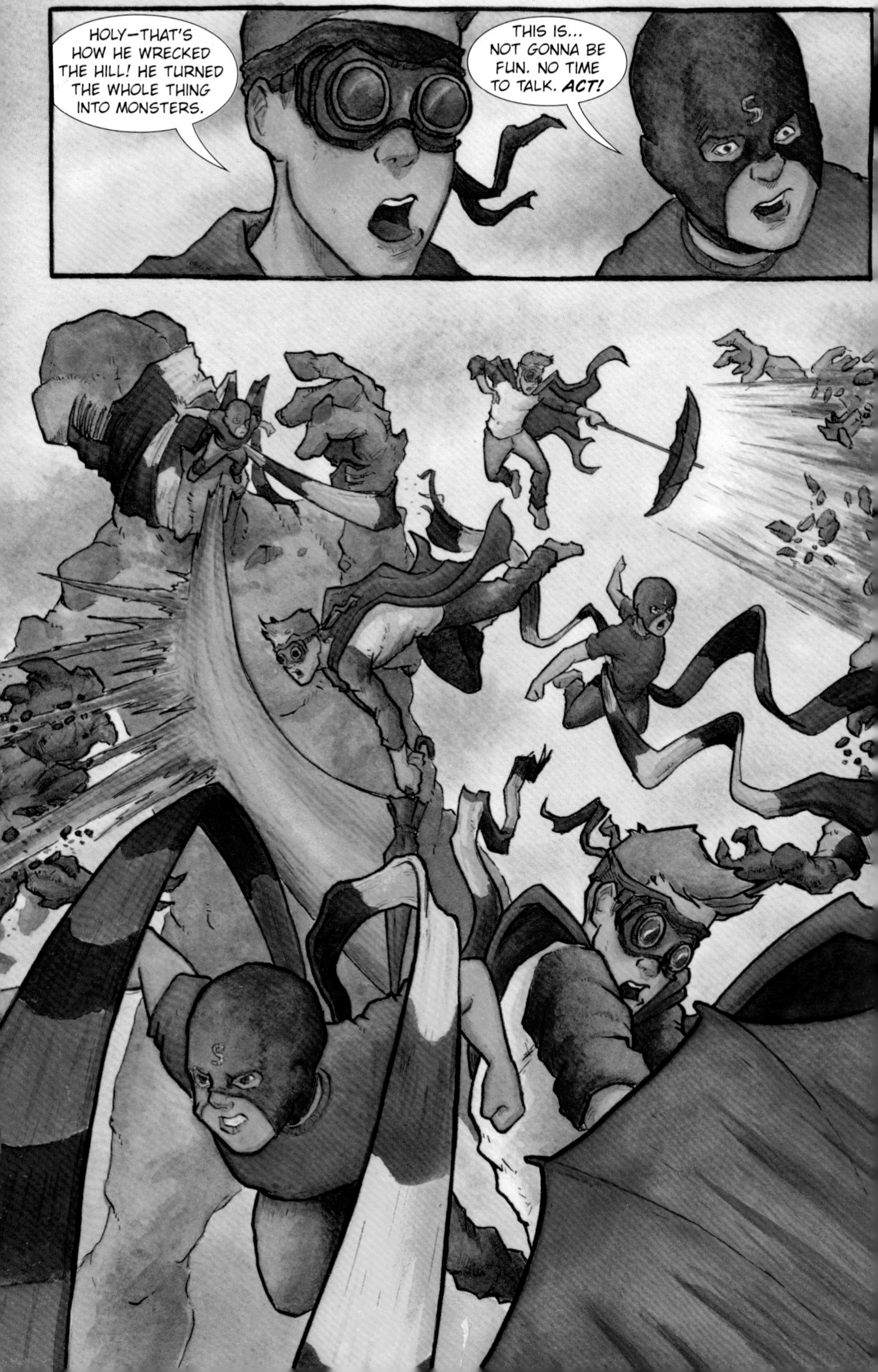
HOLY—THAT'S HOW HE WRECKED THE HILL! HE TURNED THE WHOLE THING INTO MONSTERS.
THIS IS... NOT GONNA BE FUN. NO TIME TO TALK. ACT!

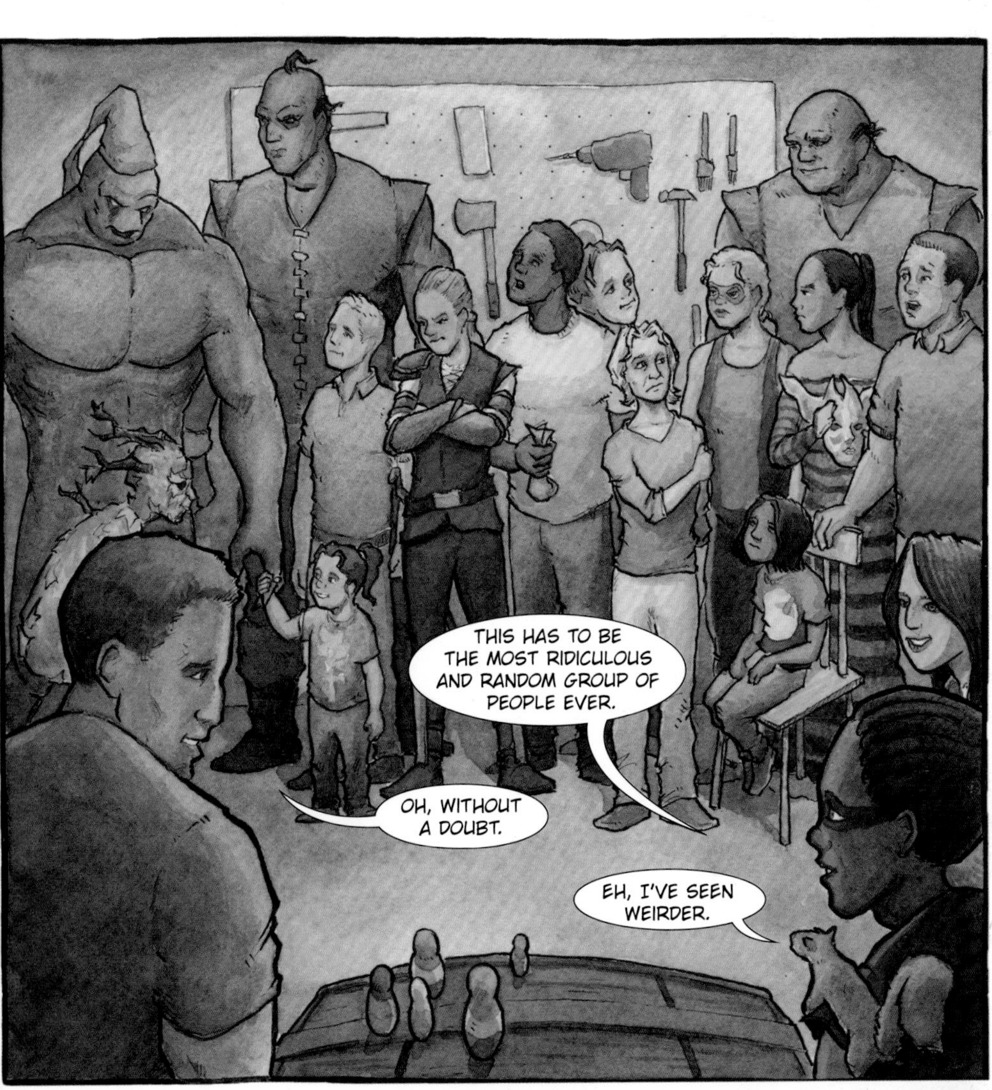
THIS HAS TO BE THE MOST RIDICULOUS AND RANDOM GROUP OF PEOPLE EVER.
OH, WITHOUT A DOUBT.
EH, I'VE SEEN WEIRDER.

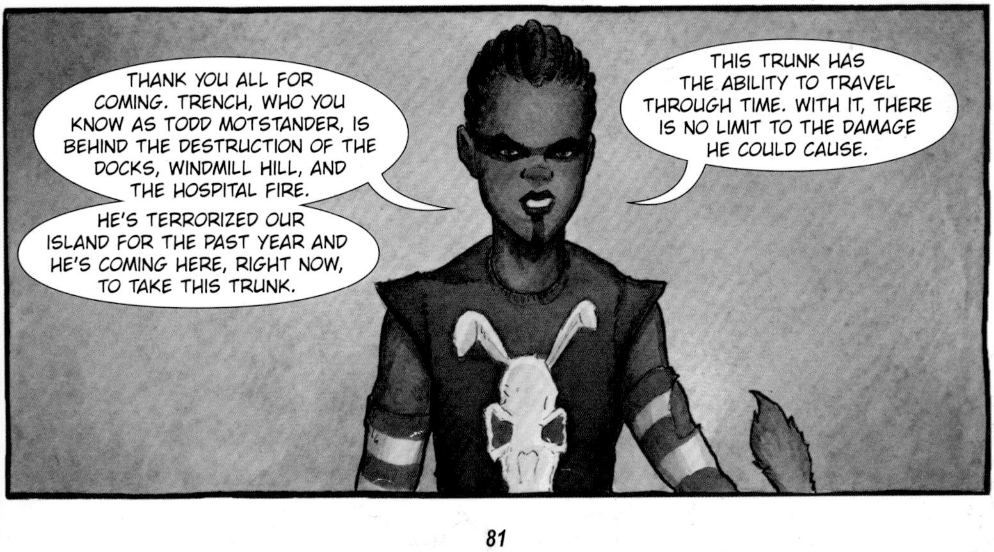
THANK YOU ALL FOR COMING. TRENCH, WHO YOU KNOW AS TODD MOTSTANDER, IS BEHIND THE DESTRUCTION OF THE DOCKS, WINDMILL HILL, AND THE HOSPITAL FIRE.
HE'S TERRORIZED OUR ISLAND FOR THE PAST YEAR AND HE'S COMING HERE, RIGHT NOW, TO TAKE THIS TRUNK.
THIS TRUNK HAS THE ABILITY TO TRAVEL THROUGH TIME. WITH IT, THERE IS NO LIMIT TO THE DAMAGE HE COULD CAUSE.

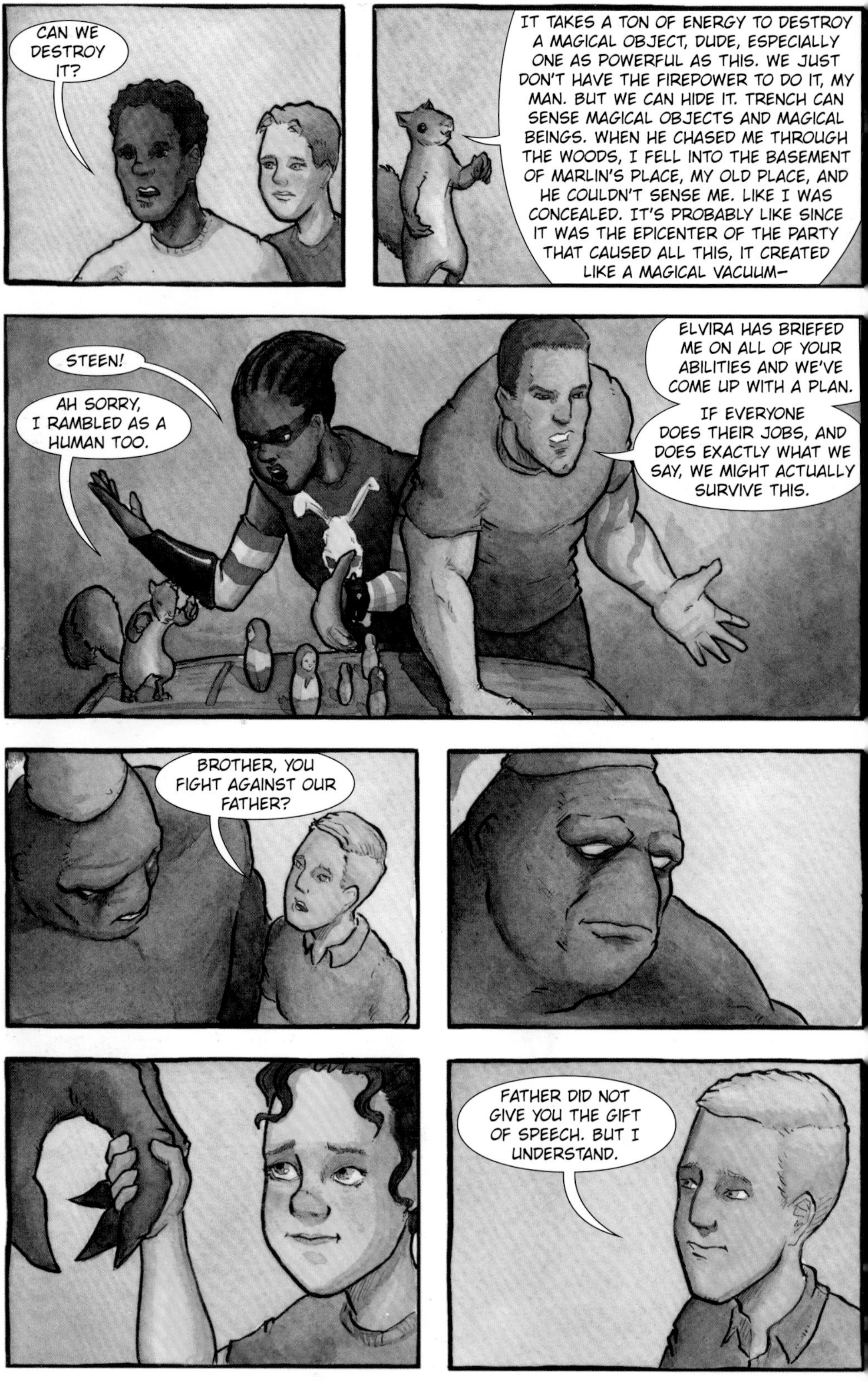
CAN WE DESTROY IT?
IT TAKES A TON OF ENERGY TO DESTROY A MAGICAL OBJECT, DUDE, ESPECIALLY ONE AS POWERFUL AS THIS. WE JUST DON'T HAVE THE FIREPOWER TO DO IT, MY MAN. BUT WE CAN HIDE IT. TRENCH CAN SENSE MAGICAL OBJECTS AND MAGICAL BEINGS. WHEN HE CHASED ME THROUGH THE WOODS, I FELL INTO THE BASEMENT OF MARLIN'S PLACE, MY OLD PLACE, AND HE COULDN'T SENSE ME. LIKE I WAS CONCEALED. IT'S PROBABLY LIKE SINCE IT WAS THE EPICENTER OF THE PARTY THAT CAUSED ALL THIS, IT CREATED LIKE A MAGICAL VACUUM–
STEEN!
AH SORRY, I RAMBLED AS A HUMAN TOO.
ELVIRA HAS BRIEFED ME ON ALL OF YOUR ABILITIES AND WE'VE COME UP WITH A PLAN.
IF EVERYONE DOES THEIR JOBS, AND DOES EXACTLY WHAT WE SAY, WE MIGHT ACTUALLY SURVIVE THIS.
BROTHER, YOU FIGHT AGAINST OUR FATHER?
FATHER DID NOT GIVE YOU THE GIFT OF SPEECH. BUT I UNDERSTAND.

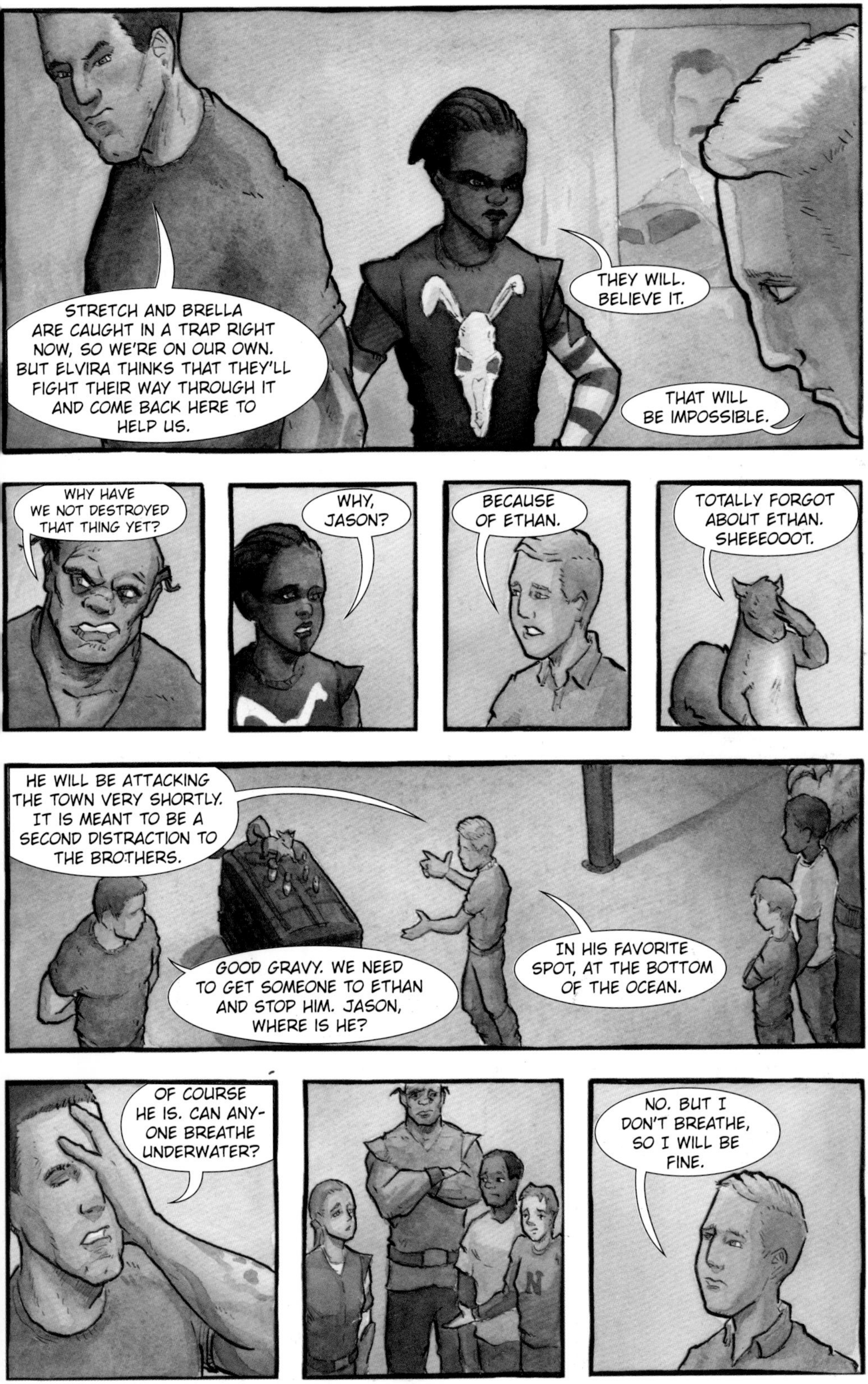
STRETCH AND BRELLA ARE CAUGHT IN A TRAP RIGHT NOW, SO WE'RE ON OUR OWN. BUT ELVIRA THINKS THAT THEY'LL FIGHT THEIR WAY THROUGH IT AND COME BACK HERE TO HELP US.
THEY WILL. BELIEVE IT.
THAT WILL BE IMPOSSIBLE.
WHY HAVE WE NOT DESTROYED THAT THING YET?
WHY, JASON?
BECAUSE OF ETHAN.
TOTALLY FORGOT ABOUT ETHAN. SHEEEOOOT.
HE WILL BE ATTACKING THE TOWN VERY SHORTLY. IT IS MEANT TO BE A SECOND DISTRACTION TO THE BROTHERS.
GOOD GRAVY. WE NEED TO GET SOMEONE TO ETHAN AND STOP HIM. JASON, WHERE IS HE?
IN HIS FAVORITE SPOT, AT THE BOTTOM OF THE OCEAN.
OF COURSE HE IS. CAN ANY-ONE BREATHE UNDERWATER?
NO. BUT I DON'T BREATHE, SO I WILL BE FINE.

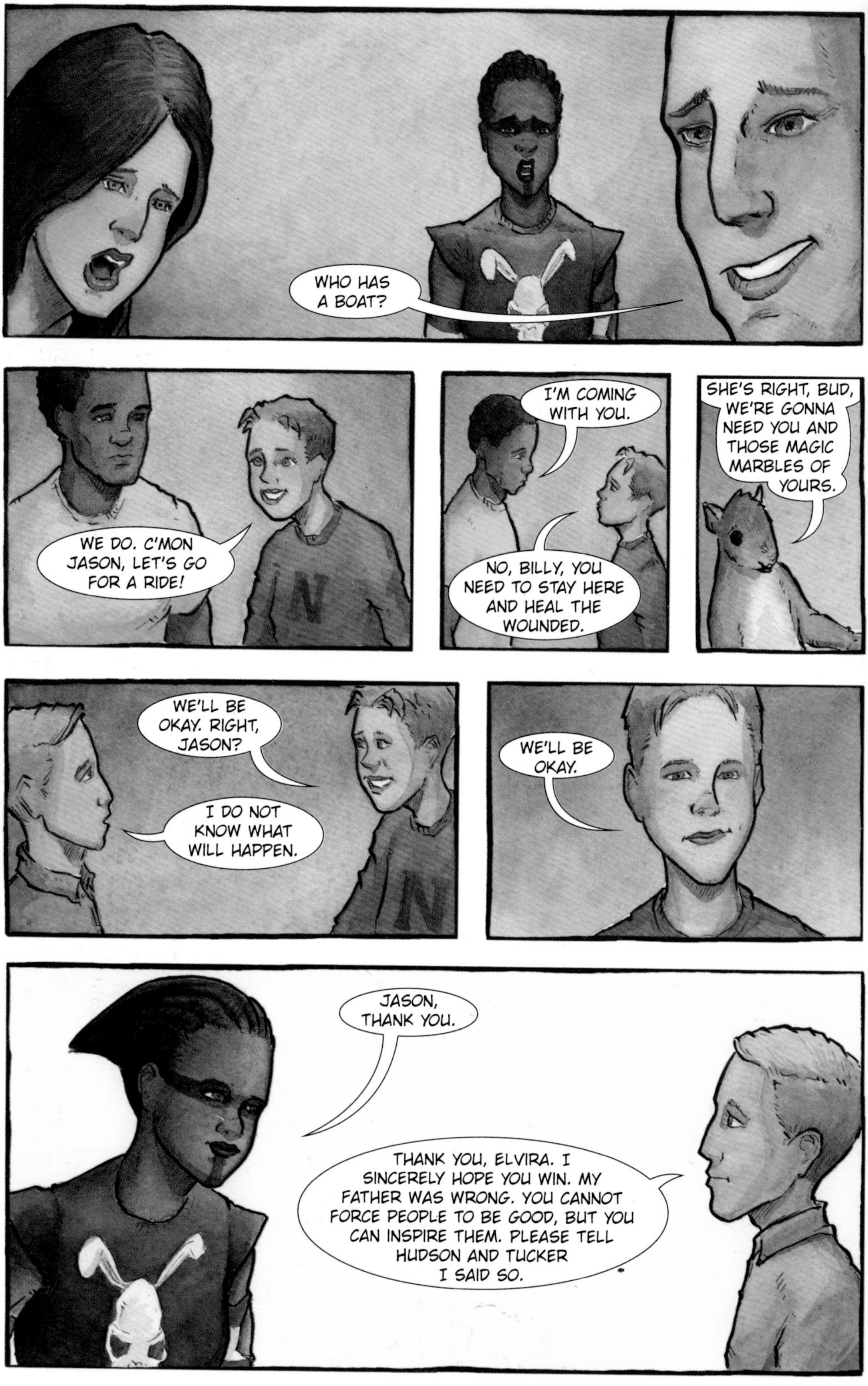
WHO HAS A BOAT?
WE DO. C'MON JASON, LET'S GO FOR A RIDE!
I'M COMING WITH YOU.
NO, BILLY, YOU NEED TO STAY HERE AND HEAL THE WOUNDED.
SHE'S RIGHT, BUD, WE'RE GONNA NEED YOU AND THOSE MAGIC MARBLES OF YOURS.
WE'LL BE OKAY. RIGHT, JASON?
I DO NOT KNOW WHAT WILL HAPPEN.
WE'LL BE OKAY.
JASON, THANK YOU.
THANK YOU, ELVIRA. I SINCERELY HOPE YOU WIN. MY FATHER WAS WRONG. YOU CANNOT FORCE PEOPLE TO BE GOOD, BUT YOU CAN INSPIRE THEM. PLEASE TELL HUDSON AND TUCKER I SAID SO.

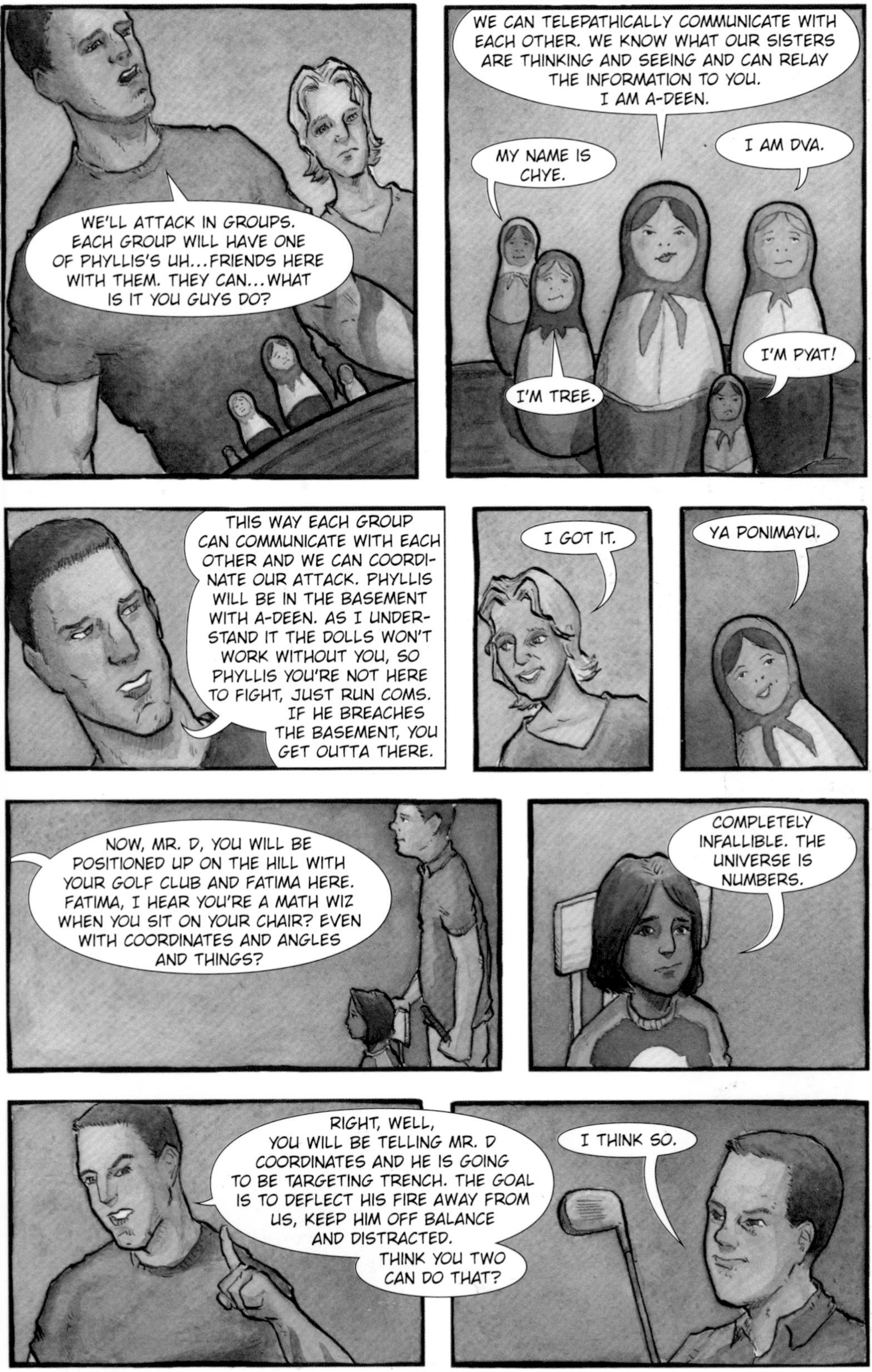
WE'LL ATTACK IN GROUPS. EACH GROUP WILL HAVE ONE OF PHYLLIS'S UH...FRIENDS HERE WITH THEM. THEY CAN...WHAT IS IT YOU GUYS DO?
WE CAN TELEPATHICALLY COMMUNICATE WITH EACH OTHER. WE KNOW WHAT OUR SISTERS ARE THINKING AND SEEING AND CAN RELAY THE INFORMATION TO YOU. I AM A-DEEN.
MY NAME IS CHYE.
I AM DVA.
I'M TREE.
I'M PYAT!
THIS WAY EACH GROUP CAN COMMUNICATE WITH EACH OTHER AND WE CAN COORDINATE OUR ATTACK. PHYLLIS WILL BE IN THE BASEMENT WITH A-DEEN. AS I UNDERSTAND IT THE DOLLS WON'T WORK WITHOUT YOU, SO PHYLLIS YOU'RE NOT HERE TO FIGHT, JUST RUN COMS. IF HE BREACHES THE BASEMENT, YOU GET OUTTA THERE.
I GOT IT.
YA PONIMAYU.
NOW, MR. D, YOU WILL BE POSITIONED UP ON THE HILL WITH YOUR GOLF CLUB AND FATIMA HERE. FATIMA, I HEAR YOU'RE A MATH WIZ WHEN YOU SIT ON YOUR CHAIR? EVEN WITH COORDINATES AND ANGLES AND THINGS?
COMPLETELY INFALLIBLE. THE UNIVERSE IS NUMBERS.
RIGHT, WELL, YOU WILL BE TELLING MR. D COORDINATES AND HE IS GOING TO BE TARGETING TRENCH. THE GOAL IS TO DEFLECT HIS FIRE AWAY FROM US, KEEP HIM OFF BALANCE AND DISTRACTED. THINK YOU TWO CAN DO THAT?
I THINK SO.

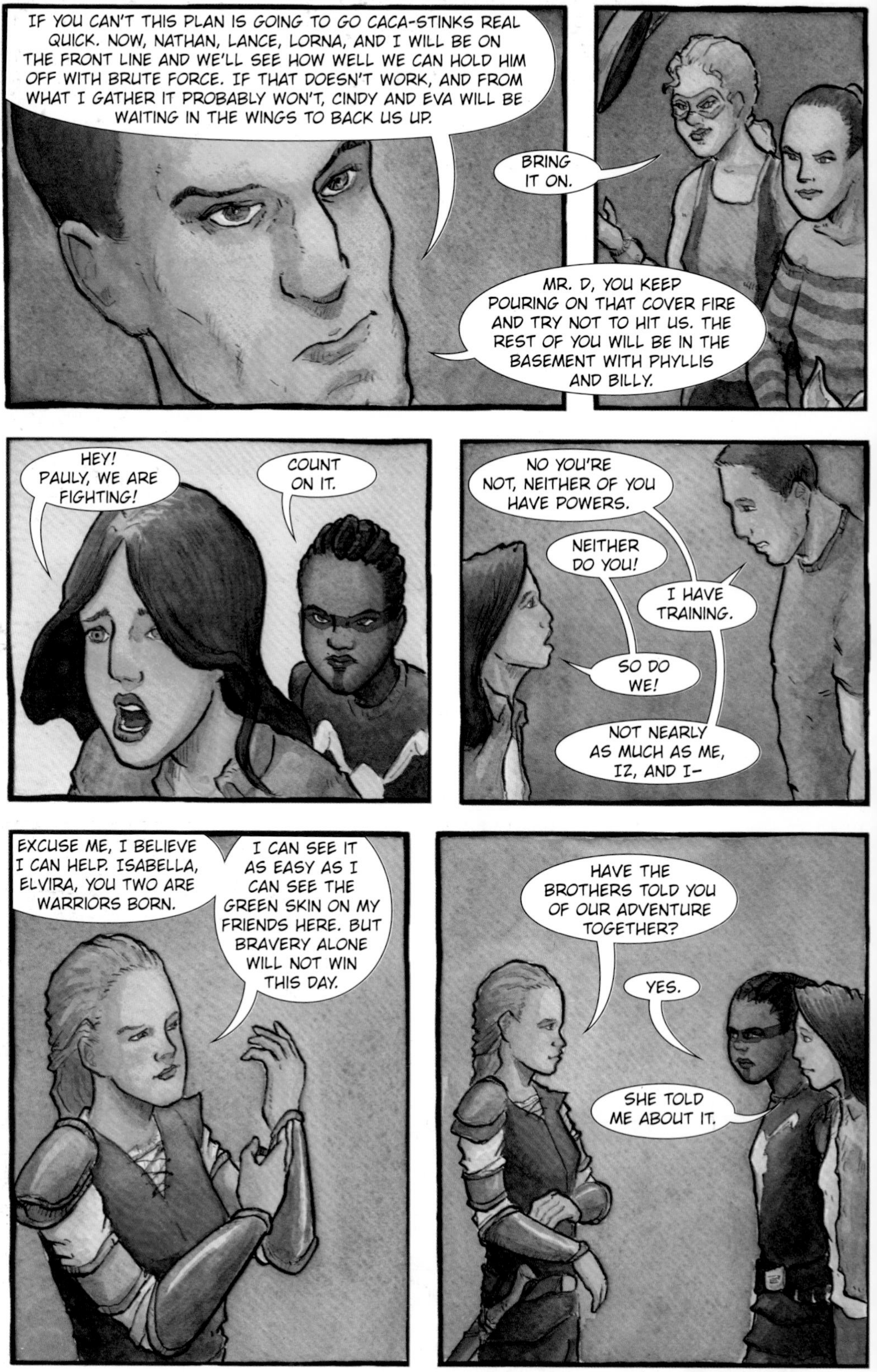
IF YOU CAN'T THIS PLAN IS GOING TO GO CACA-STINKS REAL QUICK. NOW, NATHAN, LANCE, LORNA, AND I WILL BE ON THE FRONT LINE AND WE'LL SEE HOW WELL WE CAN HOLD HIM OFF WITH BRUTE FORCE. IF THAT DOESN'T WORK, AND FROM WHAT I GATHER IT PROBABLY WON'T, CINDY AND EVA WILL BE WAITING IN THE WINGS TO BACK US UP.
BRING IT ON.
MR. D, YOU KEEP POURING ON THAT COVER FIRE AND TRY NOT TO HIT US. THE REST OF YOU WILL BE IN THE BASEMENT WITH PHYLLIS AND BILLY.
HEY! PAULY, WE ARE FIGHTING!
COUNT ON IT.
NO YOU'RE NOT, NEITHER OF YOU HAVE POWERS.
NEITHER DO YOU!
I HAVE TRAINING.
SO DO WE!
NOT NEARLY AS MUCH AS ME, IZ, AND I–
EXCUSE ME, I BELIEVE I CAN HELP. ISABELLA, ELVIRA, YOU TWO ARE WARRIORS BORN.
I CAN SEE IT AS EASY AS I CAN SEE THE GREEN SKIN ON MY FRIENDS HERE. BUT BRAVERY ALONE WILL NOT WIN THIS DAY.
HAVE THE BROTHERS TOLD YOU OF OUR ADVENTURE TOGETHER?
YES.
SHE TOLD ME ABOUT IT.

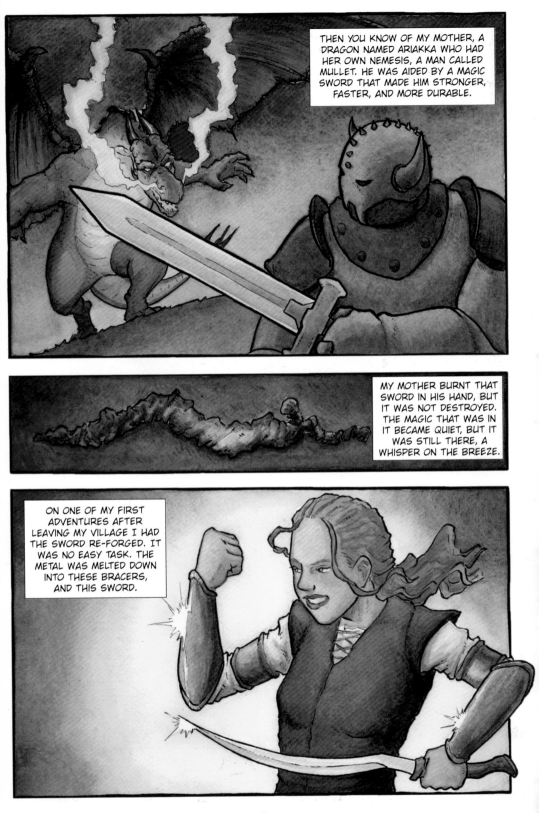

THEN YOU KNOW OF MY MOTHER, A DRAGON NAMED ARIAKKA WHO HAD HER OWN NEMESIS, A MAN CALLED MULLET. HE WAS AIDED BY A MAGIC SWORD THAT MADE HIM STRONGER, FASTER, AND MORE DURABLE.

MY MOTHER BURNT THAT SWORD IN HIS HAND, BUT IT WAS NOT DESTROYED. THE MAGIC THAT WAS IN IT BECAME QUIET, BUT IT WAS STILL THERE, A WHISPER ON THE BREEZE.

ON ONE OF MY FIRST ADVENTURES AFTER LEAVING MY VILLAGE I HAD THE SWORD RE-FORGED. IT WAS NO EASY TASK. THE METAL WAS MELTED DOWN INTO THESE BRACERS, AND THIS SWORD.

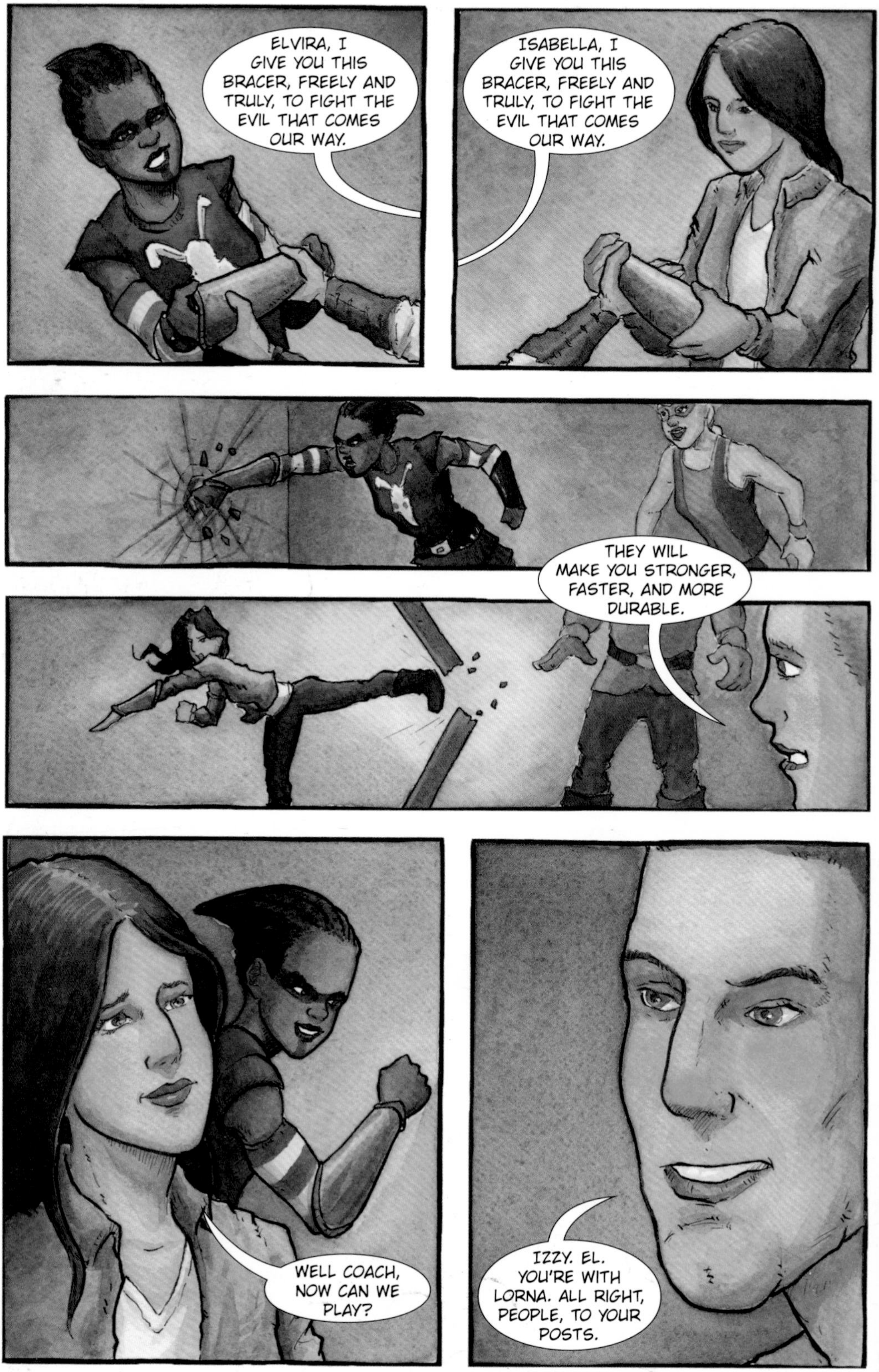
ELVIRA, I GIVE YOU THIS BRACER, FREELY AND TRULY, TO FIGHT THE EVIL THAT COMES OUR WAY.
ISABELLA, I GIVE YOU THIS BRACER, FREELY AND TRULY, TO FIGHT THE EVIL THAT COMES OUR WAY.
THEY WILL MAKE YOU STRONGER, FASTER, AND MORE DURABLE.
WELL COACH, NOW CAN WE PLAY?
IZZY. EL. YOU'RE WITH LORNA. ALL RIGHT, PEOPLE, TO YOUR POSTS.

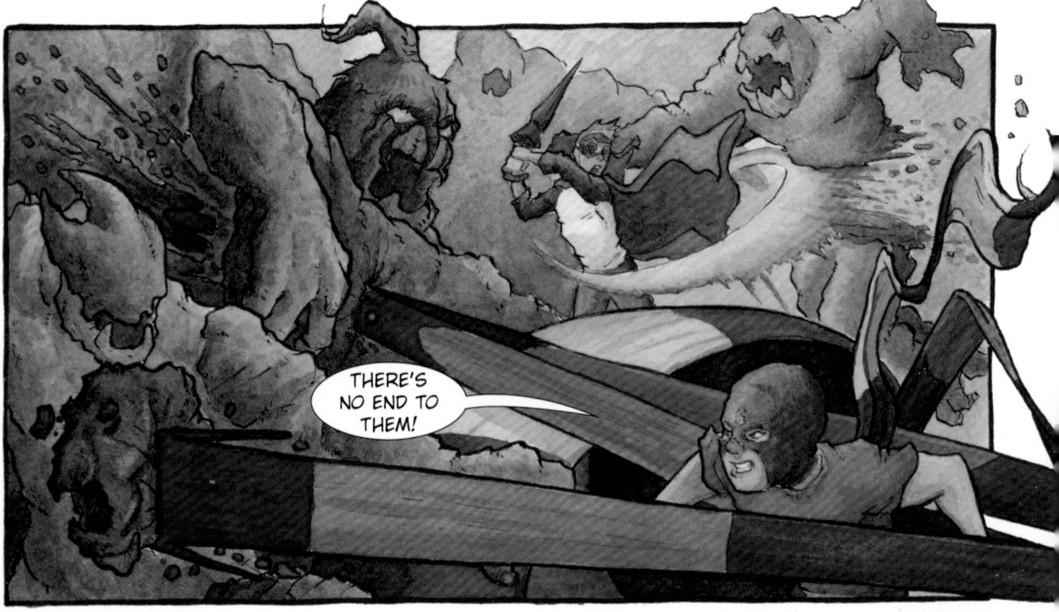
THERE'S NO END TO THEM!

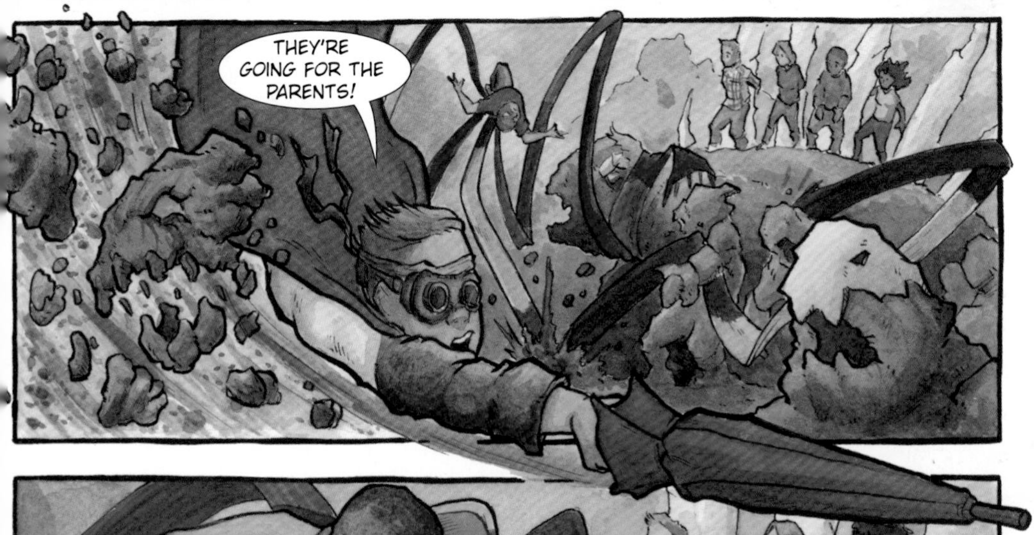
THEY'RE GOING FOR THE PARENTS!

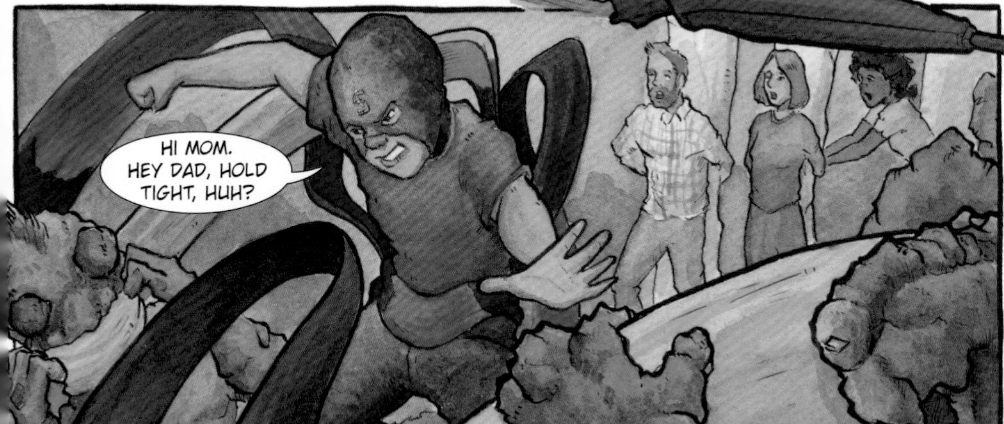
HI MOM.
HEY DAD, HOLD TIGHT, HUH?

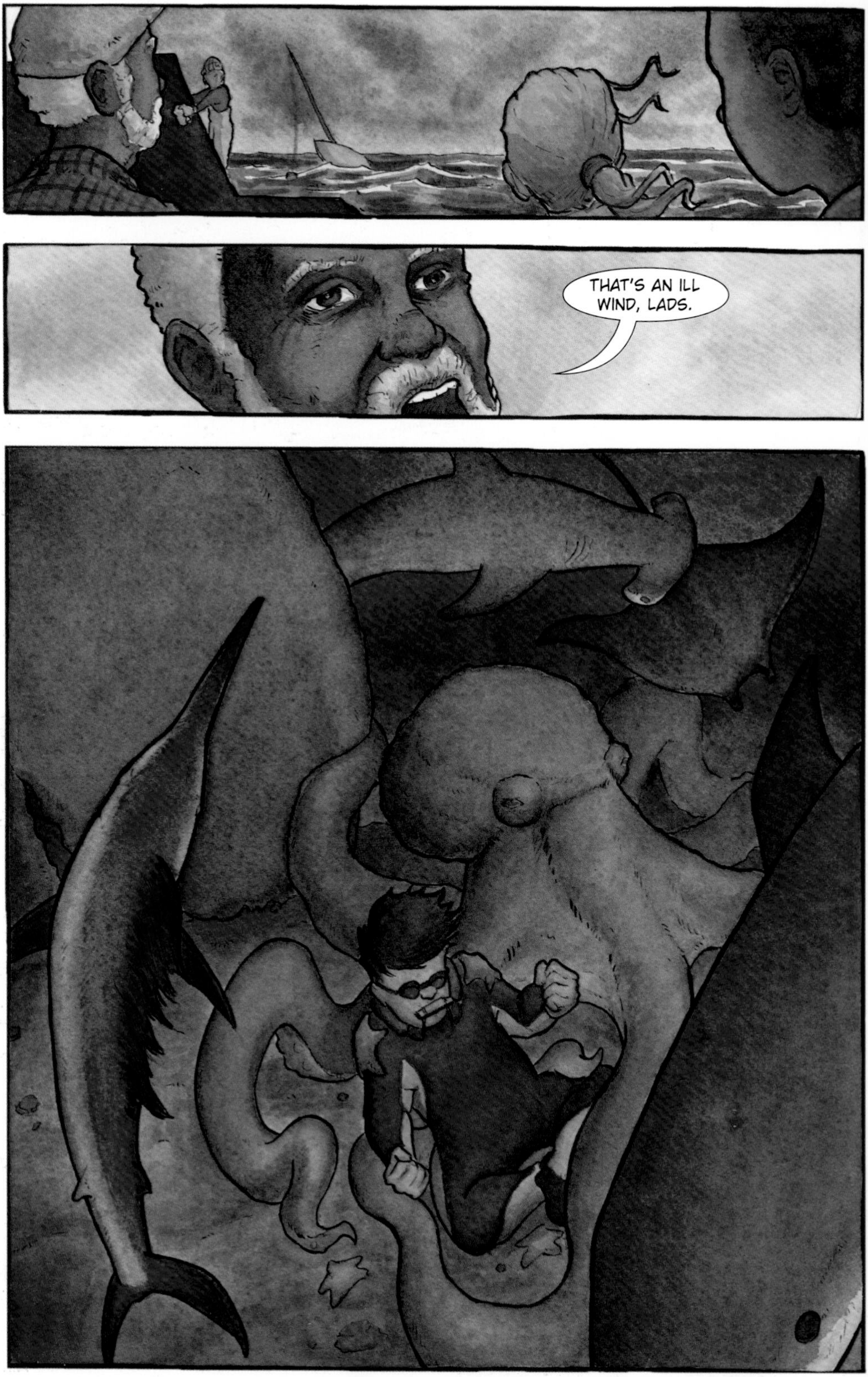
THAT'S AN ILL WIND, LADS.

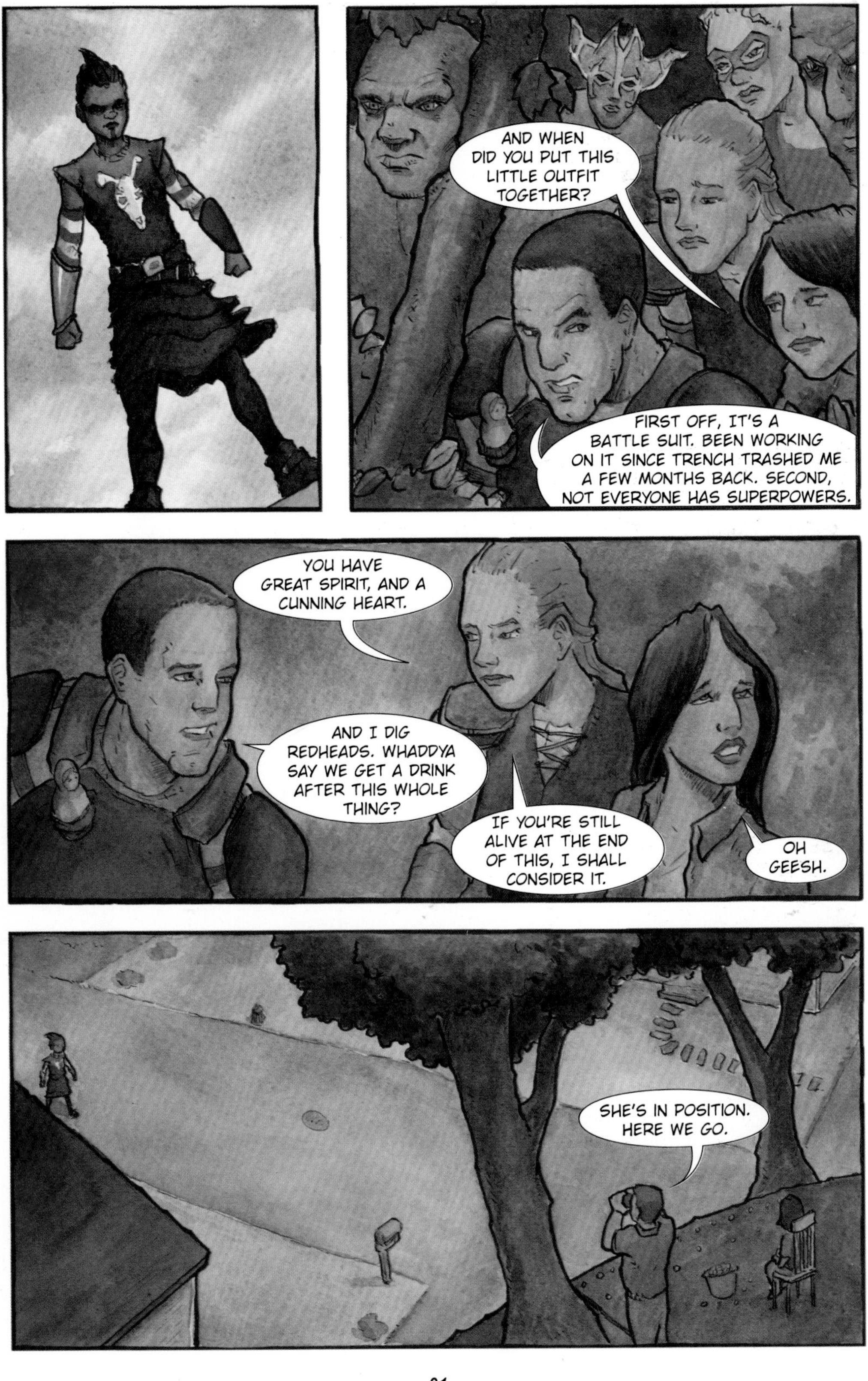
AND WHEN DID YOU PUT THIS LITTLE OUTFIT TOGETHER?
FIRST OFF, IT'S A BATTLE SUIT. BEEN WORKING ON IT SINCE TRENCH TRASHED ME A FEW MONTHS BACK. SECOND, NOT EVERYONE HAS SUPERPOWERS.
YOU HAVE GREAT SPIRIT, AND A CUNNING HEART.
AND I DIG REDHEADS. WHADDYA SAY WE GET A DRINK AFTER THIS WHOLE THING?
IF YOU'RE STILL ALIVE AT THE END OF THIS, I SHALL CONSIDER IT.
OH GEESH.
SHE'S IN POSITION. HERE WE GO.

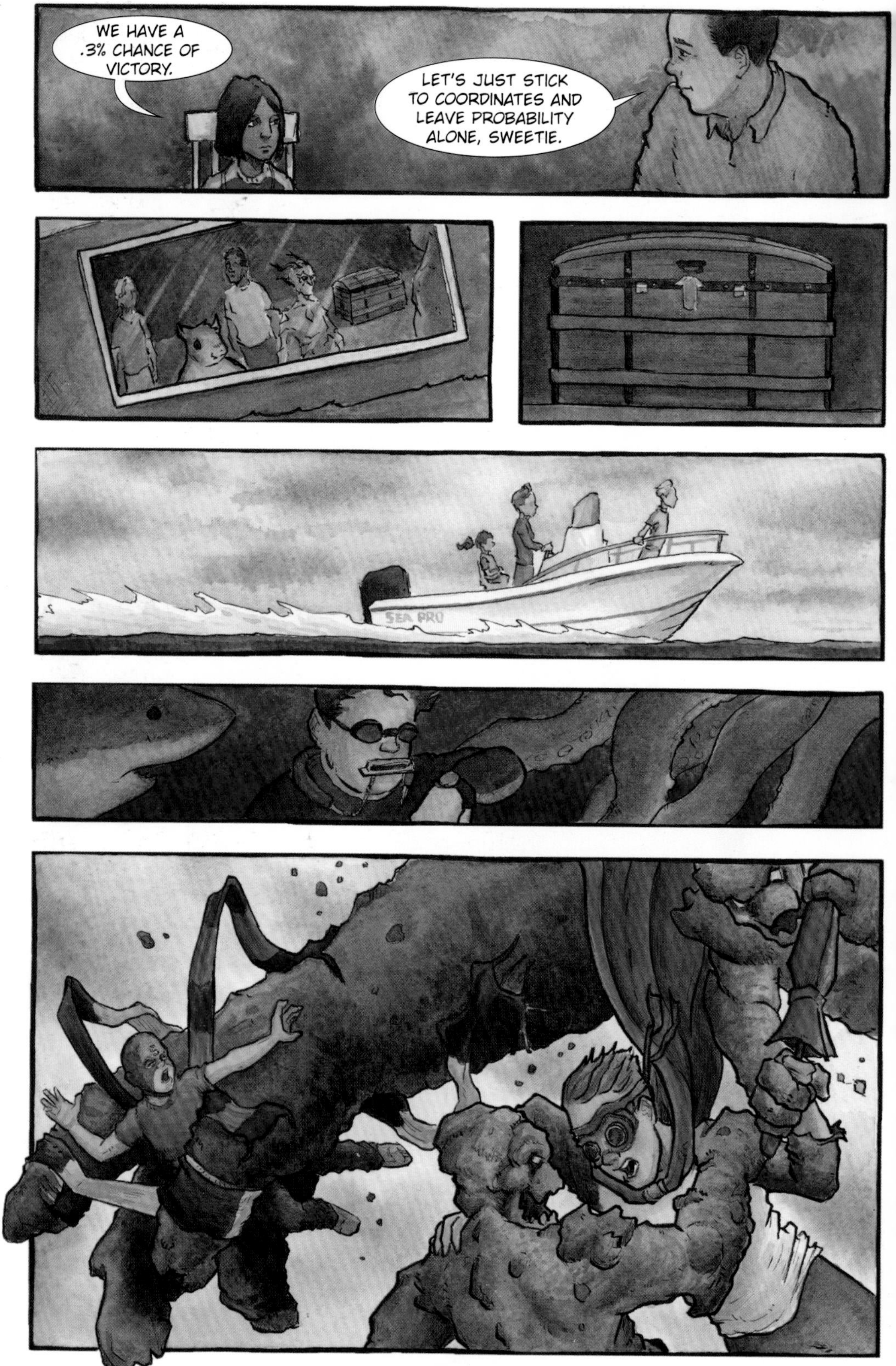
WE HAVE A .3% CHANCE OF VICTORY.
LET'S JUST STICK TO COORDINATES AND LEAVE PROBABILITY ALONE, SWEETIE.
SEA PRO

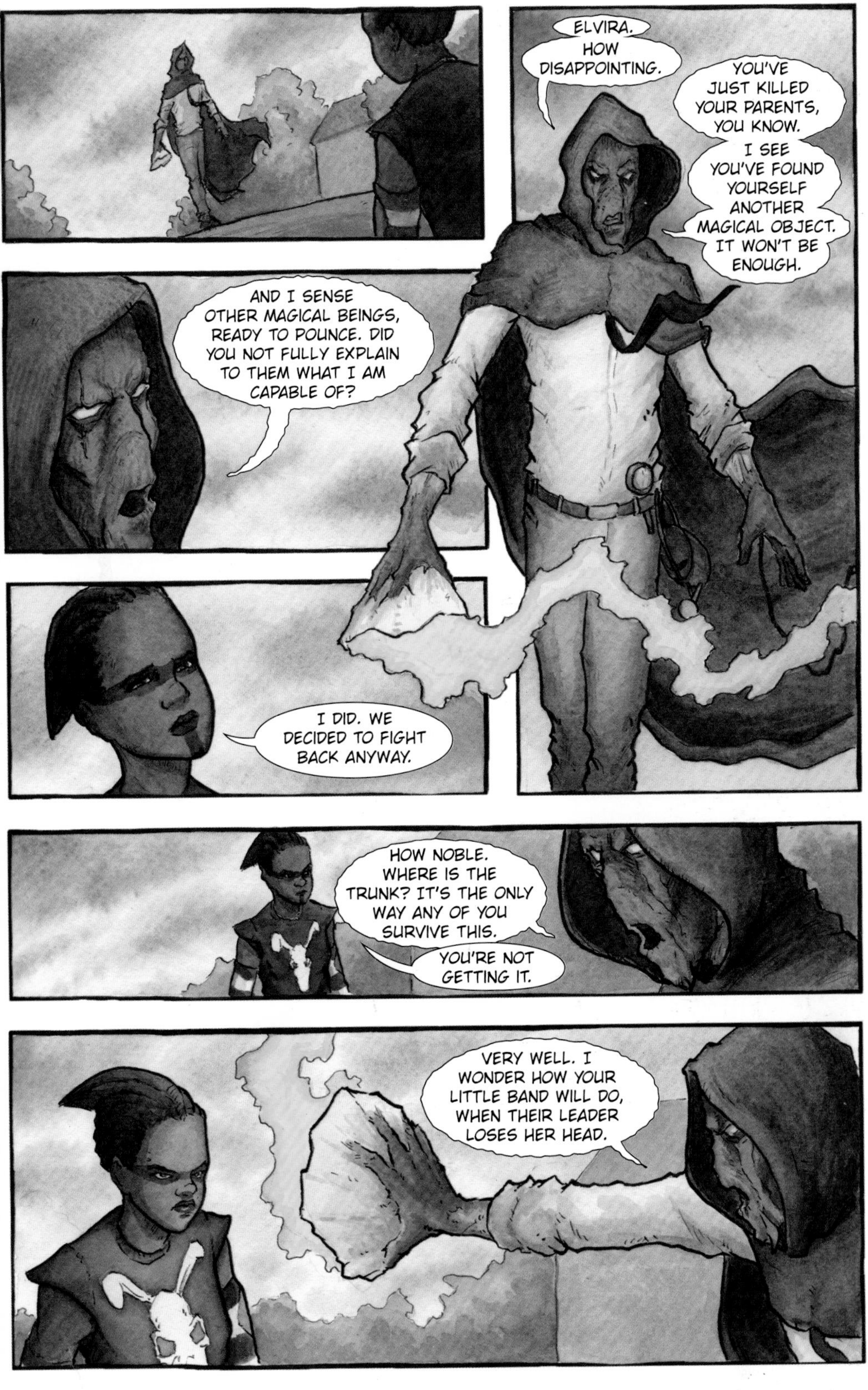
ELVIRA. HOW DISAPPOINTING.
YOU'VE JUST KILLED YOUR PARENTS, YOU KNOW.
I SEE YOU'VE FOUND YOURSELF ANOTHER MAGICAL OBJECT. IT WON'T BE ENOUGH.
AND I SENSE OTHER MAGICAL BEINGS, READY TO POUNCE. DID YOU NOT FULLY EXPLAIN TO THEM WHAT I AM CAPABLE OF?
I DID. WE DECIDED TO FIGHT BACK ANYWAY.
HOW NOBLE. WHERE IS THE TRUNK? IT'S THE ONLY WAY ANY OF YOU SURVIVE THIS.
YOU'RE NOT GETTING IT.
VERY WELL. I WONDER HOW YOUR LITTLE BAND WILL DO, WHEN THEIR LEADER LOSES HER HEAD.

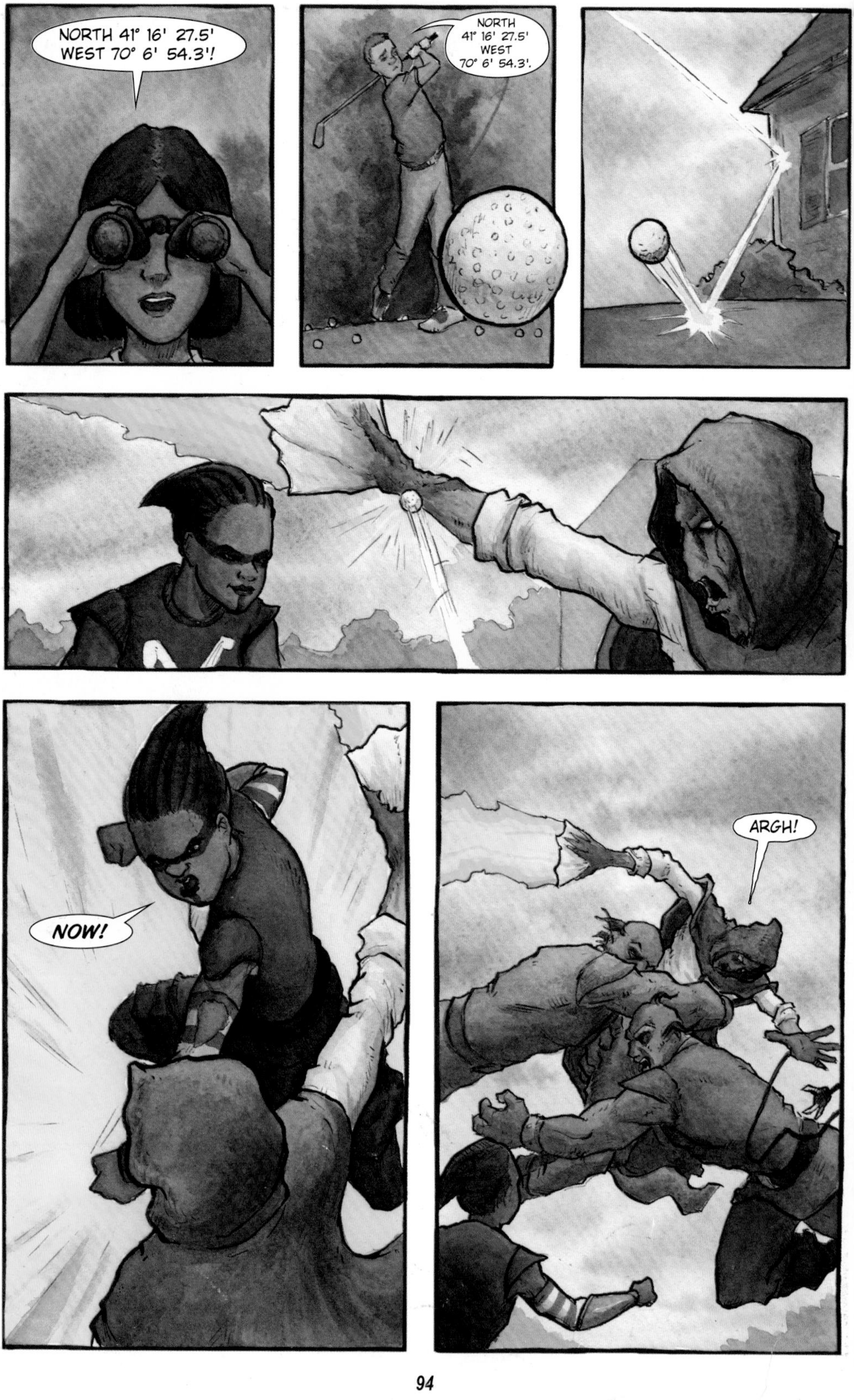
NORTH 41° 16' 27.5'
WEST 70° 6' 54.3'!
NORTH
41° 16' 27.5'
WEST
70° 6' 54.3'.
NOW!
ARGH!

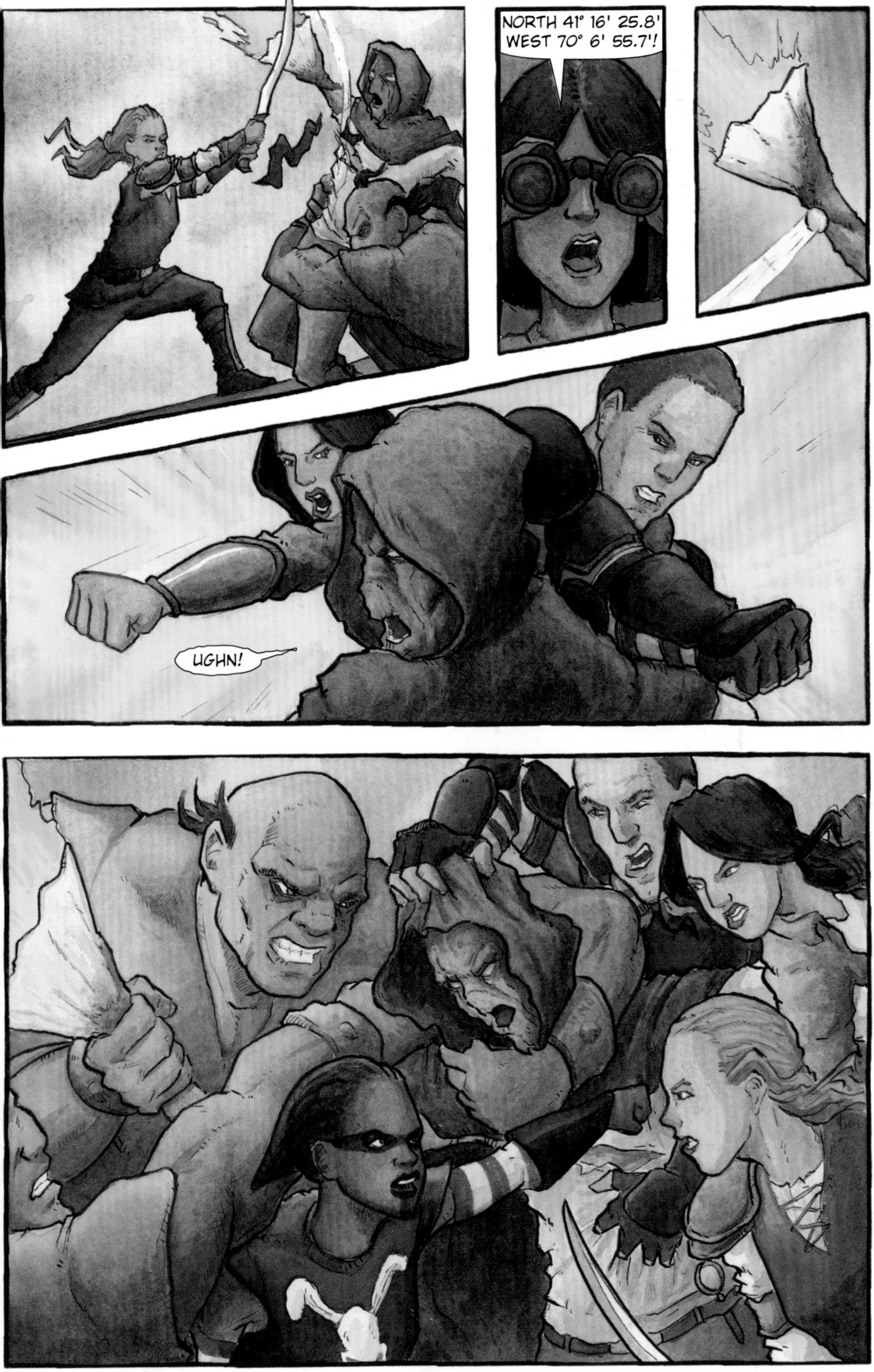
NORTH 41° 16' 25.8'
WEST 70° 6' 55.7'!
UGHN!

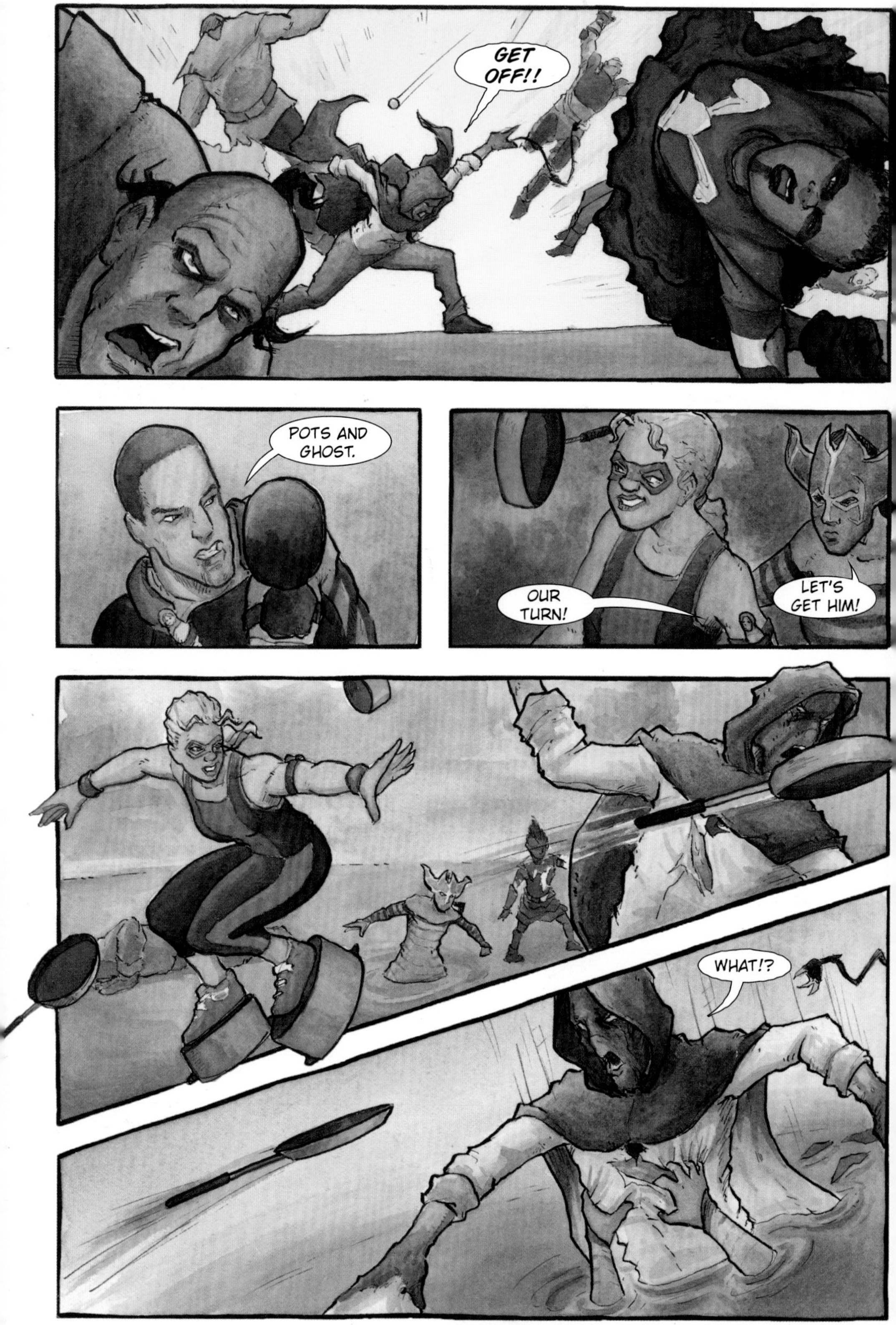
GET OFF!!
POTS AND GHOST.
OUR TURN!
LET'S GET HIM!
WHAT!?

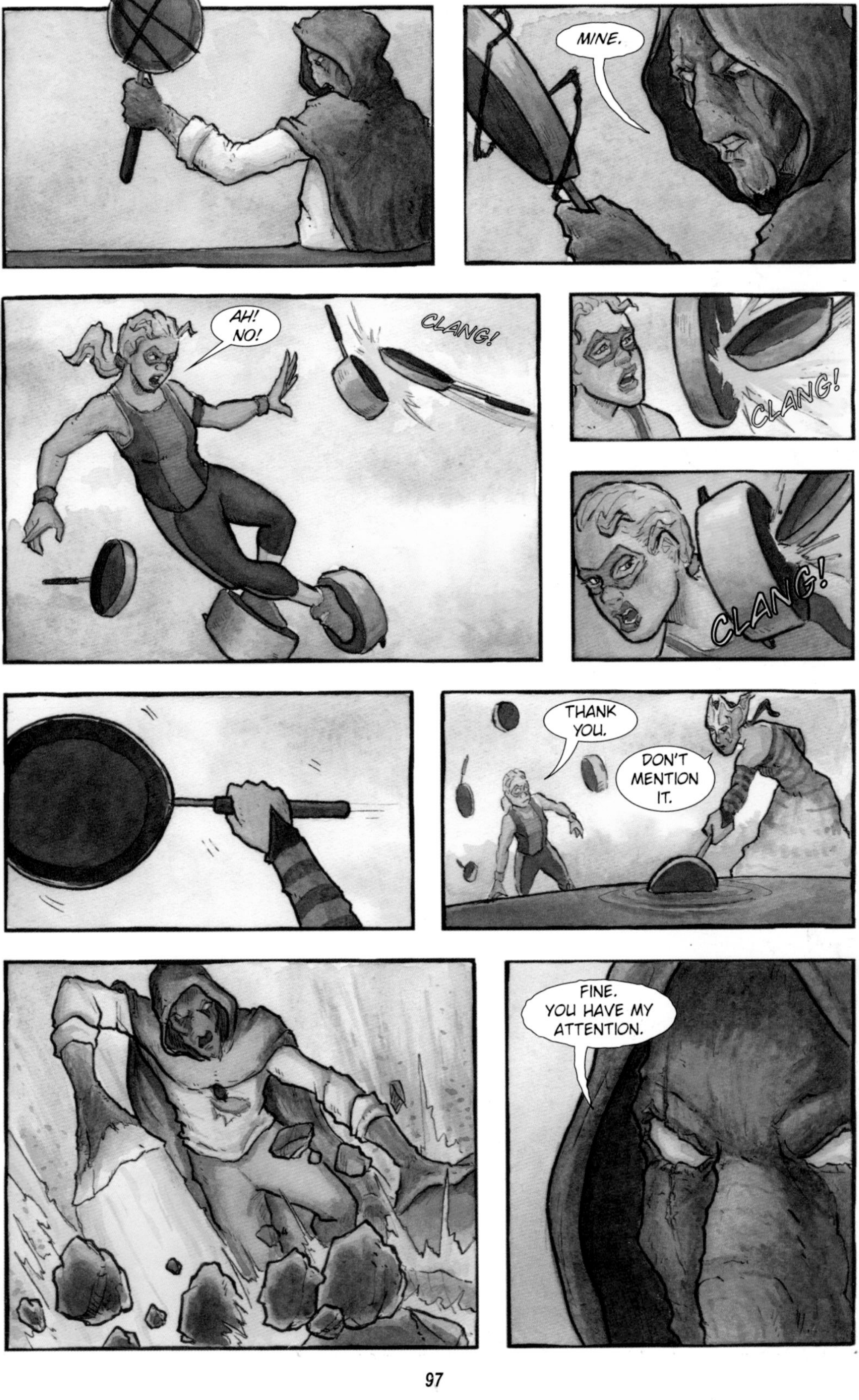
MINE.
AH! NO!
CLANG!
CLANG!
CLANG!
THANK YOU.
DON'T MENTION IT.
FINE. YOU HAVE MY ATTENTION.

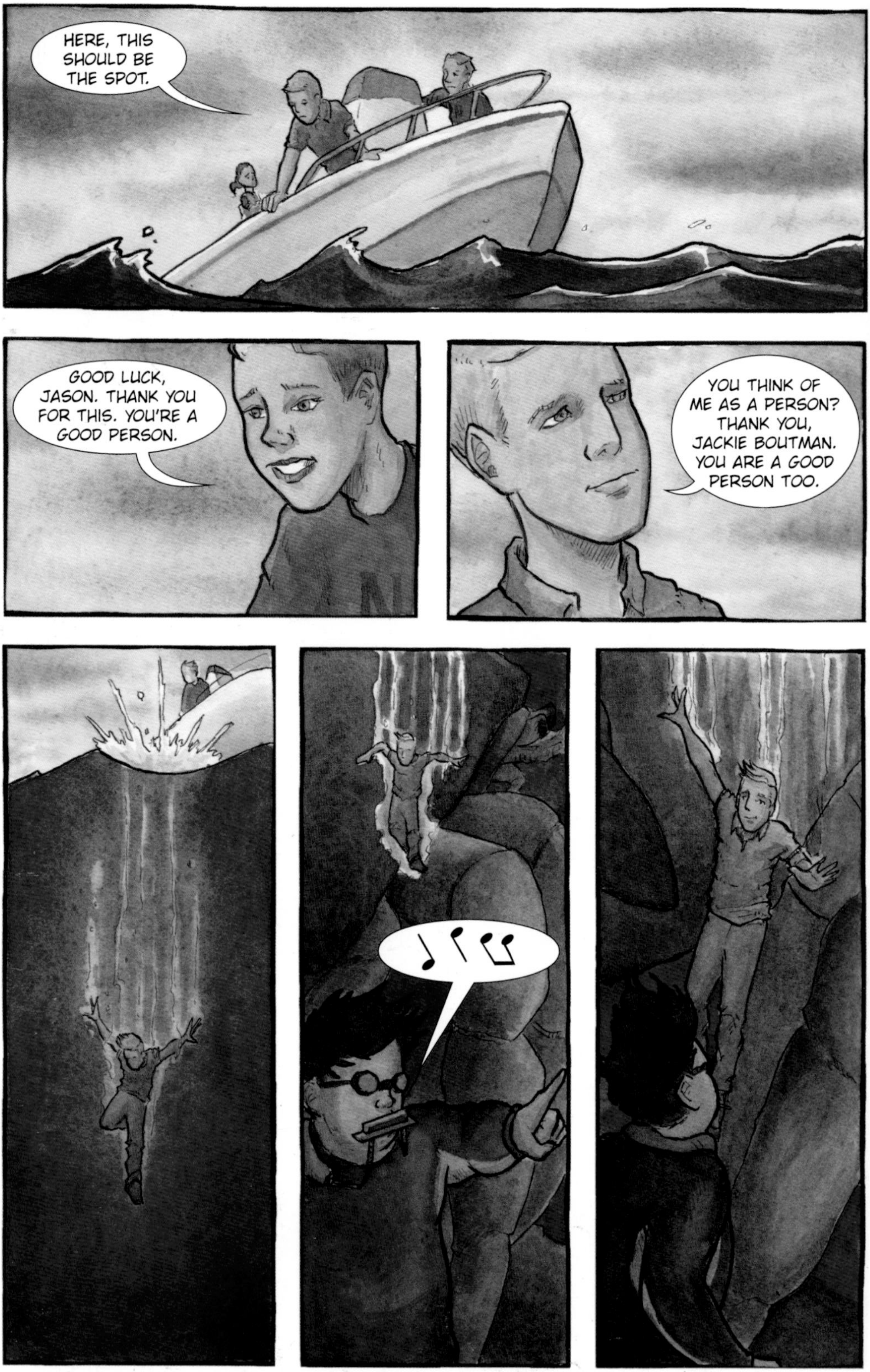
HERE, THIS SHOULD BE THE SPOT.
GOOD LUCK, JASON. THANK YOU FOR THIS. YOU'RE A GOOD PERSON.
YOU THINK OF ME AS A PERSON? THANK YOU, JACKIE BOUTMAN. YOU ARE A GOOD PERSON TOO.

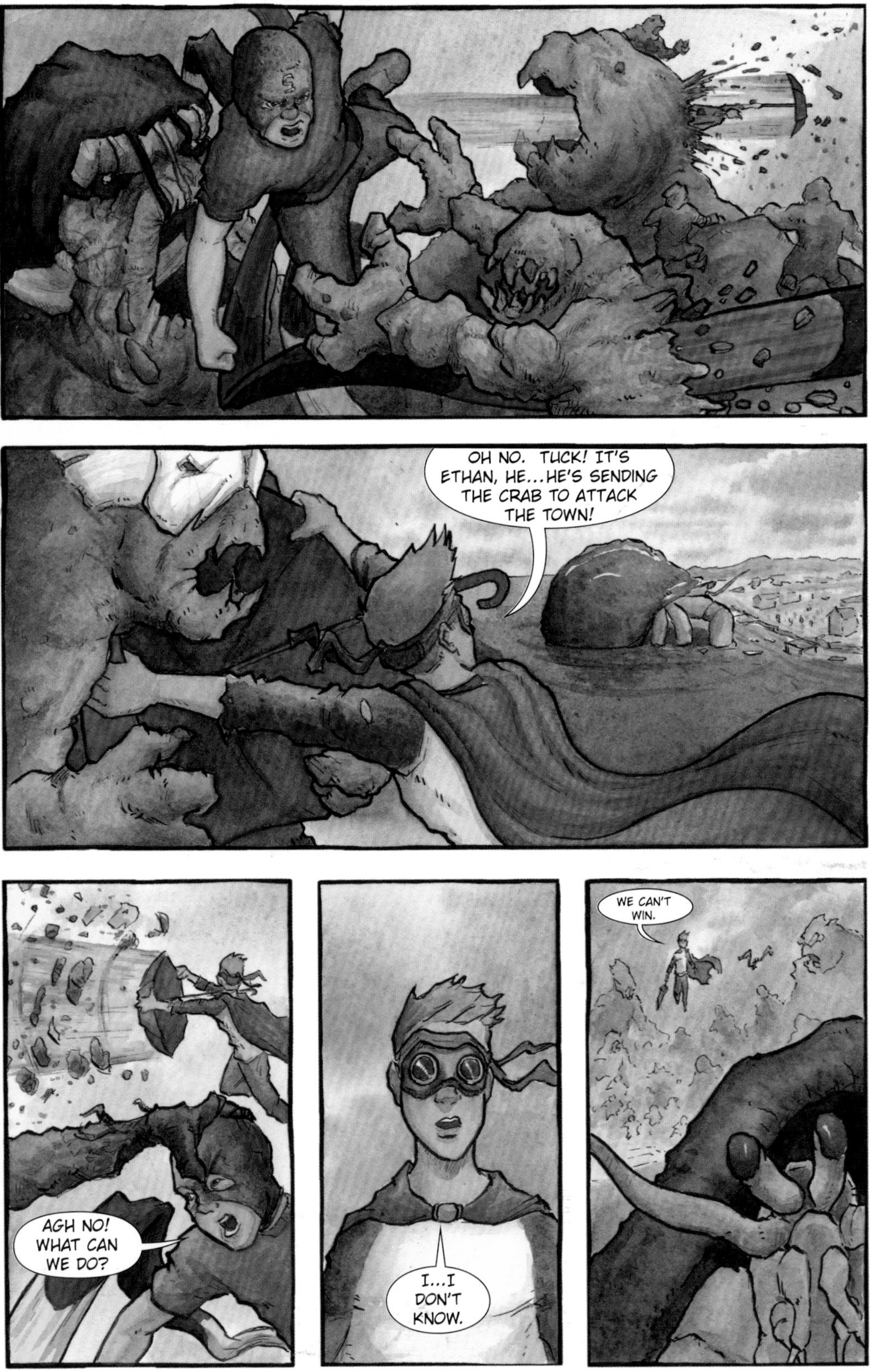
OH NO. TUCK! IT'S ETHAN, HE...HE'S SENDING THE CRAB TO ATTACK THE TOWN!
AGH NO! WHAT CAN WE DO?
I...I DON'T KNOW.
WE CAN'T WIN.

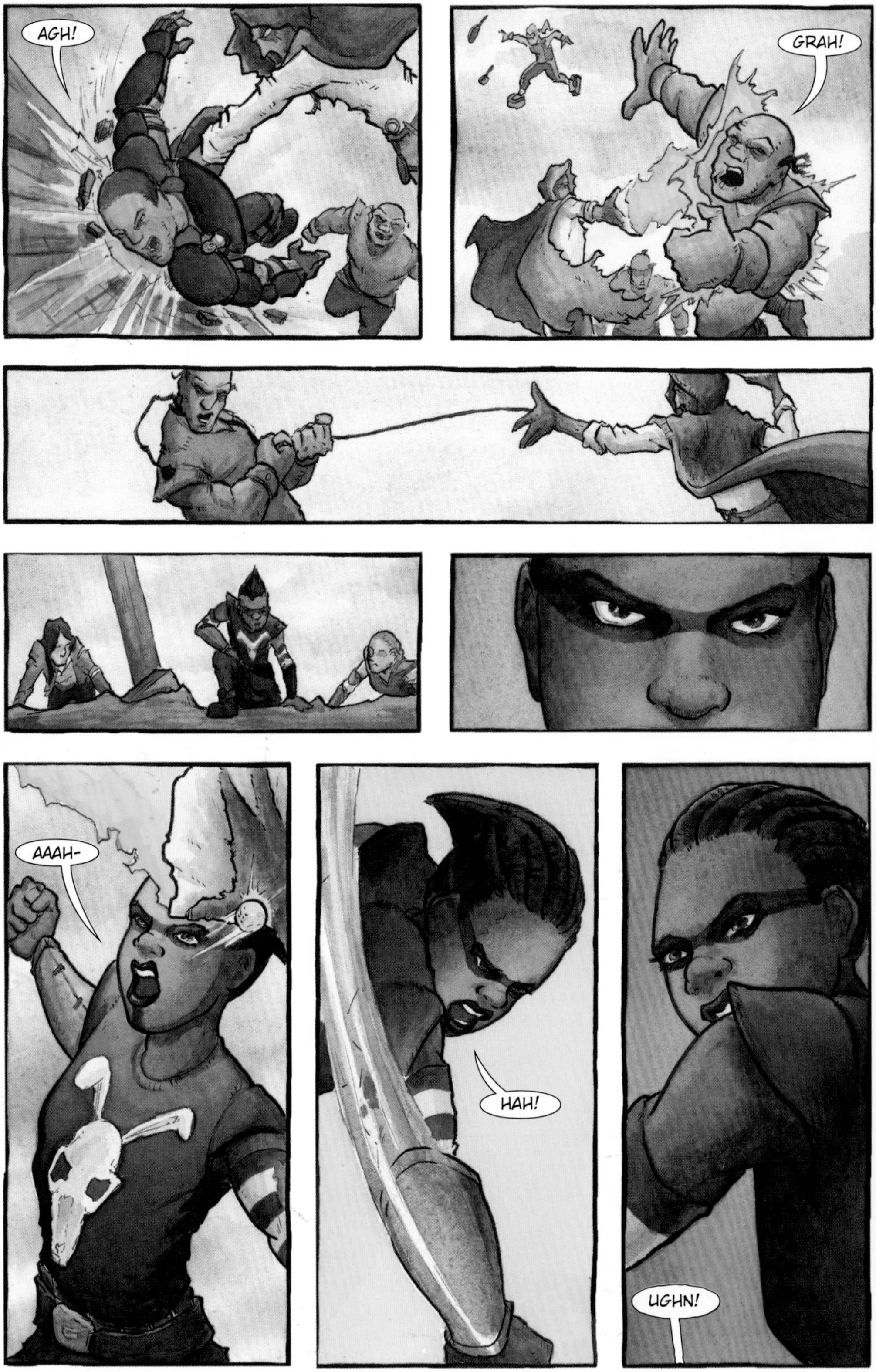
AGH!
GRAH!
AAAH-
HAH!
UGHN!

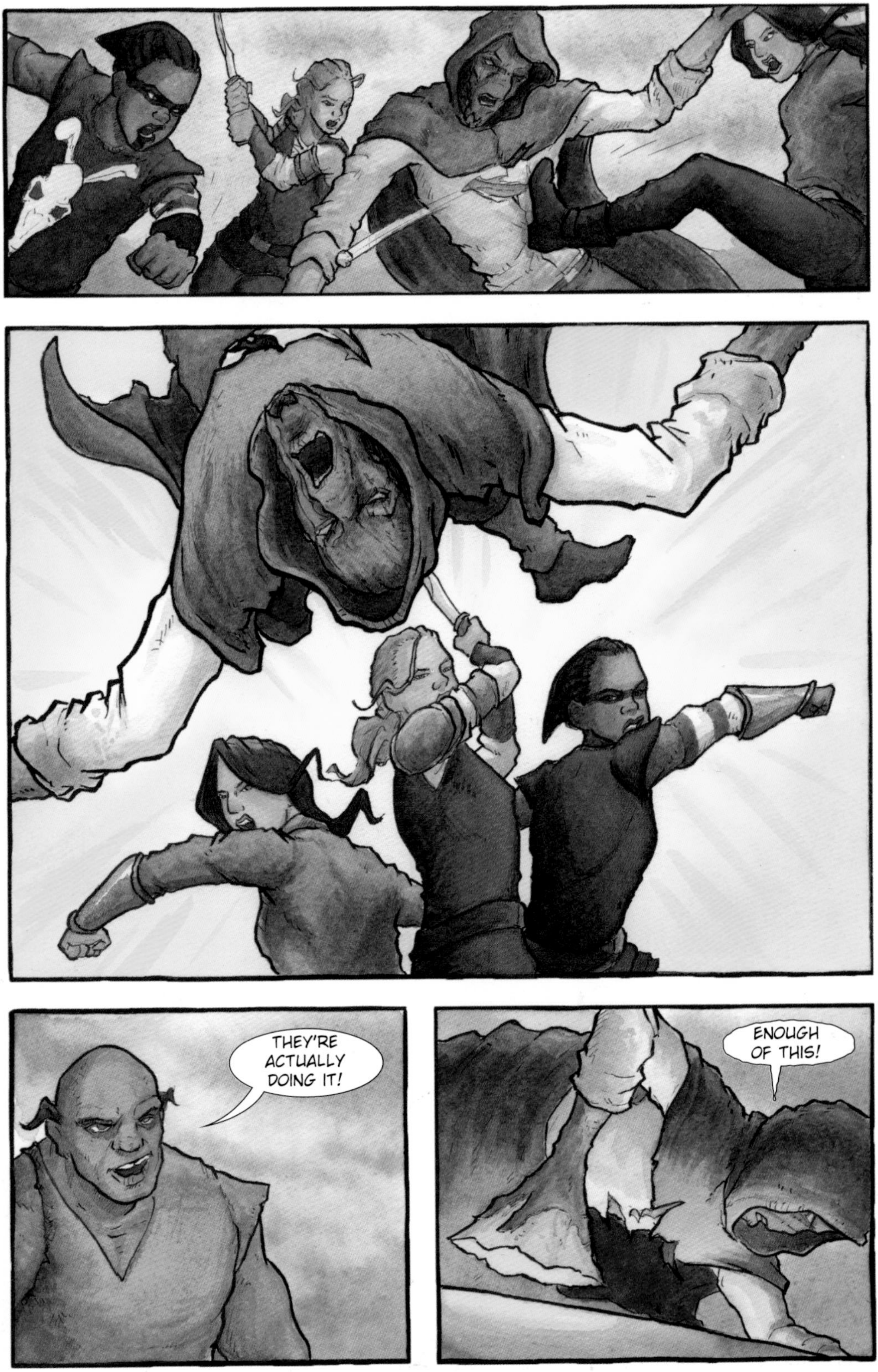
THEY'RE ACTUALLY DOING IT!
ENOUGH OF THIS!

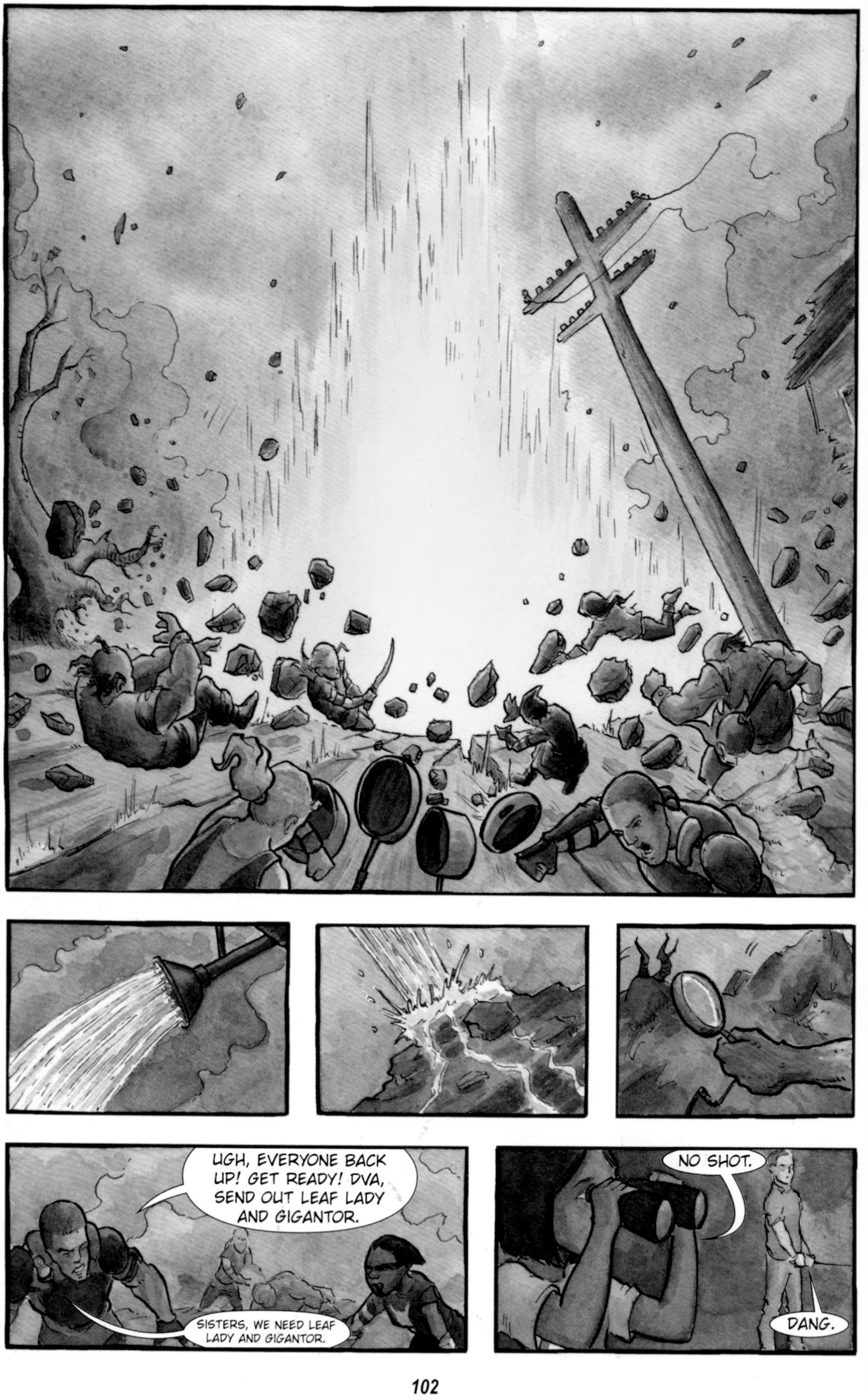
UGH, EVERYONE BACK UP! GET READY! DVA, SEND OUT LEAF LADY AND GIGANTOR.
SISTERS, WE NEED LEAF LADY AND GIGANTOR.
NO SHOT.
DANG.

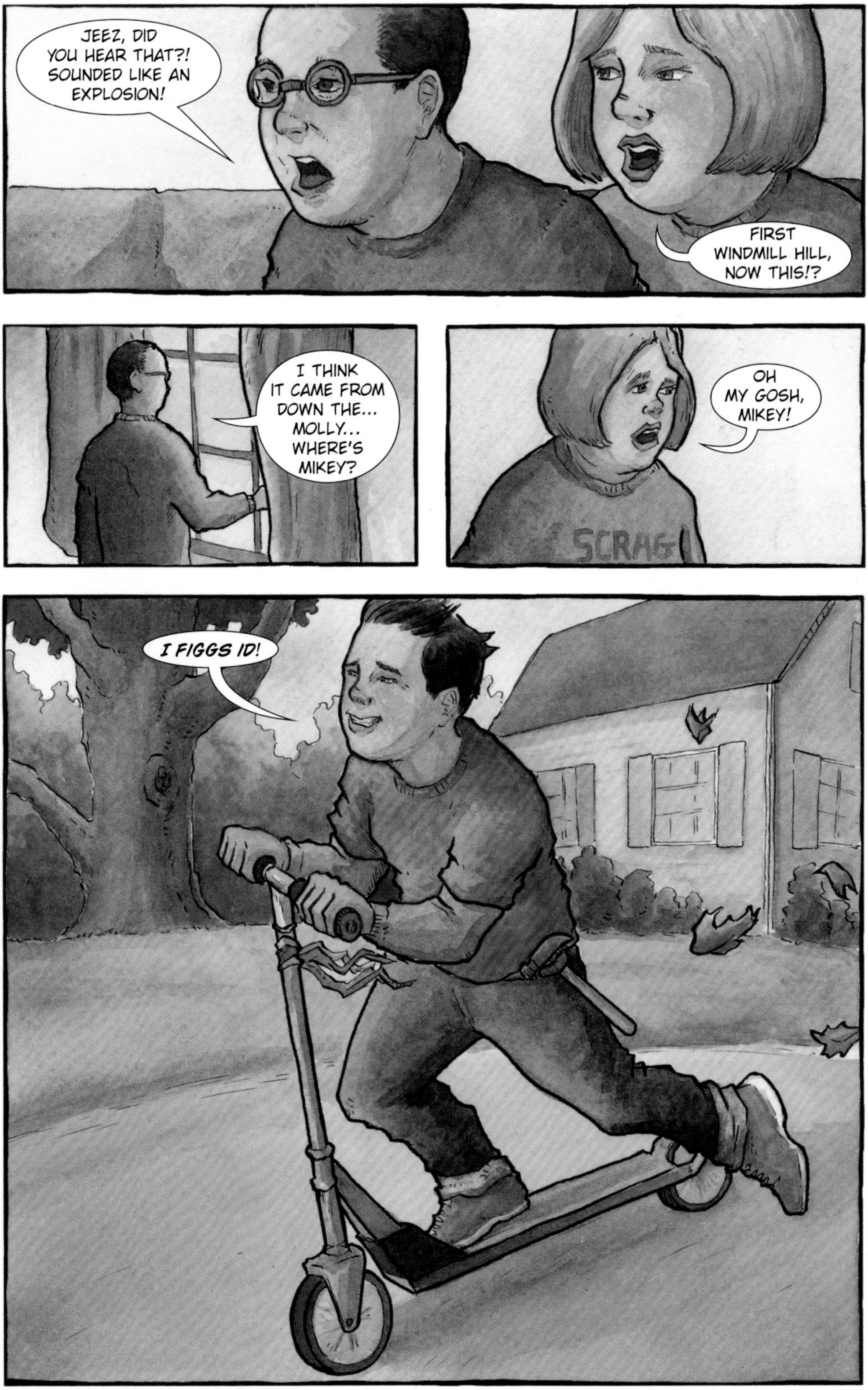
JEEZ, DID YOU HEAR THAT?! SOUNDED LIKE AN EXPLOSION!
FIRST WINDMILL HILL, NOW THIS!?
I THINK IT CAME FROM DOWN THE... MOLLY... WHERE'S MIKEY?
OH MY GOSH, MIKEY!
SCRAG
I FIGGS ID!

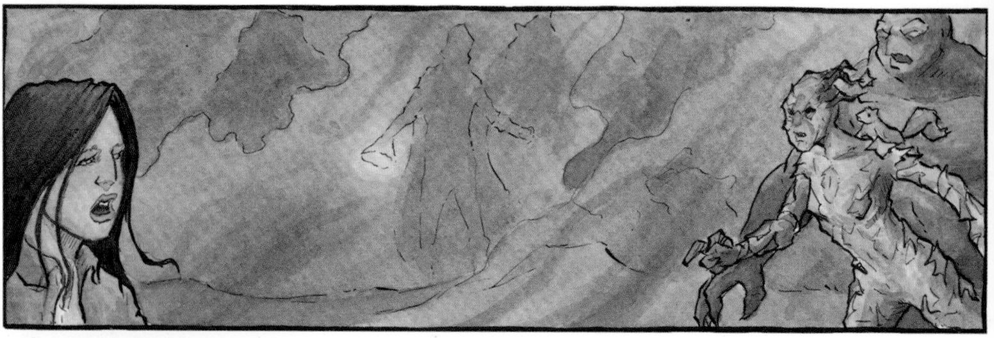

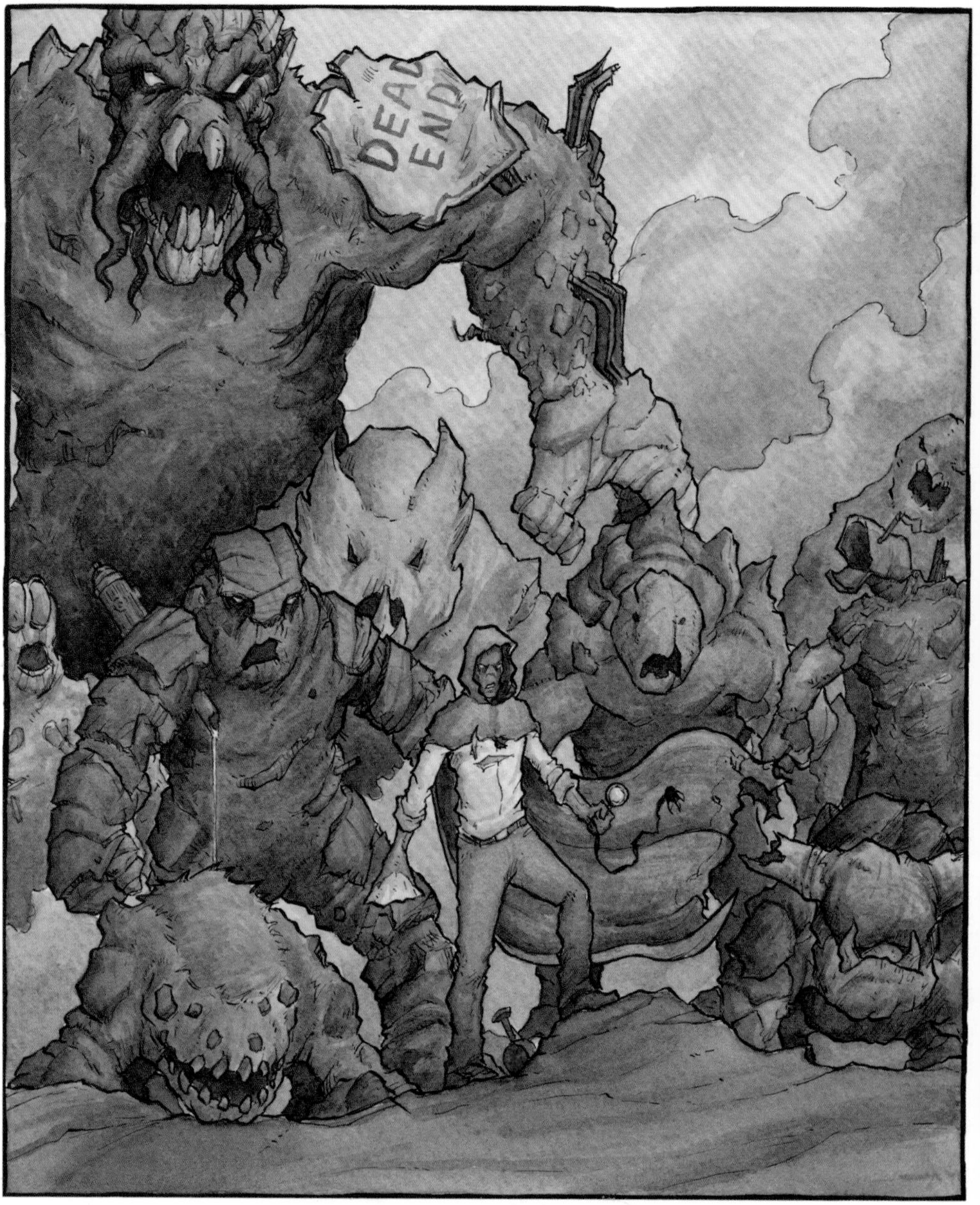
DEAD END

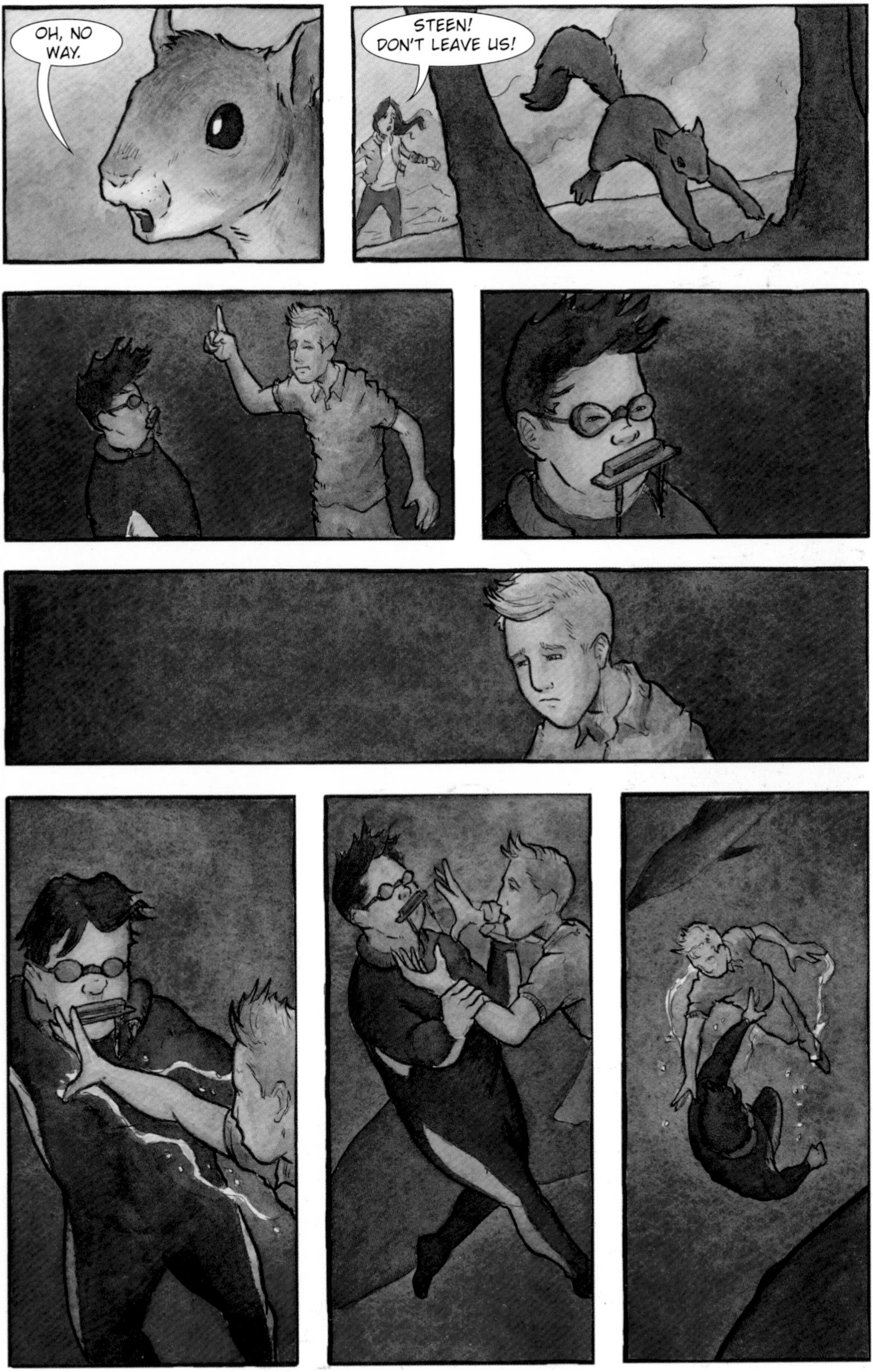
OH, NO WAY.
STEEN! DON'T LEAVE US!

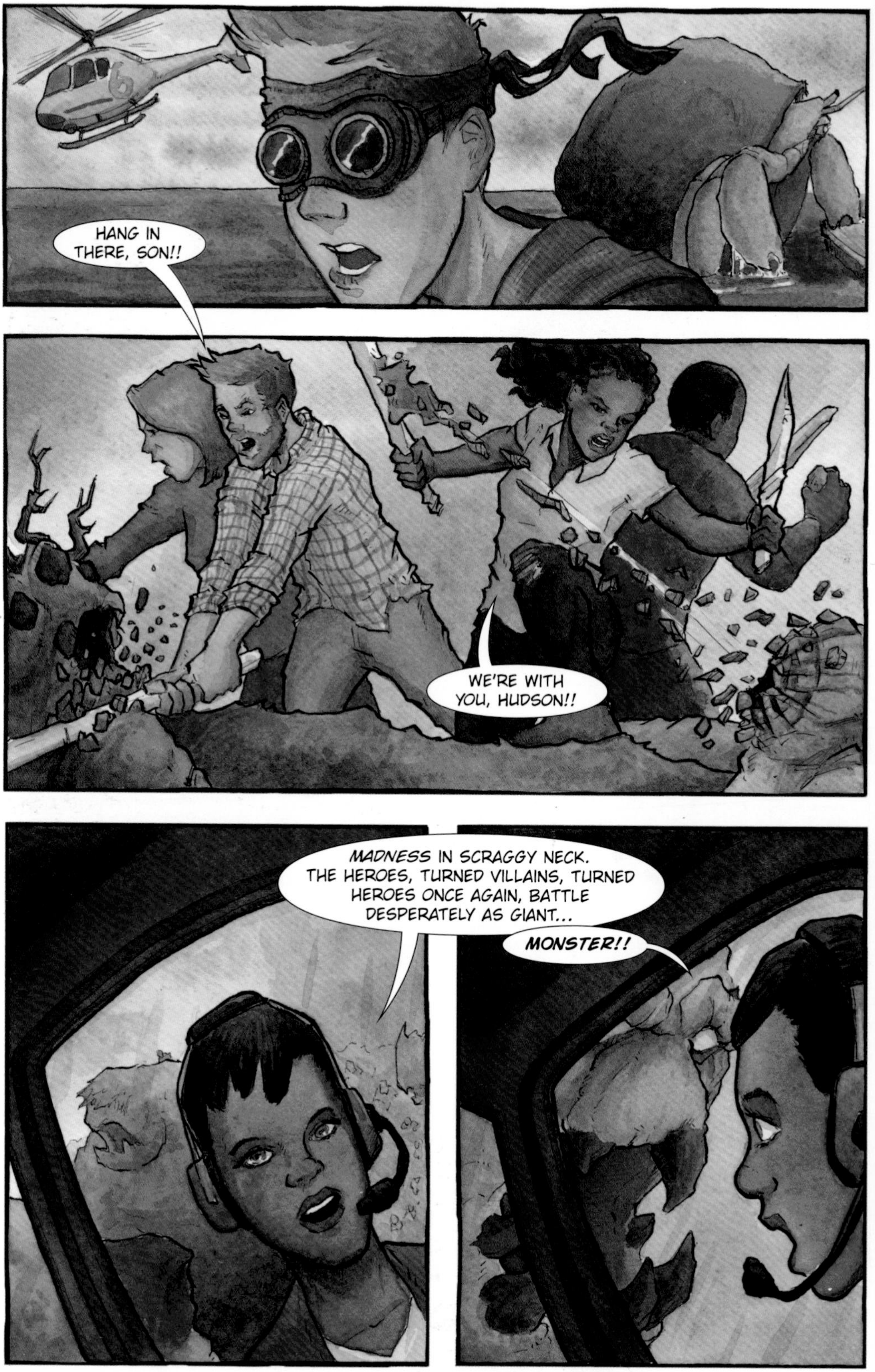
HANG IN THERE, SON!!
WE'RE WITH YOU, HUDSON!!
MADNESS IN SCRAGGY NECK. THE HEROES, TURNED VILLAINS, TURNED HEROES ONCE AGAIN, BATTLE DESPERATELY AS GIANT...
MONSTER!!

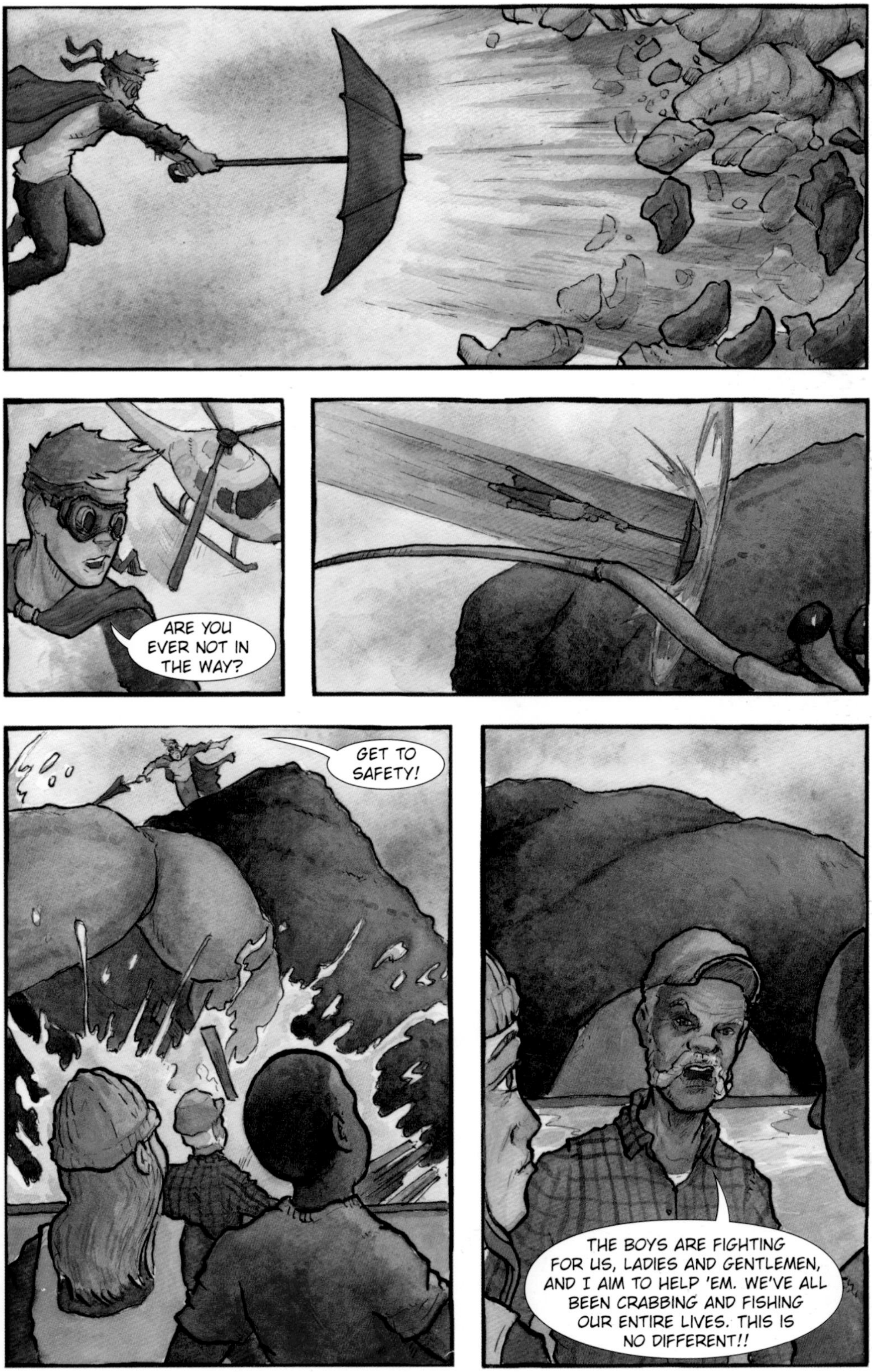
ARE YOU EVER NOT IN THE WAY?
GET TO SAFETY!
THE BOYS ARE FIGHTING FOR US, LADIES AND GENTLEMEN, AND I AIM TO HELP 'EM. WE'VE ALL BEEN CRABBING AND FISHING OUR ENTIRE LIVES. THIS IS NO DIFFERENT!!

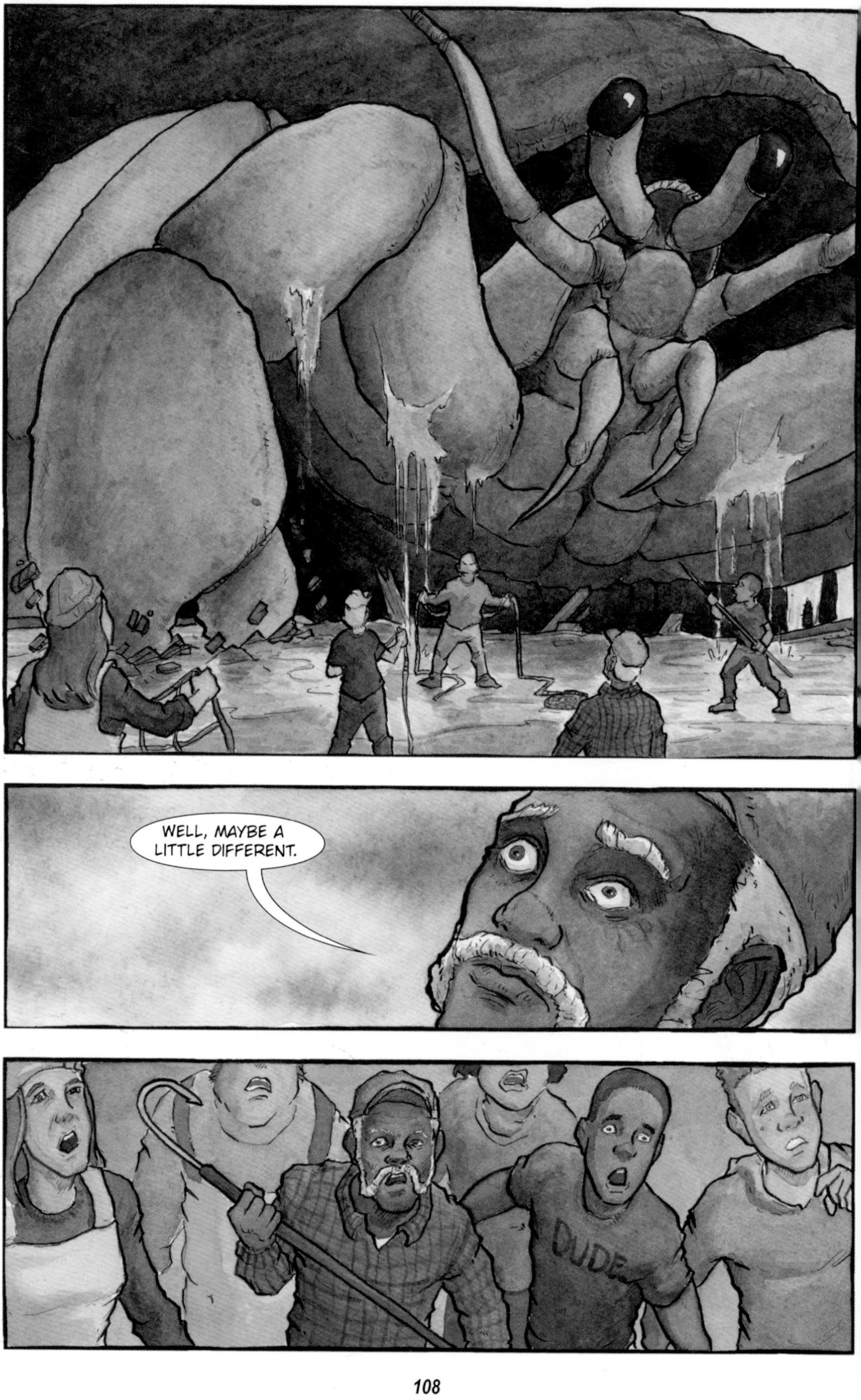
WELL, MAYBE A LITTLE DIFFERENT.
DUDE

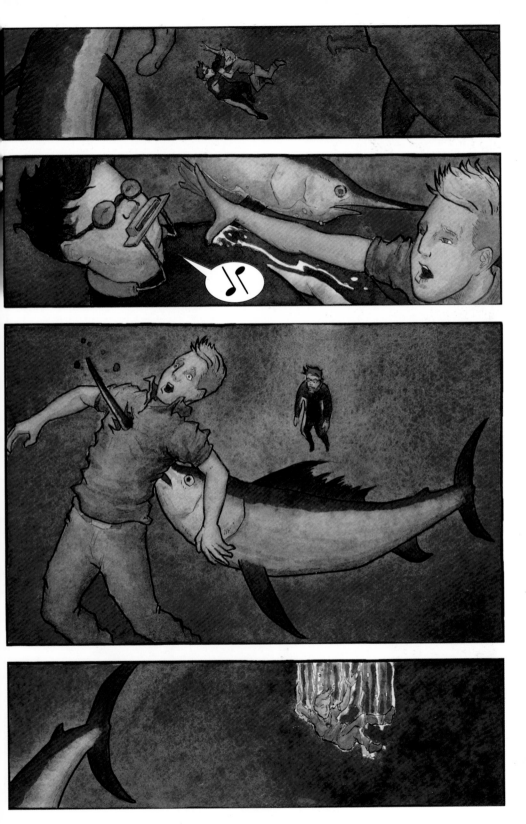

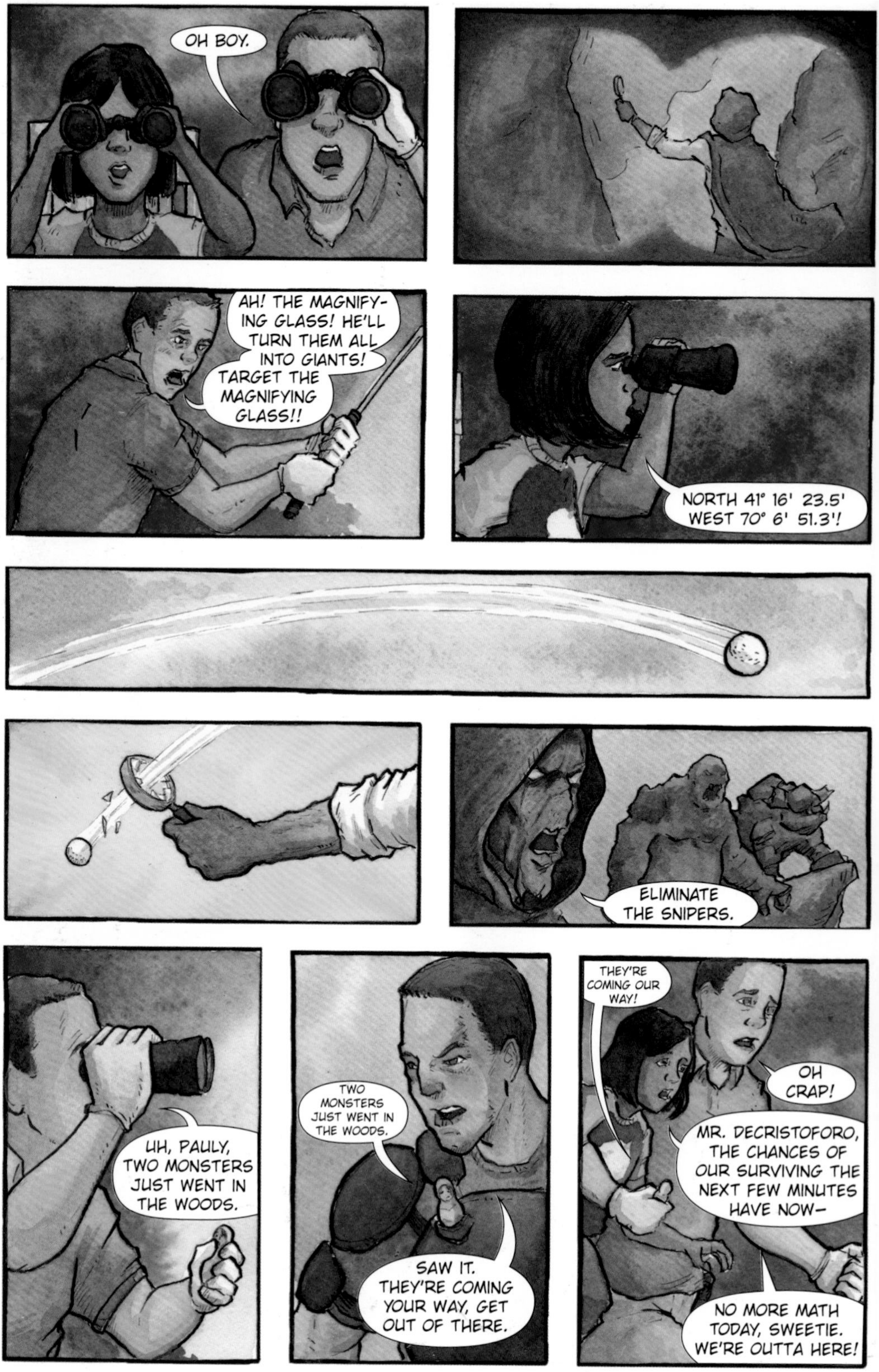
OH BOY.
AH! THE MAGNIFY-ING GLASS! HE'LL TURN THEM ALL INTO GIANTS!
TARGET THE MAGNIFYING GLASS!!
NORTH 41° 16' 23.5' WEST 70° 6' 51.3'!
ELIMINATE THE SNIPERS.
UH, PAULY, TWO MONSTERS JUST WENT IN THE WOODS.
TWO MONSTERS JUST WENT IN THE WOODS.
SAW IT. THEY'RE COMING YOUR WAY, GET OUT OF THERE.
THEY'RE COMING OUR WAY!
OH CRAP!
MR. DECRISTOFORO, THE CHANCES OF OUR SURVIVING THE NEXT FEW MINUTES HAVE NOW—
NO MORE MATH TODAY, SWEETIE. WE'RE OUTTA HERE!

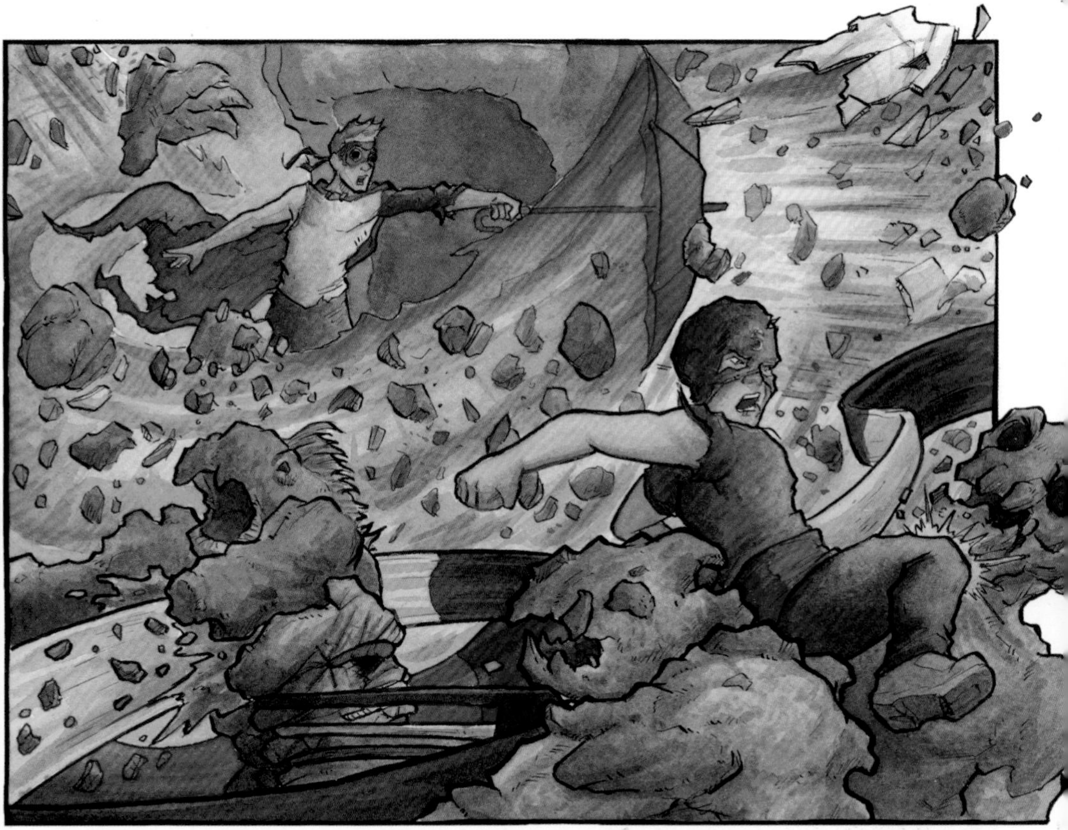

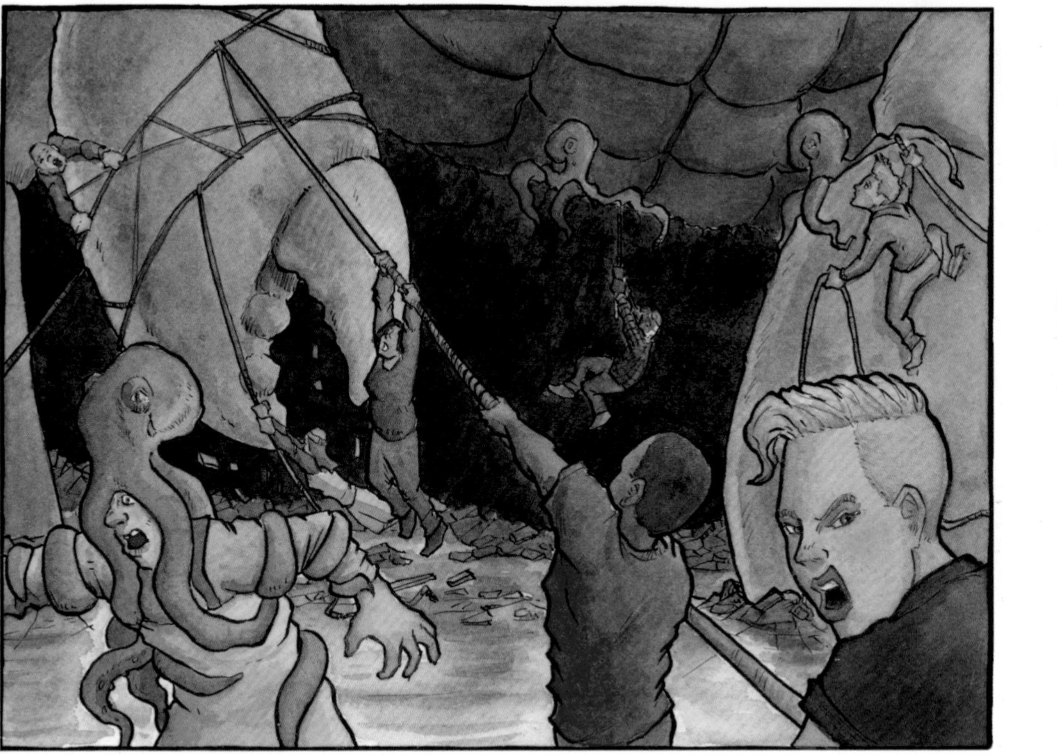

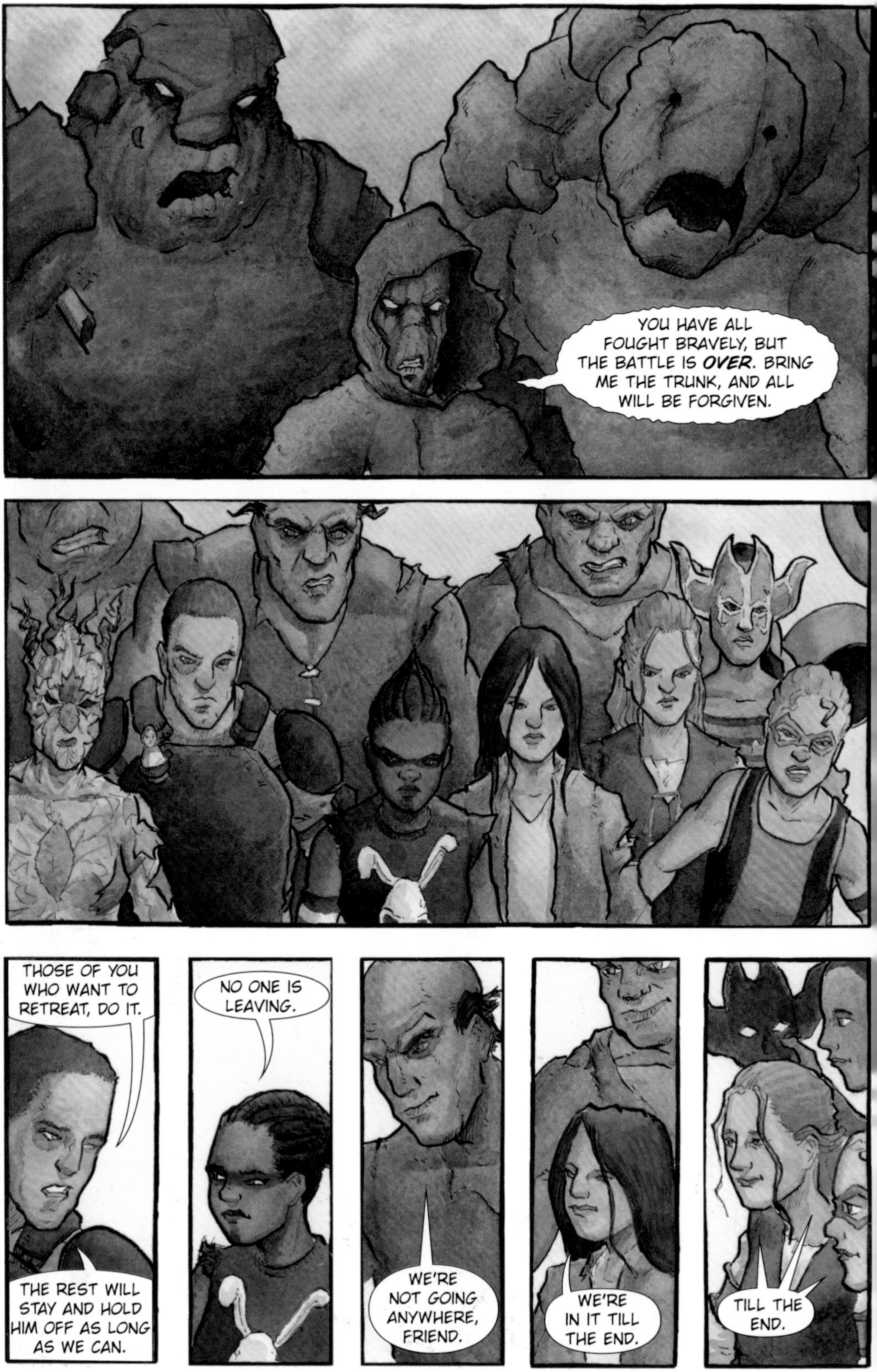
YOU HAVE ALL FOUGHT BRAVELY, BUT THE BATTLE IS **OVER**. BRING ME THE TRUNK, AND ALL WILL BE FORGIVEN.
THOSE OF YOU WHO WANT TO RETREAT, DO IT.
THE REST WILL STAY AND HOLD HIM OFF AS LONG AS WE CAN.
NO ONE IS LEAVING.
WE'RE NOT GOING ANYWHERE, FRIEND.
WE'RE IN IT TILL THE END.
TILL THE END.

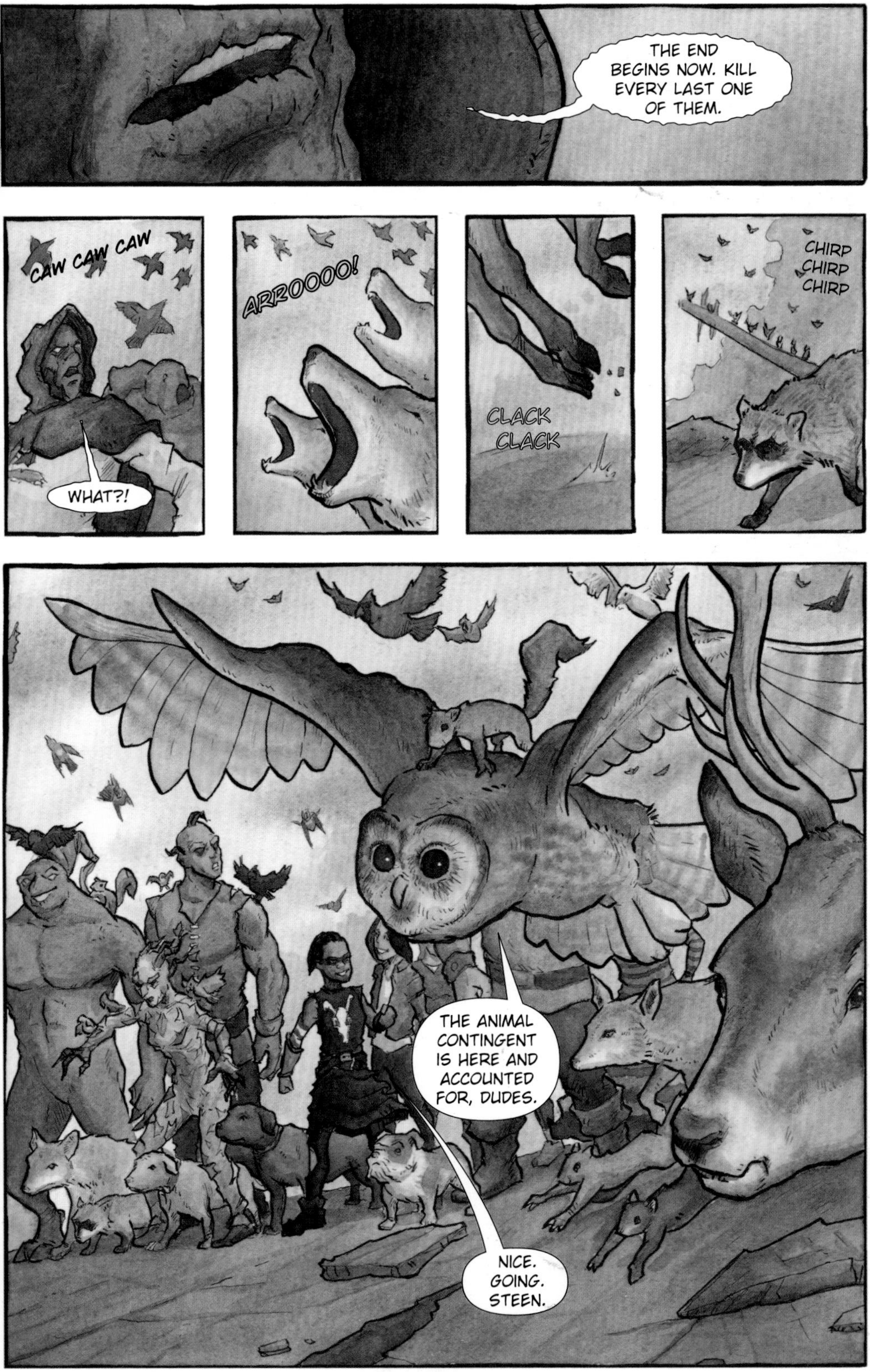
THE END BEGINS NOW. KILL EVERY LAST ONE OF THEM.
CAW CAW CAW
WHAT?!
ARROOOO!
CLACK CLACK
CHIRP CHIRP CHIRP
THE ANIMAL CONTINGENT IS HERE AND ACCOUNTED FOR, DUDES.
NICE. GOING. STEEN.

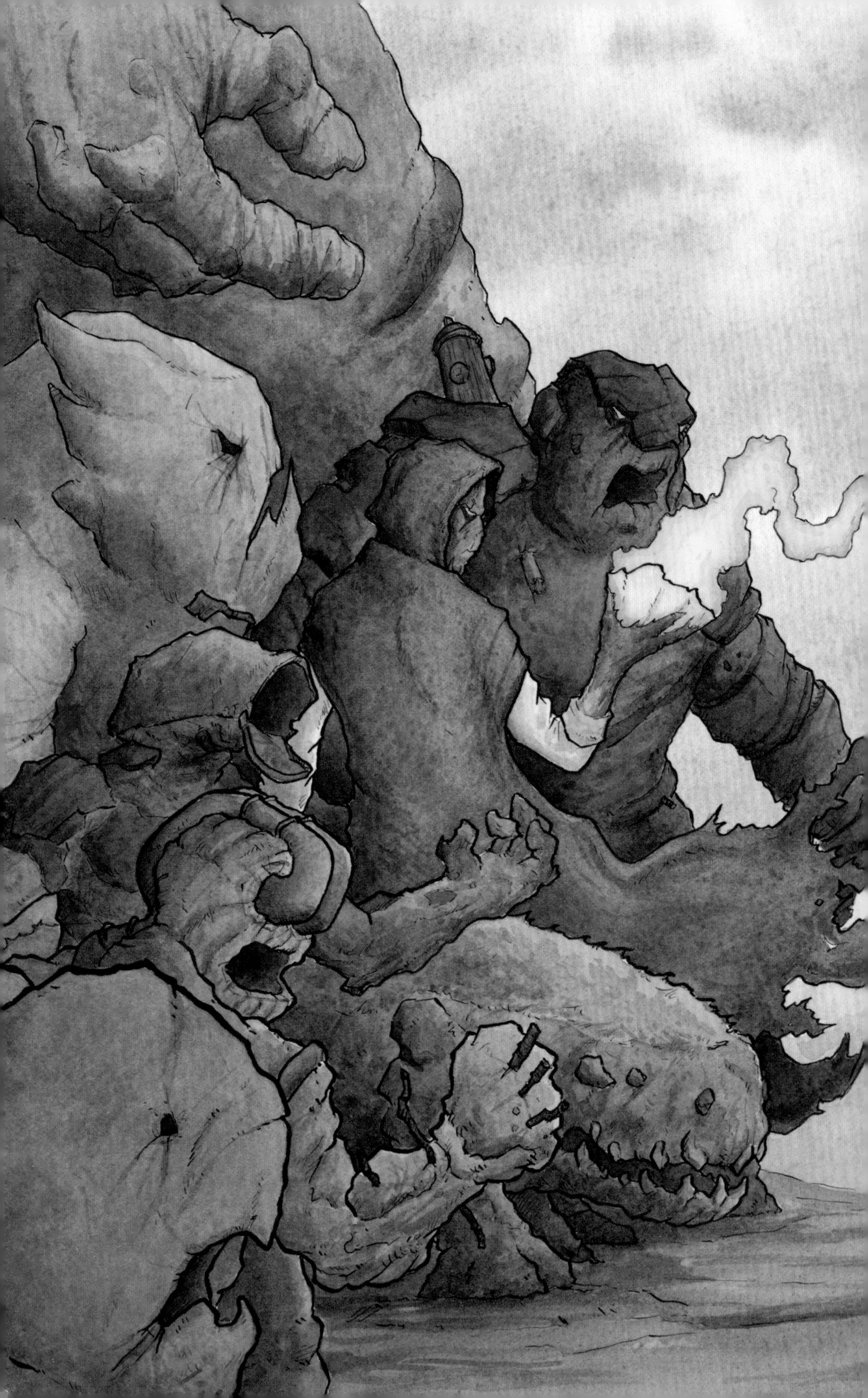

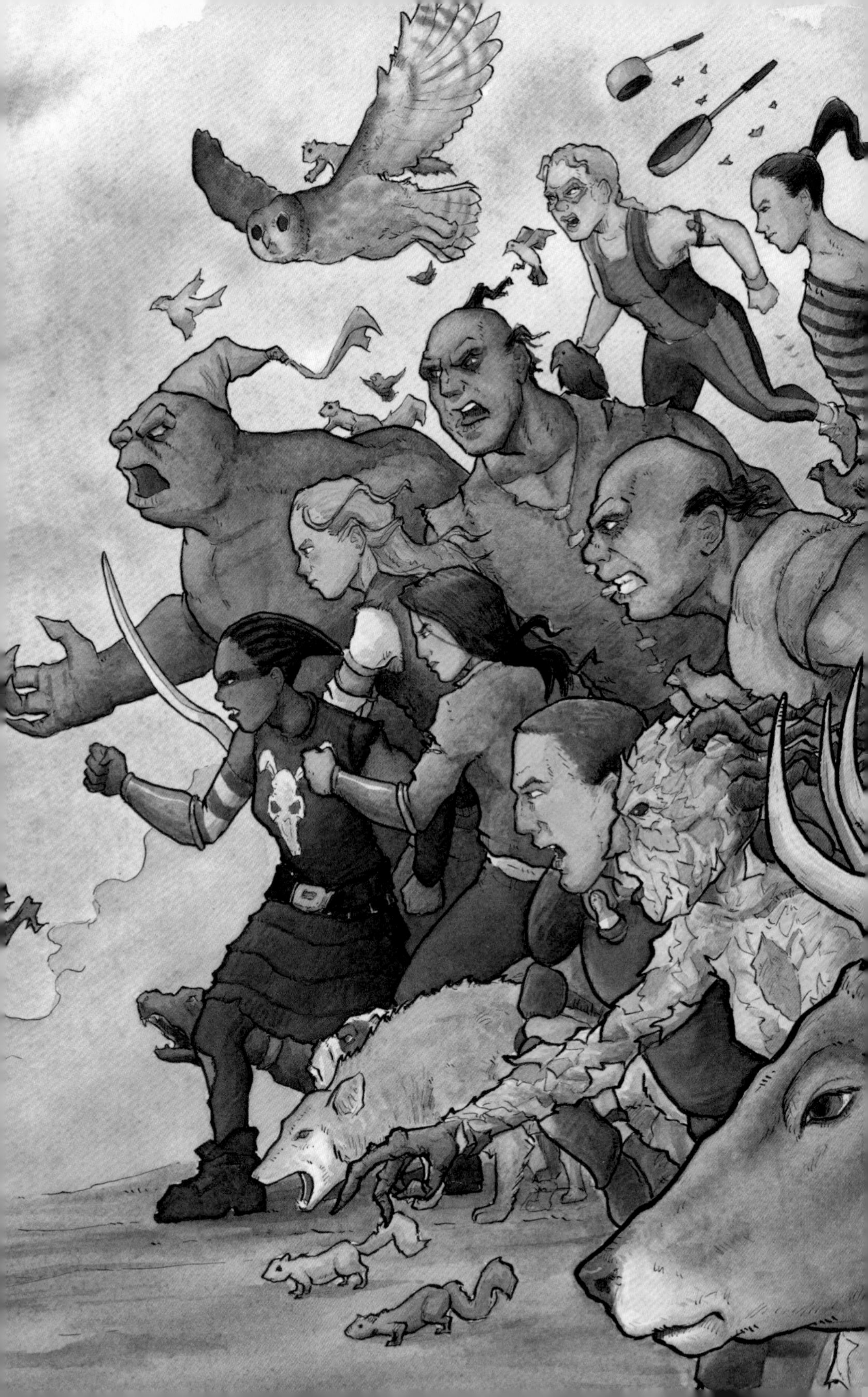

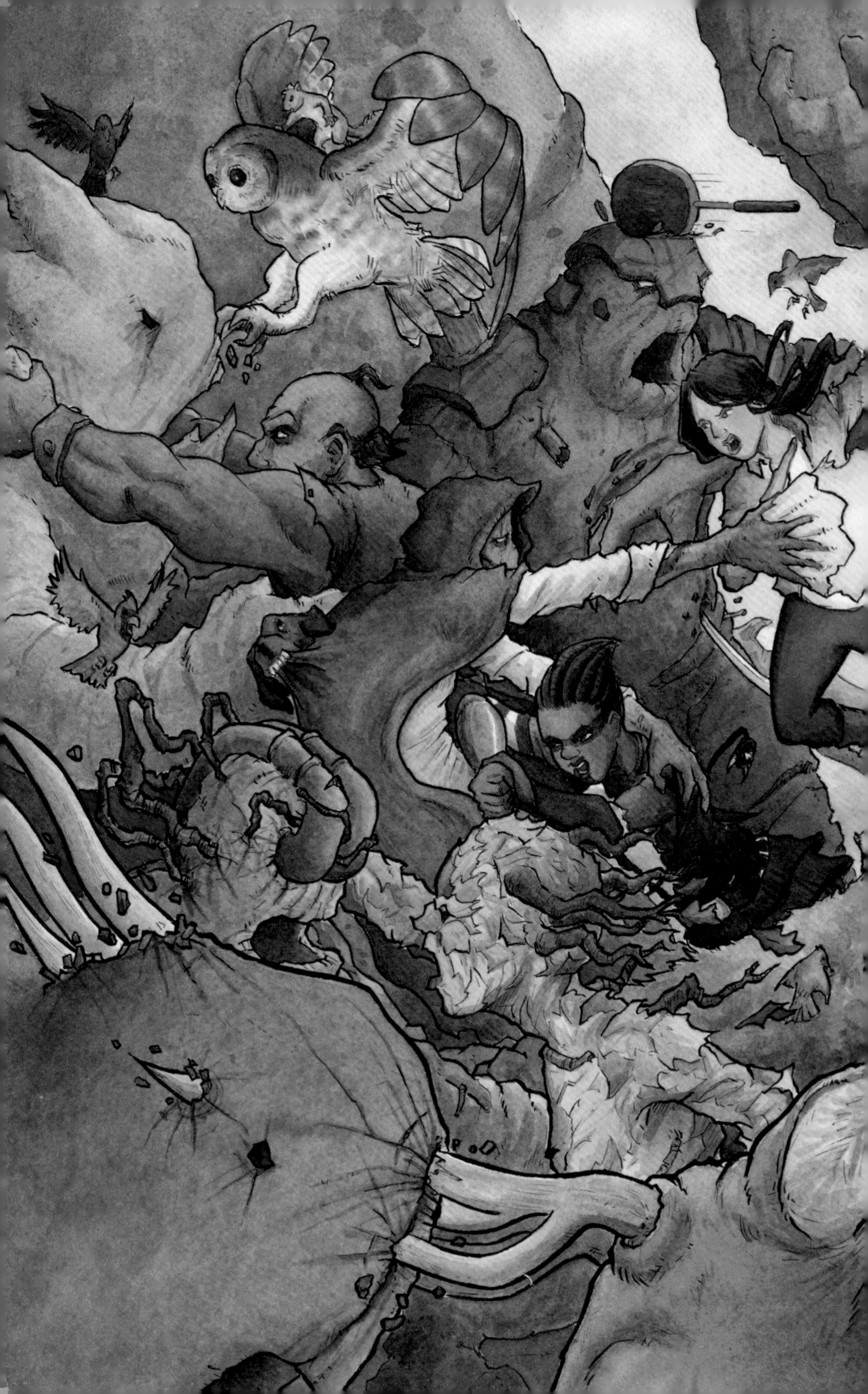

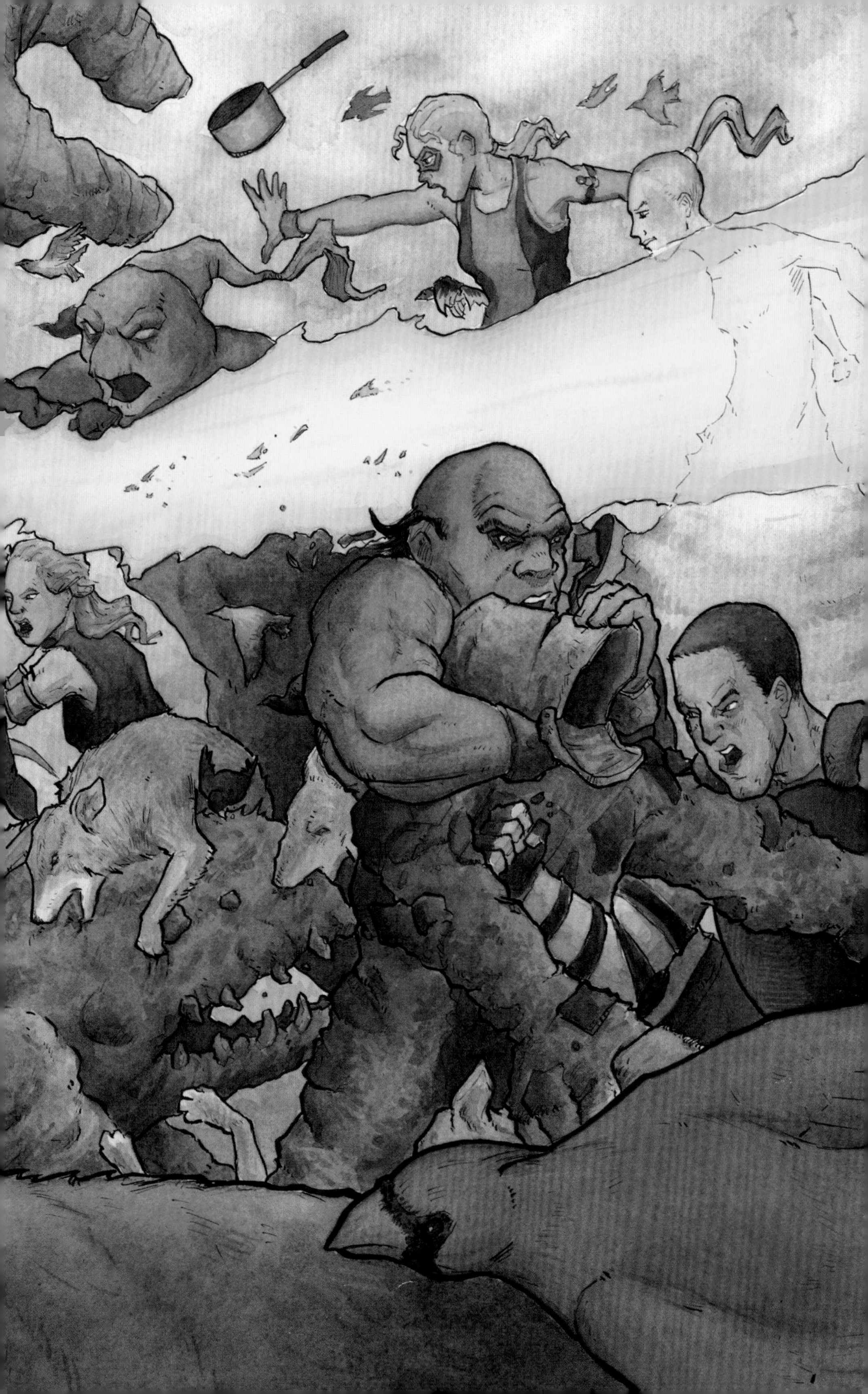

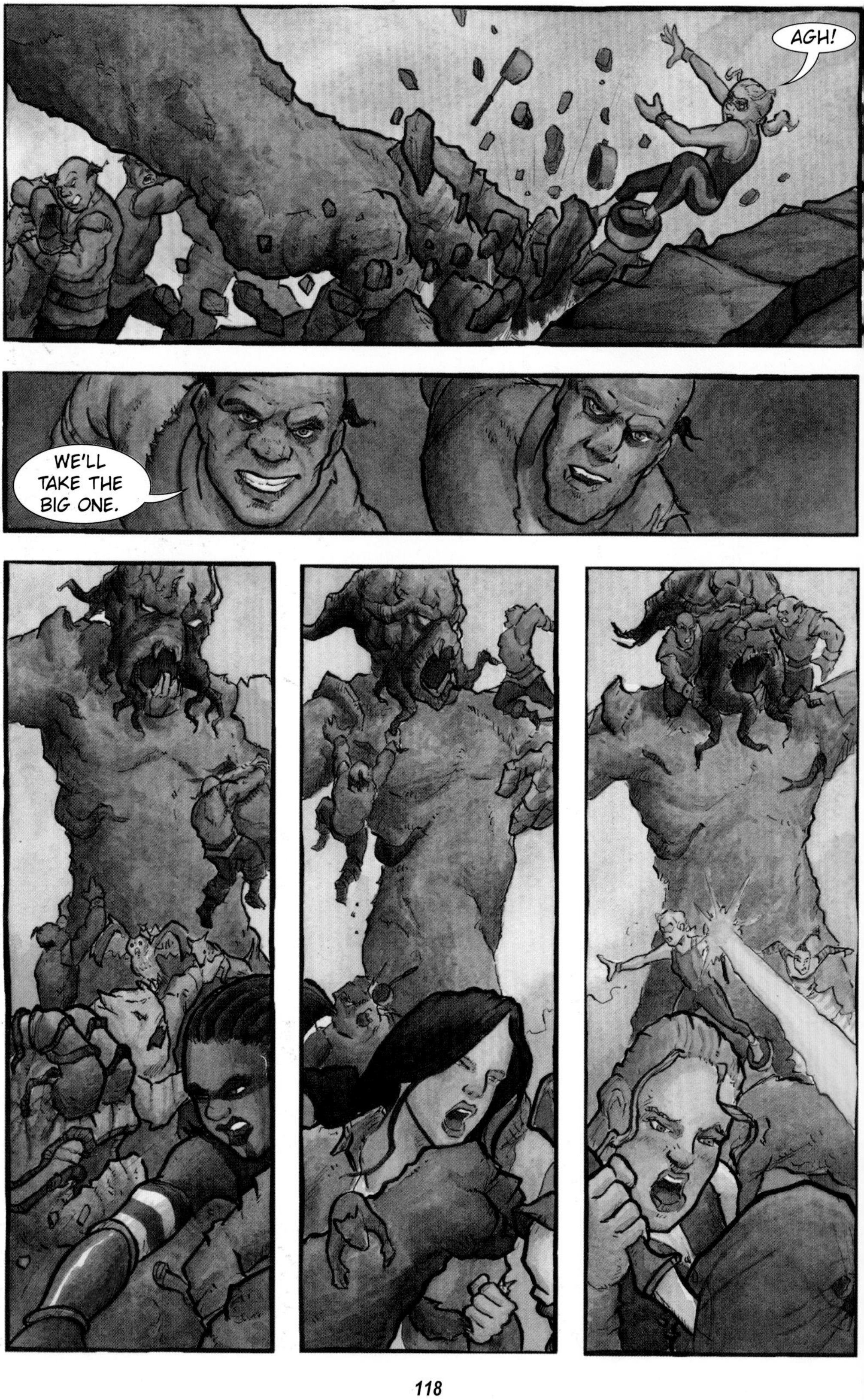
AGH!
WE'LL TAKE THE BIG ONE.

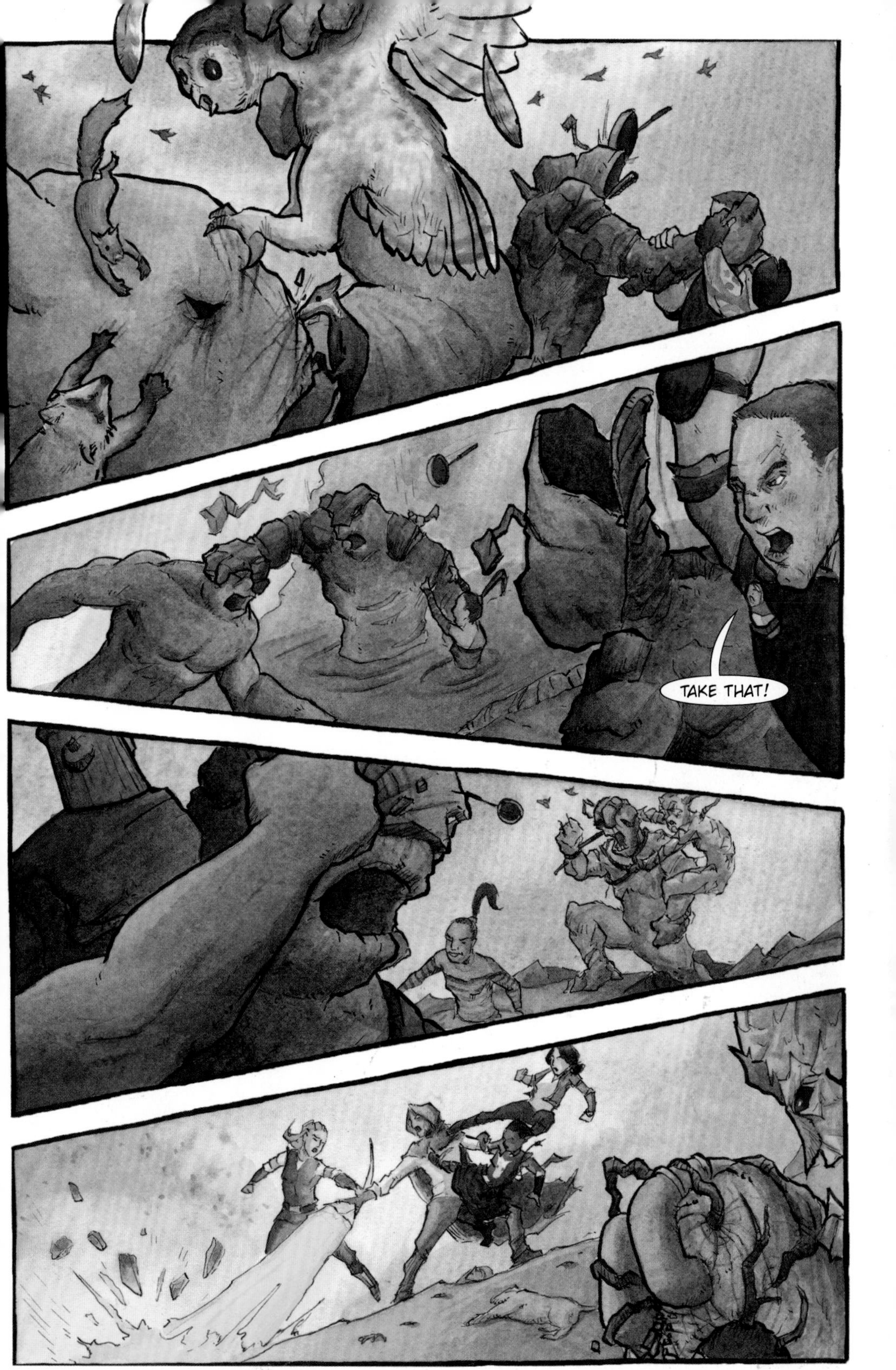
TAKE THAT!

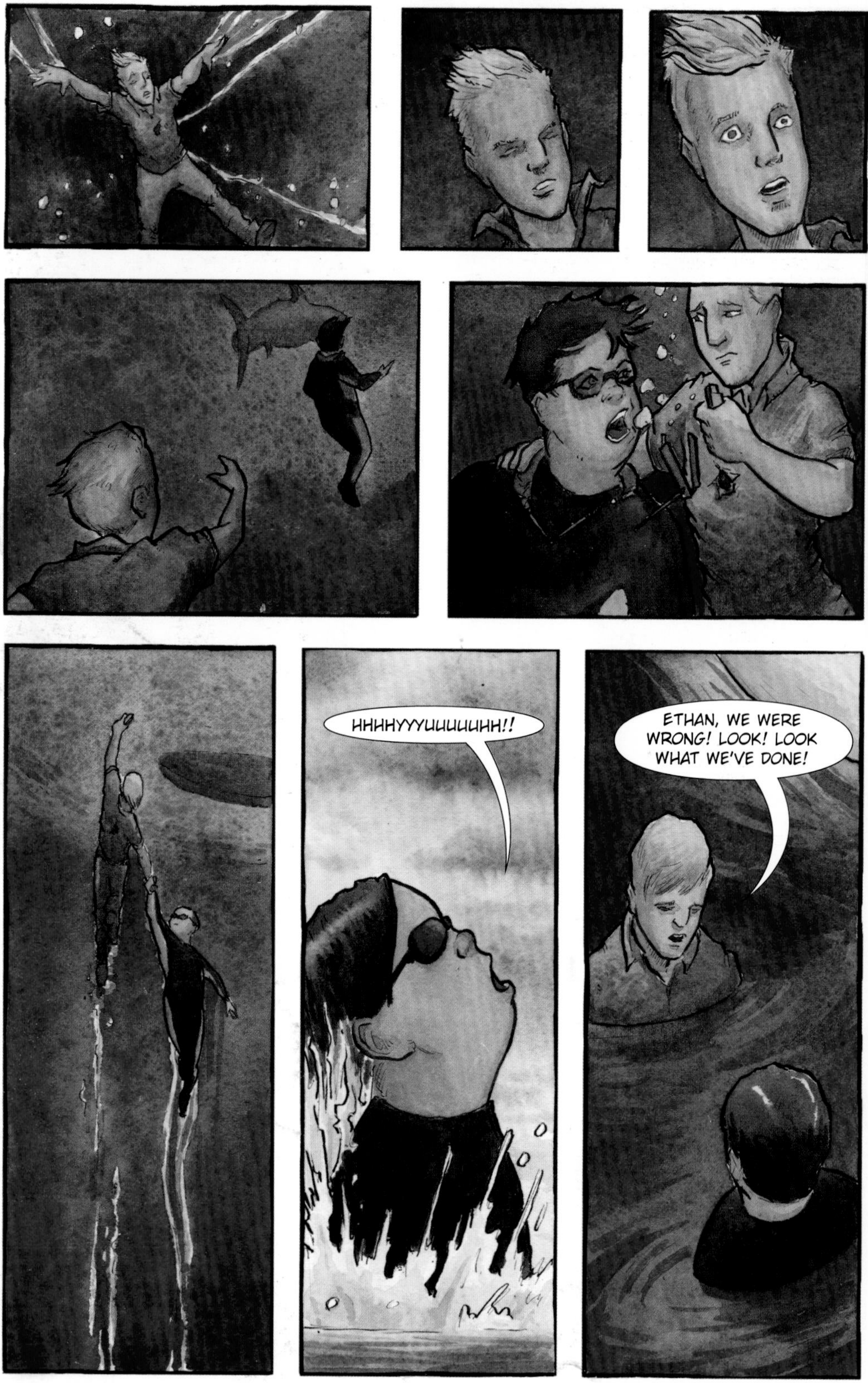
HHHHYYYUUUUUUHH!!
ETHAN, WE WERE WRONG! LOOK! LOOK WHAT WE'VE DONE!

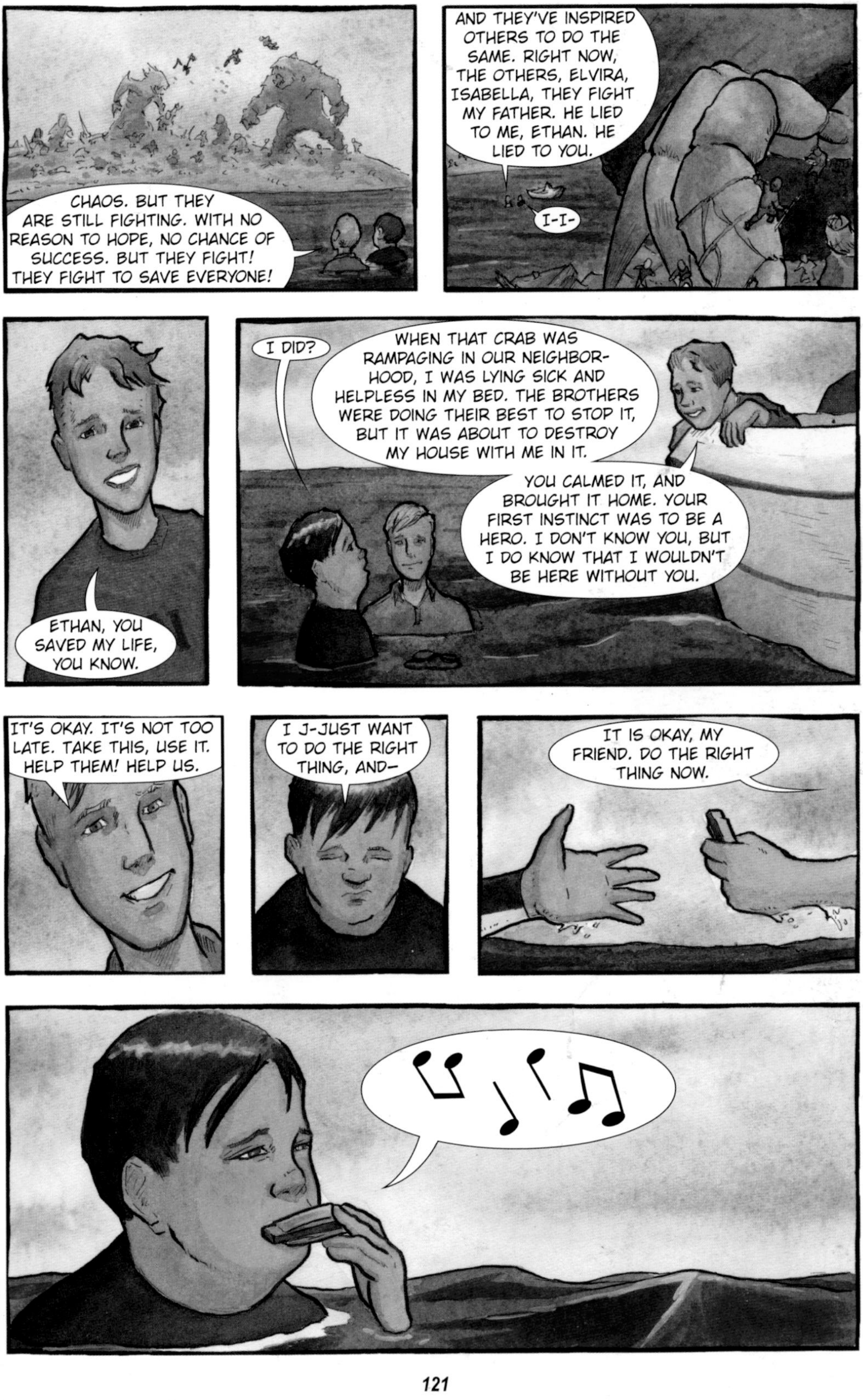
CHAOS. BUT THEY ARE STILL FIGHTING. WITH NO REASON TO HOPE, NO CHANCE OF SUCCESS. BUT THEY FIGHT! THEY FIGHT TO SAVE EVERYONE!
AND THEY'VE INSPIRED OTHERS TO DO THE SAME. RIGHT NOW, THE OTHERS, ELVIRA, ISABELLA, THEY FIGHT MY FATHER. HE LIED TO ME, ETHAN. HE LIED TO YOU.
I-I-
ETHAN, YOU SAVED MY LIFE, YOU KNOW.
I DID?
WHEN THAT CRAB WAS RAMPAGING IN OUR NEIGHBOR-HOOD, I WAS LYING SICK AND HELPLESS IN MY BED. THE BROTHERS WERE DOING THEIR BEST TO STOP IT, BUT IT WAS ABOUT TO DESTROY MY HOUSE WITH ME IN IT.
YOU CALMED IT, AND BROUGHT IT HOME. YOUR FIRST INSTINCT WAS TO BE A HERO. I DON'T KNOW YOU, BUT I DO KNOW THAT I WOULDN'T BE HERE WITHOUT YOU.
IT'S OKAY. IT'S NOT TOO LATE. TAKE THIS, USE IT. HELP THEM! HELP US.
I J-JUST WANT TO DO THE RIGHT THING, AND—
IT IS OKAY, MY FRIEND. DO THE RIGHT THING NOW.

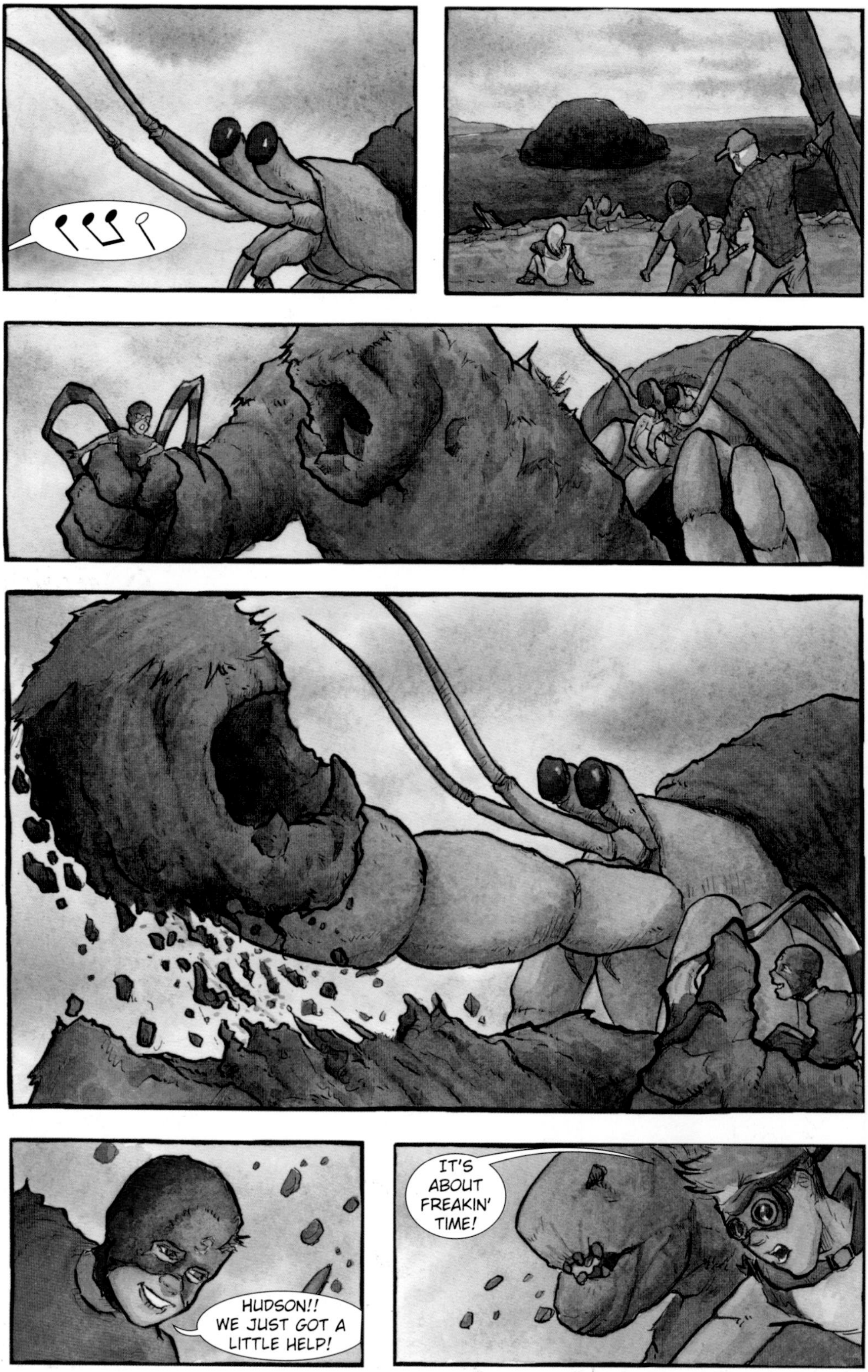
HUDSON!! WE JUST GOT A LITTLE HELP!
IT'S ABOUT FREAKIN' TIME!

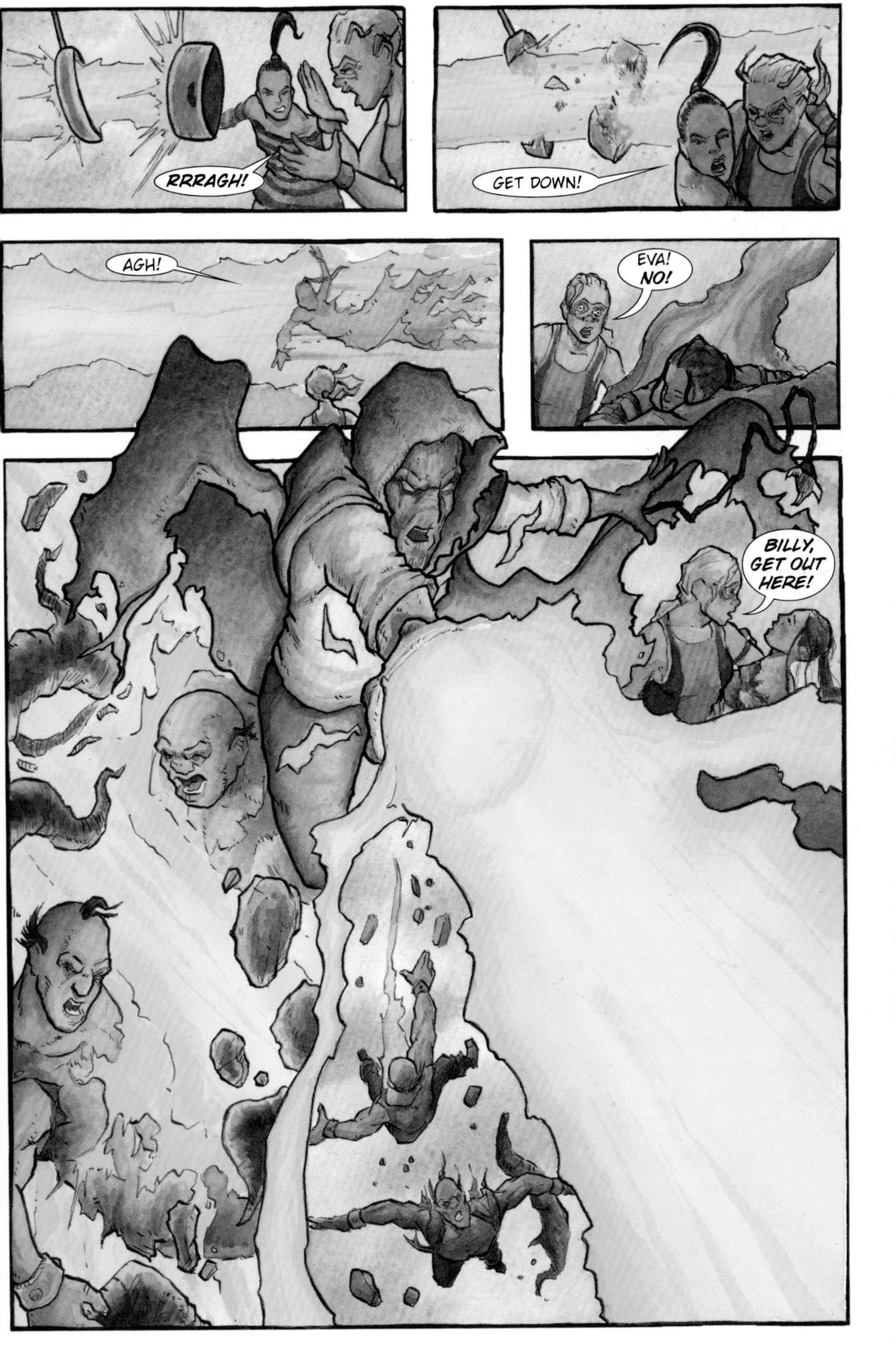
RRRAGH!
GET DOWN!
AGH!
EVA! NO!
BILLY, GET OUT HERE!

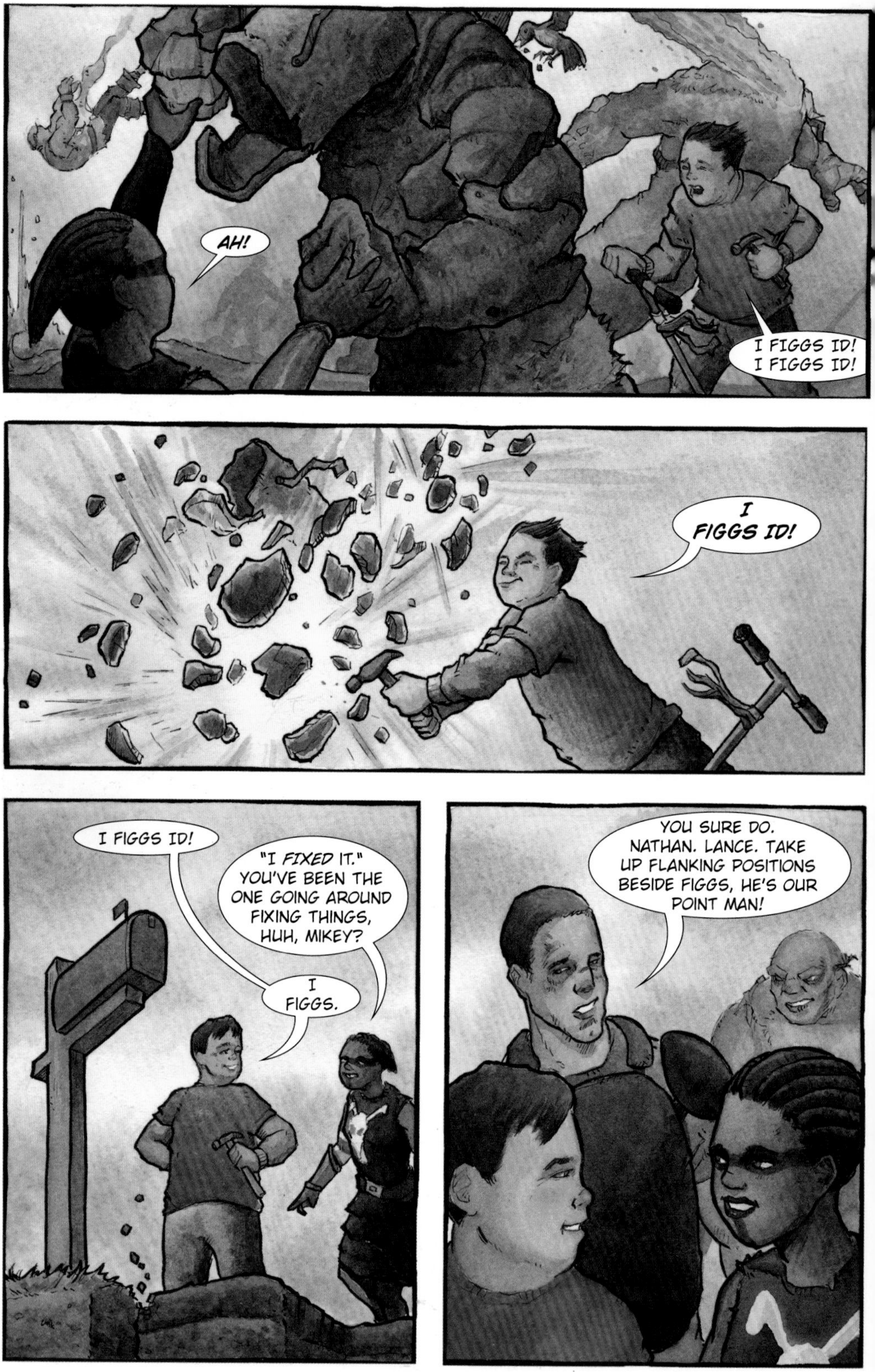
AH!
I FIGGS ID! I FIGGS ID!
I FIGGS ID!
I FIGGS ID!
"I FIXED IT." YOU'VE BEEN THE ONE GOING AROUND FIXING THINGS, HUH, MIKEY?
I FIGGS.
YOU SURE DO. NATHAN. LANCE. TAKE UP FLANKING POSITIONS BESIDE FIGGS, HE'S OUR POINT MAN!

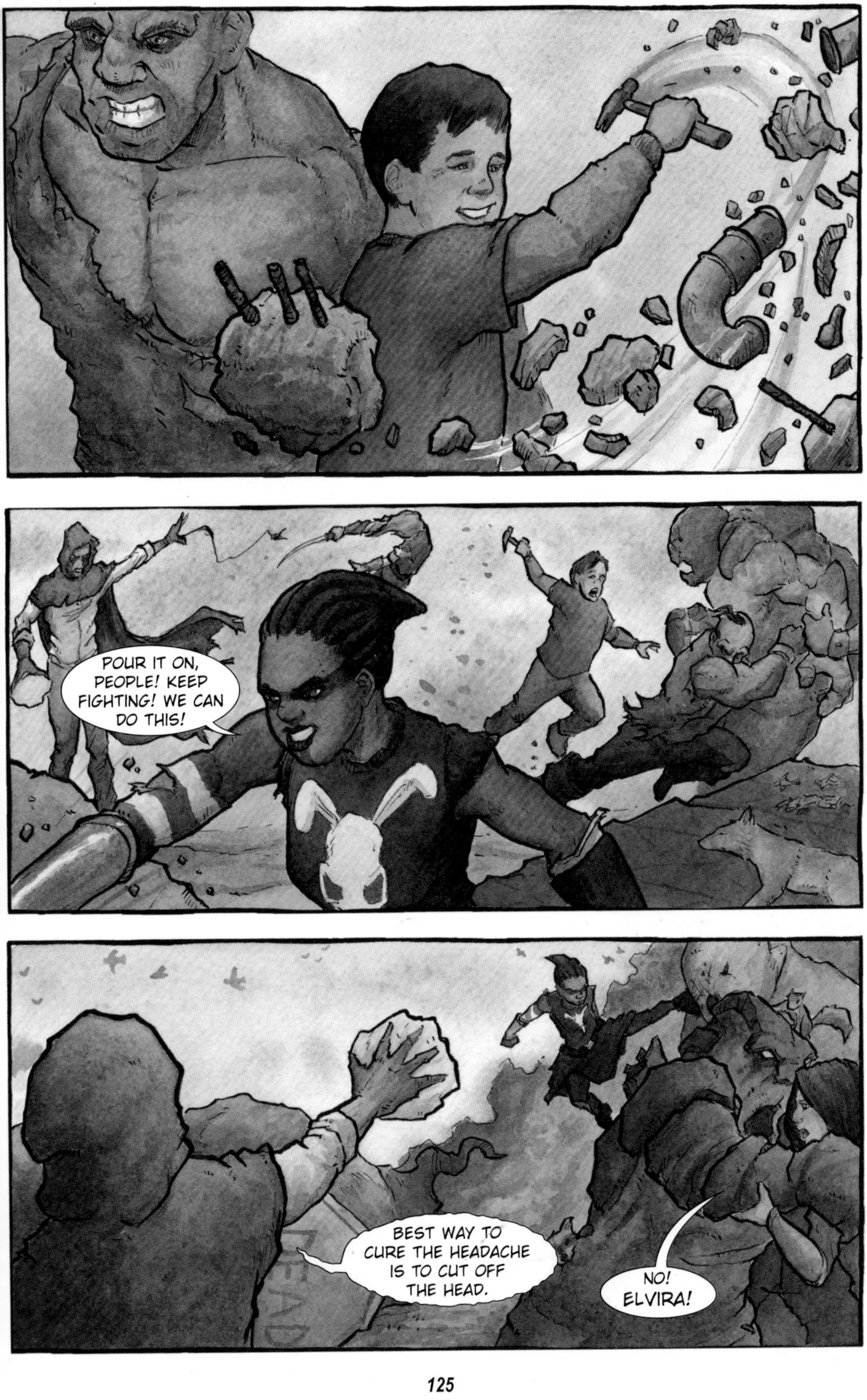
POUR IT ON, PEOPLE! KEEP FIGHTING! WE CAN DO THIS!
BEST WAY TO CURE THE HEADACHE IS TO CUT OFF THE HEAD.
NO! ELVIRA!

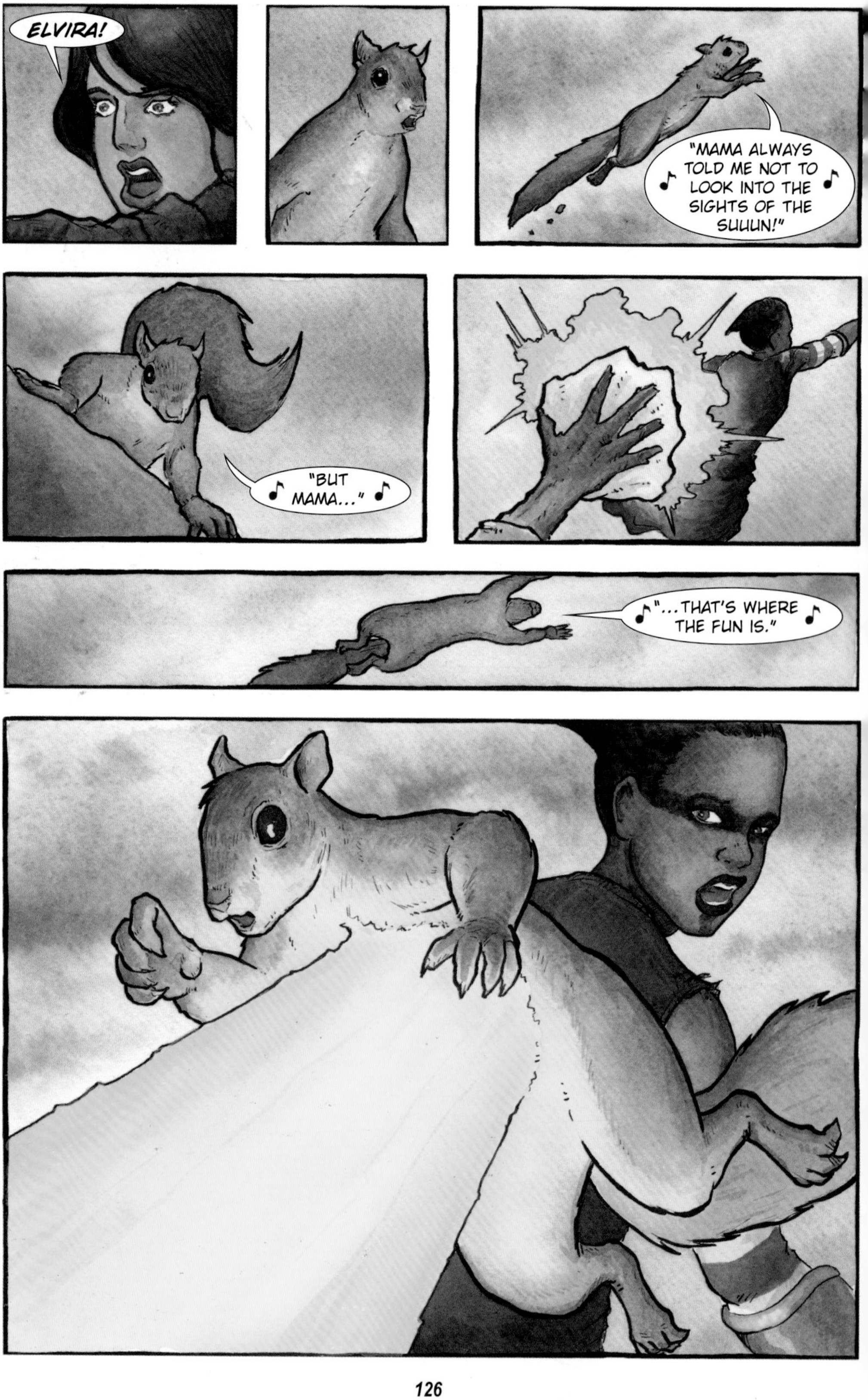
ELVIRA!
"MAMA ALWAYS TOLD ME NOT TO LOOK INTO THE SIGHTS OF THE SUUUN!"
"BUT MAMA..."
"...THAT'S WHERE THE FUN IS."

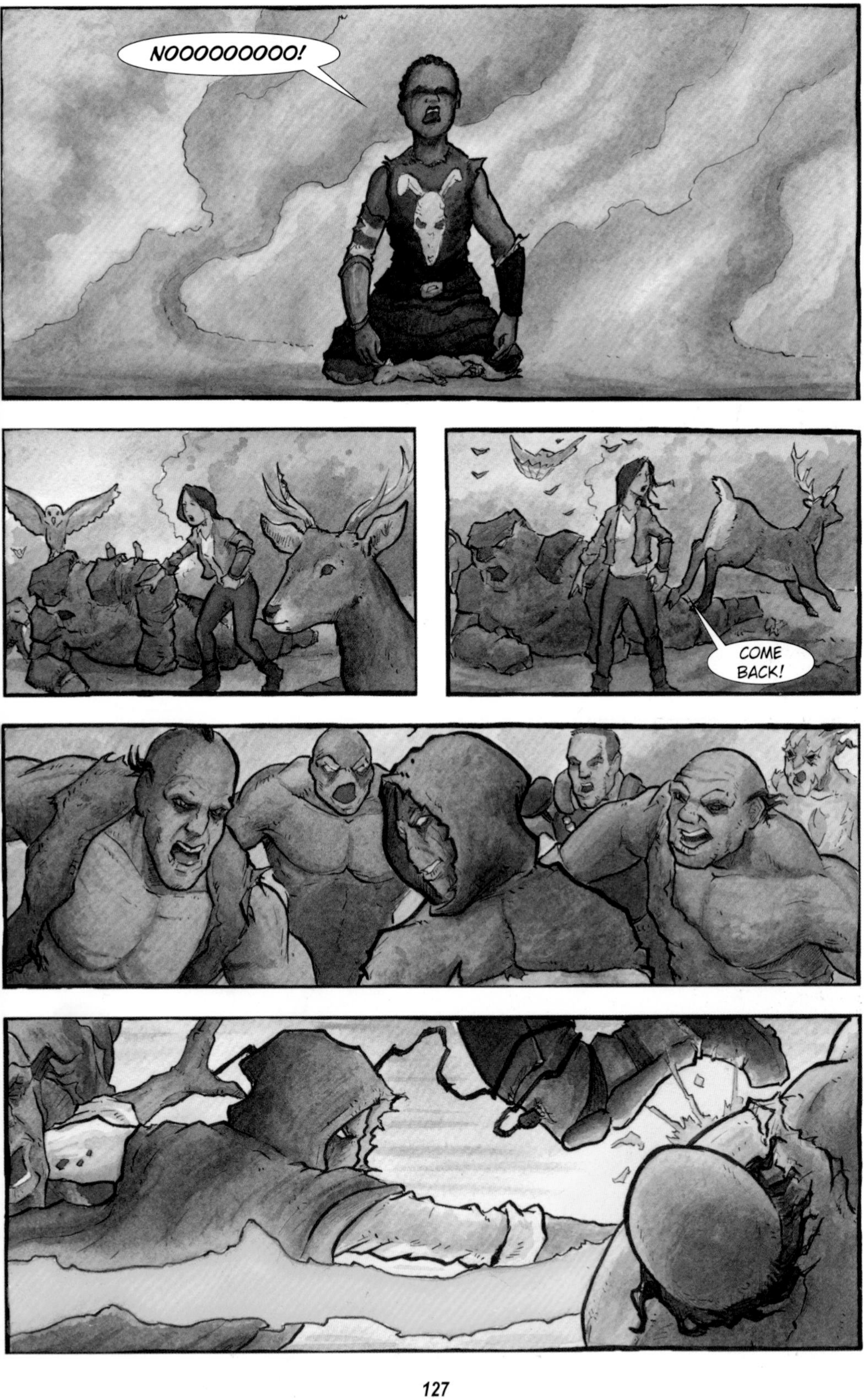
NOOOOOOOOO!
COME BACK!

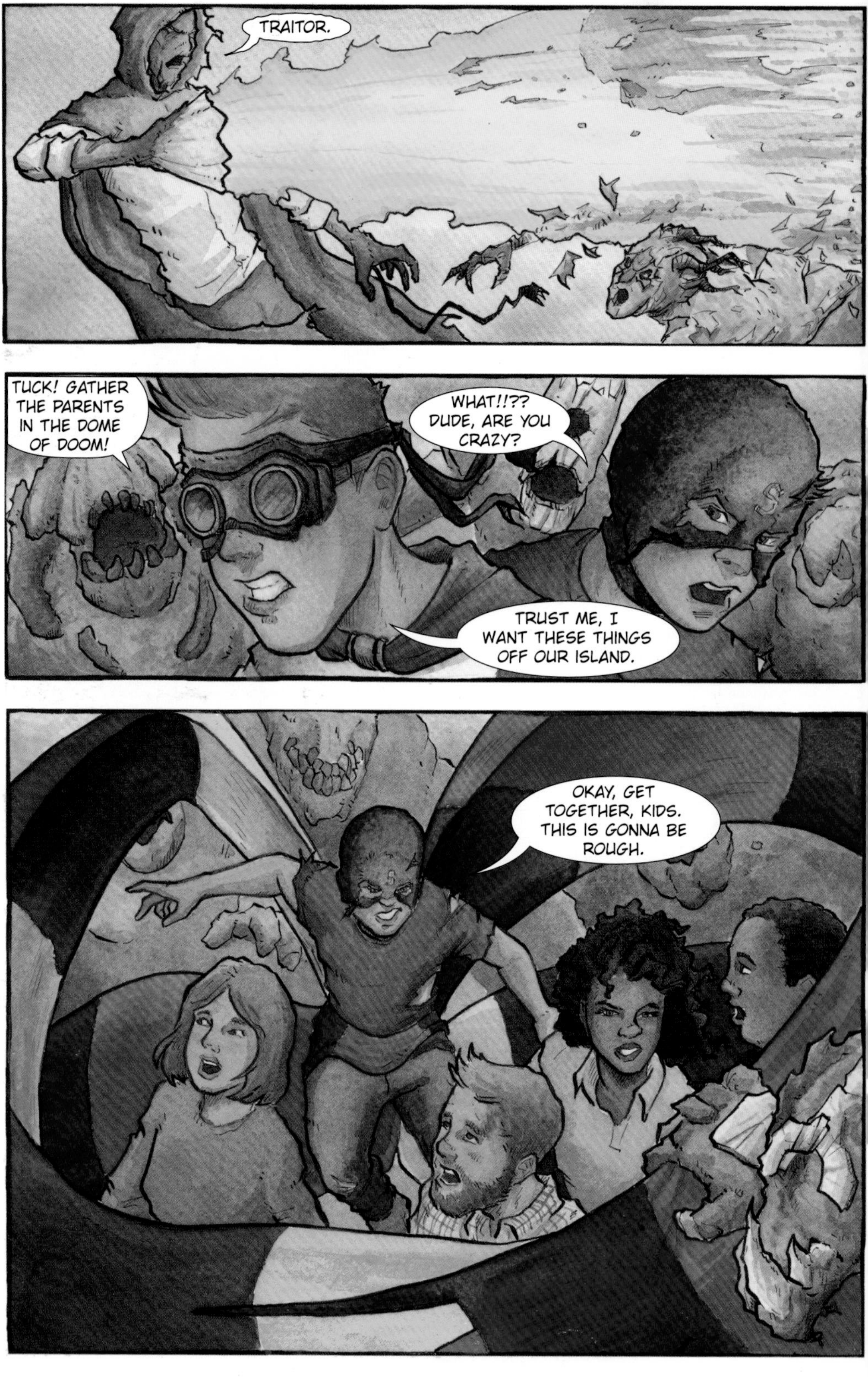
TRAITOR.
TUCK! GATHER THE PARENTS IN THE DOME OF DOOM!
WHAT!!?? DUDE, ARE YOU CRAZY?
TRUST ME, I WANT THESE THINGS OFF OUR ISLAND.
OKAY, GET TOGETHER, KIDS. THIS IS GONNA BE ROUGH.

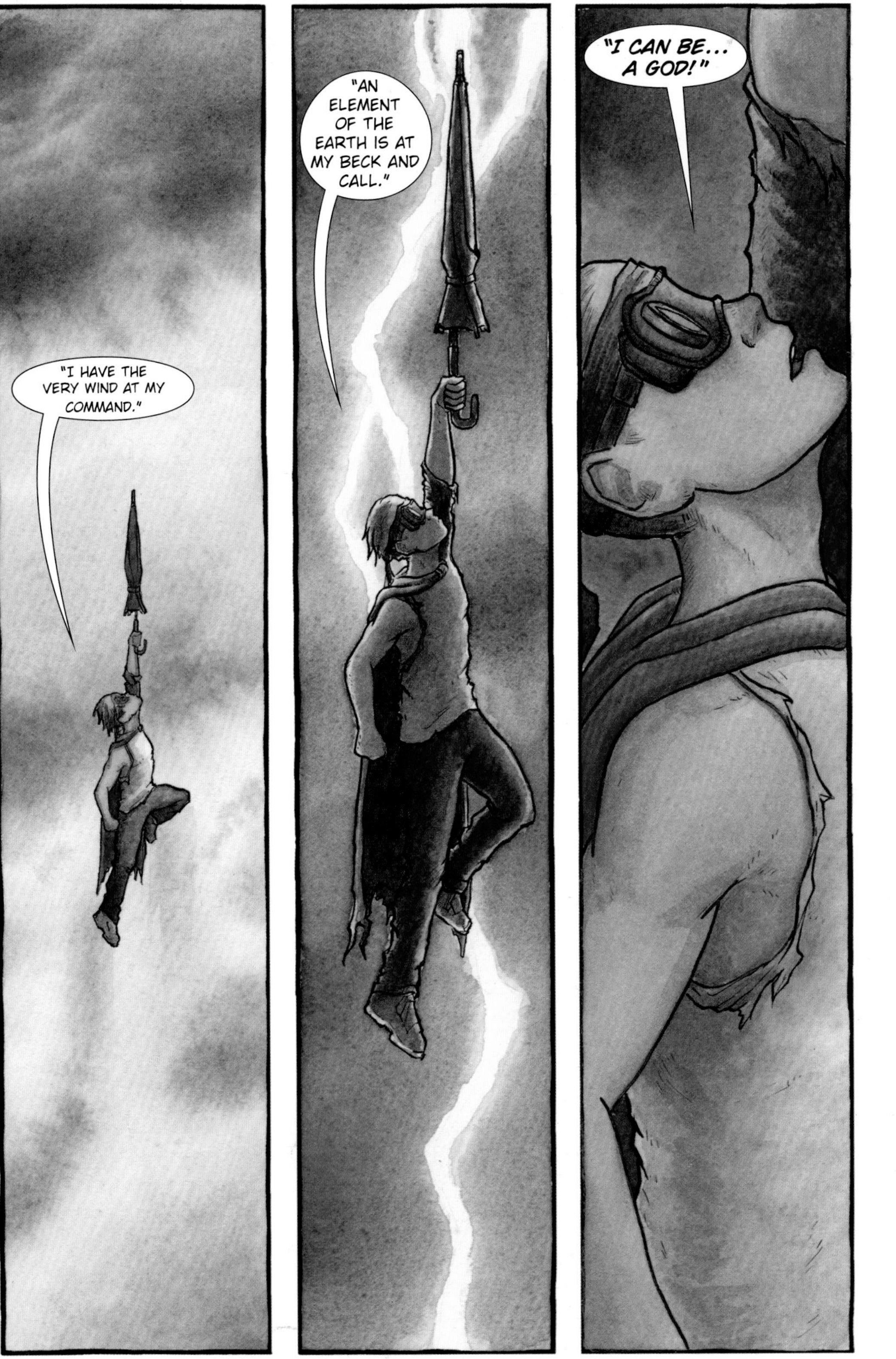
"I HAVE THE VERY WIND AT MY COMMAND."
"AN ELEMENT OF THE EARTH IS AT MY BECK AND CALL."
"I CAN BE... A GOD!"

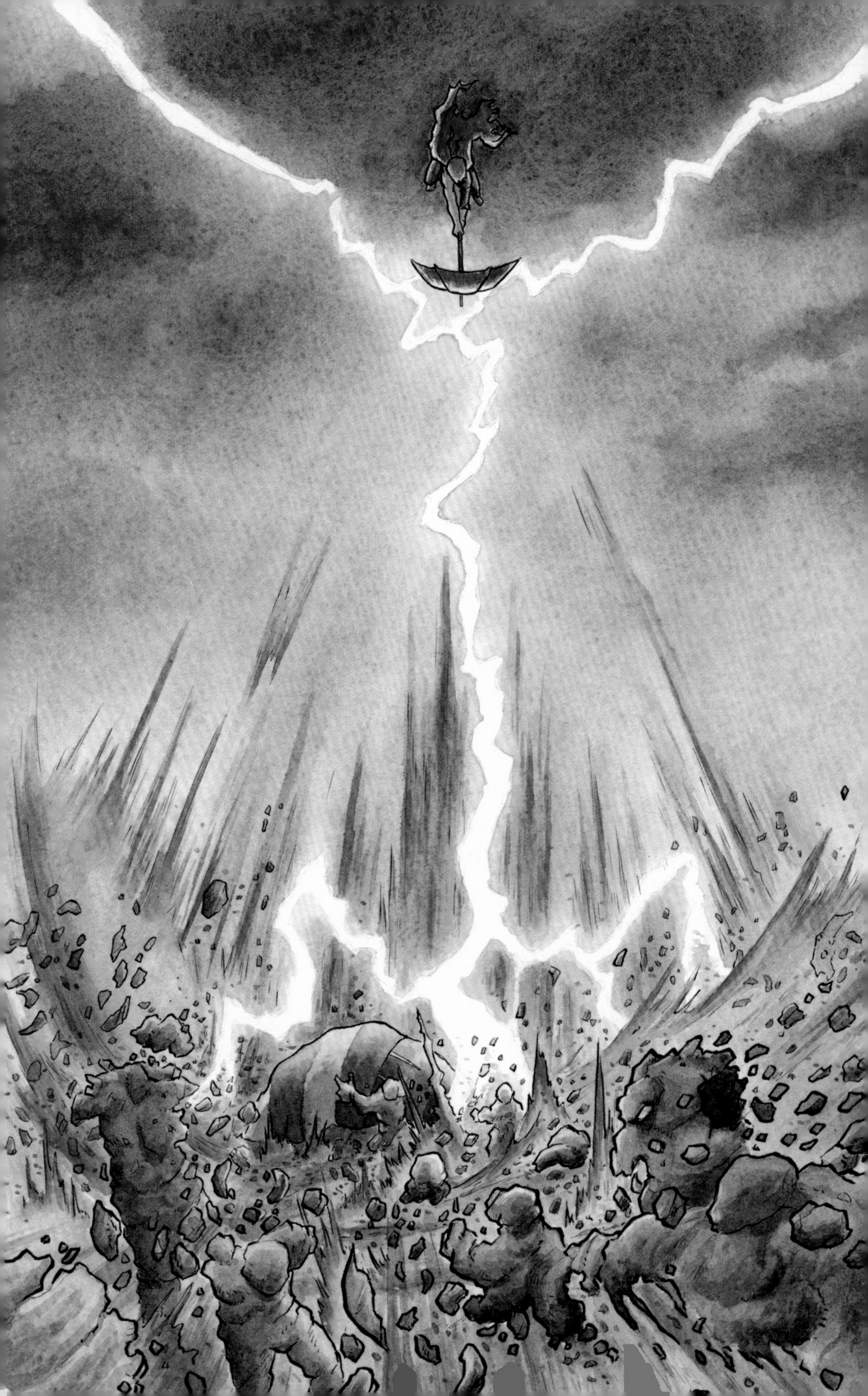

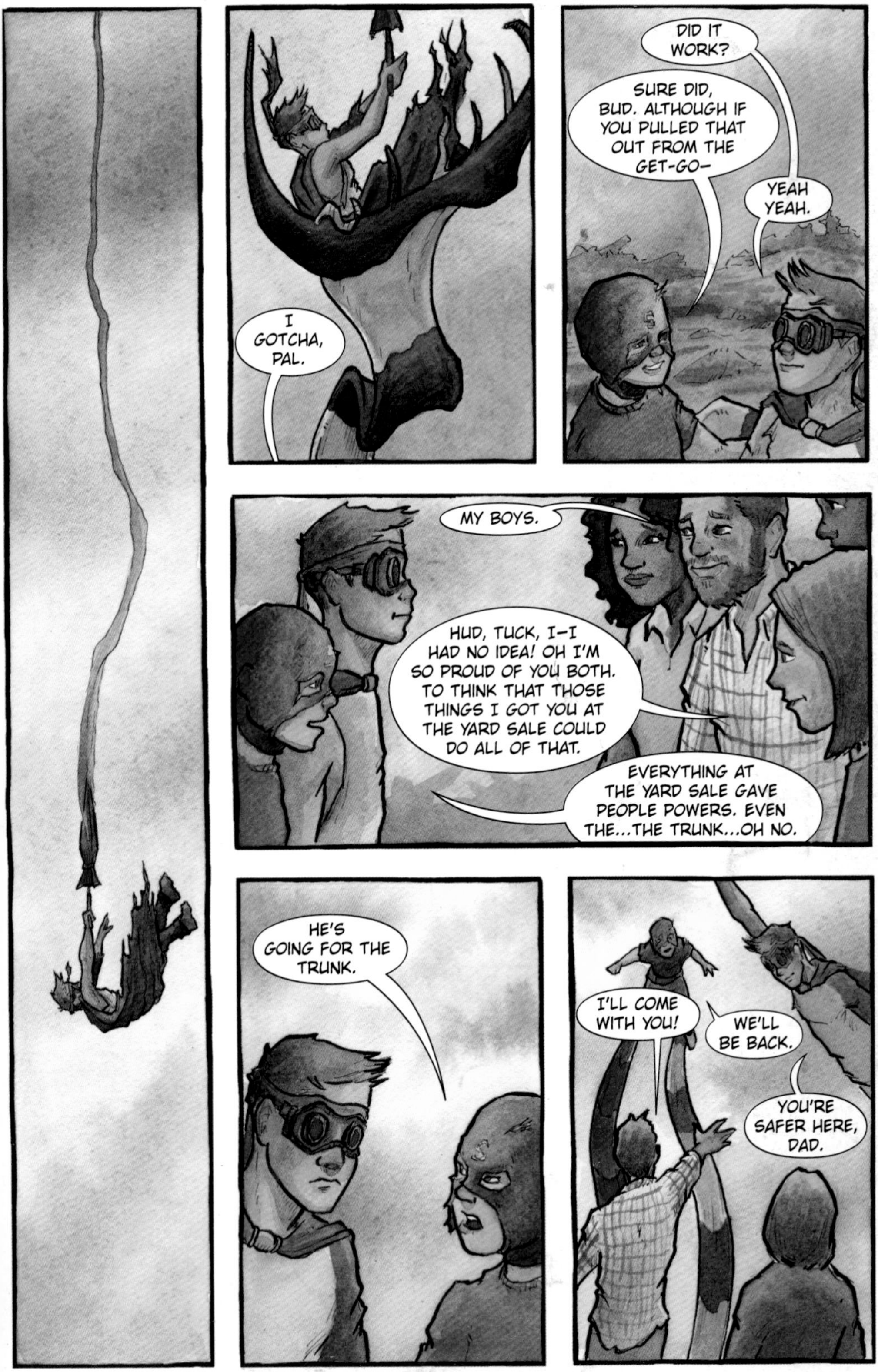
I GOTCHA, PAL.
DID IT WORK?
SURE DID, BUD. ALTHOUGH IF YOU PULLED THAT OUT FROM THE GET-GO—
YEAH YEAH.
MY BOYS.
HUD, TUCK, I—I HAD NO IDEA! OH I'M SO PROUD OF YOU BOTH. TO THINK THAT THOSE THINGS I GOT YOU AT THE YARD SALE COULD DO ALL OF THAT.
EVERYTHING AT THE YARD SALE GAVE PEOPLE POWERS. EVEN THE...THE TRUNK...OH NO.
HE'S GOING FOR THE TRUNK.
I'LL COME WITH YOU!
WE'LL BE BACK.
YOU'RE SAFER HERE, DAD.

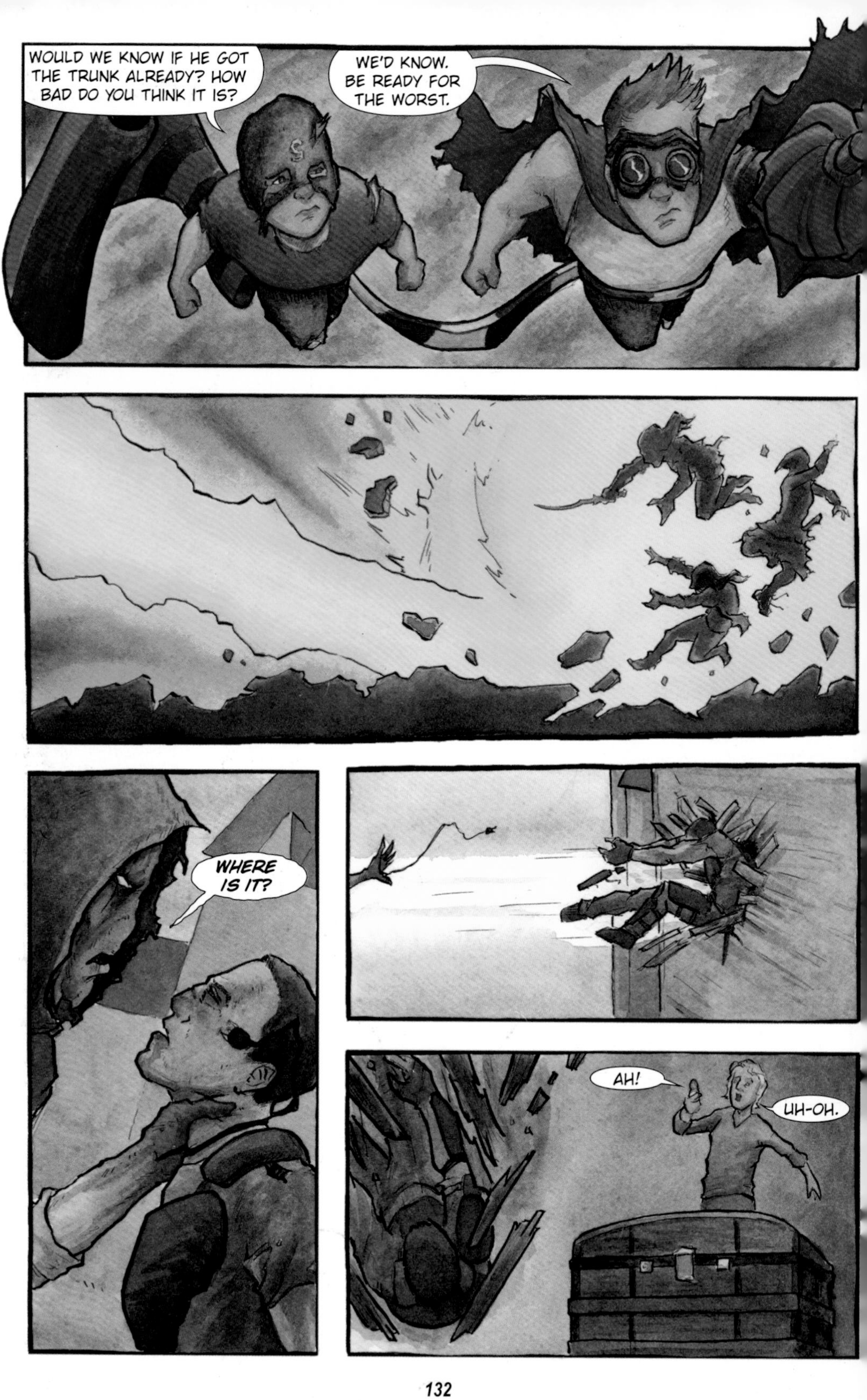
WOULD WE KNOW IF HE GOT THE TRUNK ALREADY? HOW BAD DO YOU THINK IT IS?
WE'D KNOW. BE READY FOR THE WORST.
WHERE IS IT?
AH!
UH-OH.

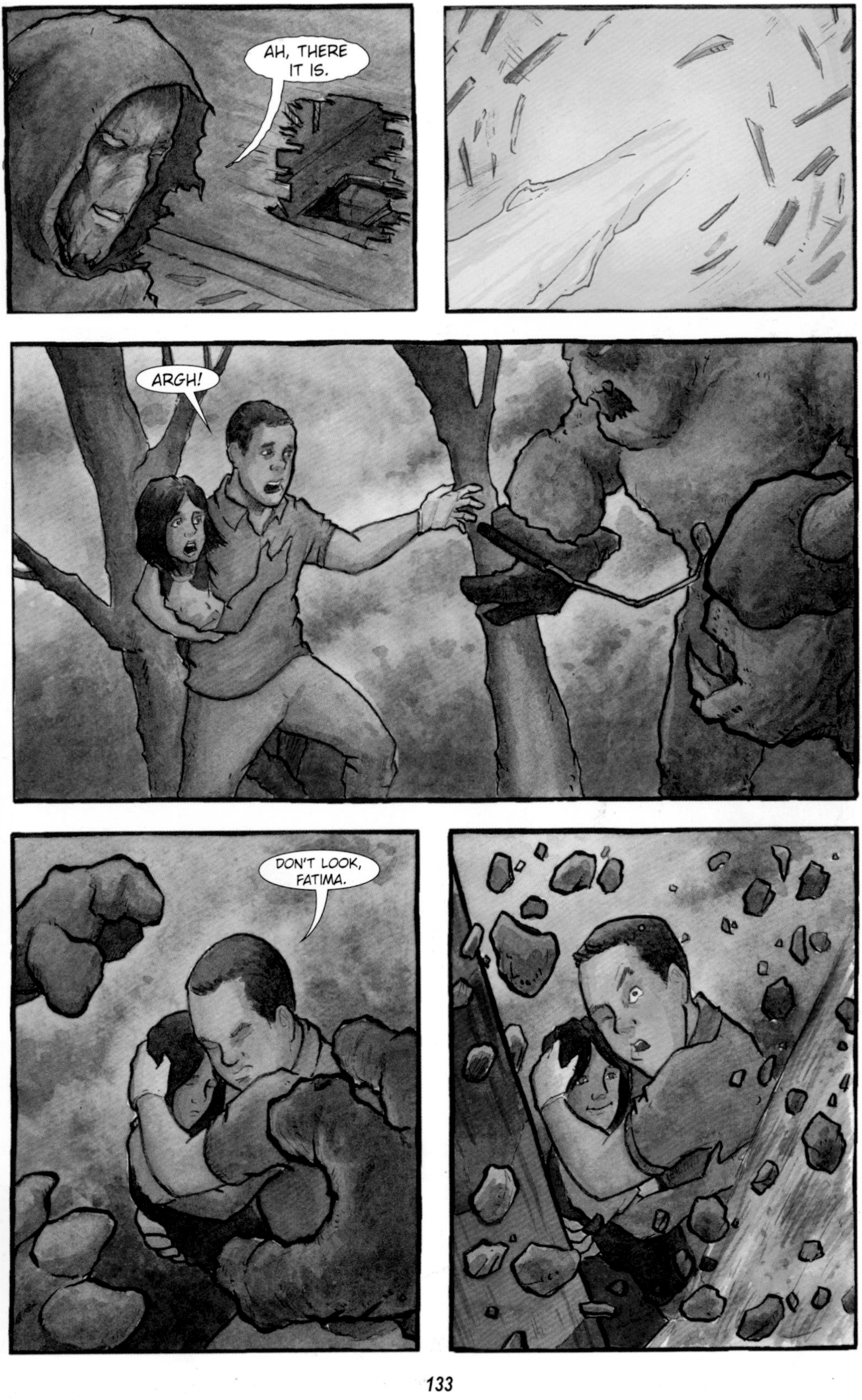
AH, THERE IT IS.
ARGH!
DON'T LOOK, FATIMA.

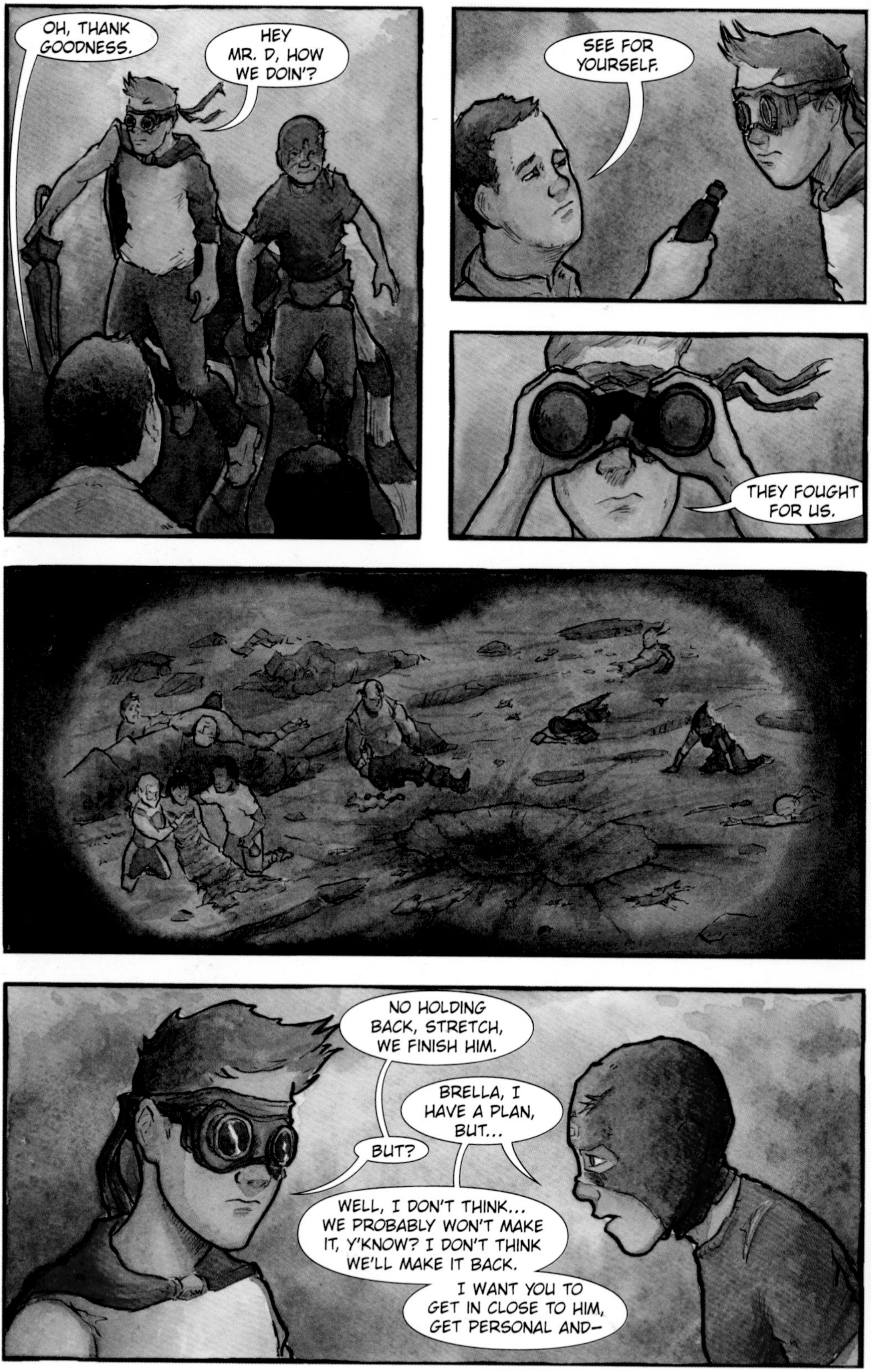
OH, THANK GOODNESS.
HEY MR. D, HOW WE DOIN'?
SEE FOR YOURSELF.
THEY FOUGHT FOR US.
NO HOLDING BACK, STRETCH, WE FINISH HIM.
BRELLA, I HAVE A PLAN, BUT...
BUT?
WELL, I DON'T THINK... WE PROBABLY WON'T MAKE IT, Y'KNOW? I DON'T THINK WE'LL MAKE IT BACK.
I WANT YOU TO GET IN CLOSE TO HIM, GET PERSONAL AND—

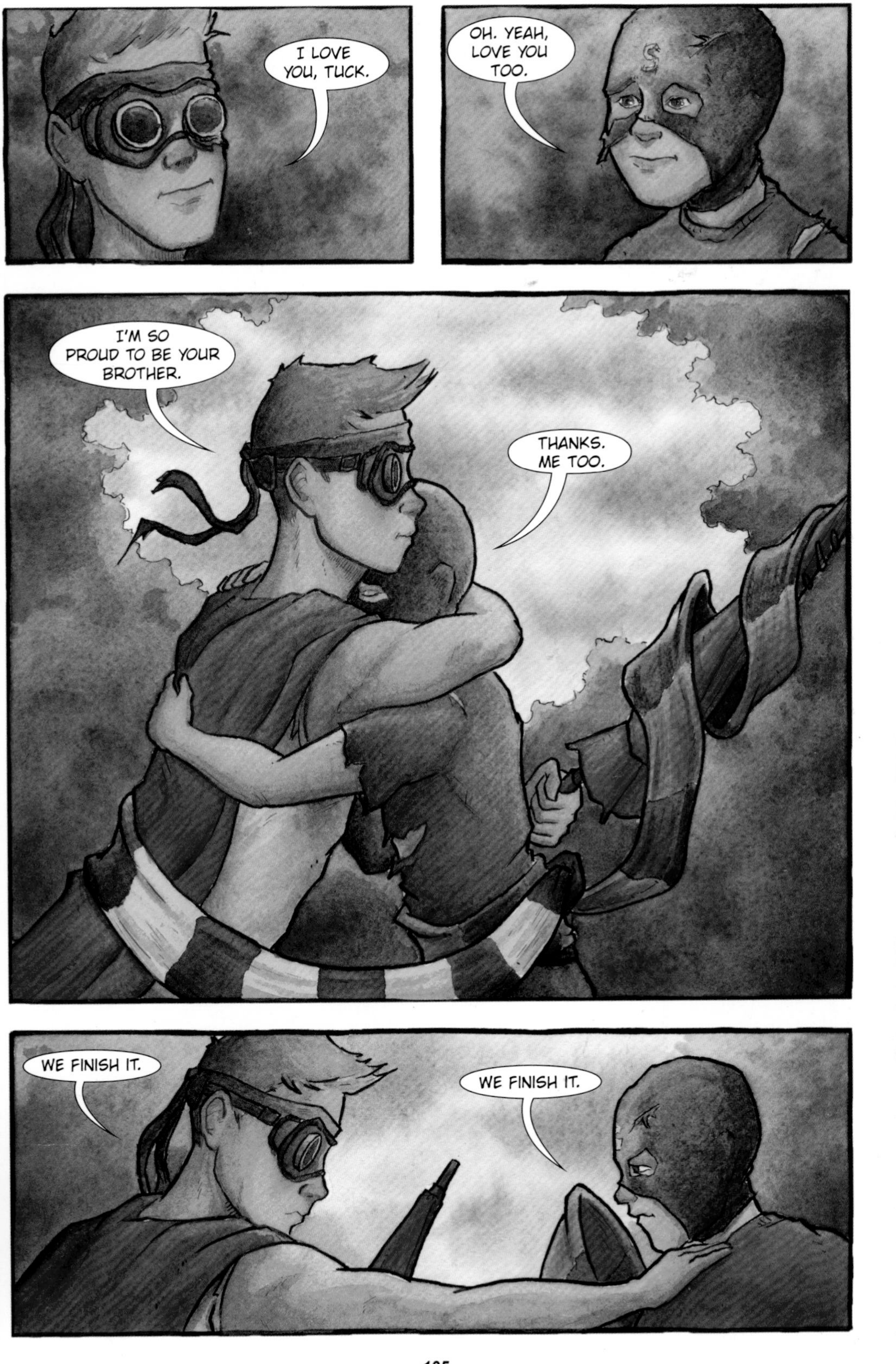

I LOVE YOU, TUCK.
OH. YEAH, LOVE YOU TOO.
I'M SO PROUD TO BE YOUR BROTHER.
THANKS. ME TOO.
WE FINISH IT.
WE FINISH IT.

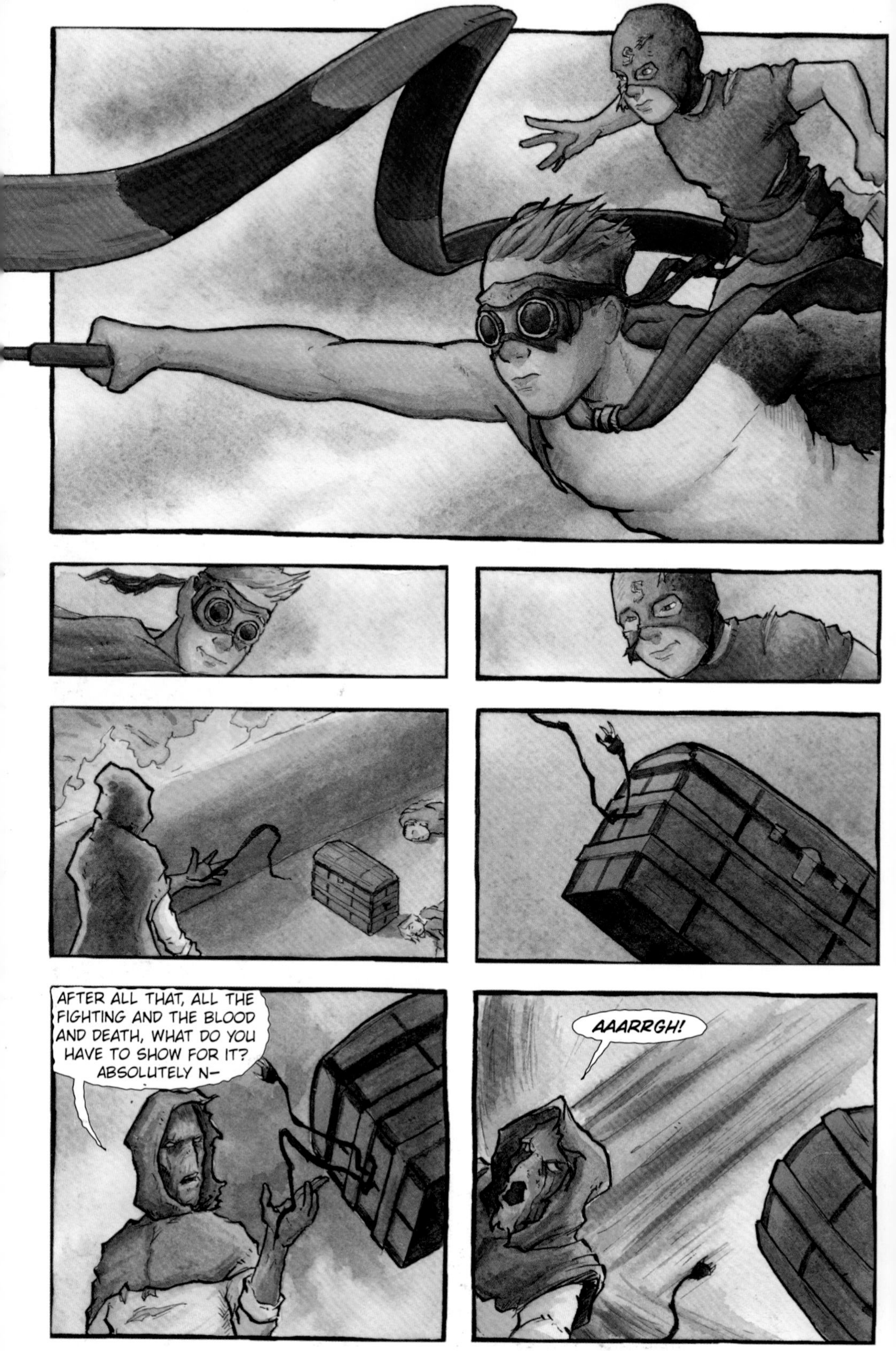
AFTER ALL THAT, ALL THE FIGHTING AND THE BLOOD AND DEATH, WHAT DO YOU HAVE TO SHOW FOR IT? ABSOLUTELY N–
AAARRGH!

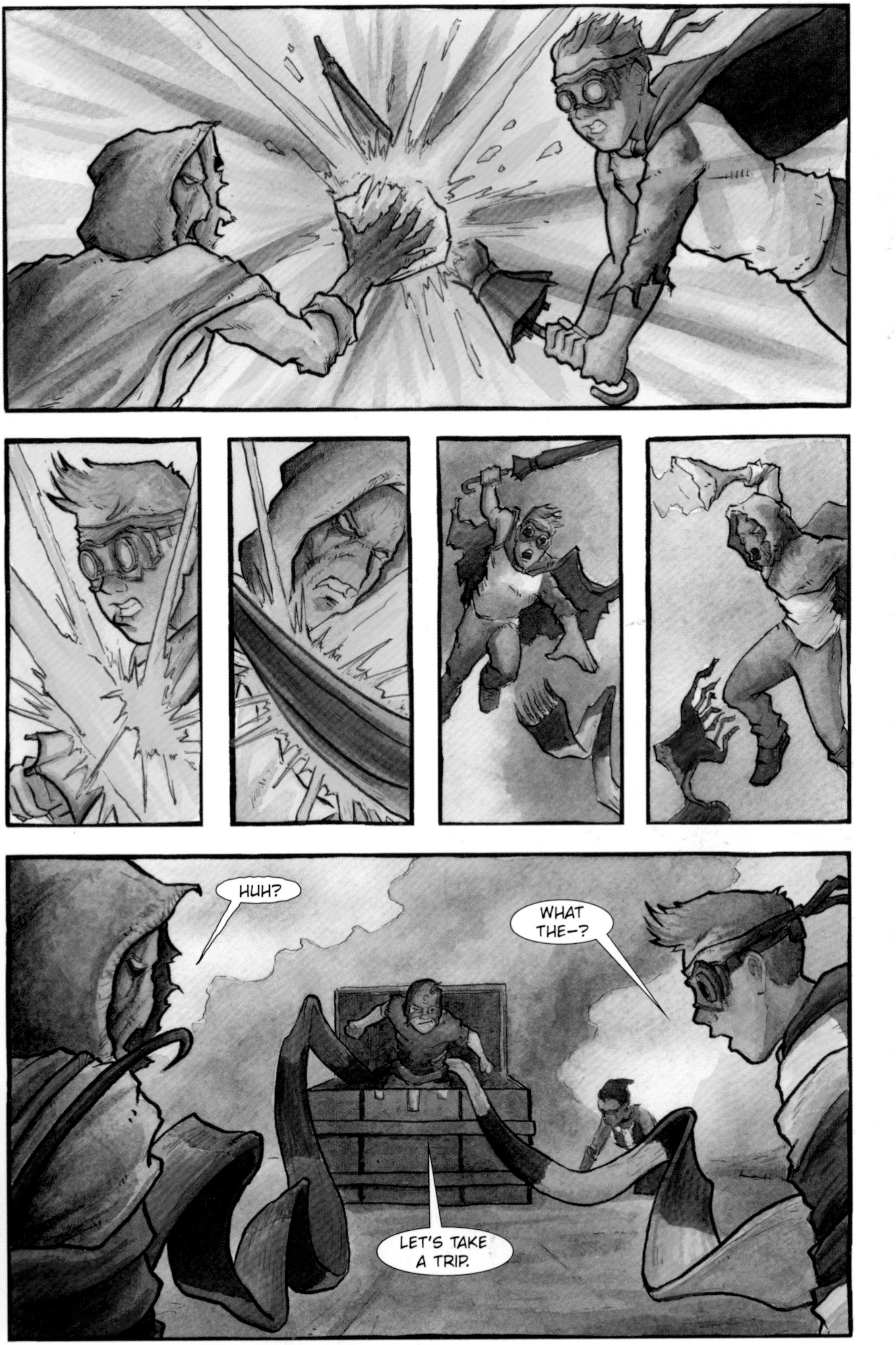
HUH?
WHAT THE–?
LET'S TAKE A TRIP.

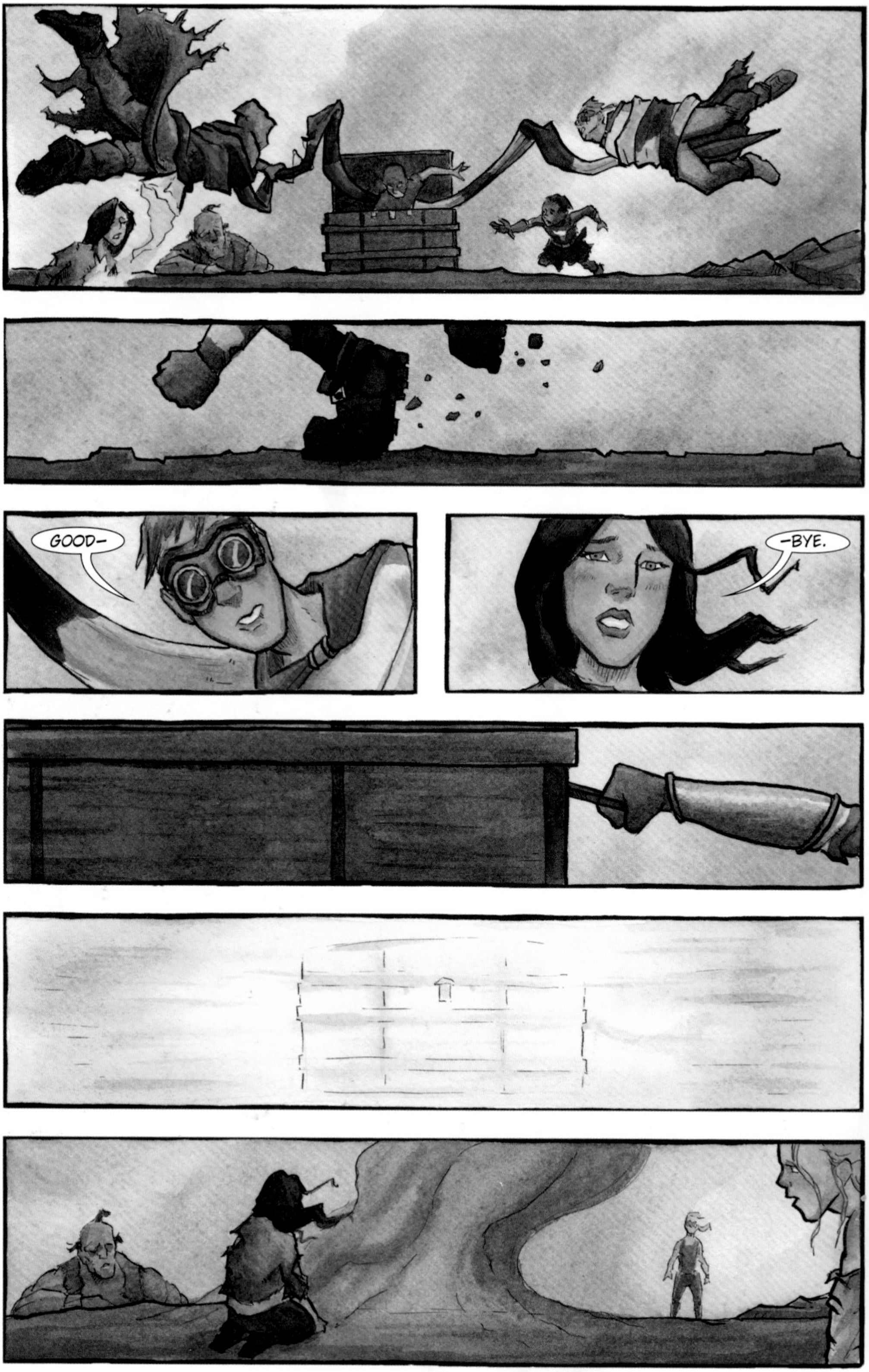
GOOD–
–BYE.

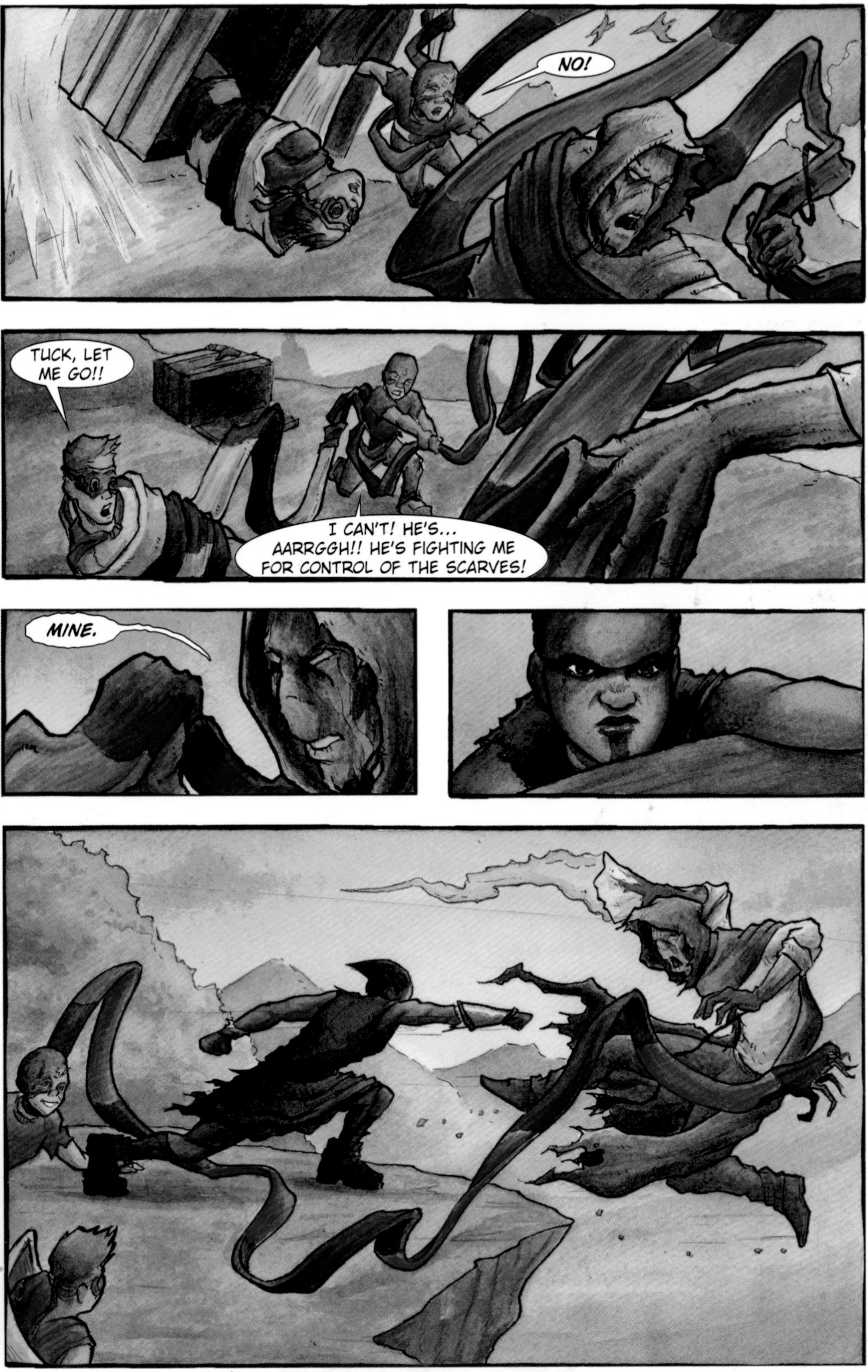
NO!
TUCK, LET ME GO!!
I CAN'T! HE'S... AARRGGH!! HE'S FIGHTING ME FOR CONTROL OF THE SCARVES!
MINE.

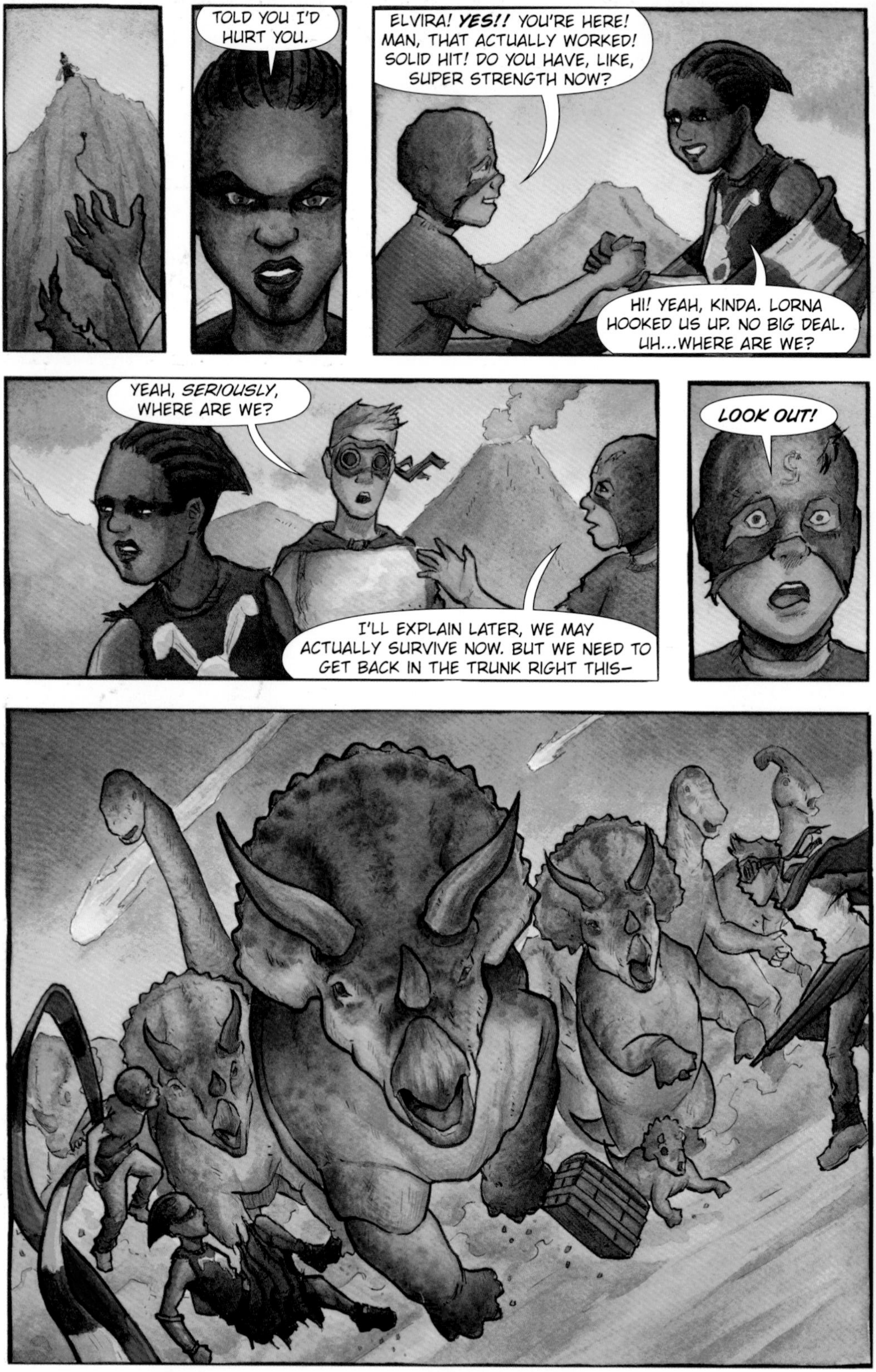
TOLD YOU I'D HURT YOU.
ELVIRA! YES!! YOU'RE HERE! MAN, THAT ACTUALLY WORKED! SOLID HIT! DO YOU HAVE, LIKE, SUPER STRENGTH NOW?
HI! YEAH, KINDA. LORNA HOOKED US UP. NO BIG DEAL. UH...WHERE ARE WE?
YEAH, SERIOUSLY, WHERE ARE WE?
I'LL EXPLAIN LATER, WE MAY ACTUALLY SURVIVE NOW. BUT WE NEED TO GET BACK IN THE TRUNK RIGHT THIS–
LOOK OUT!

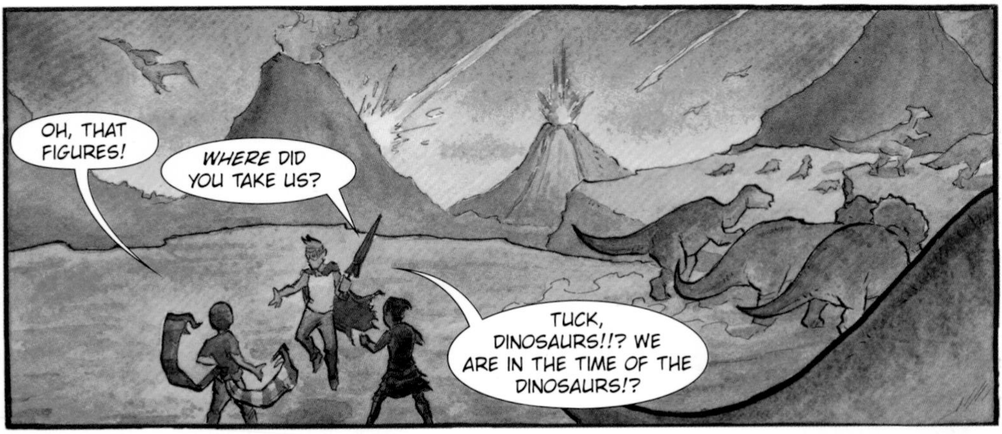
OH, THAT FIGURES!
WHERE DID YOU TAKE US?
TUCK, DINOSAURS!!? WE ARE IN THE TIME OF THE DINOSAURS!?

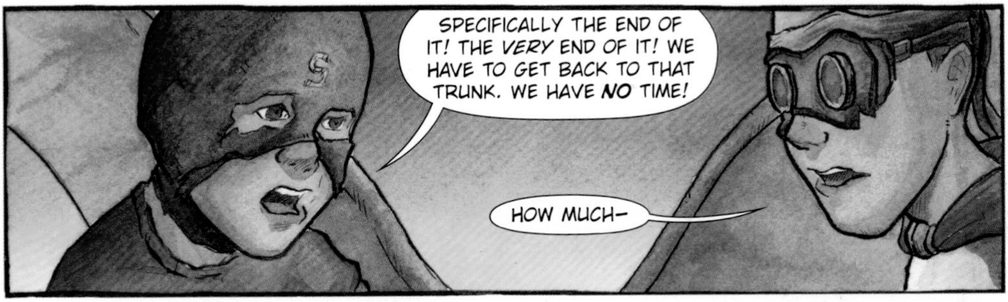
SPECIFICALLY THE END OF IT! THE *VERY* END OF IT! WE HAVE TO GET BACK TO THAT TRUNK. WE HAVE ***NO*** TIME!
HOW MUCH–

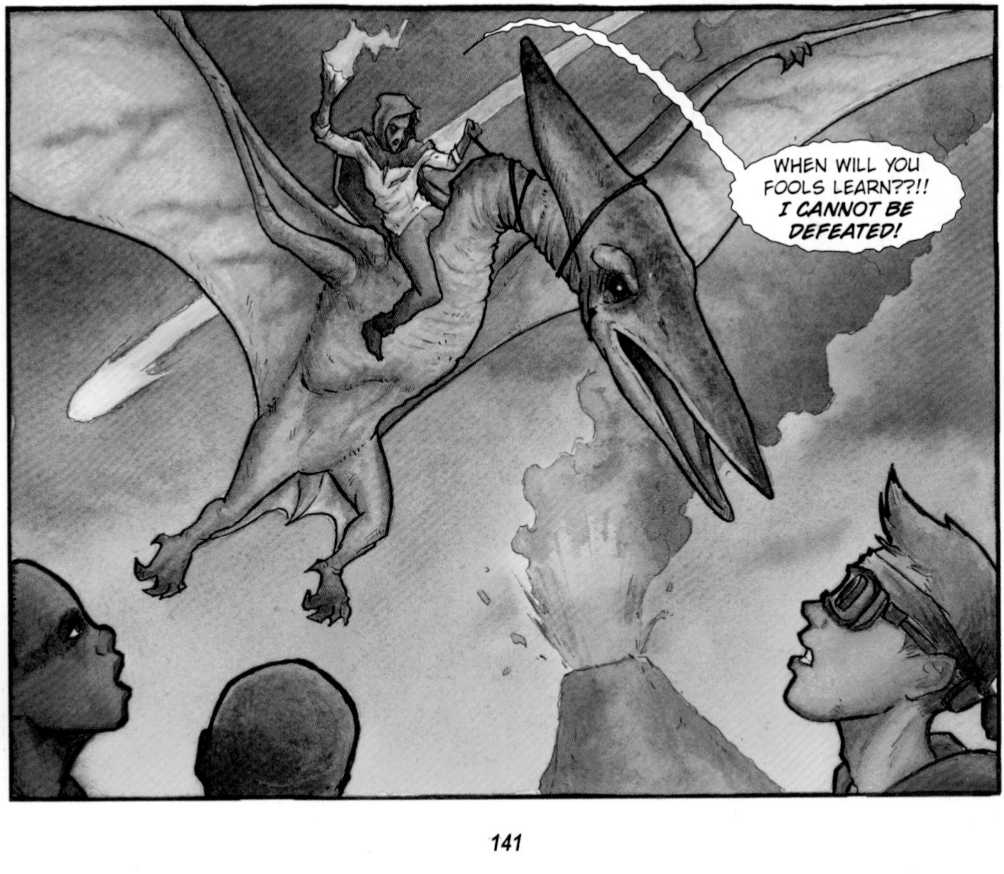
WHEN WILL YOU FOOLS LEARN??!! ***I CANNOT BE DEFEATED!***

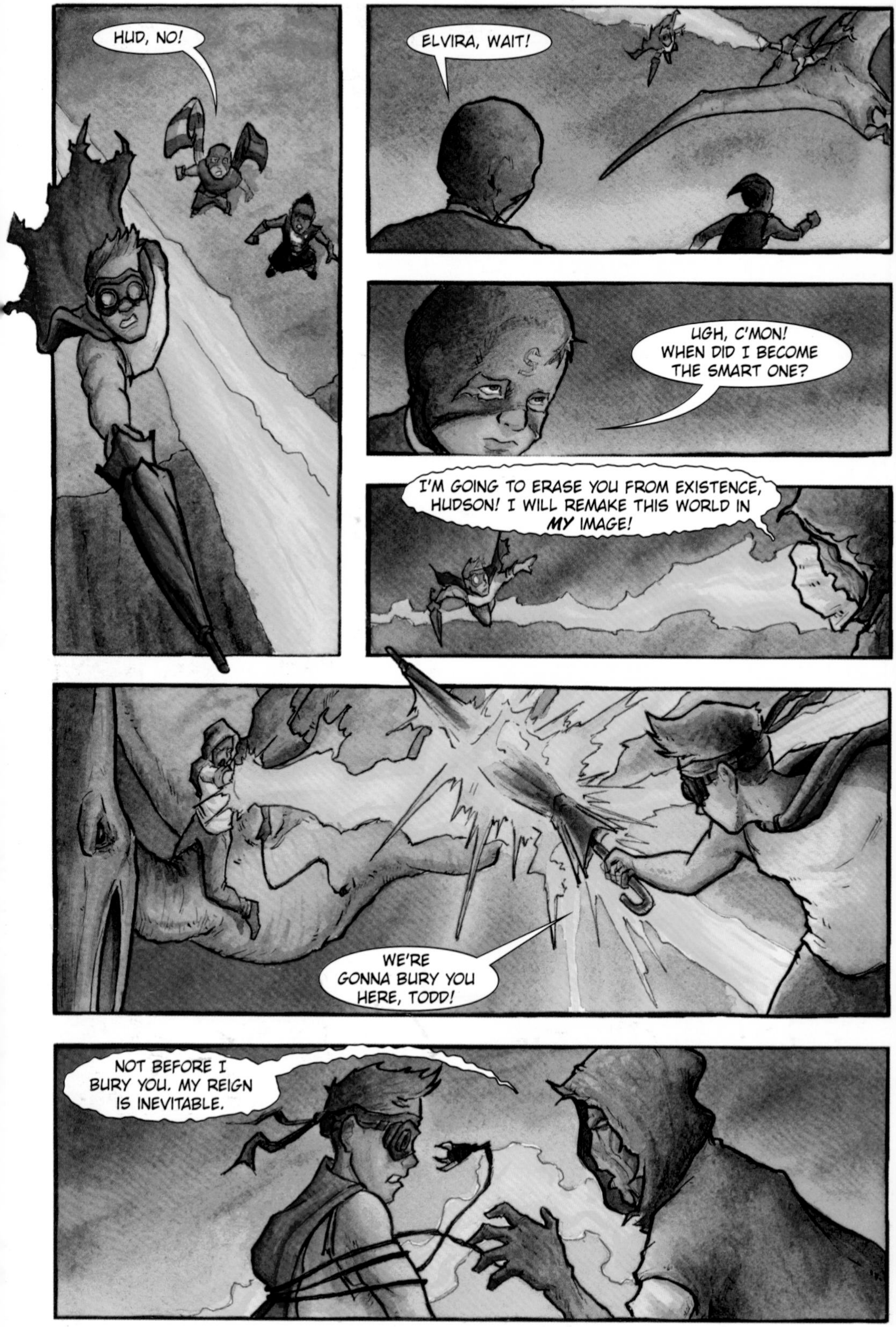
HUD, NO!
ELVIRA, WAIT!
UGH, C'MON! WHEN DID I BECOME THE SMART ONE?
I'M GOING TO ERASE YOU FROM EXISTENCE, HUDSON! I WILL REMAKE THIS WORLD IN *MY* IMAGE!
WE'RE GONNA BURY YOU HERE, TODD!
NOT BEFORE I BURY YOU. MY REIGN IS INEVITABLE.

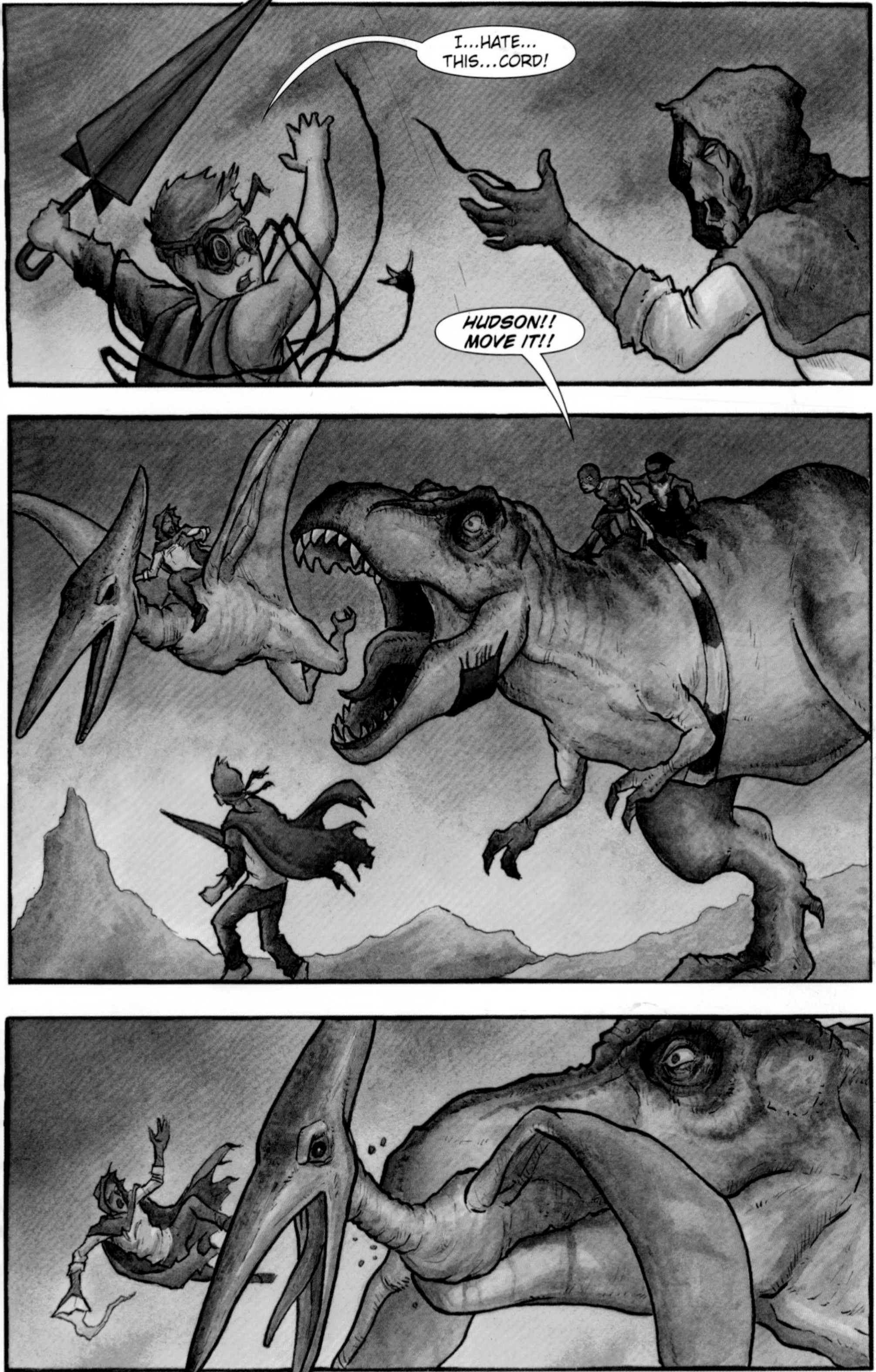
I...HATE...
THIS...CORD!
HUDSON!!
MOVE IT!!

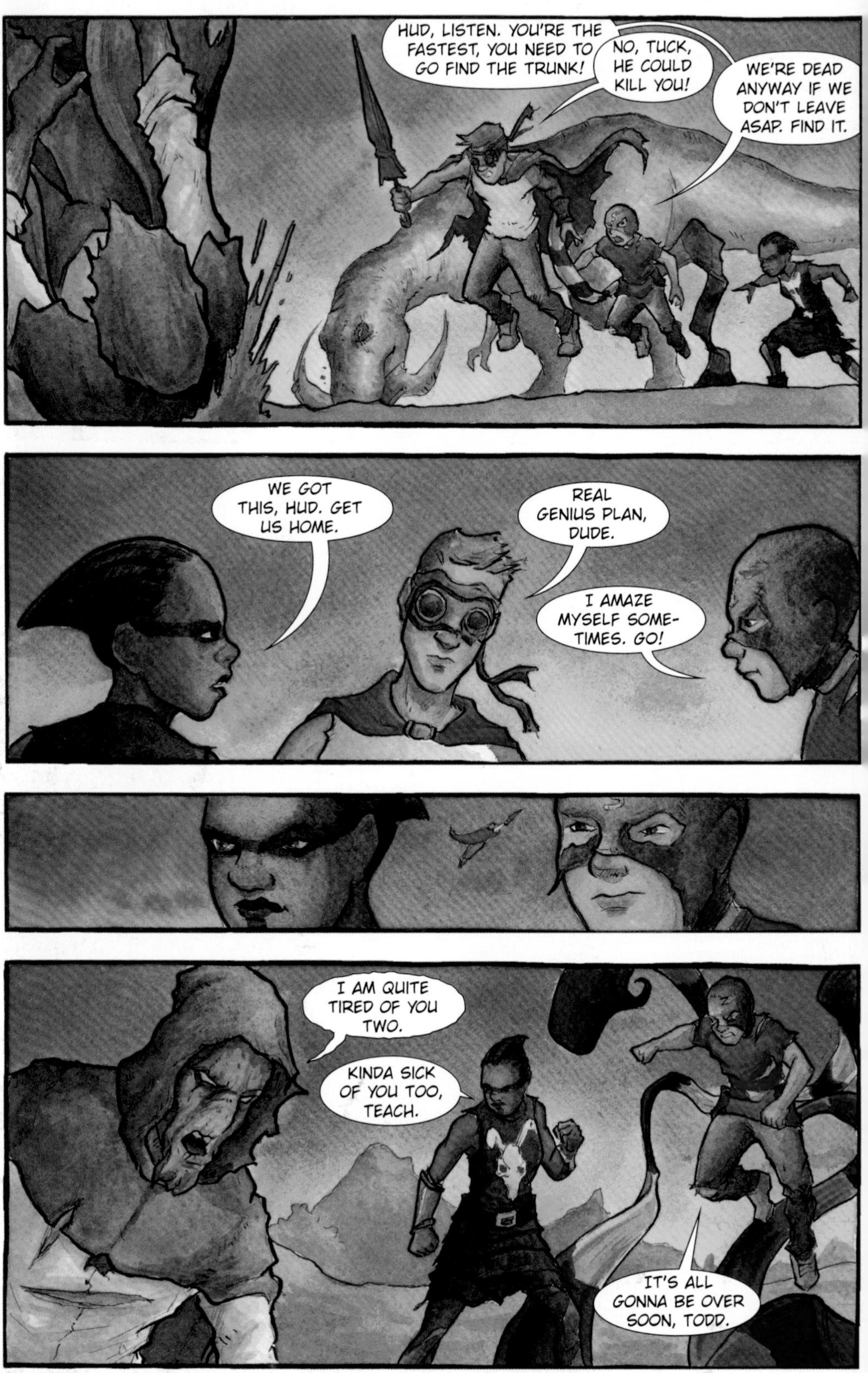
HUD, LISTEN. YOU'RE THE FASTEST, YOU NEED TO GO FIND THE TRUNK!
NO, TUCK, HE COULD KILL YOU!
WE'RE DEAD ANYWAY IF WE DON'T LEAVE ASAP. FIND IT.
WE GOT THIS, HUD. GET US HOME.
REAL GENIUS PLAN, DUDE.
I AMAZE MYSELF SOME-TIMES. GO!
I AM QUITE TIRED OF YOU TWO.
KINDA SICK OF YOU TOO, TEACH.
IT'S ALL GONNA BE OVER SOON, TODD.

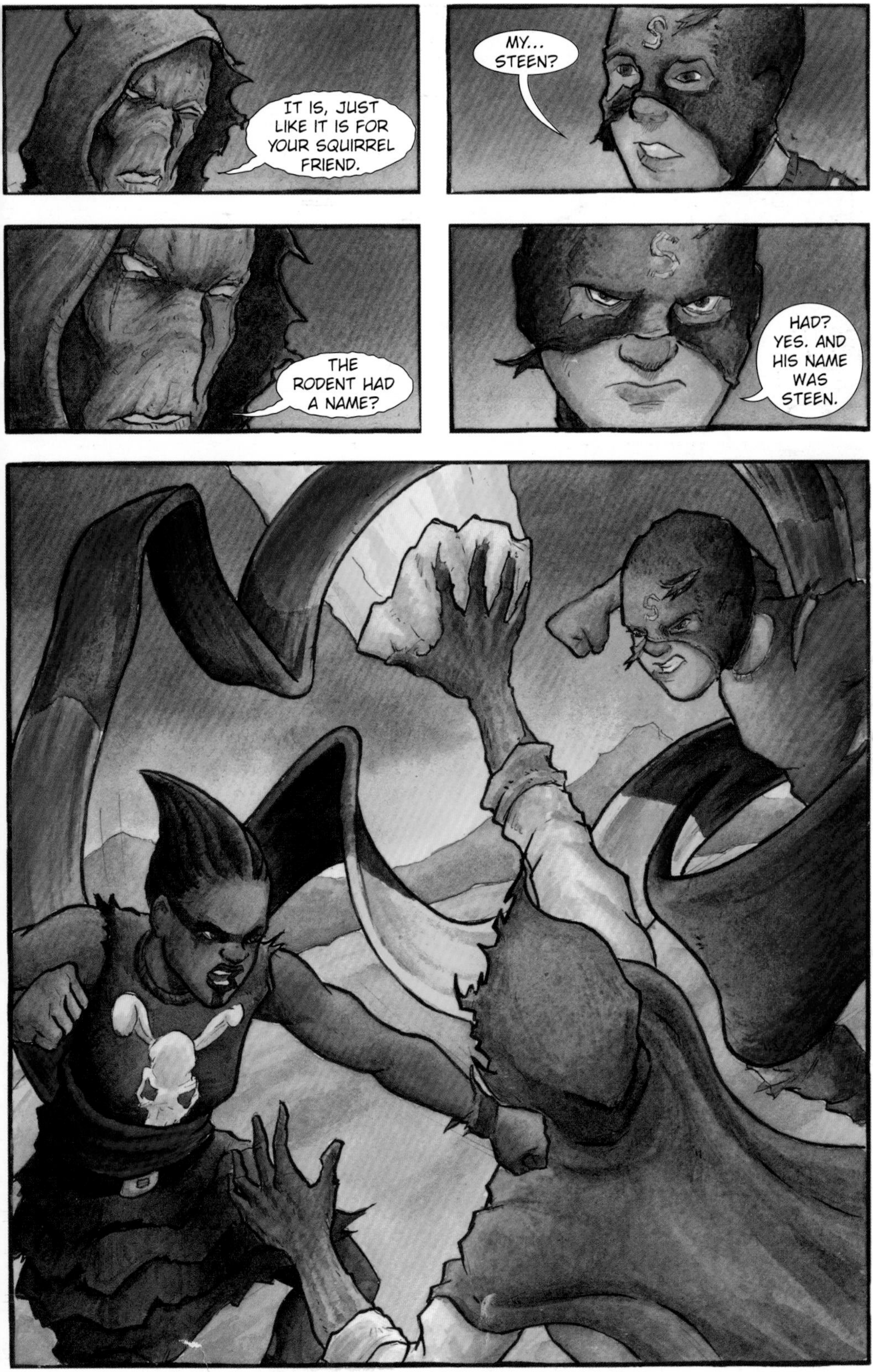
IT IS, JUST LIKE IT IS FOR YOUR SQUIRREL FRIEND.
MY... STEEN?
THE RODENT HAD A NAME?
HAD? YES. AND HIS NAME WAS STEEN.

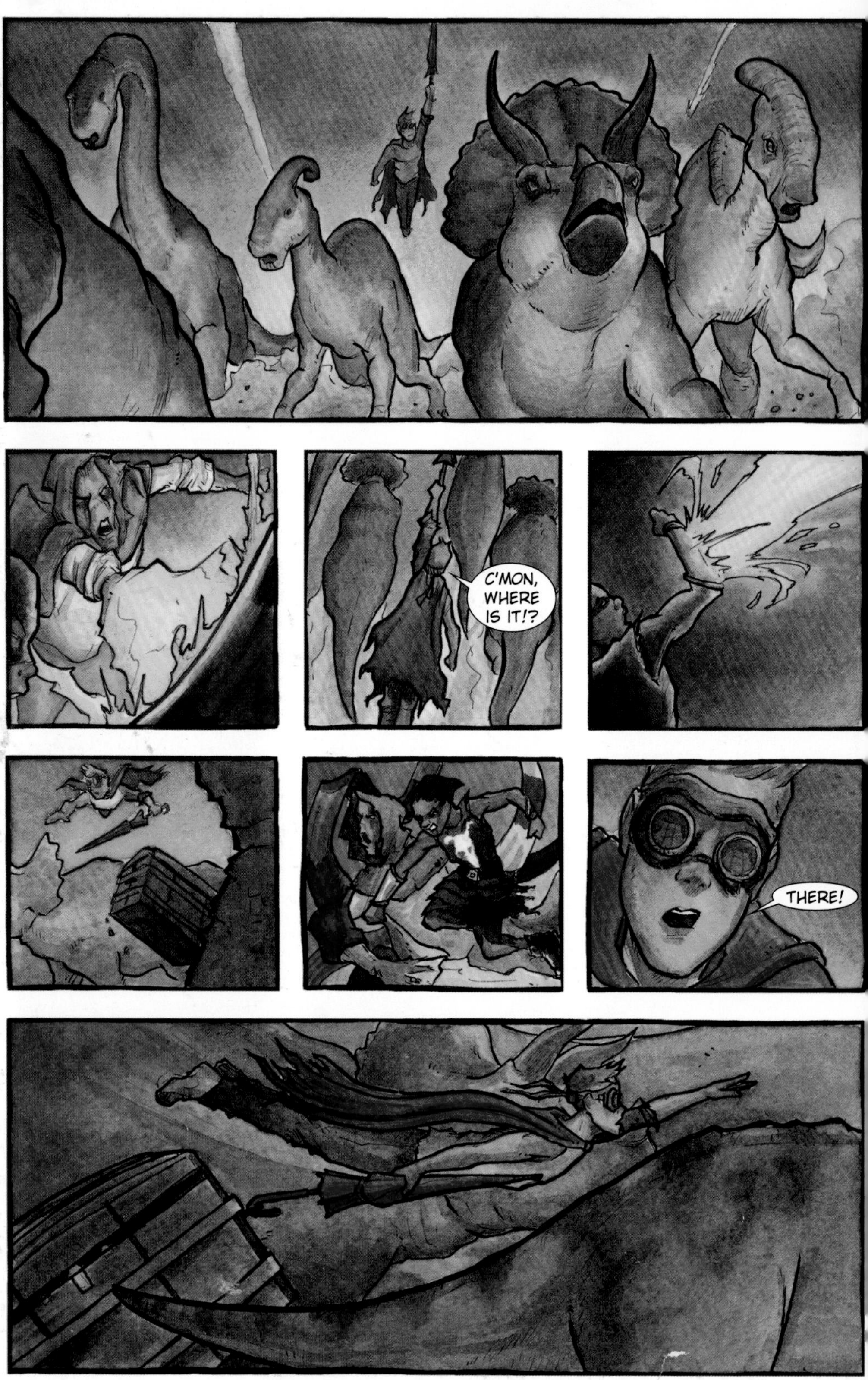
C'MON, WHERE IS IT!?
THERE!

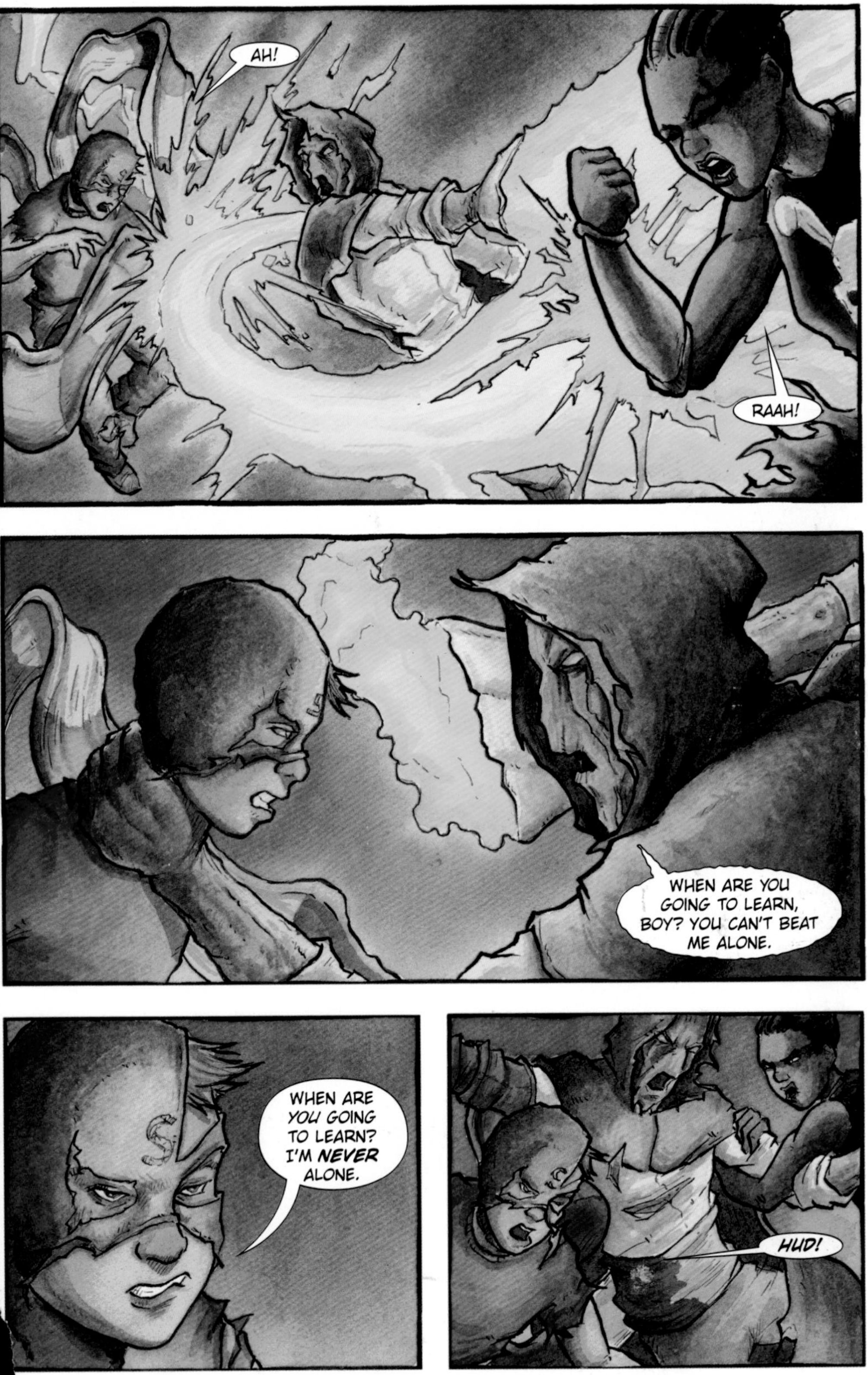
AH!
RAAH!
WHEN ARE YOU GOING TO LEARN, BOY? YOU CAN'T BEAT ME ALONE.
WHEN ARE *YOU* GOING TO LEARN? I'M ***NEVER*** ALONE.
HUD!

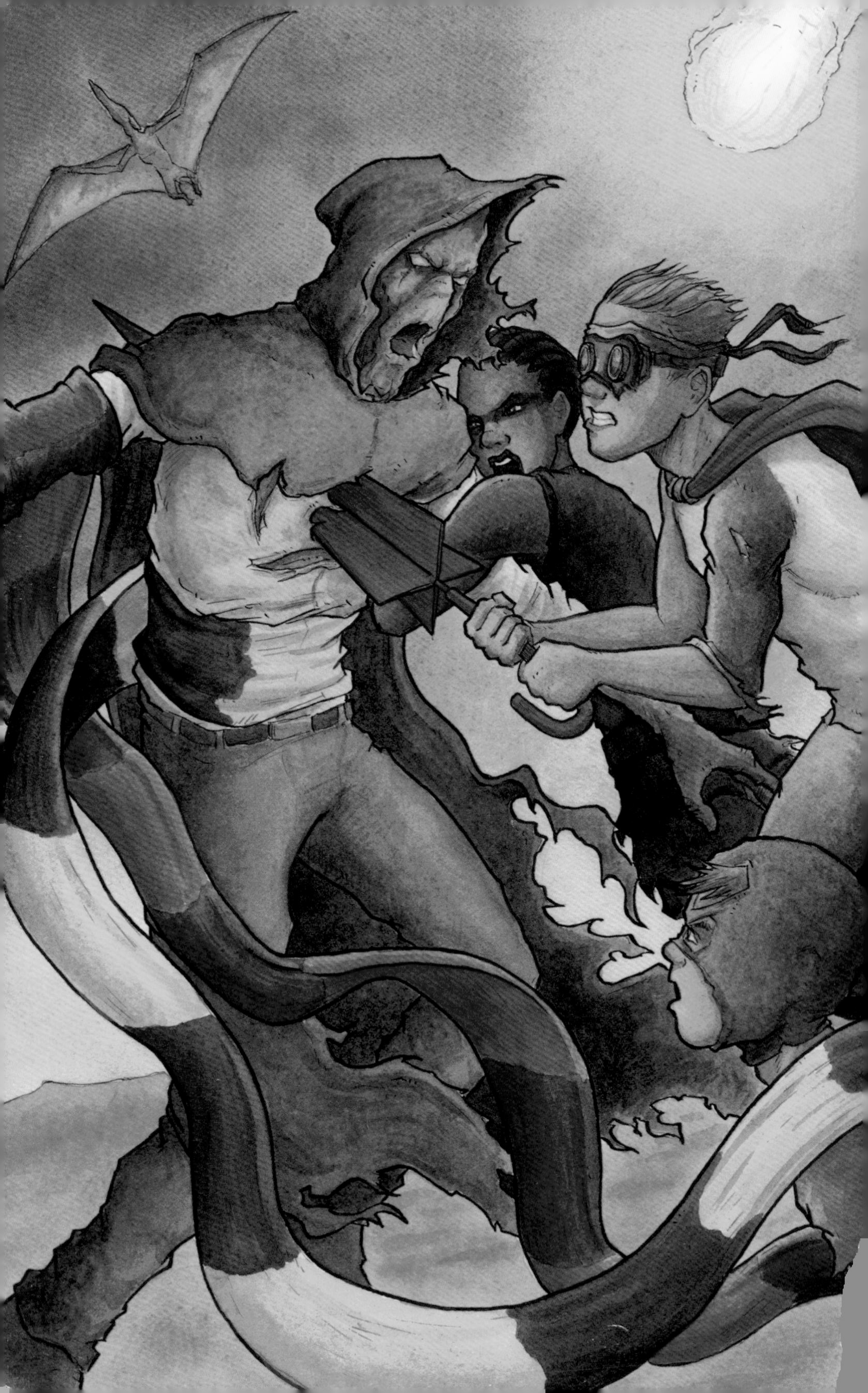

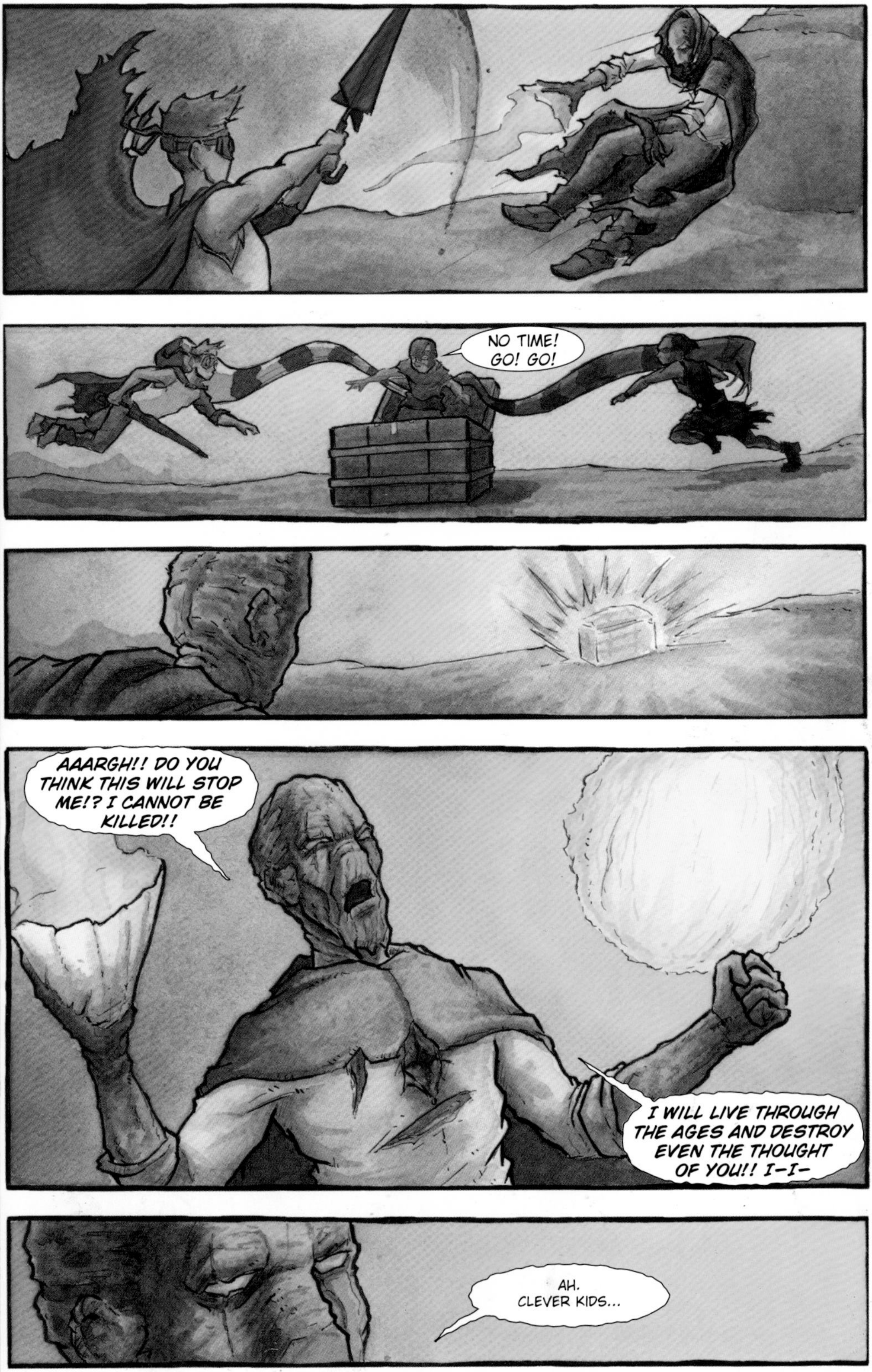
NO TIME!
GO! GO!
AAARGH!! DO YOU THINK THIS WILL STOP ME!? I CANNOT BE KILLED!!
I WILL LIVE THROUGH THE AGES AND DESTROY EVEN THE THOUGHT OF YOU!! I—I—
AH.
CLEVER KIDS...

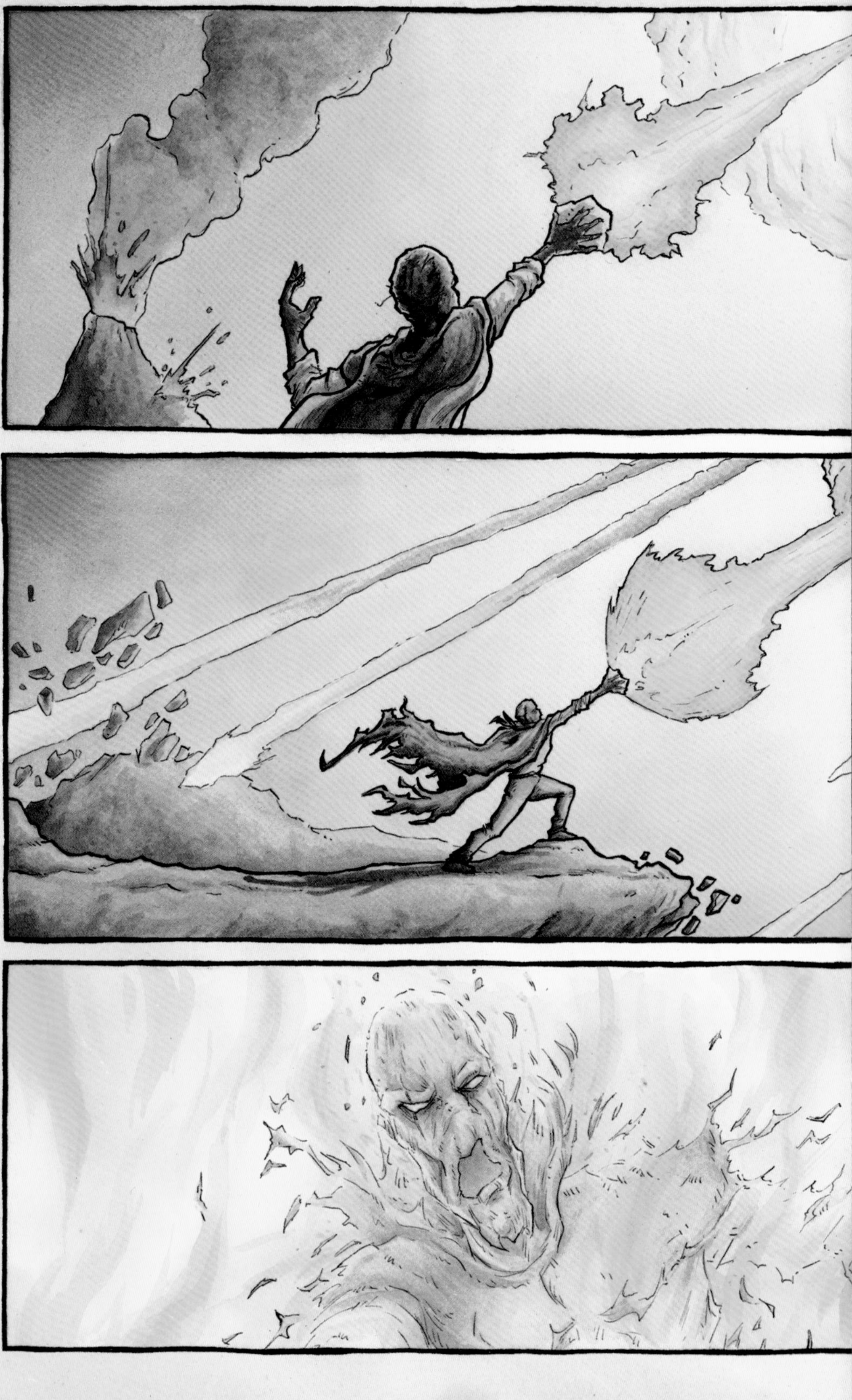

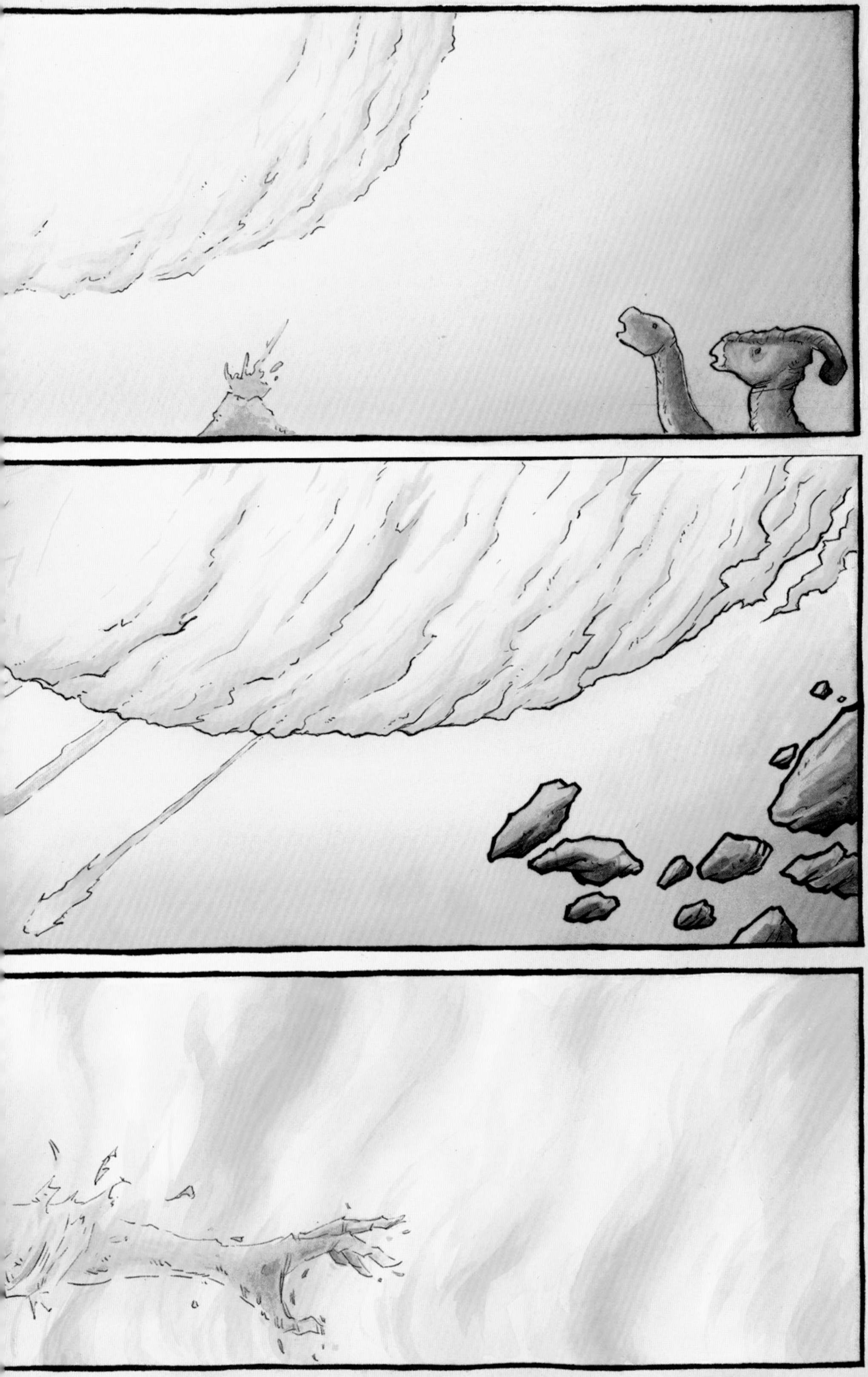

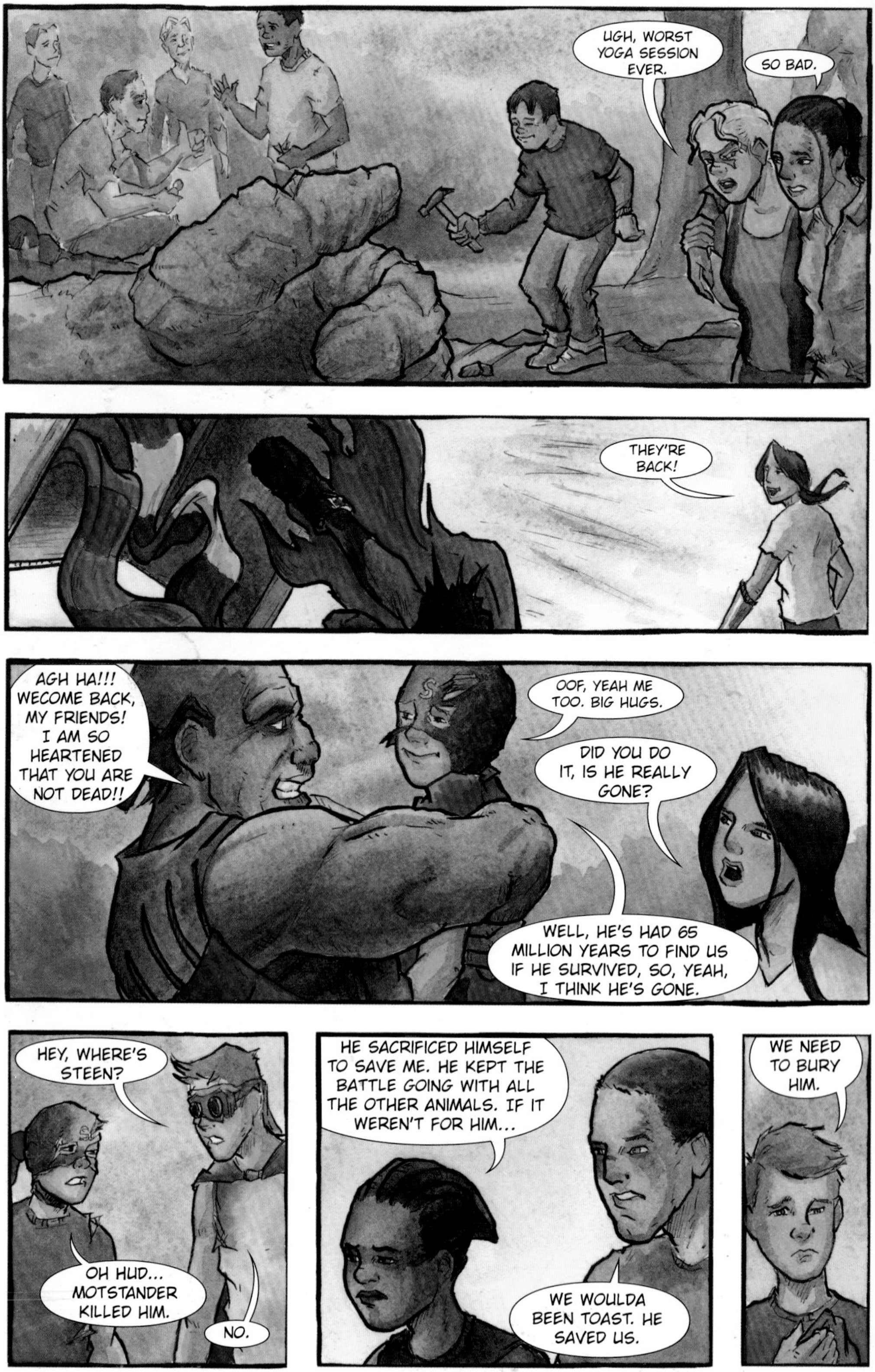
UGH, WORST YOGA SESSION EVER.
SO BAD.
THEY'RE BACK!
AGH HA!!! WECOME BACK, MY FRIENDS! I AM SO HEARTENED THAT YOU ARE NOT DEAD!!
OOF, YEAH ME TOO. BIG HUGS.
DID YOU DO IT, IS HE REALLY GONE?
WELL, HE'S HAD 65 MILLION YEARS TO FIND US IF HE SURVIVED, SO, YEAH, I THINK HE'S GONE.
HEY, WHERE'S STEEN?
OH HUD... MOTSTANDER KILLED HIM.
NO.
HE SACRIFICED HIMSELF TO SAVE ME. HE KEPT THE BATTLE GOING WITH ALL THE OTHER ANIMALS. IF IT WEREN'T FOR HIM...
WE WOULDA BEEN TOAST. HE SAVED US.
WE NEED TO BURY HIM.

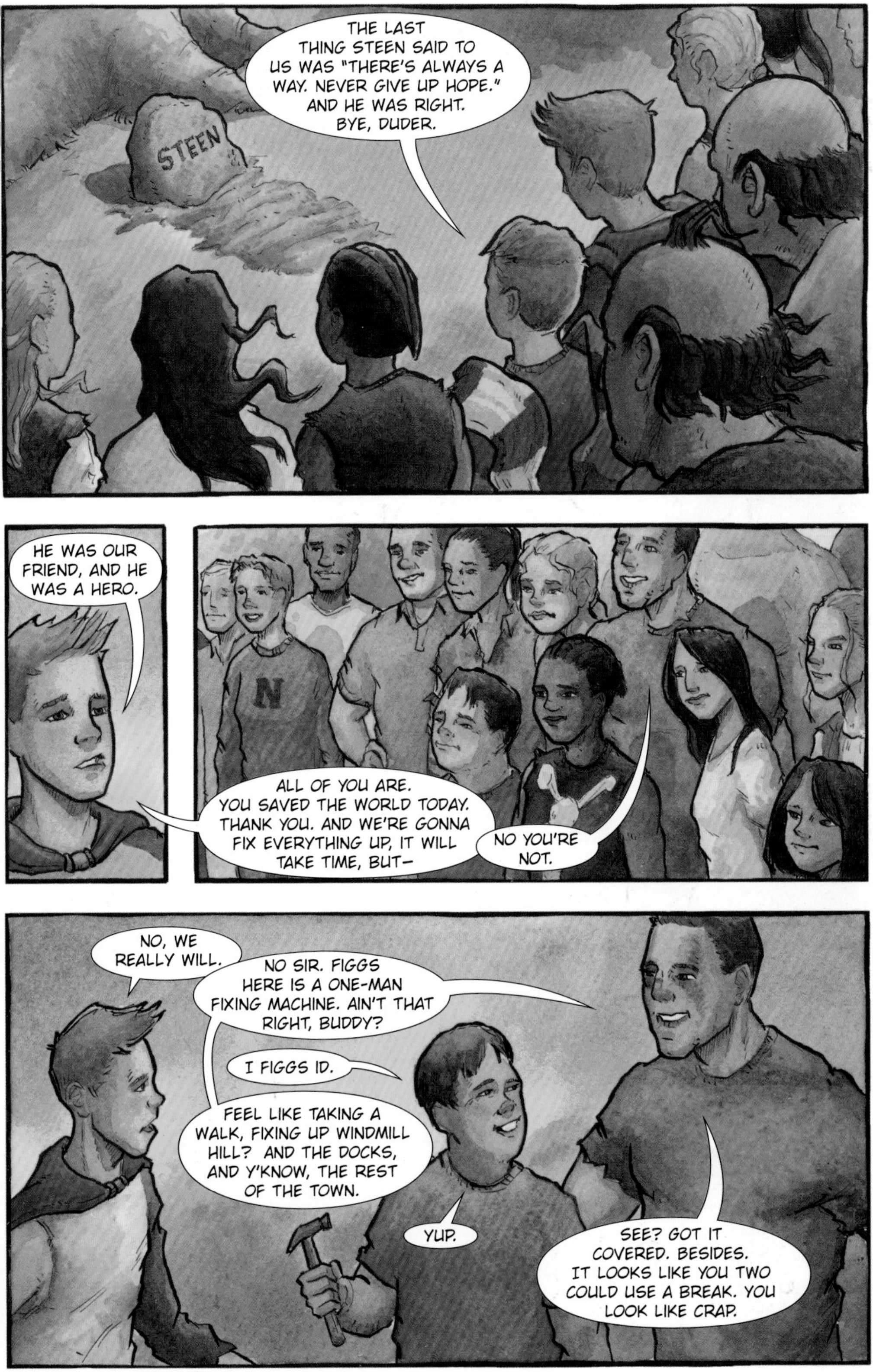
THE LAST THING STEEN SAID TO US WAS "THERE'S ALWAYS A WAY. NEVER GIVE UP HOPE." AND HE WAS RIGHT. BYE, DUDER.
STEEN
HE WAS OUR FRIEND, AND HE WAS A HERO.
N
ALL OF YOU ARE. YOU SAVED THE WORLD TODAY. THANK YOU. AND WE'RE GONNA FIX EVERYTHING UP, IT WILL TAKE TIME, BUT—
NO YOU'RE NOT.
NO, WE REALLY WILL.
NO SIR. FIGGS HERE IS A ONE-MAN FIXING MACHINE. AIN'T THAT RIGHT, BUDDY?
I FIGGS ID.
FEEL LIKE TAKING A WALK, FIXING UP WINDMILL HILL? AND THE DOCKS, AND Y'KNOW, THE REST OF THE TOWN.
YUP.
SEE? GOT IT COVERED. BESIDES. IT LOOKS LIKE YOU TWO COULD USE A BREAK. YOU LOOK LIKE CRAP.

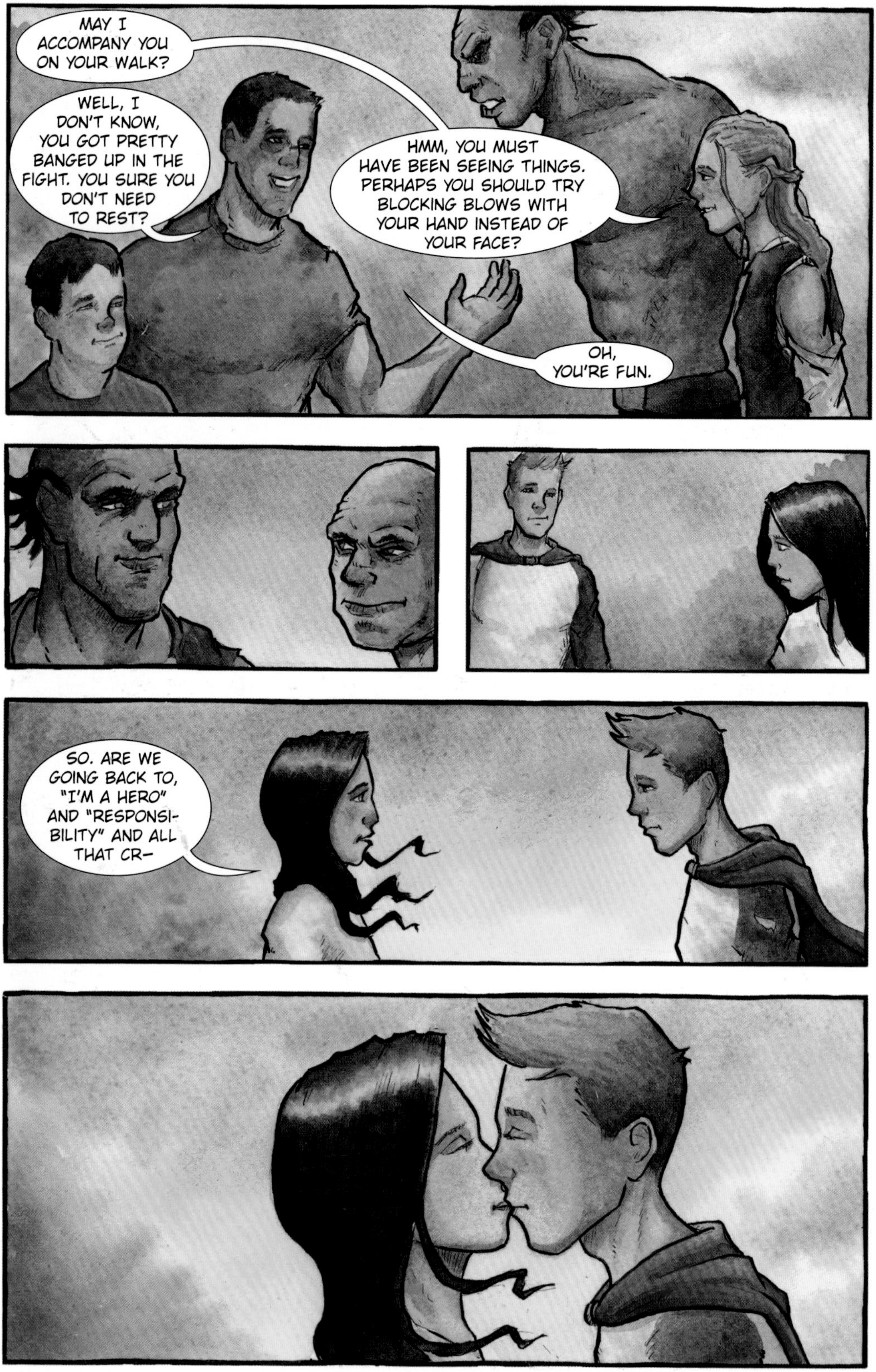
MAY I ACCOMPANY YOU ON YOUR WALK?
WELL, I DON'T KNOW, YOU GOT PRETTY BANGED UP IN THE FIGHT. YOU SURE YOU DON'T NEED TO REST?
HMM, YOU MUST HAVE BEEN SEEING THINGS. PERHAPS YOU SHOULD TRY BLOCKING BLOWS WITH YOUR HAND INSTEAD OF YOUR FACE?
OH, YOU'RE FUN.
SO. ARE WE GOING BACK TO, "I'M A HERO" AND "RESPONSI-BILITY" AND ALL THAT CR–

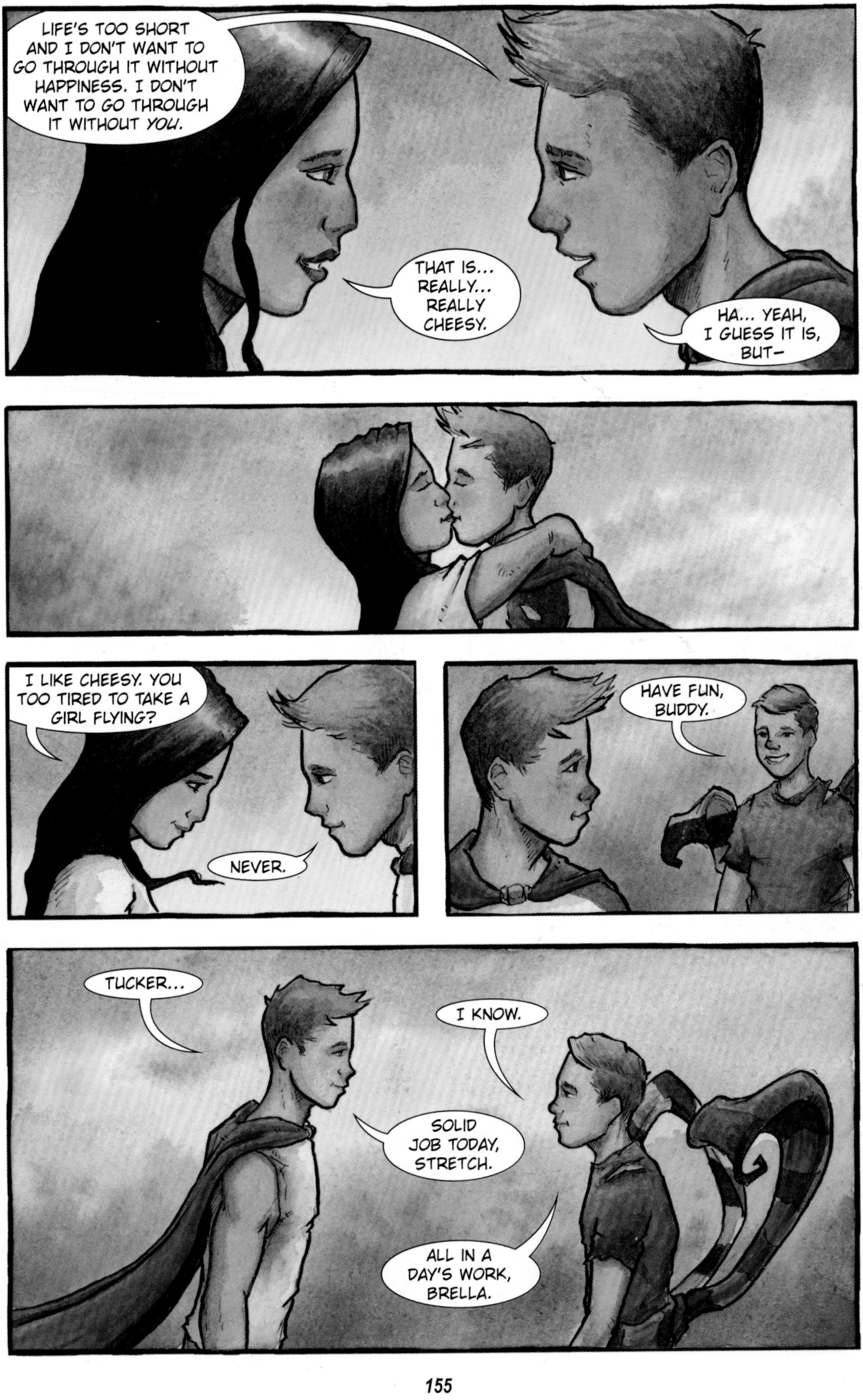
LIFE'S TOO SHORT AND I DON'T WANT TO GO THROUGH IT WITHOUT HAPPINESS. I DON'T WANT TO GO THROUGH IT WITHOUT *YOU*.
THAT IS... REALLY... REALLY CHEESY.
HA... YEAH, I GUESS IT IS, BUT—
I LIKE CHEESY. YOU TOO TIRED TO TAKE A GIRL FLYING?
NEVER.
HAVE FUN, BUDDY.
TUCKER...
I KNOW.
SOLID JOB TODAY, STRETCH.
ALL IN A DAY'S WORK, BRELLA.

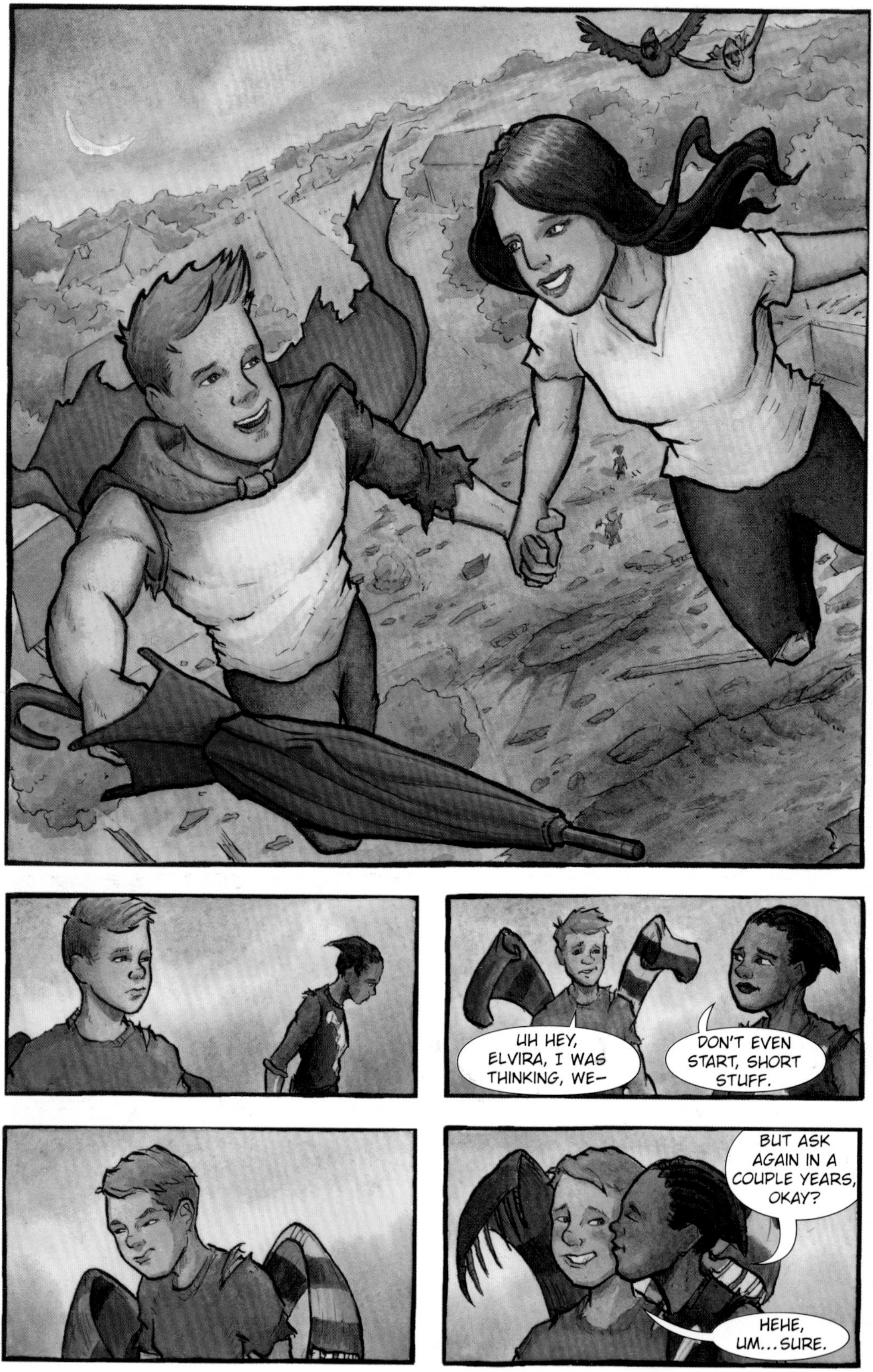
UH HEY, ELVIRA, I WAS THINKING, WE–
DON'T EVEN START, SHORT STUFF.
BUT ASK AGAIN IN A COUPLE YEARS, OKAY?
HEHE, UM...SURE.

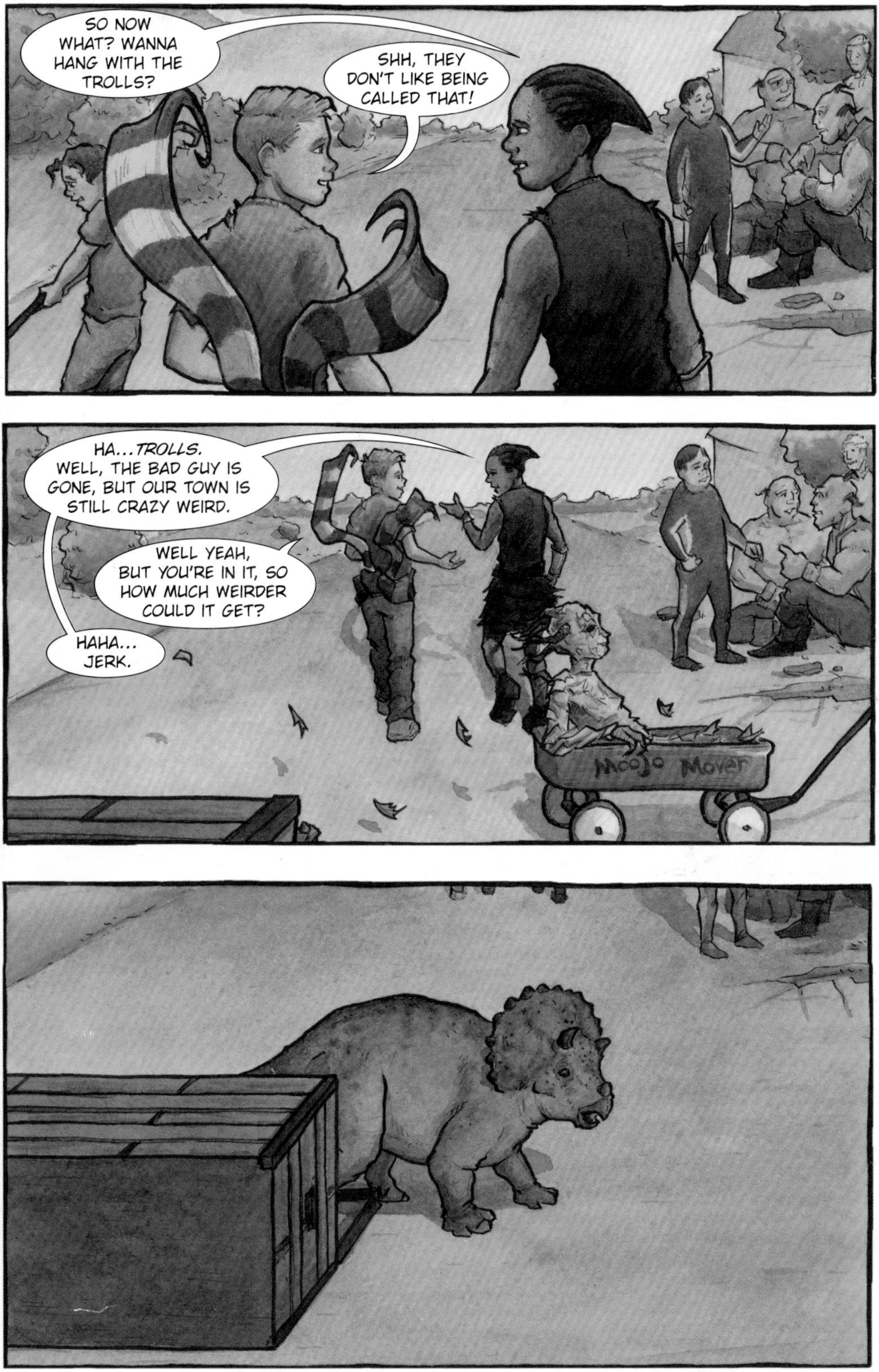

SO NOW WHAT? WANNA HANG WITH THE TROLLS?
SHH, THEY DON'T LIKE BEING CALLED THAT!
HA... *TROLLS.* WELL, THE BAD GUY IS GONE, BUT OUR TOWN IS STILL CRAZY WEIRD.
WELL YEAH, BUT YOU'RE IN IT, SO HOW MUCH WEIRDER COULD IT GET?
HAHA... JERK.
Moojo Mover

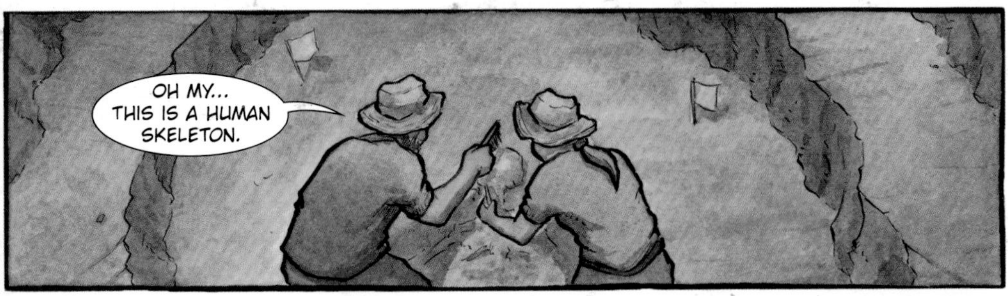
OH MY...
THIS IS A HUMAN
SKELETON.

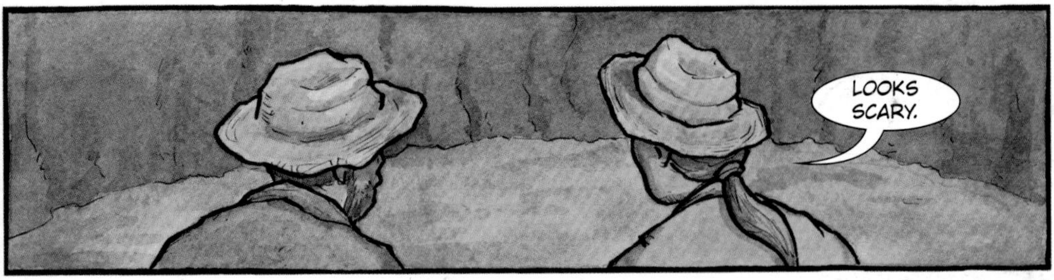
LOOKS
SCARY.

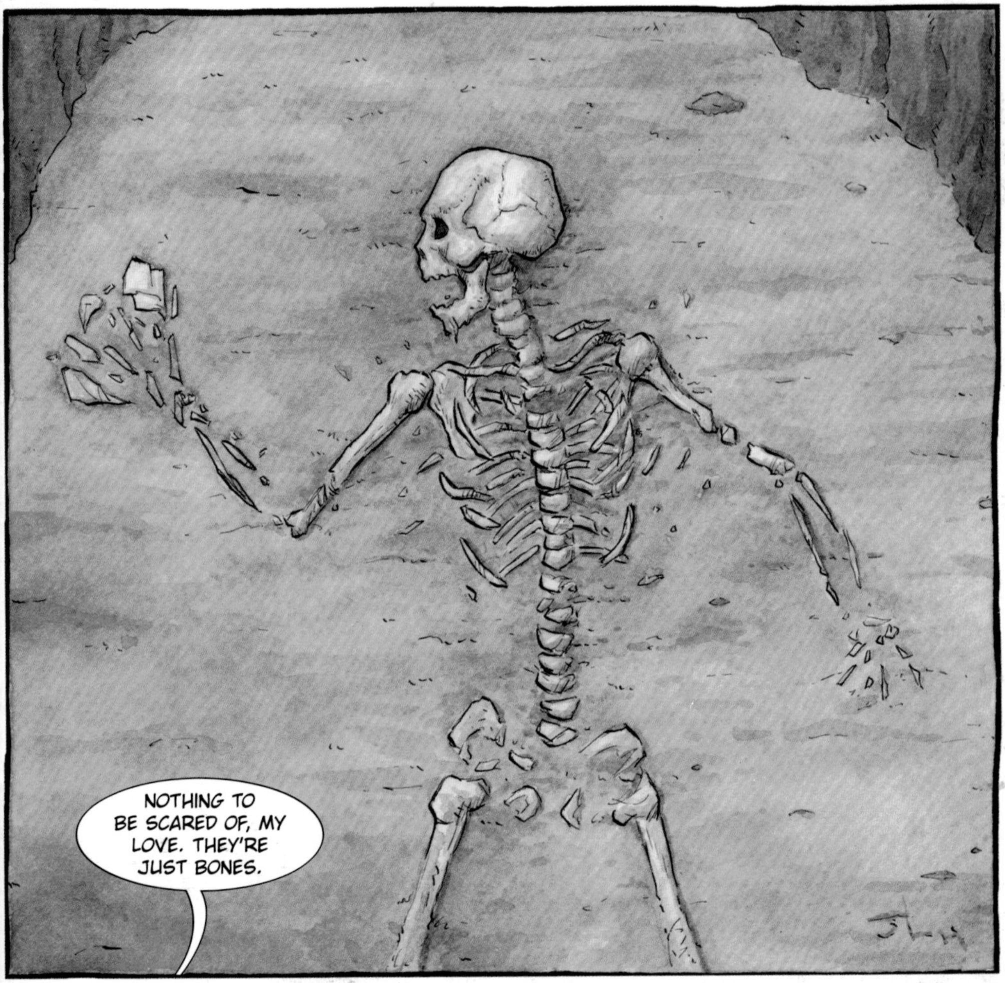
NOTHING TO
BE SCARED OF, MY
LOVE. THEY'RE
JUST BONES.

ACKNOWLEDGMENTS

WRITING, DRAWING, INKING, AND PAINTING EACH OF THESE PAGES COULD HAVE BECOME QUITE THE STRUGGLE WITHOUT AN INCREDIBLE TEAM OF FAMILY, FRIENDS, AND COWORKERS BY MY SIDE.

THANK YOU TO MY PARENTS, MY GRANDPARENTS, MY BROTHER JEFFREY, RAYDENE, AND THE REST OF MY AWESOME FAMILY. THANK YOU TO THE CATAUMET CREW FOR A LIFETIME OF MOVIE-WORTHY STORIES AND TO MY NYC FRIENDS FOR YOUR PATIENCE AND SUPPORT. THANKS TO THE PEOPLE AND PLACES OF NANTUCKET, CAPE COD, AND MILLIS FOR BECOMING MY SETTING.

A SPECIAL THANKS TO DANA CHIDIAC, JASMIN RUBERO, LILY MALCOM, LAURI HORNIK, REGINA CASTILLO, SARAH WARNER, RICH JOHNSON, AND DAVID USLAN FOR TAKING A CHANCE ON THESE BROTHERS AND THEIR ADVENTURES.

AND IF YOU'RE HOLDING THIS IN YOUR HANDS I'D LIKE TO SAVE THE BIGGEST THANKS FOR YOU. THANK YOU SO MUCH FOR GOING ON THIS JOURNEY WITH ME. I TRULY APPRECIATE IT AND HOPE YOU ENJOYED THE RIDE.